Elizabeth's

Story

Trapped by success, freed by disappointment, drawn by an irresistible love that had been there all along

Hilary Van Wagenen

D1444514

Dedication

To others who have learned that when you get the one thing necessary in place at the core of who you are, everything else fills in around it.

To all who seek with a true desire to find.

TABLE OF CONTENTS

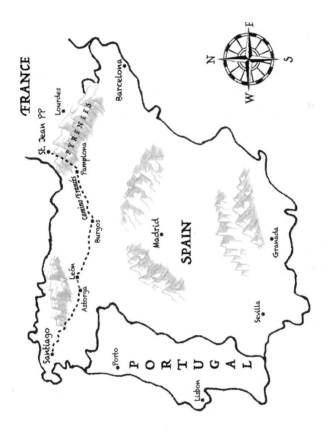

PREFACE

In 2007 my parents and younger brother set out to walk 800k (500mi) across northern Spain on an ancient pilgrim trail known as the *Camino Francés*. What happened on that adventure continues to inform all our lives.

Having walked subsequent Camino pilgrimages since then, our family has made friends all over the world who share the common bond of *peregrino* experiences. The more stories we live when we walk the Camino again ourselves, or hear from other pilgrims, the more we want to weave them into novels that entertain returning and future pilgrims. Camino lessons have a way of staying with you for the rest of your life. They are redemptive, miraculous, funny, challenging, or convicting—and often, all of those.

Even if walking the Camino holds no appeal, you can enjoy these stories. *Stories from the Way Series* will carry universal truths of real life challenges, relationships, and hope for overcoming the things in life that can weigh us down and hold us back from being the people we are meant to be.

Elizabeth's Story is the first in the *Stories from the Way Series*, and we have others planned. We hope you enjoy it.

For more information about the Camino de Santiago and the pilgrim life, check out our family business, CaminoProvisions.com, *Online Guide and Outfitter for the Camino de Santiago*. Enjoy the loads of free information and tips you find there. My mom has written a brilliant

Guidebook for the Camino to help you prepare and save money on your trip. You can order it and all our favorite Camino gear and clothing through our website store from Amazon. We donate a portion of the earnings from our sales to *Provisions with Purpose*. Through this program we contribute to non-profit groups helping pilgrims along the Camino.

PROLOGUE

Sometime in the ninth century a tomb in northwest Spain was discovered and identified as that of the Apostle of Jesus Christ known as James the Elder (brother of the Apostle John). In the centuries since then followers of Jesus and others seeking favor or adventure began traveling to the site to pay their respects. People through the ages have valued the significance of this pilgrimage in many different ways, but what we know for sure is that millions of people have made this journey, sowing the trail with their tears, laughter, and prayers of hope.

In recent years a revival of interest in walking the Camino has steadily increased, so that the number of people arriving in *Santiago de Compostela* in 2016 was more than 250,000. There are more than a few routes considered official Camino routes, but the most popular is the route known as the *Camino Francés*, which begins in a small French town called *St. Jean Pied-de-Port* and ends 500 miles away in Santiago.

Over the years a *peregrino* (pilgrim) infrastructure has provided lodging and food for those walking. The most colorful accommodations on the Camino are known as *albergues*, and range from huge dormitory style buildings with rows and rows of bunk beds, to family-run albergues offering private rooms and smaller numbers of people. Those who can afford it can even opt for the occasional luxury hotel.

The physical challenge of walking so many miles up and down mountains, through vineyards, farmland, and other beautiful country appeals to adventure seekers, and so faces on the Camino belong to those looking for an exciting summer trip, as well as dedicated followers of Jesus on Christian pilgrimage, and others from all over the world.

For information about the Camino de Santiago, visit our family business at CaminoProvisions.com.

1

ELIZABETH JANE WILTSHIRE

The chill of an April night hung in the air as Elizabeth ran up the steps to her third story Logan Circle condo. She unlocked the door, tossed her keys on the counter, and kicked off her high heels, catching a glimpse out her window of the Washington Monument peeking over the treetops a few blocks away.

Willoughby, her black and white tuxedo cat, sauntered over to say hello, yowling his displeasure at her long absence.

"I know, buddy, I'm just as hungry as you are," she said as she bent down to scratch his neck.

Her phone pinged an email alert, and she immediately took her laptop out of her briefcase and sat down to respond. Her boss wanted to know whether she had finished formatting the Baker deposition for the trial next week. She quickly typed out a reply, her stomach rumbling with hunger. Since working closely with Bruce Devon for the past several years, she'd learned to function on coffee and little else. One of the top corporate lawyers in the country, Devon had a reputation for being cunning, intelligent, and ruthless. Elizabeth admired his success, and was grateful she had the opportunity to learn from someone like him.

Willoughby's plaintive meow jolted her out of her chair to the cabinet, where she quickly poured some cat food in a bowl. She changed into her pajamas, flipped the TV on for some background noise, and started warming up some canned chicken noodle soup, keeping one eye on her laptop.

She sighed as she thought of the days in law school when she had a roommate and shared a table with someone who talked back. "No offense, Willoughby," she said, turning towards the cat inhaling his food. "Sometimes I just wish I had more stimulating conversation." Willoughby purred as she scooped him up into her lap, and she rubbed his downy head with her cheek, thankful for the warmth of his companionship.

Her soup started to simmer while she spooned peanut butter into her mouth, and as she sat down with her bowl, an image on the television screen caught her eye. Mountains green with grass, rolling hills lined with rows of grapevines, and a group of three backpackers walking on a dirt road.

She laughed to herself. It was hard not to be cynical when the last vacation she'd taken was a backpacking trip to Europe with her boyfriend, Steve, just after graduating from Furman University more than a decade ago.

As memories of the trip threatened to surface, she pushed them away as quickly as possible. It hurt too much to think about Steve. *Anyway, it was all for the best that he broke up with me. If he hadn't, I would never have been able to invest in my job this way. And it HAS been worth it*, she thought to herself.

Promotions were being announced soon, and Bruce had hinted, more than once, that she was in the running for partner. Not many 33-year-old women had the honor of their name on the marquee of one of the premier law firms in the country, and Elizabeth hadn't worked 90-hour weeks for nothing. She hoped that if she met everyone's expectations, she'd gain the credibility she needed to open her own firm and work with underprivileged women and children.

She turned her attention back to the TV, seeing images of forest paths and small towns flash across the screen. She quickly changed the channel to a soccer game, suppressing the longings and regrets that welled up whenever she thought about travel.

She opened the deposition to check that everything was in order, all the while answering emails from Bruce. Even though his constant demands grated on her, she knew he expected round-the-clock availability. "It won't always be this way," she thought. "Once I'm established as a partner, I'll have the freedom to do things my way." When she received an email from Bruce signaling the "all clear" for the day, she shut her laptop down. It was 11:30, and her 4:30 AM wake-up time was coming soon. She climbed into bed next to Willoughby, exhausted from the day's demands.

2

MIRIAM

Miriam woke with the last of a dream playing in her mind. A slender young woman with a familiar glow seemed to float toward her out of the sun. She knew this was the next one she would be helping to find her way.

It often began this way, a dream or picture in her mind of a person she had never met, but instantly knew. Something was imparted to her so she would know how to pray and prepare. Miriam sensed this one would come as many had, broken and desperate, walking the Camino de Santiago. "Lisbet," she heard in her heart. *Ahh*, prayed Miriam to herself, *Father God, thank you for Lisbet. Make her path here such that she can come to know your love and all that you have for her to be.*

She lay there a few more minutes, praying silently for her children and grandchildren, friends, and other pilgrims she had recently helped. A cold wet nose bumped her hand in the soft light, and she accepted the greeting from her little shepherdess, a black and white collie mix named Tiggy. "*Goodemorgen*, little nanny. You take such good care of me. Okay, I'm getting up. I'm getting up. Go wake everyone else." Off went Tiggy to give polite yips at the doorway of the pilgrims' rooms, until lights coming on and the sound of other voices meant that their guests were waking.

A chill and the promise of sun were in the sky as she rose from bed, wrapped herself in a thick sweater and put her feet into her slippers. She felt energy rise in her as she thought about the new beginning that came with morning. At the house next door a rooster crowed as she washed and dressed in her usual workday clothes: blue jeans, cotton print blouse and wool sweater. Warm socks and trekking boots completed her outfit. She brushed her hair, and commandeered as many wispy white curls as she could into a braid that would accommodate her wool cap. April was wet and cold, even here near Burgos at the threshold of the arid *Meseta*. She was tall like many Dutch women, with eyes that changed color with her moods and the colors she wore. Today they were blue.

We all need a fresh start often, she thought to herself. As she filled the kettle with water, she whispered words that had become a liturgy for the start of her day, "Lord, wash me clean of my mistakes, fill me with yourself, and let me love people the way Jesus did. I give you this day."

Only two *peregrinos* had stayed with her last night, and they were up finishing their morning washes, loading their packs, and tending their feet when Miriam came to the table with a steaming pot of coffee and hot water for tea in a thermal carafe. She laid out the sugar, cream, tea bags, butter, jam, and bread to help send her guests on their way. Tiggy wagged her tail in greeting as they came to the table.

They were a French couple, husband and wife, in their late forties, Miriam guessed. Bernadette and Michel had begun their pilgrimage in Paris, which meant they had been on their journey for almost six weeks and walked 1000 kilometers. When they arrived the previous afternoon they were absolutely joyful for the chance to use a washing machine and dryer, a rare combination along the Camino. Miriam smiled at the affirmation for putting the money toward the laundry machines rather than buying a vehicle, a decision that she wrestled with for weeks when she first moved to Spain six years ago.

Miriam welcomed them in French when they had checked in, and directed their attention to the "amenities of the house" written in four languages on a poster near the entrance. She was fluent in her native Dutch, English, and German, and could hold passable conversations in French, Spanish and Italian. Bernadette and Michel were either too shy or knew only their native tongue, so Miriam had spoken her less-than-perfect-French with them, eliciting more than one smile from them with her pronunciation and grammar. Tiggy welcomed everyone by putting her chin on each one's knee, a gesture that never failed to elicit an ear scratch or belly rub. Not only was the little collie a good companion and protector for her, Miriam had seen how the attention from a cuddly dog could relax even the most reserved or solitary pilgrim.

There was no café or restaurant in Miriam's tiny village, so she, like some *hospitaleros*, offered a simple meal to pilgrims for an affordable price. In fall and winter, it was a hearty soup, homemade bread, dessert, and wine, and in spring and summer a salad of boiled eggs or tuna, lettuces, and vegetables. She enlisted their help with the preparations and clean-up as an activity to break the ice, but generally pilgrims at this point in the journey opened up readily. Bernadette and Michel revealed in their dinner conversation that they were making their pilgrimage as a way to process the grief over their granddaughter's death. Only three years old, Amelie had died after treatments for her leukemia failed. In their words, "We walk and ask God to fill the hole in our hearts she left when she passed."

After dinner it was Miriam's practice to ask all those present to write out something they would like prayer for and place it in an old bowl on the mantel. "If you want to put something in, take something out first, and we will read them aloud together." Pilgrims from all religious traditions or philosophies participated. The three each plucked a scrap of paper from the bowl and prayed for those who were somewhere ahead on the Camino. The couple wrote prayers and put them with the others.

As Miriam put the ingredients for the evening's loaf into her bread machine, she said goodbye, and "Buen Camino," to Bernadette and Michel, who helped each other into their packs, smiled and waved, and called out *"Au Revoir."* She prayed silently for the two to heal and find peace.

3

DEVON, WILSON AND MOORE, ATTORNEYS AT LAW

Elizabeth woke with a start, her heart pounding and tears streaming down her face. The dream was so real. She was a little girl again, playing soccer in her front yard with her father while her mother cheered them on. Scene after scene from her childhood flashed through her mind. The final scene happened just after her sixteenth birthday. She and her father, dressed in black, standing beside her mother's grave, holding each other. Elizabeth's hand shook as she switched her lamp on. Her clock read 3:45. She hugged herself for a minute, shivering.

Elizabeth, whispered a voice. She glanced up, sure she had imagined it, but curiously calm. *Beloved daughter, I will give you rest and healing. My yoke is easy, and my burden is light.*

She shivered awake, got up to make coffee and checked her email. *No sense going back to sleep since I have to get up so soon. Maybe I can get in a few extra miles on the treadmill,* she thought. She pushed away an image that rose, unbidden, in her mind. The image was one of Jesus nestling a lamb against his cheek, a picture that had hung in the church of her childhood, Christ the Good Shepherd. As a little girl, she'd been captivated by the tender love in His expression for so small a creature. Her family had attended services faithfully when she was little, but as she got more involved in travel soccer, church often conflicted with weekend games. After her mother died, she and her father stopped going altogether.

She dumped the rest of her coffee down the drain, changed into her workout clothes, and hopped on the treadmill. *This way I'll be able to get to the office early.*

She kept the TV on to drown out her thoughts as she showered and dressed, then hopped on a bus for the short ride to work. As she stepped into the elevator, she ran into her coworker, Ellen Watson. "I just saw an email, Elizabeth. They're announcing the new partners today. I'm sure you'll be named. You're such a hard worker and do an amazing job."

I should be thankful for Ellen's good attitude, thought Elizabeth. *Really I should. But sometimes she drives me nuts. How can she be so kind to me, even though we're competing for the same recognition? It would be so much easier if she were colder.*

Out loud she said, "Oh, I don't know, Ellen. There are a lot of good lawyers here, including you. How is Frank?" she said, hoping that changing the subject to Ellen's husband would redirect the conversation. She was not disappointed.

"Oh, he's doing great. We're thinking about a trip to Spain this summer. There's this pilgrimage route called the Camino de Santiago…"

Elizabeth interrupted, "Well, I have to get some work done before everyone gets in for the day, Ellen. If you'll excuse me..." Elizabeth walked as quickly as she could to her office, poured herself a fresh cup of coffee, and waded into the morass of legal documents forwarded by Bruce.

She was distracted by thoughts of Ellen. As much as Elizabeth wanted to dislike her as a competitor, her colleague had an undeniable warmth, and she was drawn to Ellen. *Then again,* she thought, *the only person I really talk to other than people at the office is my cat, so my judgment could be a little off. Still, she's someone I wish I could get to know. It's just too hard when we're both after the same cases and positions.*

At 10:00, Donna, the front desk administrative assistant and unofficial office "mom," tapped on Elizabeth's door. "Hi, Elizabeth…just making sure you noticed the time. We better get to the meeting! Can I get you something on my way in?" The older woman's kind face was crinkled into a smile as she poked her head in the door. "You look tired, Elizabeth, are you okay?"

Elizabeth glanced up sharply. "I'm fine, Donna!" she said more sharply than she intended, and then softened her tone as hurt flashed across Donna's face. "I'm just finishing up this email, and I'll be there in a second." Elizabeth pushed "send" and scooped up her laptop and coffee mug, dribbling hot coffee on her hand and desk. She cursed and hastily wiped up the spill, flung her door open, and rushed down the hall to the conference room. Most of the other attorneys sat around the large mahogany table with their laptops open, waiting expectantly for Bruce to begin the meeting. Elizabeth sat down and felt her cheeks warm and her shoulders slump as Bruce glared at her, conveying disappointment, anger, and shame in a single glance. "Now that Ms. Wiltshire has decided to join us, I'll begin." Elizabeth looked down at her computer to avoid the many eyes--some more sympathetic than others--turning in her direction.

After letting the silence hang for what seemed like an eternity, Bruce said, "I know you're all anxious to hear about the promotions, but we have a few other items to attend to before the announcement. First of all, human resources has asked me to remind you all that any vacation and comp time not used by December 31st will be lost. Of course, as we all know, there are more important things than taking vacations." Several of the attorneys shifted in their seats and chuckled, exchanging knowing glances. Everyone who worked for this firm knew that even though vacation time may be available, few actually took it if they wanted to keep their status in the firm. Bruce continued, "I'm sure you'll all be VERY judicious with when and how much vacation you take this year."

He continued, "Next, I want reports on each case of how you are maximizing profit by using up retainer fees and extending court days. I'll start with the Anderson case." As individuals and team leaders reported around the conference table, Elizabeth's mind drifted to partnership, how proud her dad would be, how tired she was, the mention of vacations, and the dream and the impressions of Jesus she had upon waking. She hadn't thought of Jesus, church or her spiritual well-being for a long time. Bruce's sharp cough interrupted her, then he snapped his fingers in Elizabeth's direction, saying, "Please join us when you are able!"

She reported the progress on the Baker case to the group, and Bruce seemed pleased with everyone's accumulation of client hours. "Now, on to the announcement of partner," he said.

Elizabeth sat straighter in her chair, heart pounding, the idea of a vacation flitting away from her mind's eye. Bruce continued, "Several of you know what a difficult choice this was for the other partners and me, and we want you to know that a lot of thought and discussion went into this year's choice. We have chosen someone who has proven to be trustworthy, hard working, and willing to prioritize this firm above all else. Someone who is not only a successful attorney, but also a caring colleague. This year, we welcome Ellen Watson as our partner."

Elizabeth knew her own expression of shock mirrored that on Ellen's face, and did what she could to make her disappointment less obvious by looking down at her lap.

"Congratulations, Ellen. We're happy to have you on board."

Bruce continued talking, but His words no longer penetrated past the pounding in Elizabeth's ears. She felt her heart racing faster. She saw bright flashes of light and felt nauseated. "Excuse me, I need a glass of water," she said as she exited the room as quickly as she could. Bruce rolled his eyes and stepped aside so she could exit.

As she rushed down the hallway, she heard Donna call her name, but it sounded watery and far away. She felt a rush of blood to her head, and everything went black.

Elizabeth opened her eyes. She felt a cool hand on her forehead and heard someone whispering. As she regained consciousness, she heard a voice whispering a prayer: "Jesus, give this dear one rest. May she find peace in you..."

"What happened?" Elizabeth slurred, as she tried to sit up.

"Don't try to talk or sit up, sweetie. The ambulance will be here in a minute," soothed Donna.

"I need to get back to work. I'm fine, Donna." Elizabeth tried articulating the words with more certainty than she felt, but could not control the tremor in her voice.

"Elizabeth, you hit your head when you fell. You may have a concussion. You're going to the hospital to get checked, and I'm coming with you. You won't be alone."

"What about Bruce?"

Donna's eyes darkened momentarily, but all she said was, "Don't worry about him. He's already gotten someone to cover for you."

"Thank you, Donna," Elizabeth said, listening to sirens in the distance.

4

MATTEO GARCIA

Tuesday mornings were Matteo's busiest because he had to do the morning chores at his *albergue*, get the bread dough mixed and rising, and then pick up Miriam and drive to Burgos for supplies. She didn't own a car, so they shared the ride and divided large bags of staple foods and cases of other goods they both used in their *albergues*. Sharing in this way benefitted both of them in saving money buying wholesale and keeping their pantry stocked with fresher goods, and a deep friendship had developed over the past few years. He looked forward to the time with her each week, and knew she enjoyed it, too. Miriam had been quick to learn what Matteo taught her about managing her *albergue*--involving *peregrinos* in the dinner preparations, bringing their dirty sheets to the laundry--and had also adopted his system of hosting a little prayer service after dinner.

Matteo had been a *hospitalero* for more than 15 years, since his wife had left him and his son Andrés for a job and new life with her sister in León. The farm had been in his family for many generations, nearly 20 acres intersected by the Camino Francés. Matteo had grown up learning from his father and grandfather how to plant, harvest and trade, but Maria had never really taken to life in the country and marriage to a farmer. It was true that the farm had failed to pay much more than a subsistence to them, but they never went hungry thanks to the large vegetable garden and a flock of chickens, ducks and turkeys, and with profits from small crops of maize and soybeans they had always paid their taxes and had enough left over to see that Andrés had the chance at a good education. The boy had excelled at learning from the beginning and picked up languages easily from the *peregrinos* that walked the Camino through the village and asked to camp on their land.

That was what had given Matteo the idea to open an *albergue*. The number of pilgrims making their journeys to Santiago had been increasing every summer, and there weren't enough beds along the way in the peak months of June, July, and August. He and Andrés, by this time a student in secondary school, had cleaned out and converted a small barn on their property into a dormitory that held six bunk beds. These they built themselves, as well as adding basic bathroom facilities to the structure. A simple building, yes, but Matteo was pleased to have pilgrims arrive who had been referred to him by their friends, and flattered to have been mentioned in guide books for the cleanliness of the facility and friendliness of the host. By the time Andrés left for university, they had expanded the barn dormitory to accommodate 20 pilgrims, and felt this was the most they could properly serve. At peak times he had allowed a few *peregrinos* to camp in one of the small pastures, or set up a cot, but only if they were desperate for a safe place to bed down.

He truly enjoyed extending hospitality to pilgrims passing through, and hoped that he might have some positive impact on the thousands of *peregrinos* that stayed with them each year. After all, during his own pilgrimage after Maria had left, a *hospitalero* near León had introduced him to Jesus Christ, who had healed his broken heart and brought him into a place of peace with the Father. He could read the same needs on the faces of the many *peregrinos* who stayed with him. The physicality of the Camino alone primed pilgrims to open up and accept help for their feet, tired muscles, and an assortment of injuries usually seen in elite athletes. Most welcomed the blister compresses, ice packs, and liniments Matteo and Andrés offered, and accepted their prayers for their healing.

This morning Matteo gave instructions to his small helper Felipe to finish cleaning the dormitory, take the dirty sheets to his mother to wash, and feed the flock. The boy's mother needed the income these chores supplied, and was grateful that Matteo could provide fatherly encouragement while Felipe's own father was gone all week to León for work.

"Felipe, I am leaving you in charge while I am gone. Take care of everything. I will return by noon."

"Sí, señor."

"Ah, ah, ah. In English!"

"Jess, sir. I do it!"

Matteo smiled. "I *will* do it," he whispered as he patted him on the head.

A German shepherd sat at attention as Matteo was speaking, eager to hear whether he would be invited to go. "Come Rex, I need you to look after the truck." With a whistle and motion of his hand Matteo opened the back hatch and Rex jumped in. If people knew what a kind nature Rex had they wouldn't be nearly as frightened of him when he was on guard duty. Matteo had trained him well as a watchdog, but rarely had the dog ever had to use his training to protect their property or guests from a malicious intruder. However, there was the one time a couple years ago when a scream came from the women's shower room, and Rex had run on instinct from the main house faster than Matteo had ever seen him run. Matteo hurried after him to find Rex pinning a frightened man to the ground and growling a warning through bared teeth. The man was drunk and had threatened one of the *peregrinas* while she showered. The police came to take the man to jail to sleep off his beers, and Rex received grateful attention from the *peregrina*. Unless he sensed anyone was dangerous or in danger, Rex was an easy-going companion to all the pilgrims. But he always served as a noble sentry on trips and took his job seriously.

Matteo steered his little Citroën truck around a pothole on the dirt road, and pulled out onto the paved highway that connected his village to Miriam's. They were only 5k apart via the Camino, but a little farther via the highway. He turned onto a dirt road and pulled up in front of the *casa rural* Miriam owned. It was a large country house of the kind built a century ago for family groups to escape the heat of the city while they raised and put by a stock of vegetables and fruit for the winter. The house was set in the center of an acre with a small vegetable garden, fruit trees, summer kitchen, and a vacant chicken house Miriam used for starting seedlings and wintering over pots of herbs. At the back of the property were two beehives. Matteo was happy to barter eggs and vegetables throughout the year for Miriam's honey and fruit preserves.

Tiggy announced his arrival, wagging her whole body and trotting back and forth in front of the house. Matteo greeted the collie and let Rex out to say hello and have a romp before they went to town.

"Hello, Miriam! You look lovely this morning, are you ready?"

"Yes, do you need to come in first?"

"No, I am ready, and the Burgos market awaits us!"

She locked her door, and turned to see Matteo opening her car door, motioning her inside with a deep bow and sweep of his hat. She answered with a regal nod and wave, smiling at his chivalrous manners.

Matteo had the easy smile and open face of someone who was comfortable being who he was. No airs, no pretense. They were about the same age, and Matteo had stayed fit with his farming chores and homegrown lifestyle. He was the same height as she was, dressed in heavy black canvas work pants, a light blue shirt and grey wool jacket. He wore the black felt brimmed hat he always wore on market days, and hiking boots left by a *peregrino* some months back. Matteo had the brown skin of a man who had worked outdoors for all his 60 years, grey hair with a little of his original light brown color still there. His hazel eyes were wise and mischievous at the same time, and his manners were full of grace and kindness toward everyone.

As more and more of their neighbors moved closer to the city for jobs, they relied on each other for help and society. No one knew that part of the country like Matteo—its people and traditions, bargains, and food. He was a walking encyclopedia of information about anything to do with the region, and running an *albergue*.

"Did you have many guests last night?"

"A husband and wife from France. Only two. And you?"

"I had five Brits, backpacking through Europe for their gap year. Three men, two women. No problems, so that was good. Full of questions about the *Meseta*. I told them I thought the only challenge they would have with the *Meseta* in April was the rain. Not hot enough to worry about dehydration like the summer, but wet clothes and shoes can cause you to get chilled and get worse blisters. They were invincible when they left this morning, but I wonder how they will feel after walking for six hours in pouring rain?"

They both chuckled, knowing everyone is eventually humbled by the weather and terrain on the Camino. They certainly had been, and had heard the same from every *peregrino* who had stayed with them through the years.

"No rain for us today here today, thankfully. Are we headed to the farmer's market first, or the wholesaler?" she asked. Matteo had wifi at his place, and could check prices online for staples they would buy at the wholesale distribution center. They carried some fresh and frozen items too, but those were not always competitive in price with the local farmers.

"I think today we buy beans, wine, milk and butter at the market, and flour, coffee, sugar, and paper goods at the wholesaler. Let's grab a coffee at Alejandro's and go to the market first."

It was a treat for Miriam to go into town with Matteo. The merchants and farmers all knew and respected him. In her first years living in Spain her Spanish improved dramatically from these outings and the social gatherings that came from them. On each visit she learned new expressions and jokes in Spanish. It was such a colorful language! Her neighbors were eager for their children and grandchildren to learn other languages well. Parents knew that their children would benefit from knowing English. The fact that Miriam knew English well from living so long in the U.S. meant her Spanish friends were always eager to practice English with her. She had even tutored several families in her first years in Spain in exchange for their help renovating her house.

Miriam settled in with her *café con leche* near the window overlooking the street bordering the market. She always enjoyed watching people in the morning bustle. She sipped and prayed for those God seemed to bring to her attention. Meanwhile, Matteo took his coffee at the bar where he chatted with a couple of his old friends. These men trusted his counsel, and there was never a lack of problems and worries to be shared with him. She glanced over at the huddle of friends and noticed the respect they all gave him, and how intently they listened to him. Matteo cared for these men's needs through listening and prayer, but also by challenging them to accept responsibilities. They had known him long enough that they had learned much about God's love and faithfulness from watching Him walk with Matteo through the sorrows of his marriage and other losses, and had seen the signs and miracles of His presence with Matteo. It had taken dozens of years, but this little gathering of God's Church was waking up, along with their families and communities, to who God really was.

Just like God awakened me, she thought. She looked out the window, took a sip of the delicious coffee, and prayed for the little girl with the red sweater and pink school bag to meet Jesus someday soon.

5

ANDRÉS GARCIA FERNANDEZ

Andrés placed his carry-on in the overhead bin, took off his sport coat, and placed it neatly on top, then settled into seat 16 A with his laptop. He would tackle writing another couple of chapters in his manuscript during the flight to Madrid so that the first few days with his dad could be writing-free, totally focused on reconnecting with his father and helping him with any projects that needed finishing in the albergue dormitory before the busy season. His editor had given him a reasonable deadline to have the manuscript first draft finished by the end of August, and he had calculated that as long as he could work a couple of hours several days per week, he would complete it on schedule.

Working diligently during the flight except for breaks during the meal and snack time, he wrote two chapters and started the next before closing his laptop for the rest of the flight. He leaned back in his seat and closed his eyes to nap a bit, and was transported back to a happy scene at the farm, before his mother left his father and Andrés to begin a new life for herself in the city. She had broken two hearts when she left, and neither of them had ever mended completely. Andrés was thankful that his dad had leaned into the void with even more love for his son. If he had any bitter thoughts toward his wife, he had never expressed them to Andrés, neither had he given the boy false hope about having much attention from his mother in the future.

But this scene was a happy one with the three of them picnicking in early summer in the shade of the big oaks in the far pasture. They laughed at their new puppy chasing butterflies near the field of rapeseed in full bloom, and waved at the occasional peregrino walking nearby on the Camino. Andrés prayed a silent prayer of thanks for the good memory that played in his mind, since he had many of the other sort that brought him sorrow. Now that she had died, Andrés often asked God for good memories to recall about his mother. *She loved you as best as she could, my son. When she left it was because she wanted to find a life she hoped existed somewhere else. She was never as happy again as she had been with you and your father. Remember the joy and love you shared as a family. She does.*

"Sir, please bring your seat up for landing. Sir?"

Andrés blinked awake, the happy memory fading from his mind, and sat upright. "*Sí*, yes, thank you." He looked out the window at a beautiful sunrise over the outskirts of Madrid. He always loved the feeling of coming home to Spain. No matter the troubles the news reported, he always felt hope rise in his heart when he thought of Spain. He knew this was one of the gifts God had given him along with his calling to help his people by designing economic policies with government and business leaders. Hope was the foundation for the passion that spirited him through his university degrees with distinction, the essence that had gotten him noticed and sought after by corporate and governmental think tanks.

Papá, you are probably already waiting in the baggage area for me, he thought as he texted his dad that he had landed. Andrés smiled as he thought of the faithfulness of his father. He had the reputation of someone who could be counted on for help and wisdom. He had not had the educational opportunities he had sought for his son, but he had a contagious hunger for learning about the world. Andrés had often quipped, "Papá, I may have several diplomas on a wall, but you are the better educated man of the two of us!"

A little while later Andrés emerged from the international flights area with his small bag piggy-backed to his big rolling suitcase, and his backpack slung over his shoulder. He smiled at the lively Spanish chatter of the Barajas airport. As he scanned the welcoming faces he heard his father call his name.

"Andrés!"

"Papá!" The greetings came with a strong embrace as father and son enjoyed their reunion. Anyone passing by would see how Andrés resembled his father in looks, though Matteo was slightly taller.

"You look smarter and more fit every summer! How was the flight?"

"I got some work done on the book, and even a brief

siesta. You are looking robust as ever, Papá. Your joy is contagious," Andrés remarked as father and son hugged hello again.

"Let me help you with your small suitcase. Any problems getting my peanut butter through customs?" Matteo winked.

"Not at all. I brought you two big jars to last the summer. Did you drive over this morning, or come yesterday and spend the night with Tio Juan?" asked Andrés, hopeful that one day his father would make it easier on himself and come to Madrid the day before his arrival and stay with his brother Juan, rather than leave home at 3:30 in the morning to pick him up at dawn.

"Now son, you know it is difficult to ask someone to cover for me to be away that long," he debated in his good-natured way. "Besides, this way I have a good excuse to take a longer siesta after lunch!"

Andrés laughed as they walked to the parking garage, "I would be happy to catch a bus to Burgos and save you the trip."

"It is good for me to drive to Madrid occasionally. It makes me grateful for the simpler ways of the farm when I get stuck in traffic here. Here we are over in the next row," Matteo pointed.

Andrés pulled his big suitcase toward the little truck and as they got closer, was greeted by Rex's happy barks. "Hello, big fella. I'm glad to see you, too!" Andrés tousled the shepherd's head and was greeted by a polite lick on the chin, and lots of wagging. "Have you been keeping watch over the truck, big guy?"

"He is good company for the drive, and a faithful four-legged security guard. The door locks in this truck haven't been working for months."

They loaded the suitcases into the back with Rex, Andrés offered to drive, and they headed out to the A-1 north toward *Burgos*.

"Papá, I am so glad to be here. No matter where I travel or live, I will always enjoy coming home to you in Spain."

"Everything is better when you are part of it! We will see what God is up to this summer, eh? He always has interesting people to meet and good ways to serve them."

"So true, Papá. So true."

6

DOCTOR'S ORDERS

Elizabeth's pulse was still pounding in her ears as she stared at the doctor.

"Ms. Wiltshire, you sustained a moderate concussion when you fell. We have you on a fluids drip because you were dehydrated when you arrived, and we want to keep you here overnight to monitor you," said the doctor as he read her chart.

"I'm sorry, Dr…?" Elizabeth fumbled.

"Glynn," he said.

"Yes, Dr. Glynn. I'm in the middle of a big case at work. We're going to trial next week. I need to call my boss right away…I simply can't stay here." The doctor locked eyes with Elizabeth.

"Begging your pardon, but this is not a choice. Your body

is trying to tell you to slow down. It's a mercy you weren't driving when this happened, and there were people around to help you. It could have been much worse, and if you don't make some lifestyle changes, it will be next time."

Elizabeth didn't realize Donna had accompanied her to the hospital until she spoke. "Doctor, if I may. Elizabeth has a month of vacation and comp time available, and she should be able to take it this summer. Things are generally pretty quiet around the firm during July."

"Perfect," said Dr. Glynn. "I'm not exaggerating when I say your life depends on getting some rest, Ms. Wiltshire. I'll be back in to check on you later this afternoon. For now, I've given you something to help you sleep, so please do your best to relax." He dimmed the lights as he left the room, closing the door quietly behind him.

Donna got up from the corner where she'd been sitting and moved her chair closer to the bed. She picked up Elizabeth's cold hand, unfurled the tightly clenched fist, gently rubbing the fingers until they warmed. "Dear, I'll be here until you fall asleep." Tears slipped out from Elizabeth's closed eyelids. When was the last time someone had touched her this tenderly? Had cared for her this way?

As she drifted off to sleep, she heard Donna humming softly, and the beckoning voice she had heard upon waking early that morning whispered, *Beloved*. Merciful sleep overtook her.

When she woke up, pink light was coming in through the window. The sun was setting and her head throbbed. *I have to check my email. I've missed so much. Bruce is probably going to kill me.*

She pushed the call button on the side of her bed. A young nurse came into the room with a glass of water and some Tylenol. "Here you are, Ms. Wiltshire. Something for your head. If you're feeling up to it, I'll bring you a light supper."

"I need to make some phone calls. Also, could you please bring me my laptop?"

The nurse hesitated, then said, "Ma'am, the lady who brought you in took all your belongings with her. She said she would keep them safe. She said she'd be back soon, so perhaps you can ask her when she comes. In the meantime, please take this before your headache gets worse. I'll be back with some supper."

Irritated at Donna, Elizabeth did as she was told, feeling humiliated at her loss of control. *I can't wait to get out of here. None of these people know me. I'm fine. What was Donna thinking, taking my laptop with her like that? She of all people should know how much work I have to do.* Her thoughts spiraled as she watched the sun set over the city she'd called home for almost ten years.

A distant bell tolled the hour. *Seven o'clock*, she thought. How long had it been since she'd seen the sun set? She was usually at work until dark. She shut her eyes against the intensity of the beauty outside. *I can't believe Ellen got the promotion! What has Ellen got that I haven't? I'm the one that turned the tide for the Hanley case last year, and Bruce said he'd never seen such insight. I'm the one Bruce asks for help, I'm the one Bruce turns to when he has a problem he can't solve. Ellen doesn't deserve this! I do! She's probably thrilled to have me out of the office for a while so she can one up me some more.*

Elizabeth continued to assail Ellen in her thoughts, but was interrupted by a soft knock on her door. Donna entered the room with a cup of tea and a backpack. "Donna, where is my laptop? I have to talk with Bruce. What's going on at the office?"

Donna set the tea down on the bedside table, sighed deeply, and turned to face Elizabeth. "Elizabeth, I've been praying all day for courage to speak the truth to you. Honey, I know you wanted that promotion. I know it was a shock to be passed over. But I think, with time, you'll see that this is a good thing. I took everything to your place, and picked up some of your own pajamas, a few books, and some snacks to make your stay a bit more tolerable. I also called your father."

"You called Dad?" She didn't want her father to worry. He had enough to think about without being burdened by this too.

"Yes, I called your dad," Donna said slowly. "I gave him the full report, and for now he's staying in Atlanta. He has a big case going to trial tomorrow, but told me to call him if there's any change."

Elizabeth breathed a sigh of relief. The last thing she wanted to do was interrupt her father's work schedule. She'd always admired his work ethic and attention to detail. Donna sat down beside Elizabeth and took her hand again. "Is there anything you want to talk about? I'm here to listen."

"No, I'm fine. I think I just want to be left alone," said Elizabeth.

"I'm just a phone call away if you need me, Elizabeth. And I'm ready to listen anytime you want to talk." Donna stood up, kissed Elizabeth's forehead, and exited the room.

She doesn't even know me, Elizabeth thought. *Why is she doing all this for me? And what gives her the right to judge me when she doesn't know what I'm capable of and what I need? And what does she know about my job? She's just an administrative assistant.*

Elizabeth looked around the room for something to distract her from her thoughts. She noticed a stack of magazines on the corner table. She gingerly got up from the bed, not wanting to bother the nurse for something so simple. She couldn't believe how woozy she felt. As she thumbed through an outdated issue of *Get Outside* magazine, the word "Camino" caught her eye. She quickly found the article. Images of the Pyrenees mountains, vineyards, and cathedrals accompanied the article, titled "The Camino de Santiago: A Trip Like No Other." She skimmed the article, captivated by phrases such as "the trek of a lifetime" and "tests the true mettle of a person physically, mentally, emotionally." She closed her eyes to think, intrigued by what she'd just read.

Everyone wants me to take a vacation. Fine! I'll do it. But I'm doing it my way. I'm not going to just sit around on a beach somewhere. If I take a vacation, I want something to show for it.

As she perused the article, the door to her hospital room cracked open. Ellen quietly peeked in, and seeing Elizabeth awake, stepped all the way into the room. She walked over to the bed, patted Elizabeth on the shoulder, and set down a vase of pink tulips.

Wow, how did she know my favorite flowers are tulips? Elizabeth thought.

"Hi, Ellen. Those tulips are beautiful," invited Elizabeth.

"How are you feeling? Donna says they want you to stay the night to keep an eye on how you are doing." Ellen glanced at the magazine on Elizabeth's lap. "Oh my goodness! The Camino! That's what I started telling you about in the elevator this morning."

Elizabeth perked up. "Really? Have you and Frank walked it?"

"Not yet," Ellen said. "But we're considering it..." her voice trailed off and she glanced out the window and sat down. She let the silence hang for a minute before making eye contact with Elizabeth. "Everything I've read about the Camino makes me think that it's a good place to go for people who are looking for answers. Who feel like maybe there's more to life than getting up every morning and putting in hour after hour at a difficult job with difficult people."

Ellen shifted in her seat, then began to speak slowly. "Elizabeth, I'm really sorry you didn't get the promotion. I wanted it to be you. Truly. But Bruce and my dad are friends from way back. As much as I've tried to make my own way at this firm and in the legal profession, I can't seem to shake some of the nepotism that comes with family connections." Disarmed by Ellen's forthrightness, Elizabeth was quiet, shocked by what she was hearing.

Ellen and I have much more in common than I ever knew, Elizabeth thought. *Maybe I've been wrong to see her as a competitor, although it does feel very unfair that I got passed over for this promotion because of her family connections.*

"Ellen, thank you for being honest with me. I know it must have been hard for you to tell me this. Would you and Frank be up for getting dinner together sometime? I'd love to get to know you both better. We could at least commiserate about our hard jobs!" she said with a chuckle.

Ellen relaxed and smiled warmly. "Thanks, Elizabeth, we'd love that. Why don't you concentrate on getting rest for now, and we can schedule something once you've had a chance to recuperate a bit?"

"Sure, that sounds great," said Elizabeth.

"Well, I better go. I'm supposed to finish up some documents tonight. Believe me, I'd rather stay and chat with you," Ellen said with an eye roll. "Probably best for you to get more rest anyway, right? I just felt like I needed to come see you and tell you the whole story about the promotion. Plus, somehow I knew you would enjoy a bouquet of pink tulips."

"Thanks so much for coming, and for the tulips. They are my favorite. It's been a long time since anyone's gotten me flowers, Ellen. I'm really grateful. Hope you don't have to stay up too late!"

Ellen bent down and gave Elizabeth a gentle hug. "I'll do my best, Elizabeth. Rest well!"

As Ellen left the room, Elizabeth looked down at the

magazine in her lap. *Okay, I think maybe someone, somewhere is trying to tell me something,* she thought.

7

PREPARING FOR THE CAMINO

After she was released from the hospital the next day around noon, Elizabeth went straight home, thankful to have her laptop back. She opened her email, expecting to have several messages from Bruce listing all the tasks he expected her to do. She was unnerved to find only one that said simply, "Elizabeth: Ellen is handling all the work you're supposed to be doing. Hopefully you'll be back to full strength soon. Bruce."

She replied immediately, "Dear Bruce, I'm so sorry I've been out of touch for the past 24 hours. Donna took my laptop and I wasn't able to stay in touch the way I know you need me to. Please feel free to assign me any additional tasks that need doing, and please know that I'll be available throughout the weekend for anything you might need. Kind Regards, Elizabeth."

She kept her email open and googled "Camino de Santiago." "The Camino de Santiago, also known by the English names Way of St. James, St. James's Way, St. James's Path, St. James's Trail, Route of Santiago de Compostela, and Road to Santiago, is the name of any of the pilgrimage routes (most commonly the Camino Francés or French route) to the shrine of the apostle St. James the Great in the Cathedral of Santiago de Compostela in Galicia in northwestern Spain, where tradition has it that the remains of the saint are buried. Many take up this route as a form of spiritual path or retreat, for their spiritual growth. *Sounds like my kind of spiritual retreat...a 500-mile hike that begins with a trek across the Pyrenees.*

Although most of the articles she read suggested 5-7 weeks to complete the hike, Elizabeth decided to schedule four weeks. *After all, I'm in great shape. I can probably do it in three and a half weeks, but I'll allow four just to have a few extra days in case there's bad weather or something.* She spent the rest of the afternoon planning her trip, making a list of supplies she would need, and looking for plane tickets. *I like the idea that I get a certificate when I finish. That'll be a cool thing to show people when I get back so they can see what I did.*

Disconcerted by the lack of communication from Bruce that afternoon, she sent another email his way checking in. *Donna probably interfered and told him not to contact me to let me 'rest' or something ridiculous like that.* Around 7 that evening, a short missive pinged in her inbox. "Donna told me that the doctor has ordered you to take a vacation this summer. I guess some people don't hold up to this pace well. Let me know ASAP what your schedule is going to be so I can plan. Bruce"

Elizabeth quickly sent Bruce a Camino link she'd been researching that afternoon, and a schedule for her proposed vacation dates. "Do what you want as long as you're available by phone and email," he replied. Elizabeth finalized her itinerary and sent it to Bruce, along with the assurance that she would stay available to the office the whole time.

As she clicked "send" on her email, she thought, *Okay, this is really happening. I better go check my supplies so I see what gear I need.*

She went into her bedroom, pulled the step stool out from under the bed, and stretched up to the top shelf in her closet, feeling for her old backpack. A waft of dust made her sneeze as her hand clenched onto the top strap, and she stepped down from her stool carefully. "The last thing I need is another concussion, eh Willoughby?" She glanced over at the plump cat fast asleep on her pillow. *I'm going to need to find someone to watch this guy, too,* she thought, adding another line to the list she was making in her head.

She opened her pack, trying to get a feel for the size and whether it was suitable for the trek she was planning. *Well, there's not really a good pocket here for my laptop, so I should probably get something newer.*

As she probed the pack her fingers closed around a slip of paper. She pulled it out, and tears filled her eyes as she glanced down at it. A pen and ink drawing of a man and woman dancing the flamenco took her back to a night 12 years ago. It was the last night of their six-week backpacking trip through Europe, and she and Steve had planned a fancy dinner with flamenco as entertainment before they left Madrid to fly home. She'd spent the afternoon napping in their hotel room while Steve read by the pool. They had splurged on the hotel. She was just getting ready to shower when Steve came back into the room. She glanced up, blushing as she realized her thoughts had been straying towards imagining Steve proposing that night. The past eighteen months that they'd been a couple had been idyllic, and their trip to Europe had only confirmed the strength of their relationship.

As soon as she looked into Steve's eyes, a hard knot formed in her belly. His brow creased as he looked at her, and she knew she wasn't going to like what he had to say. "Elizabeth, I've been thinking…" he began.

The rest of the conversation passed in a blur, but the key phrases stood out. "Can't be encumbered by you when I'm starting medical school…college romances are fun… the last 6 weeks have been wonderful, but I don't really see us together long term." Nauseated, Elizabeth packed her things as quickly as possible, wanting to be out of Steve's presence. She vaguely remembered the concierge at the hotel helping her get a taxi and Steve running down the front steps telling her "Don't be ridiculous, you don't have to leave," as the taxi drove away. She managed to change her flight and leave that evening, and never saw or heard from Steve again.

The phone rang, jolting Elizabeth from the painful memories. She glanced down at the caller ID: Ellen. Welcoming the distraction, Elizabeth answered the phone, and answered Ellen's questions about one of the cases they were currently handling. As they finished the conversation, Ellen said, "Hey, would you like to grab coffee tomorrow? Maybe we could talk through what I can do to help cover some of your workload so you can ACTUALLY get a vacation."

"Thanks," Elizabeth said. "I'd love that." She hung up, thankful for the prospect of friendship with Ellen. She spent the rest of the evening making a list of things she would need to buy at REI in the morning, and drifted off to sleep, glad that the following day would be full of tangible goals to work towards.

The next afternoon, Elizabeth hopped into her car and drove towards Virginia, on a mission to find hiking gear. She and Ellen had ended up chatting for three hours at her favorite coffee place in Dupont Circle. After leaving, sides hurting from laughter, Elizabeth remembered a favorite saying of her mother's: You never really understand a person until you consider things from her point of view — until you climb into her skin and walk around in it. Her mom's favorite book had been *To Kill a Mockingbird*, and this quote from Atticus Finch had sunk deep into Emily Wiltshire's consciousness.

I've misjudged Ellen, thought Elizabeth. *I was so busy thinking about my own career that I let that take over everything else. I wonder how many other times I've done that? I don't want to be this way, but I feel like this is part of the grind.* Unbidden, Donna's face came into her mind, and Elizabeth realized she needed to thank Donna and apologize for the way she'd snapped at her. *I wonder how many times I've treated Donna poorly when she's been so kind to me. I feel so guilty!!!*

As Elizabeth crossed the Potomac River on I-395, she thought, *I want to do better. I need to think of others more...* Elizabeth's mind sifted through all the people she'd hurt or failed to appreciate, but she was suddenly distracted by the sunlight hitting the cherry blossoms. Streams of soft light broke through the clouds, illuminating the blossoms and creating a pinkish halo around the tidal basin. She was forced to slow down as traffic built up around lane closures due to construction. Most days, she would have been frustrated by a classic DC traffic jam, but today was different.

Deep inside, she heard, *This is for you, Beloved. This chance to slow down and see something beautiful. Drink it in. Enjoy it. Let it heal you.*

The truck behind her honked impatiently, motioning Elizabeth to merge, and she quickly did so, tearing her eyes away from the natural beauty below her, trying to refocus on her trip to REI.

As she walked into the store, list in hand, Elizabeth was surprised by how empty it seemed. She must have looked lost, because a sales associate came over. "Everyone's out enjoying the spring weather," said a wiry, middle-aged man with graying beard and hair. "I'm Dave. Can I help you?" His brown eyes creased as he smiled at her, and Elizabeth immediately felt at ease.

"Well, I'm a little daunted. I'm hiking the Camino de Santiago in July…"

Dave's face brightened into an even bigger grin. "The Camino! That trip changed my life!! You're kidding! You won't regret that decision."

Warming to his enthusiasm, Elizabeth handed over her list, and he perused it quickly. "Okay, well the most important thing I can tell you is that you want to minimize the weight you carry. This is very strenuous walk, and a lot of people don't give it the respect it deserves. I've seen it over and over. People think because they run marathons or hike a lot they won't have any problems, but then they end up with a stress fracture or something. Tell me about your itinerary," he said, continuing to look down at the list.

"Well, I'm flying out July 1st and back on August 1st. I'm starting from St. Jean Pied-de-Port. I've done several marathons and played competitive soccer most of my life. I run about 40 miles per week, so I don't anticipate this being too difficult for me," said Elizabeth.

"Okay," said Dave with a skeptical glance at Elizabeth out of the corner of his eye. "Well, the first thing we need to do is get you a good pack and some good boots or shoes." He led the way over to a wall where many packs hung.

"I'll need something that has a pocket for my laptop," said Elizabeth.

Dave turned, eyebrows raised. "That is a lot of weight! Why in the world are you taking a laptop?"

"Because my job depends on it!" Elizabeth said defensively. "I wish I had a choice, but I don't."

"Okay, sorry" said Dave. "I'm just trying to help you prevent injury. I'm glad to help you get the gear that suits you best." As Elizabeth tried on different packs, Dave regaled her with tales of his time on the Camino. "I went in October—tighten that strap there a bit—so it was less crowded than in the summer when you'll be going. The downside was that it was also colder. I almost got blown off a mountain on the hike over the Pyrenees. I could barely stand the wind was so strong. That first day from St. Jean is the toughest. It's only about 23 kilometers, that's about

16 miles, but there is also a huge elevation change--almost 5,000 feet! I made the mistake of not starting until 9:00 in the morning because I was jet-lagged and thought I'd have enough time. I barely made it to the albergue before it closed at 10:00 that night. If I could do it over again, I would've taken a few days in Paris to acclimate to the time change. Oh well, live and learn. There now!"

Elizabeth stood up straight and saluted. "It feels great, Dave!"

"Well, how about we get the rest of your gear and stuff it in there before you make that determination?" he said with a sly smile. Elizabeth tried on several pairs of hiking boots and shoes, finally settling on a pair that felt extra cushioned and seemed to have plenty of room in the toe box. After watching Elizabeth walking up and down some fake rock and jumping on and off benches, Dave pronounced the shoes a good fit.

"Of course, it doesn't matter how well your boots fit. You're likely to get the worst blisters you've ever had in your life hiking the Camino. That reminds me, let me show you a blister kit that has everything you should need in it," he said over his shoulder as he walked to another part of the store.

"That's okay," Elizabeth said as she followed Dave. "Like I said, I've done several marathons, so I know all about chafing and blisters."

Dave turned to Elizabeth and locked eyes with her. "I had done ten marathons before I hiked the Camino, and let me tell you, thinking that way can get you into real trouble on this trek."

"Okay, okay!" laughed Elizabeth. "You just keep saying I need to lighten my load, so I'm trying to figure out where I can pare things down."

"Well, there are some necessities you don't want to do without, and a blister kit's one of them."

As they walked towards the front of the store, Elizabeth stopped next to a shelf full of energy bars and gels. "I should probably get some of this stuff, huh?"

"I would advise against it. Part of the Camino experience is trusting that you'll have your needs of food and shelter met along the way. And practically speaking, we're trying to keep the weight down. This isn't the Appalachian Trail. There will be towns and villages to stop in all along the way. I know I keep harping on this, but I really want to be sure I've helped you have as realistic expectations as possible."

"Well," Elizabeth said, "who knows what the quality of the food will be over there? I feel like I just need to take some of this stuff since it's healthy and good fuel, and I have used it before."

"All right," said Dave. "It's up to you."

After loading up on clothing, to Dave's chagrin, Elizabeth felt prepared.

"Here's my card," said Dave as he helped Elizabeth to the car with her bulging bags. Don't hesitate to call if you have any more questions for me!"

"Thanks so much for everything, Dave," said Elizabeth.

51

"Your time and advice mean so much to me. Take care!"

"You too," said Dave. "And stop by if you need anything else or want to talk about your trip when you come back. I never get tired of swapping Camino stories! *Buen Camino!*"

"Sorry, what?"

"*Buen Camino!* It's a Spanish salutation you will be giving to other pilgrims and using to part company with others as you walk...it's a wish or prayer for the person you salute to have a good pilgrimage."

"Okay, thanks, Dave," Elizabeth offered as she felt her heart warming.

Elizabeth honked and waved as she drove out of the parking lot. Once she'd made three trips up and down the stairs to her apartment, unloading her purchases, she got to work putting things away, and spent the rest of the afternoon coming up with her itinerary. She was interrupted by a phone call from her dad.

"Hi Dad! Guess what I'm doing?"

Her father ignored the question. "Are you okay, Honey? I haven't heard from you in awhile and just wanted to check in and be sure you're feeling okay after everything."

"Oh, yes, I'm okay Dad. Some big things are happening that I'm really excited about, and..."

"Sorry Elizabeth, I don't have time to talk right now. I just wanted to make sure you were all right. I'm so glad you're okay and I hope you have a great rest of your weekend.

Talk again soon. Bye."

Elizabeth stared down at her phone as her dad hung up. She was used to short conversations with her dad, but it still hurt that he didn't take more time to listen to her. As she sat staring at her phone, she thought back to another conversation she'd had with her dad, years ago.

Her mother's cancer had gotten worse. The doctors had said there was nothing more they could do, and had suggested they call hospice and make her mother comfortable at home. The downstairs guest room became a temporary hospital room filled with ventilators, pain pumps, a hospital bed, and more. Elizabeth continued to go to school every day "to keep things as normal as possible," per her father's suggestion, and continued to play soccer with her team. Her father continued to work late and go to trial regularly. One night, Elizabeth collided with her dad on her way upstairs to get ready for bed.

"How is she, honey?" he asked, lines of worry creasing his face.

"Dad, I don't know. She just seems...so..." Elizabeth's voice trailed off as tears blurred her vision. She leaned her head against her dad's chest, wanting comfort, wishing she could crawl into his lap the way she had when she was a little girl. Instead, her dad took her by the shoulders and gently pushed her back. He tipped her chin up and wiped her tears away.

"Honey, Mom and I need you to be strong and keep smiling. Mom isn't going to get better if we don't stay positive!"

Elizabeth forced herself to swallow the fear rising in her throat. "But Dad, Mom is dy..."

He interrupted her quickly, as if denying what everyone else knew was coming would keep it from happening. "You don't need to worry; Mom's going to be fine! Go on upstairs and get some rest. It's after 10:00, and you have to get up early tomorrow."

Elizabeth turned slowly and trudged upstairs, wishing her dad wasn't so reluctant to let her express her sadness and fears with him. She resolved to do better, not to cause any trouble, and to stay out of the way. *The last thing he or Mom needs is to worry about me.*

Thus, to the outside world, everything seemed to be fine. Sometimes after soccer, before her father got home from work, Elizabeth would go to her mother's room to be near her while she did her homework. Her mother slept most of the time, but occasionally she'd open her eyes and smile at Elizabeth.

One conversation stood out powerfully in Elizabeth's memory and came back to her as she processed her Dad's abrupt retreat just now on the phone. Elizabeth came to tell her mom she was home from school, and to check to see how she was.

"How was your day, Sweetie?"

"Oh Mom, it was okay. How are *you* Feeling?" Elizabeth asked.

"I'm okay," she smiled. "Looking forward to being with Jesus."

"Mom, don't say that! You have to keep fighting! I just read an article about someone who had Stage IV ovarian cancer and they sent her home, but she ended up recovering."

"Honey, I know those things happen," said her mom. "But I also know this is my time. I want to tell you some things before…"

"Mom, I said stop it!" she interrupted. "Nothing is going to happen to you. You'll see! Dad and I know you're going to pull through this!" She grabbed her backpack and ran upstairs, slamming her bedroom door. *I KNOW she's going to be okay! I can't believe she's giving up like this!* Elizabeth paced back and forth across her bedroom.

The phone rang, and she quickly scooped it up. It was her soccer coach. "Elizabeth, have you decided what you're going to do about the tournament in Chattanooga this weekend? Please don't feel like you have to come if it's not a good time…"

"No, I can totally come. Mom is fine. I'll see you Friday afternoon," she said with forced cheerfulness.

As she hung up the phone, she heard a whisper. *Beloved, stay home this weekend.*

No way, she thought. *I'm definitely going. I need to get away for a few days anyway.*

When her father got home from work at 10:00, he supported her decision to go to the tournament, so she packed her things Thursday night. Friday morning she popped her head into her mother's room before leaving for school. Her mother was asleep, so Elizabeth blew her a kiss from the door and raced down the driveway, hurrying to catch the bus. *I'll see her when I get back.*

Upon arriving in Chattanooga, Elizabeth and the rest of the team spent the evening in the hotel pool, and then got to bed early because their first game was at 8 the next morning. Elizabeth scored two goals in the first game, feeling fully alive for the first time in weeks.

After her team cruised to victory, Elizabeth rushed off the field to get a snack, a wide smile on her face. Her team manager met her on the sidelines. "Your dad just called. He asked that you call him back as soon as possible." Elizabeth ran into the field house and asked to use a phone. Her father answered after the first ring.

"How was your game, Elizabeth?"

She noticed a tremor in his voice. "Dad, what's wrong? What's happened?"

"Your mother passed away this morning."

"WHAT! No! You said she was going to get well. How is that possible?"

"I know. I didn't expect it." There was a catch in his throat. "The coach says one of the parents there offered to bring you home now. I've got to go call the funeral home. See you in a couple of hours." The line clicked and went dead. Elizabeth sank slowly to the ground, still holding the phone in her hand, oblivious to the dial tone beeping incessantly. She stared at nothing, tears streaming down her cheeks, somewhat aware of happy voices, whistles blowing, a squeaky air conditioner nearby. She could smell the freshly mown grass and mud stuck to her soccer cleats. Her hands shook uncontrollably. Someone called her name, but she sat there weeping silently, her back slumped against the cabinet, her jaw clenched against the sobs threatening to rip from her chest. Her anger at this bitter injustice kept the wrenching grief at bay.

"Elizabeth! Elizabeth? Are you in here? Is it your mom?" Her friend Amy turned the corner and almost stepped on Elizabeth. "Elizabeth?" Her voice trailed off as she looked from the phone receiver to Elizabeth's pale face and closed eyes. She sank to her knees beside her friend and tentatively touched her shoulder. "Elizabeth, I'm so sorry." Amy's voice trembled as she began to cry.

Just then Coach Miller, and her teammate Camille Huntley walked in followed by her parents carrying Elizabeth's sports bag. They all hugged her, crying, and said they were sorry for her loss. Elizabeth didn't know if she could handle the onslaught of sympathy she was about to receive from teammates, their parents, and her friends in the coming days.

She didn't remember much about the two-hour trip home. She felt strangely frozen between anger and tears. The Huntleys sensed she didn't want to talk, and left her to her thoughts.

Staring out the car window, she wrestled inwardly. *Hold it together, Elizabeth. Don't fall apart. Be strong. Be a help.* The incessant thoughts tripped over one another, coming quickly. *But what about me? How will I bear this? Don't be selfish, Elizabeth. Everyone needs you.*

And so Elizabeth resolved to be the person everyone needed her to be. She organized a lunch following the Friday morning funeral, spent the weekend entertaining guests, and went back to school on Monday after her dad left for work. His hours at the office increased, and by the time Elizabeth graduated from high school, she rarely saw her father beyond the impromptu kitchen chat or occasional times he left work to come to one of her soccer games.

He had retreated so far from her now, Elizabeth realized she had lost more than her mother, and wept.

8

HOLLY

~~~~~~

Elizabeth was surprised to see the light turning golden outside her kitchen window, suggesting the sunset was only an hour or so away. Feeling the need for some physical activity, she decided to break in her new hiking boots and walking poles on a trail in Rock Creek Park. As she walked out of her building, she met her downstairs neighbor, Holly. Although they rarely exchanged more than cursory pleasantries, Elizabeth greeted her enthusiastically, hoping human contact would help her shake the melancholy meanderings of the afternoon's thoughts about her mom.

"Wow, where are you headed, Elizabeth? You look pretty serious!"

"Just breaking in my new gear for a trip I'm taking this summer." On a whim, Elizabeth invited, "Hey want to walk with me? I'm just going over to Rock Creek Park and back."

Holly looked Elizabeth up and down, and seemed to come to a decision. "Okay, I might be able to keep up with you since you're not going too far. Let me change my shoes. Here, come on in for a bit." Holly opened her door and flicked on a lamp. The light illuminated a slightly messy, simply furnished apartment.

While Holly trotted to the bedroom to grab her running shoes, Elizabeth glanced at the framed picture on the end table by the couch. Holly stood with a tall, dark haired man, in front of the Eiffel Tower. The same man was prominently featured in several other photos throughout the apartment, and Elizabeth realized she'd always assumed Holly was single. "Would you like something to drink, Elizabeth?" Holly called from the bedroom.

"No, thanks. I'm fine!" Elizabeth answered, wishing Holly would hurry up since daylight was waning.

After another few minutes, Holly came out wearing running shoes and hiking pants. "Sorry, I've put on some weight in the past year and was having a hard time finding something that fit," Holly said with a sheepish look. "You've probably never had a problem with that! You're so thin!"

Embarrassed, yet slightly pleased at Holly's appraisal of her looks, Elizabeth said, "Okay, you ready? We're losing our daylight!"

As the two women exited the building, Elizabeth shot a sideways glance at Holly. She realized Holly might, in fact, have a difficult time keeping up with her long strides. Holly's head reached just above her shoulder, and she didn't seem like someone with a regular exercise schedule.

Resigning herself to a slow walk that may or may not reach the goal she had in mind, Elizabeth decided to find out more about her neighbor. "So how is school going? Are you enjoying your students?"

Holly taught at a local Montessori school, and Elizabeth could only imagine how much stamina she must have to teach a classroom filled with small children all day long. "Oh, we've had a good year. There have been a lot of changes in the staff, but the children are so resilient they do well no matter what. The administration can be hard on the teachers, though. It's actually led me to want to go back to school so I can transition into the administrative side of things. So often administrators are out of touch with grassroots level education, and I want to change that. But I'd miss the daily contact with the children. If only I could do both!" Holly said wistfully. "What about you? Tell me about this trip you're taking!"

For the next 45 minutes, Elizabeth told Holly about the Camino, her itinerary, and other plans. The more she talked, the more proud and excited she felt. Holly was obviously impressed, especially when Elizabeth said, "Yeah, they say to allow five to six weeks for the trip, but I can't be away from the firm for that long."

"Well, I wish you the best, Elizabeth. That sounds incredible. I don't think I could ever do something like that," said Holly.

Feeling that perhaps she had sounded too superior, Elizabeth said, "Of course you could, Holly. You'd just need to train for it. It looks like you've done some traveling yourself. Who's that handsome man in the picture with you at the Eiffel Tower?" She gave Holly a gentle nudge in the ribs and a wink as she asked the question, expecting a giggle and a blush.

Instead, Holly's expression was masked, and her tone deadened as she answered simply, "That's Jake. We were engaged, but we're taking a break for a few months while he's traveling." A heavy silence hung between the two women, punctuated by the urban din of honking, car alarms, and helicopters. Elizabeth turned to look straight ahead, focusing on her posture as her hiking poles clicked on the sidewalk. *Sheesh, I shouldn't have brought that up. Sounds like he's stringing her on...*

As the silence wore on, Elizabeth glanced back down at Holly, who was starting to look winded and pink cheeked from the brisk walk. "You know what, Holly? How about we turn around here? We can grab some sandwiches on our way back home and eat at my place if you don't have plans."

"That sounds good," Holly said gratefully. For the rest of the walk back, Holly and Elizabeth swapped work stories. Elizabeth was taken aback when Holly mentioned, in passing, her fluency in French and her master's degree from the Sorbonne. *Wow, here's another person I've misjudged and made assumptions about.*

As they walked into Elizabeth's condo, Willoughby came happily out to greet them, and Holly immediately scooped him up. "I hope this is okay. I probably should have asked before I picked him up! What's your name, handsome?"

"Oh gosh, you're welcome to pick him up," said Elizabeth as she grabbed plates and cutlery from the cabinets and two beers from the fridge. "Sometimes I think he's more dog than cat. He loves attention! Actually, I need to figure out what to do with him while I am in Spain. Hey, would you be interested in watching him while I'm gone? I'm not sure how you feel..."

Before she could even finish her sentence, Holly interrupted and said, "Oh, yes, yes, yes! I'd love to! I grew up with a cat just like Willoughby. I've wanted to get a pet, but haven't found the right fit. Thank you so much for asking!"

The rest of the evening was full of laughter as the women painted their toenails, watched some wedding shows on tv, and talked about clothes. As Holly tromped back downstairs, Elizabeth said, "Come visit Willoughby anytime, come walk with me anytime, and I'd love to spend another evening pretending I'm in seventh grade again!"

Holly's merry laugh was audible all the way up the stairs. "You've got it, Elizabeth! Don't worry, next time I'll bring my 'Teen Beat' magazine! See you soon!"

9

BEGINNING

The next few months were so busy at work that Elizabeth barely had a moment to think about her trip. She took an occasional hike, and continued to run on her treadmill, reassuring herself she'd be physically ready for the trek ahead with all the miles she was putting in. She and Ellen met for lunch whenever their schedules matched up, and Elizabeth was delighted at the unexpected gift of having a friend at work. She and Holly also enjoyed some dinner-and-a-movie nights and short hikes together, and she was grateful when Holly offered to take her to the airport to catch her flight to Paris. When the time came for her departure, Elizabeth gave Willoughby one last squeeze, gave a last glance around the apartment, and locked the door. She couldn't help feeling anxious, even though she knew Holly would be checking on things, getting her mail, and using her car while she was gone. She hoisted her pack onto her shoulders, grabbed her handbag, and held her dress up with one hand as she walked gingerly down the stairs. Dave's warning echoed in her mind, "Be careful not to carry too much weight. Don't take anything you don't need. Ideally you shouldn't carry more than ten percent of your body weight."

She pushed away the anxiety brought on by her 30-pound pack as Holly opened the door and said brightly, "Ready to go?"

At the airport, Elizabeth waved from the curb as Holly pulled away, and promised to email as much as possible to check in. "I'm sure it'll be easy to keep in touch since I'm bringing my laptop," she reassured Holly.

"Maybe I'll set up a webcam so you can watch Willoughby while you're gone," Holly joked.

"Sounds riveting," said Elizabeth, laughing. "Please do!" She walked purposefully into the airport, found her gate, and spend the time before her flight emailing with Bruce and prepping for a deposition that had recently landed on her desk. Just before she shut her laptop down to board, an email pinged in her inbox. *John Cunningham! Gosh, I haven't heard from him in ages! He was always one of the nicest of my dad's lawyer friends. He really seemed to care about me as a person, not just about my achievements. I wonder why he's emailing me?* She skimmed the email.

Dear Elizabeth,

I know it's been a long time since we've been in touch, but I've kept tabs on you through your dad, and have always admired your work ethic, caring nature, and people skills. I remember when I wrote your law school recommendation you were interested in working with victims of domestic violence, and that you had the ultimate goal of opening your own firm someday. I know you've been working in the field of corporate law for some time now, and am not sure whether you've decided to continue on that trajectory or not. I have an opportunity you might be interested in if you'd like a change. You may remember that I've done pro bono work for domestic violence victims in the Atlanta area for a number of years, and the group for which I've worked, "Firm Foundations," would like to start a branch in the DC area. A number of private donors have already committed funding, and we have a few grants coming through in the next six months. Your role would be heading up the branch. Initially, it would only be you and an administrative assistant, but as the branch (hopefully) grows, you'd be able to hire more staff and expand. We wouldn't be able to pay the salary you're currently receiving, but hopefully we can pay enough for you to be comfortable. Please let me know if this is something you're interested in, and we can talk more.

Sincerely,
John L. Cunningham, Esq.

John Cunningham's kind, round face swam into her mind. His daughter, Sarah, had been a few years younger than Elizabeth in school, but their paths had still crossed regularly.

Mr. Cunningham had never missed a chorus concert, had always come to every awards ceremony, and had sat, beaming with pride, in the front row of every activity. *I wonder what it would have been like to have my dad so excited to be with me?* Elizabeth quickly pushed away the unbidden thought. *My dad had to work hard; besides, he always said John Cunningham didn't seem to understand what the job really demanded.* She quickly tapped out a reply,

Dear Mr. Cunningham,

Thanks so much for your email! It's lovely to hear from you. I'm on my way out of town for a month, but wanted to get back to you before I left. I appreciate your offer so much, but I'm very happy at my current job and plan to stay there for the foreseeable future.

Tell Sarah hello for me...

Take care,
Elizabeth

As she closed her laptop, she heard the voice again, *Are you really happy, beloved? Is this really the life you want? Come to me...*

She hurried over to join the line of boarders snaking around the seating area. *I really need to make partner before I try to take on something like that. Maybe in a year or two, but not now.*

Resolute in her decision, she found her seat, took out her neck pillow, and watched her fellow passengers board. She was fortunate to have a window seat, and planned to sleep for as much of the flight as possible.

She was just shutting her eyes when she felt her arm jostle and straightened up in her seat. A small, blonde boy was sitting down and stowing his backpack, chattering in French to his mother and baby sister, and leaning over Elizabeth to look out the window. *"Regardez! Regardez les hommes et les camions!"* His mother, a pretty woman who looked to be about Elizabeth's age, hushed him when she saw Elizabeth was trying to sleep.

Pushing back her annoyance, Elizabeth forced a smile and

said, *"Pas de problem,"* in her rusty college French.

"Merci, merci," said his obviously fatigued mother, and she and the little boy settled into their seats. The boy opened his backpack, extracted two rather worn matchbox cars, and handed one to Elizabeth. As he began a litany of engine noises, Elizabeth forced herself to stay calm and play along, smiling as her eyes met those of his grateful mother. Despite his mother's near constant admonitions of, *"Guillaume, arrête!"* the boy continued to lean over Elizabeth as they took off, exclaiming at all the *"petite choses"* below, clearly delighting in the novelty of flight. All expectation of sleep gone, Elizabeth couldn't help but delight in the child's infectious joy, and spent the time before dinner playing with cars, assorted rubber animals, and coloring with Guillaume, whose backpack seemed to contain an endless collection of action figures, cars, crayons, and stuffed animals. He was wholly unconcerned by the language barrier, and kept up a near constant stream of dialogue in his sweet, high voice. When their meals came, Elizabeth helped Guillaume cut his meat, hoping his mother wouldn't mind receiving a stranger's assistance. His mother said in heavily accented English, "Thank you very much. I am not able to be 'elping 'im and his seester. We 'ave traveled from Caleefornia today, and are very tired."

Elizabeth felt a sudden rush of warmth towards the woman, and said, *"Je m'appelle Elizabeth. Et toi?"* That's all the French I know, by the way," she said, smiling.

The woman smiled back and said, "I am Marie, this is Guillaume (Elizabeth chuckled as Guillaume began dancing his stuffed bear on her forearm), and this is Vianne." The chubby, pink-cheeked baby squeaked happily when

69

Elizabeth reached over and tickled her under the chin. As the flight attendants cleared their meals, Elizabeth assisted Marie with bedtime preparations, holding Vianne, helping Guillaume find the essential stuffed animals, and stowing his shoes and cap in his backpack. As his long eyelashes drooped, he popped his thumb in his mouth and leaned his head against Elizabeth's shoulder. Taken aback by the sweetness of his trust, Elizabeth's eyes momentarily filled with tears. Even though she had consciously chosen to devote herself to her career after her breakup with Steve, she had always hoped to be a mother. Unfortunately, the men she'd dated in the past several years had never stayed around past the initial spark of infatuation, and though they'd warmed each other's beds for a few months, Elizabeth had yet to find someone with whom she could truly be vulnerable. Not liking the direction her thoughts were taking, she gingerly leaned over on her neck pillow, moving as little as possible so as not to wake Guillaume, and closed her eyes again.

Strange dreams played across the stage of her mind: her father and Bruce laughing and talking about her trip to Spain, John Cunningham asking her to reconsider the job, Guillaume and Willoughby dancing and riding a merry-go-round.

She awoke to light streaming in her window, and felt small fingers on her arm, patting it. She looked down into Guillaume's sky blue eyes, and he cheerily said, "*Bon matin! Vous êtes prêt à jouer?*" Elizabeth was drawn back into Guillaume's imaginative world, one which lasted until his fork had handily defeated hers at breakfast, the flight attendants had collected the meal trays, and the plane landed at Charles de Gaulle airport.

Elizabeth was surprised at how bereft she felt as she watched Guillaume, Marie, and Vianne walk toward the immigration line for French citizens. As she turned to find the line for non-EU citizens, she felt a tug on her skirt. Guillaume was standing, holding up one of his treasured little cars to her. "For me?" Elizabeth asked.

"*Oui! Je vous aime!*" said the little boy, hugging her around her legs, and then trotting back to his mother. Marie waved at Elizabeth as they turned away, and Elizabeth inspected the sticky car through tears. Wiping her eyes, she looked up at the connecting flight board, confused that her flight wasn't listed.

The line edged forward for the next half hour, and finally she was stamped through passport control and hurried toward the baggage carousel to pick up her backpack and get through customs. Grabbing it from the carousel, she stood in line for the customs check and scanned the flight boards for her flight to Biarritz.

The customs agent waved her through the doorway, and she hurried to the security officer tending the conveyor receiving baggage being rechecked for connecting flights. "Excuse me, Monsieur. I do not see my flight to Biarritz on the board, but here is my ticket. Can you tell me what gate I need to find?"

He looked at her ticket, and then furrowed his brow. "Madame, this flight leaves from a different airport. You will have to catch a bus or taxi to get there. It is outside the city."

"What?" panicked Elizabeth. "My flight leaves in less than two hours! How long will it take to get there? What am I going to do?"

The line built up behind her as she struggled with what step to take next. The security guard said gently, "Madame, if you go to the information desk over there, they might be able to help you with another plan."

Passengers pushed past her as she mumbled an embarrassed, "Thank you," and ran with her backpack to the Information desk.

The woman at the desk looked up and smirked as Elizabeth screeched to a halt in front of her. After Elizabeth explained her dilemma, the woman said, smugly, "Your ticket is for the only flight to Biarritz today, and Orly airport is too far to make that flight. You will have to stay in Paris tonight and take the flight tomorrow morning."

"I HAVE to get to get to St. Jean Pied-de-Port tonight!" Elizabeth said, her volume increasing with her frustration level. "Ahha, *une pèlerine!*" The woman looked at her computer screen for the information to give Elizabeth. "Well, there is a flight leaving in one hour. Yes, there are a couple of seats left, and you will arrive in Toulouse at 10:55. From there you would take a train leaving at 13:04, which arrives in Bayonne at 17:32. From there you take a taxi to St. Jean if there is one." She indicated these options on a map, and Elizabeth nodded, feeling more frustrated.

She looked up at the clock on the airport wall, her sense of adventure rising to take on this new challenge. It was 8:25. "Where do I get my ticket and which gate?"

After the woman gave her directions and a plan, Elizabeth set out toward the ticket counter at a sprint. *"Merci,"* she called over her shoulder, hoping that she'd make the flight, the train, and find a taxi in order to make it to her hotel in St. Jean before it closed down for the night.

The flight was just over an hour, a taxi took her to the train station in Toulouse, and when she had bought her ticket to Bayonne, she still had a few minutes to get a snack in the cafe and board the train without jogging to the platform. Elizabeth stowed her pack in the luggage shelf on her train car, she settled into her seat with a big sigh of relief. This was the first time she had been on a European train since her backpack trip with Steve 12 years ago. A pang of nostalgia swept over her. Memories from their summer together played through her mind. What were these feelings she was having? Not regret, not anger. It wasn't that she missed Steve. The pain from his rejection after they had shared so much left her feeling unsure of her ability to read people. She did not miss the man who treated her this way. She realized that what she missed was the intimate relationship won from sharing hours of adventures and dreams. The attention of someone with common interests and goals, who had truly seemed interested in spending time with her. Her mother had always made her feel special in that way, but her dad was always too busy at the office for much of anything else.

The lunge of the train starting to move away from the platform jogged her back to the present. She downed the soda and sandwich she had bought at the station, and got out her laptop to check email. The slowness of the Internet on the train was annoying, but at least she could do some catching up at a snail's pace. She answered all of Bruce's emails first, and then let her dad, Holly, and Ellen know that she had made it this far.

She stared out the window as the pretty French countryside whizzed by. It was a beautiful day. This was not the plan she made, but she had to admit she was enjoying riding on the train and seeing the country. She would have been enjoying herself a lot more if she weren't so anxious about getting to her *albergue* in time to check in and find something for supper. She was travel-weary, but knew she needed to stay awake so she didn't miss getting off at Bayonne.

Finally they were slowing for the Bayonne station. Elizabeth pulled her backpack down from the luggage rack, loaded her laptop into its sleeve, and hoisted the pack onto her back without buckling the hip belt. She swung down onto the platform and rushed through the little station house to look for a taxi. It was 5:30 p.m., but the sun was still high.

A taxi! She hurried over to the curb out front, and as she arrived, three other people wearing hiking clothes and carrying packs hurried up as well. A jovial driver was hopping out speaking in French and some English while he opened the trunk of his car. Elizabeth realized she would be sharing this ride.

"My name is Pierre. I will take you to St. Jean Pied-de-Port. The cost will be 30 euros each. One of you in the front, and the rest in the back. Packs go in the trunk. Everyone in the taxi. We meet everyone when we get in."

While Elizabeth outwardly went along with the arrangement, she noticed again the unsettling feeling she had earlier of going along with something she had not planned, and hoping it would work out as the train ride had, an unexpected joy. Still she worried about getting to the room she had reserved.

She climbed in the front seat as Pierre closed the trunk and got in. The other three people tucked into the back. "*D'accord, allons-y*! Let's go!" said Pierre, as he started the engine. "Okay, America, what is your name, and where are you from in the States?" he asked Elizabeth.

Is it that obvious I'm American? thought Elizabeth, as she said, "I'm Elizabeth, and I'm from Washington, DC."

"*D'Accord, bon*. Okay, Good. Next..."

The others introduced themselves. A soft-spoken mother and college-aged daughter from Seoul, South Korea, whose names sounded something like Eenmo and Ungee. And a middle-aged man with an angular face and perfect English spoken with a Germanic accent, Gerald from near Frankfurt.

"Pierre, I have a reservation at the albergue close to the Pilgrim's Office. What time will we arrive?" asked Elizabeth, hoping to stake her claim to be dropped off first.

"Mademoiselle, you sound very worried. You will learn something on your *chemin*, your Camino, your pilgrimage. You will learn that we make our plans, but God directs our steps. He knows best what we need, and the sooner we learn to get along this way, the better it goes with us. We will get to St. Jean around 18:30. The Pilgrim Office is open until 22:00. If you need to purchase your *credenciál*, your pilgrim passport, you go there to do that, and to get your *credenciál* stamped if you already have it. Also, there are several *albergues* on the street there. The doors will be open until 22:00, but I cannot tell you if your room will still be available."

The matter of fact way Pierre said this annoyed Elizabeth. "But I made a reservation..." she said, with a whining tone she instantly regretted.

"Another lesson to learn...the Camino has many things you might find on vacation, like lodging and cafes, but it is not the same in many ways, too. *Albergues* serve all pilgrims in the best ways they can. The *hospitaleros*, the hosts, work very hard, long hours from Easter until autumn. They can make a living this way, even to cover the months there are no *pèlerins*. They have learned that even when someone makes a reservation, if they have not arrived by 16:00 they will most likely not arrive. At this time of year, when they are serving many, many *pèlerins*, they might reassign a reserved room if pilgrims needing beds come asking. You will find out where you are staying when you get to your *albergue*. It may not be what you had planned, but God always provides what pilgrims need...maybe not what they want, but what they need."

Elizabeth wanted to believe this was true, but it felt very new. She didn't know if she could get used to this. Her expectations were formed from what she knew of hotels in the U.S. and clearly the rules were different here. Gerald added with an air of certainty, "If you know you will be late, you can call ahead before 2 and tell them you are still coming, and they will keep it for you."

Mother and daughter whispered to one another in Korean, but otherwise were silent.

Pierre began asking where people wanted to be taken in

St. Jean. Gerald was going to the Municipal *albergue*, and Eenmo and Ungee to the Pilgrim Office. The taxi began slowing as it approached streets with more traffic, and it looked like they must be coming into St. Jean. A quaint town lay before them with beautiful green mountains framing it, and Elizabeth saw dozens and dozens of *pèlerins*, pilgrims, walking along the sidewalks and streets.

"There are only about two thousand people living here full time, but many more passing through as pilgrims," Pierre informed them.

He pulled over to the curb as soon as they drove past the ancient wall of the city. "Gerald, here you are." Elizabeth looked at the big building displaying the word "Albergue" in bright yellow. She watched people of all ages walking in and out, with and without backpacks strapped on their backs, and heard German, French, and Spanish being spoken by couples and groups walking by the taxi. Pierre hopped out to open the trunk, and Gerald reached in for his backpack, paid his share, and called out *"Buen Camino"* to the taxi. Everyone echoed *"Buen Camino"* in reply, and they started slowly up the street. The town was small, but with so many pilgrims out walking around, they stopped several times for pilgrims to cross the street.

"I will pull in here, and you must walk over to that street and look left. Your *albergues* are both just a little way down. The street is not easy for cars, and it is now just for pedestrians. I wish you all a *"Bon chemin! And Buen Camino!"*

The women got out of the taxi, paid Pierre, shouldered their packs and set out in the direction he had pointed. This was a very pretty town--window boxes and flower pots lining walls, brimming with red geraniums, pink and yellow flowers Elizabeth did not recognize, and lots of other flowers. She looked at the address of the albergue on her phone, and began counting down the addresses she read over doorways. She passed restaurants, shops, patisseries and residences. People stopped ahead of her to read a menu posted at the entrance to a restaurant, local children dribbled a soccer ball back and forth in the center of the street. Two old women walked on the sidewalk uphill arm in arm deep in conversation.

Here is Number 42! Albergue du Pyrenees! She smiled at the pot of flowers in an old hiking boot at the doorway. Hurrying inside Elizabeth found a man at a desk just inside.

"*Bienvenue, Mademoiselle!* May I help you?" The young man had a kind face, and Elizabeth noticed he was taking in her bedraggled, fatigued appearance.

"Yes, please. I have an individual room booked for tonight under the name Elizabeth Wiltshire."

The young man's face fell. "I am so sorry, *Mademoiselle*. Because we are in the busiest season, we must give rooms away if our patrons have not arrived or contacted us by 16h. We have no more rooms available this evening."

"Oh no! I missed my flight from Paris to Bayonne, and had to make other arrangements. I had planned to be here by noon. I didn't know I had to call to confirm." She felt herself losing control and getting louder. She sank into the chair nearby, tired, hungry and out of ideas.

The young man, now clearly uncomfortable with both the situation and the volume of Elizabeth's voice, said, "I am sorry to report that I have just heard from the Pilgrim

Office that the lodgings in St. Jean are all "complete" tonight. The church has opened to receive the overflow to sleep on their floor."

Elizabeth felt a hand on her shoulder. She jumped and saw a woman with a grey braid and green eyes standing at her left elbow. "You are very tired, I think, miss...Elizabeth? I am staying in a private room and have an extra bed. Would you like to stay with me?"

Something like the feeling produced by stepping under a warm shower at the end of a long day came over her as the woman spoke. Elizabeth looked at the tiny woman in front of her and nodded assent with a smile.

She was suddenly ashamed of how she must have sounded, and turned to apologize to the man at the front desk. "I'm so sorry. I just didn't know the policies."

"Of course, Madame. I understand. Rest well, and *Bon Chemin.*"

"Jacques, please make a place for Elizabeth at dinner. I will take her upstairs."

She surprised herself by accepting the woman's offer and following her benefactress up the stairs, taking in the woman's sinewy legs and pink rubber flip-flops. Elizabeth's pack bit into her shoulders with every step, and she was grateful to deposit it on the floor when they arrived in their room. The room was simple and clean, with a window between two beds made up with bottom sheets and pillows. A small table between the beds held a lamp, with two folded blankets on a shelf underneath.

"I am Clare, born in Italy, but now living in Spain. May I walk you over to the Pilgrim Office so you can get your *credenciál*? Just bring your small bag with your valuables and passport. Your heavy pack is safe here after I lock the door. They serve supper at 19:30, and we should be back in time. Shall we go?"

Elizabeth nodded and put her bag over her shoulder across her chest as she had learned to wear it when traveling. She noted where the hall bathroom was as they went back down the stairs.

Clare spoke in French to the host on duty, saying they would be back in time for dinner, and out the door and across the street they went to the pilgrim office. A few *pèlerins* milled around the small space reading bulletin boards and looking at the maps of the routes posted on the walls. Volunteers sat behind long tables and beckoned the pilgrims forward to receive their *credenciáles* and stamps. A petite woman with short white hair and decades of laugh wrinkles at her eyes invited Elizabeth and Clare to sit. "Elizabeth, Lydia will help you now, and I will see you at dinner. *Merci, Lydia, à bientôt!*"

"You wish to purchase a pilgrim *credenciál*? That will be 2 euros, " said Lydia as she took a folded card from a box behind her. Elizabeth found a 2-euro coin and paid. "What name do you wish me to write?"

"Elizabeth J. Wiltshire, *s'il vous plaît*."

"Would you spell it for me, please?"

Elizabeth spelled out her name, and answered Lydia's questions about where she would begin walking and where she planned to end her pilgrimage, recorded her home country, and then asked what her reason was for doing the *chemin*, the pilgrimage. "Are you walking the Camino for religious reasons, Elizabeth?"

She paused, caught off guard with a question about religion. Seeing her hesitation, Lydia offered, "Or is it for adventure, or health?"

"I would say, for 'adventure.'"

Lydia recorded her answer on a form, and gave Elizabeth a page diagramming elevations and distances for the route *Napoléon*, or *Camino Francés*. "The weather looks clear for the French side of the mountains, but they forecast rain on your descent. It will be good to start as early as possible tomorrow. Let me stamp your *credenciál*. This is what entitles you to stay in the municipal *albergues*, it certifies you are a *pèlerine*, or in Spanish, *peregrina*. You will have each place you stay or pass through give you a stamp to qualify you to stay at the next place. Do you have any questions?"

Lydia positioned the Pilgrim Office stamp over the fresh page on Elizabeth's pilgrim passport and pushed down firmly. "Your first stamp!" she said with a wide smile.

Elizabeth was too tired to think of any questions, but thanked the little woman and headed back across the street to her *albergue*. She walked into the common room on the first floor where the other 20 or so people gathered around tables of varying sizes. As tired as she was, her mouth watered as she smelled and saw the bowls and platters of food on the tables. People smiled and pointed to an empty place for her, as Jacques came in carrying several baskets of sliced bread and asking for everyone's attention.

Jacques spoke slowly in English, "Welcome, pilgrims. You have traveled far. You are from many different nations, cultures and beliefs. One thing we may all agree about is that we gather here in a spirit of thanks and gratitude for our food and bed and safety. Let us take a moment of silence to consider these things. Many bowed their heads in prayer or reverence, some made the sign of the cross from head to heart, shoulder to shoulder, some folded hands in prayer, and others stood quietly staring ahead. Elizabeth bowed her head. *Lord, I haven't done this in a while, but I want to say thank you for this food and for the way things worked out to get here and have a bed. Amen.*

There were eight people at Elizabeth's table, five women and three men, three French, one Polish, two Germans, and an Italian. Everyone spoke either French or English in addition to their native tongues, and she found her French coming back to her as she practiced with a woman from *Vessely*, who spoke only French. Incredibly, Agnes had walked from her doorstep, a distance of nearly 1000k, and was continuing on to Santiago. She already had a suntanned face and hands, which Elizabeth would soon discover were clues to how long a pilgrim had been walking. The food and wine were delicious, and the conversation in the room became louder and merrier as the meal progressed. Summer vegetables, pasta, and pork were the stars of one the most delicious home cooked meals Elizabeth had eaten in a very long time. There was even homemade pear compote served over vanilla ice cream for dessert. It reminded her so much of the way her grandmother and mother cooked and the same joy at table with this pilgrim family as she remembered at her own family holiday gatherings.

Merry and relaxed from the wine, full of good food, and tired from their journeys to reach St. Jean, people began to clear their dishes then disperse to their beds, or go out for an evening stroll. Clare made her way over to Elizabeth. "I will be going to bed early. How about you? Shall we both go up and get ready for sleep?"

"Yes, I am very tired. I'll come up with you," responded Elizabeth, and went upstairs. The room had cooled off with nightfall, but was still warm. A faint chattering of voices steadily drifted through window on a puff of breeze. Clare pulled closed the curtains for privacy.

"May I share some tips that I have learned when I have walked sections of the Camino other years?"

"Oh! You have walked before? Yes, please tell me," she answered, eager to hear from a seasoned *peregrina*.

"It is good to get into the rhythm of the Camino life, and you will be able to focus on things other than physical hardship and worrying about your basic needs. It might be easiest to tell you these things by showing you my backpack." Clare reached down beside her bed and picked up a pack that was not more than the size of a kindergartener's school pack.

Elizabeth couldn't keep from exclaiming, "Oh my gosh! That's your whole pack for this walk!" She took it from her as Clare handed it over, and Elizabeth tested its weight in her hand and guessed it was less than 10 pounds. She handed it back, and Clare continued.

"The clothes you see me wearing, plus one more shirt, two pairs of socks, a rain jacket, one more underpants and my sun hat are the only clothes I have with me." Elizabeth studied the outfit Clare was wearing more carefully. A long sleeved, blue gingham button up shirt, olive green Capri length hiking pants with cargo pockets, pink discount store flip flops and a rose floral wrap scarf of light cotton worn as an evening wrap around her shoulders. Around her neck she wore a yellow cotton bandana. Her braid was held by an elastic. She unzipped her pack and pulled out a plastic storage bag with the other clothes she had mentioned, and a second plastic bag with toothpaste, toothbrush, plastic comb, a small tube of sunscreen, and a small bag with a tiny soap bar. Next, she took out a small Bible in a plastic bag, a case for her spectacles, and a recyclable bottle of water.

"And now I will show you what I carry in my pockets." One by one she reached into her hip pockets and cargo pockets to show her passport, pilgrim *credenciál*, and some cash in a small zippered wallet, a rosary, a package of tissues ("for the call of nature on the path," explained Clare). "My boots are there with my walking stick," she pointed to the corner near her bed where a pair of worn high top boots and a smooth, sturdy length of tree branch waited for morning. "I have not always lived so simply, but am learning to enjoy this way of life, and find ways to take it home. For me, walking the Camino is about setting aside all that weighs me down in my heart, mind, and spirit. Setting aside as many material things as possible reminds me to lay aside burdens I was never meant to carry, and trust God to supply what I need. And now you should get ready for sleep. I will go finish in the bathroom, and you can be next," she said as she took her toiletries bag, her clean shirt, and underpants and left the room.

In a flickering sort of way Elizabeth saw the wisdom and love the woman had shared. She was drawn to the simplicity and freedom of Clare's way, and she felt the warming sensation again. She felt affection for Clare, who shared her room and knowledge so freely and without compensation or judgment. But judgment rose up from somewhere inside her, *Here is someone else telling me what I should and shouldn't do. I don't see how I could live that simply. My life is more complex.* She did look into her pack to find a few extras she took out--pajamas, a dressy skirt and top, a pair of heels. Now that she had had a small taste of Camino life at dinner, she realized she would be sleeping in her hiking clothes, and never be dressing up on this trip. She put these items under the lamp table and found a clean hiking outfit, her toiletries, and her camp towel.

Clare came in, fresh from a shower, wearing her clean shirt, her floral wrap as a skirt and with damp hair. She closed the door for privacy, draped her freshly washed hiking pants, bra, and underpants on the bed frame. She whisked off the makeshift skirt, and hung it over the window that was swung open into the room, picked up her Bible and rosary, and then slipped into a sheet sack that served as her travel bedding. She propped her head on her pack and put on her glasses to read and pray.

Elizabeth watched Clare's routine with admiration and fascination, as she gathered her things for her trip to the bathroom. "Clare, I am learning so much from you. I am embarrassed to ask, but where is your towel?"

"Ah yes, such are the uses of my flowered cloth--it is a wrap for additional warmth, a temporary skirt or top for modesty sake, and my towel! It is thin enough to dry quickly, and long enough to wrap and provide privacy even in municipal *albergues*."

Elizabeth felt clean and even sleepier when she returned
to the room. She hung up her damp underwear and towel,
and added her travel dress to the stack of give-aways,
unrolled her hiker's sleep sack onto the bed, and got in.
Clare had her eyes closed, and her Bible and glasses were
on the bedside table, but her fingers moved along the
rosary. She hesitated to interrupt, but Clare opened her
eyes and smiled. She turned to look at Elizabeth as she
moved her pack beside the bed.

"Elizabeth, tomorrow's walk is long and very strenuous.
I plan to get up and leave at dawn to walk as much as
I can while it is cooler. It will take me all day to get to
Roncesvalles."

"Thank you so much for your kindness, Clare. You don't
even know me, and you helped me."

"But Jesus knows you. And so I know you. And that is
enough. Don't worry. God will take care of you. Rest well.
I think maybe we will see one another again. At least I
hope so."

Elizabeth's eyes closed, and she fell into a dreamless sleep.

10

OVER THE PYRENEES

The next morning, Elizabeth woke with a start. She was surprised to see Clare's bed empty, and looked at the time on her phone. 9:00 am! She threw things into her pack, made a quick trip to the bathroom and took the stairs two at a time. Jacques glanced up as she into the reception area. "I need to pay the bill from last night," she shouted breathlessly as she extracted her money pouch from the front of her pack. "Your bill has already been paid. Clare paid yesterday, and left this note for you." Momentarily rooted to the spot by Clare's generosity, Elizabeth was jolted back to the reality of her hike as Jacques said, "*Madamoiselle*, you should go now. The hike to Roncesvalles is very long and *difficile*, and it will perhaps rain later today. Here is a small lunch Clare asked us to pack for you. *Bon Camino!*" He handed her a small bag, she waved gratefully, and followed the brass scallop shells embedded in the road out of town, hoping the cloudy sky would cool things off rather than slicking the trail with rain as she feared.

It was 9:15, and she figured if she covered four miles per hour, she would have no problem making Roncesvalles by early afternoon. The road ahead stretched over green hills, and despite the cloudiness, visibility was good. This was a green she had never seen, as if someone had saturated the color with photo editing. Sheep dotted the hillsides, and she could hear the tinkling of bells around their necks and the bleating of the lambs. Even though she was breathing hard from the uphill climb, she was struck by the deep peace and beauty of the scene before her. She remembered a line from an old song, "He makes me lie down in green pastures, He restores my soul..." The phrase echoed again and again through her mind as she walked, and a quiet voice said, *This is what I want to give you, dear one. Rest easy.*

She increased her pace, willing these unbidden thoughts to leave. Her heart rate increased as the elevation climbed sharply, and Elizabeth pulled harder on her walking poles to grip the road, hoping to take some of the workload off her legs. After a solid two hours of going up steadily, muscles straining, she spotted three pilgrims up ahead, colorful packs bobbing, and walking poles clicking a steady rhythm on the road. When one of them finished singing a happy sounding tune, the other two doubled over with laughter and hurrahs. It sounded like they were playing some sort of game.

They smiled as she drew up alongside them and the man in the group said in a thick Irish accent, "Hi there, young lady! Lovely day isn't it? I'm Christopher, and this is my wife Eileen and daughter Mary." The two women grinned at Elizabeth, and she immediately felt at ease.

"I'm Elizabeth from Washington, DC. May I join you for a bit?" she asked, struggling to keep her breathing even as the angle of the path increased even more steeply. They all nodded their assent, and Elizabeth fell into step beside Mary, impressed that her breathing seemed barely labored at all even though she looked to be only about 13 or 14.

They chatted about their plans, and when Elizabeth told them she planned to finish in Santiago in 26 days, Christopher whistled and said, "Good luck, girlie. Be careful. It's best to take rest days here and there, and bus if you need to. This is my third time on the Camino. The first time out of the gate, I tried to do the whole thing as fast as I could. I was so focused on passing other pilgrims that I missed a lot of opportunities for friendship and learning along the way. Thankfully, the good Lord afflicted me with tendinitis in both knees and slowed me down. I ended up stopping in León, and didn't make it to Santiago. Three years later, with a newly humble heart, Eileen and I decided to hike together to celebrate our 40th birthdays. That time we made it to Santiago, and now we're back with Mary. Just remember, Lizzie, it's not about speed. Or even where you end up. It's about letting the Lord have his way with you, and keeping your heart and spirit open. Listening. Few places in the world allow for the type of listening you can do on the Camino. It's what the Celts used to call one of the 'thin places': a place on earth where you can easily see heaven."

"I suppose it helps if you're in pretty good shape?" asked Elizabeth, expecting to be reassured in her assumption that her own fitness level would set her up to achieve her goal. "I'm used to running some pretty high mileage every week back home, so I hope I can keep my schedule. I can't take any more time away from my job."

Eileen asked about her life in DC, and Elizabeth shared the basic information about herself--law practice, hoping for partnership soon, single, enjoys the outdoors..."That's why the Camino appealed to me. It's kind of an adventure vacation with pretty scenery and plenty of activity."

They walked on together swapping information about their lives back home. Christopher was an accountant, Eileen a schoolteacher, and Mary a student who had just completed the Irish equivalent of American sixth grade. Now and again the family would pause to take in the view over a valley, or note a pretty vegetable garden at a *casa rural* they passed. They were cheerful walking companions and folded Elizabeth into their family as they clocked another hour of walking. Up they went, spotting the yellow arrows and scallop shells pointing the way to go, seeing new and prettier views of the countryside as they went higher. They came around a long winding curve in the road and Christopher announced, "Ah, here we are!"

Up ahead, Elizabeth saw a sign for *Refugio Orisson*, noting the distance to Roncesvalles as more than 13k more, and her heart sank. "Wait, we've only gone 8k since leaving St. Jean? But I've been hiking for almost two and a half hours!"

"Aye, Lizzie, but you've climbed quite a lot of elevation, so it feels like more distance. Of course your pace will be slower. You'll stop here with us, right? Even if you've not made a reservation here, we can ask if they have a bed for you," said Eileen, laying a hand on Elizabeth's forearm.

Elizabeth paused, struck yet again by the kindness of the pilgrims she'd met so far. She was feeling completely exhausted, and an ache in her right knee had steadily grown for the past hour. Still, she had a reservation in Roncesvalles for that evening, and she'd only been hiking for a few hours. "Thank you so much for asking, but I think I'm going to continue on to Roncesvalles. I have a reservation there for tonight. I enjoyed meeting you and walking together. Buen Camino!"

Christopher stepped close to Elizabeth and laid a hand on her shoulder. Mary and Eileen followed suit, clearly accustomed to his actions. "May the grace of our Lord Jesus Christ be with you, and may God hold you in the palm of His hand and bring you peace and healing. Amen." He made the sign of the cross on Elizabeth's forehead, and the family turned and walked inside to check in. Elizabeth watched them walk in, remembering the priest making that same sign on newly baptized Christians at her childhood church, and the memory brought with it a pang of homesickness for her old priest, Father Matthew. *It's not too late, Beloved. You can stay with them and learn from them. Rest. Don't be afraid.*

Obviously I'm not afraid, she thought, willing this persistent voice to be silent. *I'm going on. If I were afraid, I wouldn't be doing that,"* she thought.

She went inside to the Refugio bar to buy a bottle of water and use the restroom, and walked back to an open-air deck across the road to eat some of her lunch overlooking a beautiful green valley and mountain. Others were also having lunch or a beverage as a break from walking to Roncesvalles. When she sat down, she noted with some concern the increase in dark clouds and drop in temperature. She unzipped her pack, took out the sack lunch, and layered on another long sleeved t-shirt. She propped her right leg on the railing of the deck as she ate half of a ham and cheese sandwich and drank the water. *This really is beautiful,* she thought as she chewed and stared out at the valley. *But break time is over.* She stood up, *Okay, you can do this, Elizabeth*, she thought as she hoisted her pack back onto her shoulders and turned back to the path.

She resolved to increase her pace and not stop for the next few hours. Mist drifted in shrouding the mountains around her, and decreasing visibility so that she could only see a hundred yards or so of the path. The paved road disappeared and often now she was walking on trails of dirt, rocks and grass. Now and again, she passed fellow pilgrims always exchanging the greeting of "Buen Camino!"

Hour after hour she walked, and she was still going up. Occasionally the path would level out for a quarter mile or so, but then upwards again. The backs of her legs and glutes were super sore, but that reminded her of getting in shape at high school soccer camp. What worried her most was the throbbing in her right knee. She stopped briefly to find some ibuprofen in her pack, toss back a couple with some water, and begin again. Her pack felt twice as heavy when she put it on this time, and she felt a raw spot on both collar bones from the weight and friction of the straps. She couldn't deal with that now, she had to keep moving. Then came an hour of descent and more level ground, and Elizabeth thought it must be the downhill to Roncesvalles. She stopped at a water fountain beside the path where some other pilgrims were refilling bottles and camel backs, and looking at maps.

"Not much longer now, I hope, " said Elizabeth as she filled her water bottle.

"About 4 more kilometers to the peak and then 4 more to Roncesvalles," said a dark skinned man with an Italian accent. He pointed to their location on his map, and Elizabeth realized she had only walked 16k out of 24.

Some of the others looked as spent as she was. Some were getting their rain gear on or treating blisters. Elizabeth managed a "Buen Camino" to a few still at the fountain, and started walking.

It was getting darker. At first she thought it was the rain clouds, but now she realized even though she couldn't see the sun because of the cloud cover, that the sun was lower in the sky. She was hungry and stopped on the lee side of a rock outcropping to dig out the rest of the lunch, and drink some water. As she crested the mountains, rain began to fall and she donned her poncho, thankful that she'd already covered her pack. The next few kilometers passed in a haze of deep mud and steady rain, and Elizabeth was grateful for the balance her hiking poles gave her, but wishing she'd bought the rain gaiters Dave at REI had recommended to keep her socks dry.

The descent began as a relief from the work of the uphill pull she had been doing, but she soon found how difficult this new challenge was. Now she had to shorten her stride, and let her poles swing out to steady her foot plant on each downhill step. Now the strain was on the fronts of her legs, and her right knee complained more than ever. Suddenly she slipped on some wet gravel and landed on her right knee. She rolled onto her side, wincing from the pain of the fall and assessing the damage as she lay still. Rain fell on her face, mixing with tears from the pain. After a few minutes, she tried to sit up, but felt more like a turtle on its back with her pack on. She unclipped the straps and sat up, her poncho getting momentarily stuck under the weight of the pack. Blood spread quickly on her rain soaked pants, but rolling up the pants for inspection showed only a superficial cut. Using one of her walking poles as a crutch, she stood up slowly, putting all her weight on her stronger leg. Gingerly she tested some body weight on the injured leg, and nearly collapsed.

She eased back down on the path, not knowing what to do next. *I am with you, Beloved. I love you. You are safe.* The inner whisper strengthened her, and she responded by getting back to her feet, putting on her pack, and turning towards Roncesvalles. She would make it. One step at a time. One foot in front of the other. Her mind cast about for something to distract her from the shooting pain in her knee, and she began singing, "Amazing Grace, how sweet the sound, that saved a wretch like me..." The pain in her knee didn't stop, but she was able to bear it.

By the time she arrived at the *albergue* in Roncesvalles, she had been hiking more than 12 hours, was soaking wet, shivering, and had lost count of the number of times she'd run through "Amazing Grace" in her head. She flung open the door, lowered her pack to the floor with a slight thump, and sank down on a bench opposite the deserted reception desk. Where was the desk clerk? She opened her eyes when a voice said, "Miss? Let me help you." A young man with soft brown eyes wrapped a warm towel around her shoulders and offered her another for her muddy face. "I've already taken your pack upstairs and dried it off. It's next to your bed waiting for you. Can I help you up the stairs? Here, lean on me." He offered his arm, and Elizabeth leaned against him gratefully, wincing with each step.

The man had dry clothes ready for her, and waited outside the bathroom while she changed and washed. She leaned on his arm as she limped to her bunk. He held an ice pack and bandages in his other hand. She sat down on the bed with her right pant leg pulled up to expose her bloody, swollen knee. He gently applied the ice, and then went to work bandaging the cut and blisters. He hummed softly as he worked, and Elizabeth ceased shivering and felt her body relax. The lights were out in the dormitory, and pilgrims around the room were already snoring.

"What's your name?" Elizabeth whispered, not wanting to disturb the sleeping pilgrims in the bunks nearby.

"You can call me Saadya."

Elizabeth chuckled. "Saadya? I've never heard that name before."

"It means 'God's helper,'" he explained, smiling back at her as he handed her a glass of cold water and a plate of roasted almonds, cheese, and some slices of pear from a tray on a nearby table. "I brought some extra pillows so you can keep your knee elevated as you sleep, and I've registered you here and stamped your *credencial*, so you may rest easy."

He refilled Elizabeth's plate and glass, and she said, "You know a lot about treating injuries, you must have some medical training. How long have you worked here, Saadya?"

"I come when extra help is needed," he said in his lightly accented English.

"Are you Spanish? I can't place your accent," said Elizabeth, puzzled by his strange reply.

"I've traveled a lot," Saadya, said as he removed the icepack and wrapped her knee in a compression bandage. "This will keep the swelling down. You can wear it as you walk. Just see how it feels when you wake up in the morning. It has been a pleasure meeting you, Elizabeth. I wish you Godspeed on your journey." He rested his palm lightly against Elizabeth's cheek for a moment, then gathered the empty dishes and bandage trimmings and exited the room.

Elizabeth lay quietly, touched by Saadya's kindness, then remembered with a pang of fear that she hadn't contacted Bruce in almost 48 hours. She leaned off her bunk, unzipped her pack, and pulled out her laptop, fearing Bruce's wrath. As she tapped out replies to his many queries, and apologies for her tardiness, a few of the pilgrims in bunks around her rolled over and sighed loudly, clearly perturbed at being awakened by the light glowing from her computer screen. She responded as quickly as possible to each item and shut down. She sank into the pillows. *God, thank you. Thank you for Saadya. Thank you for a warm place to sleep and for helping me make it here.* Her eyelids closed as she welcomed sleep.

11

TO LARRASOAÑA

Elizabeth awoke to an incessant beeping. She quickly looked for her phone, confused at the source of the noise, and then realized the alarm was coming from the opposite side of the room. It was still dark. A man turned off the alarm, switched on his headlamp, and began rummaging through his pack, dressing quickly, but not quietly. She shot him an annoyed glance. On his way out of the dorm he walked past her. "Maybe next time you not stay up so late working, eh? See how it feels? Buen Camino!" His footsteps echoed down the stairs, and Elizabeth sank back against the pillows. Every muscle in her body ached, although her knee had stopped throbbing. Loud snoring around her indicated that not every pilgrim had been awakened by the alarm, and Elizabeth tried to go back to sleep. She finally gave up. She was fully awake, and her mind was racing ahead to her day. It was nearly 28 kilometers to *Larrasoaña*. She swung her legs over the bed, and stood up carefully. Her knee was stiff, but not painful, and she silently gave a prayer of thanks for

Saadya and his help. After dressing in her own clothes she folded the ones Saadya had let her wear and loaded her pack. She shouldered her pack and went downstairs to the reception desk. A young woman was behind the counter checking something on the computer. *"Buenos Días,"* she said as Elizabeth approached.

She smiled and returned her greeting. "Is Saadya here this morning?"

"Saadya? I don't know anyone by that name," said the woman as she handed a helper some keys, and stamped a *credenciál*.

Elizabeth felt goose bumps on her arms. "But he helped me last night...he checked me in, got me food, helped me with bandages, got me ice for my knee. Are you new here?"

"We have no ice here," the woman corrected. "I have worked here for almost three years." She nodded toward other pilgrims who were leaving, and the familiar salutation of *Buen Camino* was offered back and forth.

Elizabeth stood there in the commotion of an *albergue* morning, not knowing what to make of this. She bent her right knee, assuring herself that the compression bandage was still in place, and recalling the details of the treatments and kindness of the man who greeted and helped here the night before, the man who had been very real, but whom this *hospitalera* did not know. She thanked the woman, and walked out into the rosy light of early morning. She looked up at the soft colors in the brightening sky. Then came the whisper, *I care for you, Beloved. I sent Saadya. There is even more going on that you cannot see.*

Breathing deeply, Elizabeth began walking, feeling a mixture of fear and awe as she pondered the events of the last 24 hours. She tried to wrap her mind around her encounter with Saadya. *This is definitely unlike any vacation I expected.* Her knee and muscles began to feel better as she walked, and she hummed to herself in rhythm with her pace, treading more carefully on the muddy path to avoid repeating her fall of the day before. After a few hours, she spotted a flat boulder in the shade where she could sit and elevate her knee while she had a snack. She found one of the energy gels and her guidebook in her pack, and while she ate and drank some water she looked at the map. Larrasoaña was about 15k farther. She returned her water bottle to its pocket on the pack, and turned her face towards the warmth of the sun, grateful the weather had changed for the better.

As she stood to resume walking, a greeting of "*Hola, Señorita!*" rang out behind her. Turning, she saw a group of three men gaining on her and eyeing her appreciatively. She blushed under their gaze, but was flattered by the attention. One said something in Spanish under his breath, and the other two laughed and cast sideways glances at her. The tallest of the men held his hand out to take hers, and said dramatically, "I am Marco." He kissed her hand, his dark eyes meeting hers, and she felt her stomach drop. The other two men, Pablo and Nico, kissed her hand as well, then said, "You walk with us, Señorita?"

"I'm Elizabeth. I am not moving at a very fast pace today," she said as she pointed to her bandaged right knee. She was not sure whether she was safe with these guys, but then she thought about the fact that there were many others on the path today, and rarely did five minutes go by without others passing her, so she figured it was okay. She was no stranger to men's attention, and had never lacked for male companionship when she wanted it. Still, she had learned to be cautious, and hesitated as they began walking. Marco placed his hand gently on her elbow and said, "Do not worry, Elizabeth. I'll take care of you. You be safe with us." Cheeks warming as they made eye contact, Elizabeth fell into step beside Marco.

The men set a blistering pace, and after five kilometers, her knee resumed its throbbing. They barely seemed winded, however, and Elizabeth refused to complain. Marco asked her lots of questions as they walked, and she was surprised at how quickly they were opening up to one another. They had many things in common, despite growing up in different cultures an ocean apart. He knew Atlanta well, having studied engineering at Georgia Tech on a Fulbright scholarship before going back to his family's home in Madrid to work in urban planning. He was currently transitioning into a different position, and had some time off before starting his new job, so he and his friends decided to hike from Roncesvalles to Pamplona for the festival of *Sanfermines* and the running of the bulls.

"You're not actually going to run with the bulls, are you?" said Elizabeth, a teasing glint in her eye.

"Why not? You have to have fun and be happy in life. Why not take a risk once in awhile? Besides, someday I want to tell my grandchildren I ran with the bulls in Pamplona." Marco's eyes swept over Elizabeth again in a way that made her slightly uncomfortable, but she shook it off and deflected the moment with another question.

"I can't imagine ever doing something like that. You Spanish men are crazy! I can only imagine what my father would say if he found out I was planning to do something that dangerous."

"What about your mother?" said Marco. "Is she so protective of you as your father?"

"My mom died when I was sixteen," Elizabeth choked out, not used to showing her emotions.

"Oh, I am sorry. My mother, too, is with the angels in heaven now. My father and I get along the best we can, but every day I miss her," Marco said, brushing a tear from Elizabeth's cheek as they walked on in silence for a few minutes, both letting memories of their mothers play in their minds.

Elizabeth focused on her poles and feet keeping rhythm with the other footfalls and clicking of walking poles and sticks, and a memory of a long ago conversation with her mother swam into her mind. She didn't know why she remembered the story, but it was one she had come to appreciate.

She was fifteen years old when one of the most popular boys at school asked her to prom. She couldn't believe Jason Stiles had asked *her*, a sophomore, to his junior prom! She couldn't wait to tell her mother. She rushed in the door after soccer practice, full of news, and found her mother sitting at the kitchen table, reading her Bible. She immediately looked up when she came in and smiled, patting the chair beside her and giving her a hug.

"You look like you're ready to burst, sweetie! What happened at school today?"

"Jason Stiles asked me to prom! I can't believe it! All the girls like him. He's so hot!"

She had been surprised and hurt by her mother's lack of enthusiasm. "Jason Stiles? Some of the things you've told me about him make me think he's not a good person for you to spend time with, Elizabeth. He sounds pretty wild."

"Mom, you don't know him! He's so polite, and he was really sweet when he asked me. Please let me go with him."

"Elizabeth, I know this is going to be hard for you to understand now, but your father and I can't allow you to go out with a boy we barely know and spend lots of time alone with him. If he'd like to come spend time with you at our house so we can get to know each other, that would be fine. You are such a treasure, darling girl. You are beautiful, kind, compassionate, funny, intelligent, and loving. You are still so young, and we don't want you to be with any boy, or man, who doesn't fully appreciate the gift that you are."

Elizabeth glanced at Marco, appreciative of the silence that allowed her to review the memory. "I remember how loved I felt by my mom, despite my frustration at not being allowed to do some things I wanted to do." *Anyway, Mom was right. Jason Stiles did turn out to be a jerk, and I'm glad I didn't waste my time with him.*

She and Marco had slowed their pace while they talked about their mothers, not wanting to share those things with the other two men, who grinned and elbowed each other when they looked back and saw Marco with his hand on her cheek. She thought about the men she'd dated since Steve, and how disappointing the breakups were. In her frustration, she'd given up on dating, despairing of ever meeting the right man. *Maybe I shouldn't give up. Maybe it's not a waste of time*, she thought as she felt Marco's eyes on her.

They walked through some beautiful forests and past dairy farms, more flocks of sheep, and saw lovely wild flowers. Elizabeth had to stop to rest several times in the last couple of hours, elevating her right painful right knee and drinking water at each opportunity. She apologized for her speed and told the guys to go on ahead, but Elizabeth could tell they were tiring, too, and thought they were secretly glad to slow down a bit.

They arrived at *Larrasoaña* around 16:00, and Elizabeth waited patiently on a bench while the men went to make arrangements at an *albergue*. A short while later, they returned laughing and jostling each other, and Elizabeth marveled that they had enough energy for any nonessential movement.

"Señorita!" Pablo said gallantly, with a bow. "There is no room in the inn. We must go back to *Zubiri* for our beds!" Elizabeth's mouth fell open in shock.

"What do you mean we have to walk back to *Zubiri*? That's almost 8 kilometers! My knee is killing me!"

"Everyone's knees are killing them, Elisa!" said Nico with a hand to his forehead. "We must be strong!"

Elizabeth looked to Marco for support and said, "How about Marco and I catch a taxi to the next town and find a place, and you all can walk back to *Zubiri*, then we meet up with you in the morning?"

Nico fell to his knees dramatically and said, "The three musketeers cannot be separated! Marco must come with us! He is our fearless leader!"

Elizabeth looked at Marco pleadingly, but he laughed at Nico and said, "Yes, I must stay with my friends, Elizabeth. Let me see your knee...it looks like you will be able to walk a bit more, yes? Come with us!"

Frustrated by Marco's lack of compassion, Elizabeth was tempted to smack him with her walking pole, but remembering their earlier conversation and the way he'd opened up to her, decided to give him a break. *After all, he has planned this time with his friends, and I just joined them today.* She groaned as she pulled her pack on, and Pablo said, "Just like a woman. What do you have in there, Señorita? All your makeup and shoes?" The other two men laughed, but Elizabeth stayed silent, too tired to laugh off the disrespect.

As they trudged back to *Zubiri*, Elizabeth silently counted down the kilometers and when at last they arrived at the *albergue* and dropped their packs off, she wanted nothing more than a warm shower, ice for her knee, food and bed.

"Okay, now it's time to party, Elisa!" said Nico, taking her hand and swinging her in a circle.

She forced a smile and said, "I want to shower first! Where are you guys going?"

Marco waved his hand in the direction of the town center and said, "We'll just see what's open! Come find us when you're ready!" The guys clomped back down the stairs, and Elizabeth got her shower things and went to the bathroom to clean up. Thirty minutes later, cleaner than she'd been in days and glad that she'd brought her little black travel dress and a pair of sandals, she walked down the stairs, every muscle aching.

Only a few places were open in the town, and she walked into the closest one. Marco, Pablo, and Nico were seated near the back of the café, flirting with three *peregrinas* who sized Elizabeth up as she approached. She sat down next to Marco, who made room for her at the small table and introduced her. "Elisa, these are our new friends Amina, Maria, and Isabella." The women gave her an appraising glance, and then continued their conversation with the men in Spanish. Elizabeth was left on her own to decipher the menu and order her own food and drink since the others at the table had already done so. It was evident that even though she hadn't taken long to meet them, they had already had a few drinks before she arrived. She ate her food when it came, but as shadows lengthened into evening, Elizabeth had had enough. Exhausted from the day and feeling rebuffed and confused by Marco's actions, she stood up and announced, "I'm going to head back to the *albergue*. Anyone want to come with me? We've got an early morning tomorrow, especially since we have to do that extra 8k again."

Everyone shook their heads, so she limped back to the *albergue* alone, dressed in her hiking clothes for the next day, and got into bed, catching up on necessary emails to Bruce before turning over and going to sleep. At 2 AM, she awoke to loud snoring coming from both sides of the dormitory. Nico and Marco seemed to be conversing through snores, a condition exacerbated by their alcohol consumption a few hours before. She pressed her pillow over her ears, silently willing them to stop snoring and wishing she'd brought earplugs with her. She finally dropped back to sleep and woke to rain splattering on windowpanes. The men were still sleeping, but she prodded them awake, saying, "We've got to get going. You said you want to get to Pamplona today, and if we don't leave now, we won't make it."

Nico groaned, cursed, and rolled over. Pablo put his pillow over his head, and Marco blinked at her and rubbed his eyes as he sat up. She threw her pillow at each of them in turn. "Get up! We've got to go! I'm going to wait downstairs and have some breakfast." She sipped her *café con leche* and nibbled a croissant while she waited, frustrated at their immaturity. *I was right about men. They really are all the same. Overgrown boys who need a woman to tell them what to do. No wonder I've stayed single for so long. I can't take this. I really thought Marco was different.*

The last thought dissipated as Marco came downstairs, smiling his easy grin and looking at her intensely with ebony eyes. *"Buenos Días, chica.* Sorry about last night; my friends, well, you know. They're a little crazy, and sometimes I don't say 'no' when I should," he said, giving her ponytail a gentle tug.

Her resistance melted at his gaze and slow smile, and she heard herself say, "Forget it. No problem. I'm looking forward to the walk today."

"Me too," said Marco. "Perhaps when we get to Pamplona, we can spend a little time alone." Elizabeth felt her cheeks warm and quickly glanced away. What was happening to her? She couldn't let herself fall for a Spanish man she barely knew!

She shouldered her pack and said, "Hey, why don't you go get your buddies? I'll get my rain gear on." He obligingly thumped back upstairs as Elizabeth drained the rest of her coffee. *I have to be careful or I could end up physically and emotionally bruised from this trip. Why am I responding to Marco so enthusiastically? I guess it's been awhile since I felt desired or worth something other than what I can produce for my job. Maybe I should just see where this goes.*

Beloved, I desire you. You are beautiful. I have loved you with an everlasting love and drawn you with loving-kindness. The gentle voice had been growing steadily more insistent on the Camino, and she slowly began to recognize it as the voice of the God she'd been trying to ignore for the past several years. She felt a momentary pull to leave the *albergue* and start walking without the men, to listen for more of the still, small voice, but she checked herself. *It'll be more fun if I'm with other people, and I really think something could develop with Marco.*

She waited patiently by the front door, and was about to go upstairs to rouse the men again when they came stumbling down the steps, clearly hung over from last night's indulgence. "The guys want to get a little coffee and breakfast, okay? They told us to go ahead, *chica.*" Marco waved a hand at his friends, and he and Elizabeth stepped out into the drizzle.

"At least it's not pouring like it was when I went over the Pyrenees," said Elizabeth as Marco pulled on his poncho. She was determined to ignore the steadily increasing pain in her knee, and Marco took no notice of the way she compensated as she walked, nor did he offer to help her adjust her pack or cover.

After hiking a few kilometers in silence, Marco said, "I've been a friend with Nico and Pablo since I was a little boy. We all grew up together in Madrid, and they were there for me when my mother passed. I know they seem immature, but they're good guys." Elizabeth nodded in agreement, unwilling to verbally agree with Marco's statement. "What about you?" Marco asked. "Did you have any close friends that helped you when your mama died?"

"No," Elizabeth said bitterly. "My father and my mother's sisters all wanted me to be strong, be happy, keep it together. 'Be good, Elizabeth. Don't get into trouble. Don't cause any problems. Help everyone.' So, no, I didn't get the luxury of crying with my friends." The words tumbled out before she was able to stop them, and she was surprised to see Marco's eyes glisten.

"I'm so sorry, Elisa. I'm sorry you weren't able to grieve your mother. Would you like to talk about anything?" he said, laying a hand on her shoulder.

"No, I don't think so. I'd rather talk about something else," Elizabeth murmured, caught off guard by his display of emotion.

"Okay, I'll listen when you're ready, okay?" Marco said as he started walking again. Elizabeth watched him hunch his shoulders against the rain and followed, a new, piercing pain starting at the top of her knee. After another hour in which they debated the merits of Euro-league football (Marco passionately refused to accept that any team could ever match his favorite, Real Madrid, despite Elizabeth's deep love of Manchester United), they stopped for lunch in the tiny village of *Iróz*. The rain had stopped, and water drops glistened on the grass beside the trail as they crossed the river *Arga*. A small outdoor café unfurled its awnings and opened just as they walked by, so they claimed a table outside where they could watch the river. Elizabeth felt as though she'd stepped back several centuries. A teenage girl drove a few cattle down the narrow street and across the bridge, and a man drove by in a cart pulled by a donkey. Rays of sunshine broke through the clouds and shone on the terra cotta rooftops, the light sparkling off the river. A gentle breeze blew and ruffled Marco's hair, and he jokingly ran his fingers through it so it stuck up even more. "I hope you like porcupines," he said as Elizabeth chuckled.

The easy conversation continued through lunch, and as they finished their wine, Elizabeth said, "Now I'm ready for a nap."

"How about when we get to Pamplona, we get a hotel room? Just you and me?" said Marco. He leaned in and put his palm on Elizabeth's cheek. "You can have a nap, and then we can do other things too," he said suggestively. He kissed Elizabeth's forehead, then her mouth. As their kiss deepened, Elizabeth felt her resistance crumble.

All her logic, her concerns at some of Marco's earlier behavior, her worries about the future, melted, and she said, "Yes. Okay, I'll stay with you for a night in Pamplona." He smiled and stroked her hair.

"Okay then. Let's get to Pamplona. Shall we?" he said, motioning with his hand, and off they went.

Feeling contented and peaceful as they walked, Elizabeth said, "So, Marco, why haven't you settled down and gotten married?" That question prompted a discussion of their past relationships, and they laughed as they shared their worst breakup stories.

"Wait, you left Steve in *Sevilla*?" Marco said in disbelief. "Good for you! He didn't deserve a woman like you, anyway." For the first time, Elizabeth was able to laugh about the way she'd packed her suitcase and rebooked her flight at warp speed, leaving Steve behind.

"I wonder if he's still standing there with his mouth open," Elizabeth said, laughing until she hiccoughed. "No, I'm sure he has his perfect life with a perfect wife, 2.5 children, and an SUV in the suburbs. It's what he always wanted. Good for him. I hope he's got it."

Marco interrupted her reverie by pointing at a waymark showing distance to Pamplona, "Look, only 5 kilometers!"

"Good, my knee is really starting to bother me again."

"Maybe you should just stay in Pamplona with us for a few days, eh? Why do you need to go all the way to Santiago?" he asked with one eyebrow raised.

"Well, for one, I don't fancy getting trampled by a bull the way you all seem to, and I have to reach my goal. I mean, that was the whole point of the trip!" countered Elizabeth.

"Yes, but you didn't know what would happen on the trip," said Marco. "You didn't know what walking all day would be like, the towns, who you would meet..."

"Yes, no, uh, I don't know. Okay, I'll think about it," stammered Elizabeth.

Just then someone whistled loudly from behind them. Nico and Pablo waved and jogged to catch up with them. Elizabeth's heart sank. She preferred Marco without his friends. She immediately felt guilty for her thoughts. *These guys really do love Marco. They're just carefree because they're on vacation.* She took a deep breath and smiled as the men pounded each other on the back and launched into rapid Spanish.

Elizabeth resigned herself to being ignored for the rest of the way to Pamplona, and thought ahead to all the emails she would need to respond to as soon as she had wireless internet. *Hopefully I won't have a problem getting online in a city the size of Pamplona. Bruce sent me a lot of documents to look over. Maybe I'll let the guys go ahead to get some food again while I do a little work. After all, it's only mid-afternoon.*

As they walked into Pamplona, Elizabeth was struck by the size and noise of the city. After a few days in the quiet countryside, the crowds of people and vehicles speeding past felt chaotic. She stayed close behind Marco as they walked into the city center, hoping he would take the lead and find them a nice place to relax. The pain in her knee had become almost unbearable, and as she pushed herself to keep up with the men, her foot caught on a curb and she went down, her heavy pack landing on top of her. White-hot pain shot from ankle to knee, and Elizabeth bit her lip to keep from crying out. Marco signaled Nico and Pablo to go ahead, and turned to help her up.

"Are you okay? Can you walk, or shall I call a taxi?" Elizabeth tried to put weight on her knee and found she couldn't walk, even with Marco supporting her. He whistled for a taxi, and one immediately drove up. Marco gave the driver instructions, and he tore off into the steady stream of traffic down the street. A few minutes later, the taxi came to a halt in front of a large hotel. "Hopefully we won't have a problem getting a room. There are many tourists in town for the festival. You wait here."

As he disappeared into the hotel, Elizabeth clutched her knee. It was swelling again, and she wondered if she should try to find a doctor. Now her ankle was throbbing to match. Fear curled like a snake in her belly. *What if I've really hurt myself? I'm in a foreign country where I don't speak the language, have no way of getting around, and am dependent on a man I barely know. What am I going to do?* She looked up as Marco came back to the taxi and flung open the door. "They've got a room for us. The last one." He helped her out of the taxi and put his arm under her shoulders to support her to the elevator. "Someone is coming to get our bags." When at last Marco threw open the door to their room, Elizabeth was nauseated from the pain in her leg. She collapsed on the bed, and took deep breaths to calm herself while Marco received their bags from the porter. Marco turned to her, worry creasing his brow. "I need to phone Nico and Pablo and tell them where we are. Will you be all right for a bit?" Elizabeth nodded, in too much pain to even verbalize a reply.

Marco left the room, and didn't come back for what seemed like an eternity. Elizabeth had tried to elevate her knee and ankle, but found it difficult to reach all the pillows she needed while lying down. Her knee had reached an alarming size, but she managed to yank out her laptop and Google search medical treatment options in Pamplona. When Marco finally returned to the room, he avoided Elizabeth's eyes. "Do you need anything?" he said softly.

"Yes, some ice and a doctor," said Elizabeth.

"Okay, I'll find you some ice and tell you how to get to the doctor before I go."

"Before you go? What do you mean, before you go? You're not going to leave me here, are you?" Elizabeth fought back panic.

Still not looking at her, Marco said, "Nico and Pablo reminded me this trip was supposed to be about the three of us. I promised I'd be with them in Pamplona and run with them before we go on to Santiago. You will be fine if you rest for a day or two here."

Seeing he was already decided on the matter, Elizabeth shut down her emotions and said, "Fine. I can take care of myself. Just go."

"I'll get you what you need before..."

"No, I mean it. Go. I don't want you here. Enjoy your time with your friends."

"Goodbye, Elizabeth. Thank you for walking with me. You are a wonderful person." Elizabeth wondered if Marco realized how hollow his words sounded. She turned her face towards the wall as the door clicked shut behind him. Tears slid down her temples into her hair, and she reached for her phone. Dialing the front desk, she managed to communicate the need for ice, and the next moment a knock sounded on her door. Unable to walk to answer it herself, Elizabeth said loudly, "Come in!" hoping whoever was on the other side knew enough English to follow those directions.

The door opened, and a young woman walked in holding a bag of ice. "Oh, Señorita! You are badly hurt. I will call a doctor." The woman picked up the phone beside the bed, dialed a few numbers, and spoke rapid Spanish into the receiver. She set the receiver down with a click, and then turned back to Elizabeth. "Let me help you. I work for the hotel, but I am training at the university here to be a nurse, and I can help you until the doctor gets here." She stacked pillows to elevate Elizabeth's injured leg, and then packed the ice tightly around her knee and ankle, being as gentle as possible. "I will be right back," she said as she squeezed Elizabeth's hand. She came back ten minutes later with a plate of food, water, and more pillows. She propped Elizabeth up with the extra pillows, then handed her the food and water.

"How did you get here, Señorita?" Before Elizabeth could stop herself, the whole story of Marco tumbled out, along with a torrent of tears. Hating herself for confessing her foolishness and for crying in front of a complete stranger, Elizabeth abruptly fell silent after describing Marco's departure, embarrassed at how much she'd shared. The young woman squeezed her hand, her dark eyes full of sympathy and sadness as she looked at Elizabeth.

She closed her eyes for a moment and whispered something, then opened them and looked back at Elizabeth. "My shift is almost over here. I will stay with you tonight and tomorrow morning until I have to work again. I am Manuela. And you are Elizabeth, yes?"

"Yes," said Elizabeth, trying to remember if she'd told Manuela her name.

Manuela seemed to guess her thoughts, for she said

instantly, "Jesus told me your name." For the second time in just a few days, Elizabeth felt the hair on the back of her neck stand up and goose bumps on her arms. What kind of people were these? These people who talked with Jesus, with God, as though he was in the room with them? As though he was just another friend?

Manuela had dampened a cloth with cool water and was wiping Elizabeth's face. "Manuela, why are you helping me? You don't even know me. I hate to trouble you. I'm sure you need to rest before you work again. Please don't spend anymore time here. I can take care of myself."

Manuela cast another look at Elizabeth, and she felt as though Manuela could see past her body into her soul. "Elizabeth, you must understand. Jesus wants me to care for you. It is my joy to serve Him and you this way. Ah, here is the doctor."

Manuela answered the knock on the door and a small elderly man entered, carrying a bag and wearing a white coat. "Dr. Rodriguez will take good care of you. He's been a dear friend for many years."

The doctor smiled at Manuela and said something in Spanish to her. She leaned over Elizabeth and gently folded up her pants legs, took off her shoes and socks, and Dr. Rodriguez stared at her knees. "How did this happen?" asked Dr. Rodriguez in heavily accented English. His eyes widened as he compared the size of her knees.

Elizabeth shared the story, beginning with the hike over the Pyrenees, her fall in the mud, and tripping over the curb a few hours before. He touched the swollen knee lightly, and Elizabeth inhaled sharply. He attempted to bend the knee, and Elizabeth cried out in pain. "Señorita, you likely have a partial or complete meniscus tear," he said. "I suggest you come to the hospital for more tests. You may need surgery. Let me check your ankle. He rotated her ankle first in one direction, then the other. "This is just a slight sprain. We can wrap it and it should be fine in a few days, but the knee is very concerning."

"But Dr. Rodriguez, I can't have surgery now. I have to finish the Camino. I played soccer for a number of years, and I know plenty of people who have had meniscus injuries who were able to heal without surgery. Do you have some sort of brace or something I could wear to give me extra support?"

Dr. Rodriguez took off his glasses, rubbed his eyes, and gave Elizabeth a hard look. "Señorita, you could injure yourself even worse if you don't take care of this knee. I cannot advise you to continue hiking. If you injure your meniscus further, other ligaments in your knee could give way as well."

"Doctor, I simply cannot stop here. I *must* continue."

When he realized he wouldn't be able to sway her, he exchanged a look with Manuela, and then said, "Okay. I'm going to prescribe an intensive regimen of ice, an anti-inflammatory and painkiller, and I'm going to come back tomorrow morning with a brace for you to try. If you insist on continuing your hike, I'll do everything I can to keep you from injuring yourself further." He dropped four pills into Elizabeth's hand and gave her a cup of water. "Take these every four hours. This should help with the swelling and the pain. Remove the ice in 10 minutes and let Manuela wrap your knee and ankle."

Manuela moved to the side of the bed and took Elizabeth's hand. "Try to stay off of it for the rest of the day. Manuela will call if there are any changes or problems, and I will be available. I am leaving these crutches here to use only to get up for the bathroom. Do you understand?"

"Thank you for your kindness and expertise, Dr. Rodriguez. I'll be careful, I promise. How much do I owe you for this visit?"

"You are most welcome, Elizabeth. I will pray that God strengthens you for the rest of your journey, wherever it may end. No charge for the visit. I was finished for the day at my clinic and on my way home, and as I said, I am a good friend of Manuela's family." He laid his hand on her forehead briefly, and then walked with Manuela to the door, speaking soft Spanish.

Elizabeth shut her eyes and swallowed the lump in her throat, trying not to weep in front of her sweet nurse. Manuela came back, dimmed the lights, and said, "Is there anything else at can get for you?" Elizabeth shook her head. "It would probably be best if you rest. I'll wrap your knee and ankle in a few minutes, and then perhaps you can sleep." Even though it was early in the evening, Elizabeth knew she would have no trouble sleeping. She nodded, and Manuela said, "Can I pray for you?" Not trusting her voice, Elizabeth nodded again.

Manuela rested her hand lightly on Elizabeth's hair and said, "Father in heaven, we thank you for Elizabeth and her life. Thank you for bringing her here to Pamplona. Thank you that Dr. Rodriguez and I have met her and are able to help her. Please bring rest and healing to her body and soul. We pray that she would see herself as you see her. Your beautiful child. Help her sleep now." Manuela continued in Spanish, and Elizabeth listened closely, loving the sound of the language as Manuela spoke. When she finished, she removed the ice bags, wrapped Elizabeth's knee and ankle snugly, and kissed her on the forehead. "Rest now, Elizabeth. I'm going to leave you for a bit to go home and get my things. I'll be back in a few hours. I will leave my phone number on the table beside the bed if you have an emergency and need to call me."

"Thank you, Manuela. You are an angel sent from God," said Elizabeth.

Manuela laughed softly. "No angel, Elizabeth. Just an ordinary woman who loves Jesus."

"Okay, whatever you say," said Elizabeth as she sank back down onto the pillows, grateful for the soft bed and quiet room.

A few hours later, Elizabeth woke to shouting outside her window. Raucous singing and laughter floated up from the street below, and Elizabeth hobbled over with the crutches to the window, wondering what was going on. Manuela unlocked the door just as she got out of bed, exclaiming, "Elizabeth! What are you doing out of bed?"

"I wanted to see what was going on down there. It's so loud!" said Elizabeth as she returned to bed as quickly as was safe.

"Yes, we Spaniards and our festivals! We are always celebrating one saint's day or another. This is my least favorite. Every year at least one person is seriously injured or killed by the bulls. People lose control when they've had too much to drink." She fell silent, and Elizabeth glanced back at her over her shoulder.

"Manuela, are you okay?"

She unwrapped some fruit pie on a plate, and offered it to Elizabeth, who gratefully accepted it. As Elizabeth enjoyed the homemade dessert, Manuela said, "Yes, I'm just remembering. Perhaps I'll tell you. About ten years ago, my older brother Miguel decided to run with the bulls. I was only twelve years old at the time, and he was just starting at university. So full of life, so funny! He taught me how to dance flamenco. All the stomping drove our parents and our downstairs apartment neighbors crazy!" She giggled at the memory.

"Miguel had so much joy, but did not always make good decisions, especially when showing off for his friends. He declared one night at dinner that he was going to run with the bulls. I begged him not to. I had a bad feeling that something was going to happen. He laughed at me and said, 'Manuelita, so many people do this every year! Do you know how many get hurt or die? Almost none! It is all for fun and show!' Still I asked him not to, but he did not listen. I decided to go with him to watch. That morning it was so crowded; the streets were full of people. Everyone was in such a happy, fiesta mood. Still, I couldn't stop the dark feeling I had. I tried one last time, and asked Miguel not to go. He gave me a big hug and said, 'Manuelita, imagine! One day our children will play together and we'll tell them about the time I ran with bulls.' I could tell he'd been drinking. Perhaps it was his way to silence the voice of reason inside him. You can probably guess the rest. The bulls were released. I pushed my way through the crowd and saw him round a corner, then heard a scream. I knew it was Miguel. I screamed for someone to help me, and Dr. Rodriguez came. That was how we met. We managed to get Miguel to a hospital, but he had been gored deeply and had lost too much blood. I held his hand as he died. My parents got there as quickly as they could, but they did not get to say goodbye."

Manuela paused for a moment and glanced at Elizabeth. Tears were pouring down Elizabeth's cheeks, and she absentmindedly brushed them away. "Can I ask you something, Manuela? You speak to Jesus so freely, as if He's right here with you all the time. Yet your brother died. Where was Jesus then? Why did He let that happen?" Elizabeth almost yelled the last sentence, the gnawing pain she'd he'd been holding at bay threatening to burst the dam.

"I did not know Jesus then, Elizabeth. It was Dr. Rodriguez who introduced us. As I sat weeping and holding my brother's hand, Dr. Rodriguez laid his hand on my shoulder. 'Jesus also wept, and He weeps now for your family,' said the doctor. I had never heard about a Jesus like this. Jesus cares about my family this way? I thought He was far away. I wasn't even sure I believed He was real. Dr. Rodriguez prayed for me, and when my parents arrived he prayed for them, too. In the darkest time of my life was the beginning of my relationship with Jesus. I still do not know why God let Miguel die. But I do know He was there and wept with us, and that He's never left me. I know He feels everything we feel, but even more deeply, and that He loves us even more than we can imagine. Not a day goes by that I don't miss Miguel, but Jesus has given me the strength to bear it. And I do know death is not the end, that someday, Jesus will make all things new."

"Do you really believe that, Manuela?" Elizabeth said, now attempting to hold back sobs from escaping her chest.

"With all my heart, Elizabeth. He will never leave me. And you are also His beloved child. Would you like me to teach you to pray to meet Him?"

Elizabeth hesitated. Could it really be true? She'd been disappointed so many times by the people who were supposed to love her. What if Jesus turned out to be another disappointment? Would He abandon her, too?

As if reading her thoughts, Manuela took her hand and said, "Elizabeth, you can trust Him. He loves you, and He is good. So good."

Manuela's eyes were shining with the truth of what she said, and Elizabeth said, "Oh Manuela, I don't even know where to start. What should I say? What should I pray?"

"Just tell Him anything that's on your heart. He loves to listen. Do you want me to stay with you?"

"Yes, please," said Elizabeth. Slowly, she began to pray. "Jesus, you've brought me safely to Pamplona. I don't even know how I got here, but I see now You've put people in place to take care of me. I'm not sure how I feel about You. I have so many questions. But when I see people like Manuela, like Clare, like my Irish friends, like Saadya, I have to believe there's more to my life than what I can see. That I've been wrong about You all this time. So help me believe, God. I need You. Thank You for bringing me here." Elizabeth leaned her head on Manuela's shoulder and released her sobs while Manuela gently stroked her back. "I don't know what to think, Manuela."

"It's okay, Elizabeth. He knows. This is only the beginning of your new life with Him. And now, I think you sleep some more." She reached in her pocket and grinned. "Here, I brought you some earplugs. It's impossible to sleep through this festival unless you have some!"

Manuela rewrapped Elizabeth's knee, gave her another round of anti-inflammatory and pain medicine, then unfurled her own sleeping bag on the floor. "Sleep well, my friend!"

Elizabeth lay back onto the pillows, inserted the earplugs, and closed her eyes, a smile playing on her lips. *Okay, God. You win.*

12

ALTO DE PERDÓN
(HILL OF FORGIVENESS)

When Elizabeth stirred the next morning, Manuela was still fast asleep on the floor beside her. Although her knee felt stiff, the pain was gone, and her ankle seemed to be almost normal sized. She cautiously got up to go use the bathroom, and was happy to find that she could put a bit of weight on her knee as long as she kept it straight and didn't bend it too deeply. She decided to take a quick shower and did so as quietly as possible, but when she came back into the room, Manuela was awake and beaming at her.

"How are you this morning, my friend?"

"I'm better," said Elizabeth.

"Let me call Dr. Rodriguez and tell him we're awake. I know he wanted to see you on his way into the clinic this morning."

As she dialed the doctor on her phone, Elizabeth thought about the night before. *All along you've been talking with me, God. And I think about, even now, how something that could have gone badly wrong ended up working for my good. I could have ended up in a bad place with Marco, but you brought me Manuela and Dr. Rodriguez in spite of my bad decisions. Thank you.*

"He says he'll be right over, so we'd better get dressed," said Manuela. The two women dressed hastily, and Manuela ran downstairs to get them some breakfast. After a few minutes she and Dr. Rodriguez walked into the room together, chattering happily in Spanish.

"Greetings, sister!" said Dr. Rodriguez, hugging Elizabeth tightly. "Manuela tells me you had a talk with Jesus last night."

Elizabeth's eyes filled with tears at this kind man's enthusiasm, and she said, "Yes. I'm still pretty new at all of this, but I'm excited and hopeful."

"Oh yes, He is everything, Elizabeth. You will see. He is simple enough for a little child to understand and love, but deep enough that you can swim far beyond the shore into the ocean of His love. This is a new beginning for you. Now let me check that knee while you drink your coffee!"

Manuela handed her a steaming mug of coffee while the good doctor gently probed her knee. "It seems much better than yesterday. Does this hurt?" he asked, gently bending it slightly.

"It's tender, but nothing like yesterday," smiled Elizabeth. "The sharp pain is gone."

"I've brought you a brace to try."

He helped Elizabeth put it on, and she stood up. The brace seemed to support her knee in all the right places. "Wow, this is amazing! It feels so much better!"

"Hand me your pack, dear," said Dr. Rodriguez. "Oh, my," he said as he lifted it. "What do you have in here? Another person?" He chuckled and passed it to her. She settled it on her shoulders and felt the bruises on her shoulders ache as she strapped it down.

"Can you empty anything out of this?" Manuela asked timidly.

"Well, I have to keep my laptop, obviously. I need all of these clothes..."

"I've taken all your dirty clothes and washed them. They're in the dryer now."

"Thank you so much! They were getting pretty smelly," laughed Elizabeth.

"Why don't I mail some of these things back home for you? That way you don't have to keep carrying so much." Dr. Rodriguez and Manuela helped Elizabeth sort through her pack and keep what was essential.

Manuela held up her black dress and sandals and started laughing. "Really, Elizabeth? You thought you were going need this?"

Elizabeth snatched it back and thought with a pang of Marco and his friends. Even though it had been less than

24 hours since Marco left, it felt like a distant memory. "Okay, okay," she joined in laughing, "all of this can go home. Here's my address." She spelled out her address and was relieved to feel how much lighter her pack was after the downsizing. "What was I thinking!"

"You are not the first pilgrim to make this mistake. I see many *peregrinos* every year just like you who bring too much. People do not realize this journey is about the inner person, not the outer."

"Yes. I see that now, thanks to the two of you, and others I met in the past few days. How can I ever thank you? How can I ever repay you?"

Dr. Rodriguez stepped forward, laid his hand on her shoulder, and said, "You can share God's love with others. That's why Jesus came, and that is what He hopes we will do. Never be afraid to speak of it. Always share the hope you have. May He give you peace and strength, dear child." He brushed away Elizabeth's tears with his thumb, and she turned to Manuela.

Manuela stepped close to Elizabeth, put her hands on her shoulders, and said, "I have a word for you. As you walk today, you will come to *Alto de Perdón*, the Hill of Forgiveness. It is a steep climb, but God has healing for you there. May He bless you and keep you today."

Manuela and Dr. Rodriguez held Elizabeth's hands and prayed with her, first in English, then Spanish. Feeling strengthened, Elizabeth exited the room with her two friends, and said, "I will never forget you. Thank you so much for showing me Jesus, and for helping me. Manuela, how do I pay for the room?"

"No need to pay," said Manuela. "My family owns this hotel. When I told my parents about you, they are happy we can help you. Just knowing you and getting to serve you has been a gift."

"Thank you, Manuela," said Elizabeth, giving Manuela a quick hug.

As she left the building, Dr. Rodriguez said, "The climb up and down *Alto de Perdón* is very steep. Rest as much as you need to and use your poles."

Elizabeth promised and waved goodbye. As she walked out of the city into the morning sunshine with a lighter pack, a hymn came into her mind, one she remembered from childhood.

> *This is my Father's world,*
> *And to my listening ears,*
> *All nature sings and round me rings,*
> *The music of the spheres.*
> *This is my Father's world, I rest me in the thought.*
> *Of rocks and trees, of skies and seas,*
> *His hand the wonders wrought.*

As birds chirped happily in the trees beside the path, she remembered the second verse:

> *This is my Father's World*
> *The birds their Carols Raise*
> *The morning light, the lily white*
> *Declare their maker's praise*
> *This is my Father's World*
> *He shines in all that's fair*
> *In rustling grass, I hear Him pass*

He speaks to me everywhere.

She hummed as she walked back into the countryside, grateful to be out of the frantic pace and noise of the city. *Gosh, how will I ever survive going back to DC after this?* She smiled at the change in herself. *This city is tiny compared to what I'm used to dealing with...try not to feel overwhelmed by that thought. I'll deal with culture shock when it happens and not worry now.*

The path stayed mostly flat for a time, but then started to climb sharply. *I must be on my way up the Hill of Forgiveness.* After an hour of steady walking and her knee complaining, Elizabeth sat down by the path for a rest. *Okay, God. I'm done pretending you don't exist, and that you don't care. Please help me make it up this hill. Manuela said you had something for me there, so if that's true, you're going to have to get me to the top.* She took a long drink from her water bottle, ate a handful of almonds, and stood up again. *I'm going to have to ask my knee for forgiveness by the time this day is over. Man, I feel like an old woman. I wonder how all these people in their 60's handle this hike? Okay, let's do this!*

She stood and looked up to the top of the ridge. She could see huge white windmills turning slowly in the wind along the ridgeline of the mountain, generating electric power for the residents in the area. As she squinted at them turning and turning, she could barely make out the hill's famous *peregrino* sculptures. She had learned in this rolling country that even if you could see a destination you hoped to reach soon, it could be miles away, and in the case of the *Alto de Perdón*, it was nearly straight up.

Her pace was slow, and with several switchbacks in the path going up the mountain, it took much longer than she had imagined. The level parts were a welcome break from pulling uphill, but the zigzags doubled the distance. The closer she got to the top, the more impressed she was by the size of the windmills. At each pause she turned to take in the whole view of what was below her. Coming into view on other peaks, were dozens and dozens of the giant three-bladed windmills.

She was working and breathing very hard to get to the top. Even her lighter pack was feeling very heavy again. She pulled hard on her poles to take the stress off her aching knee, and slowed down even more, with short breaks every few steps. Looking down at the beauty of miles of green patchwork crops and wild flowers brought a sense of joy to the difficulty. As she came to the top of the hill, there at last were the famous metal figures and the bases of the gigantic windmills.

Sit down, Beloved. Obediently, Elizabeth walked to the fringe of the sculpture area, and sat, listening. For a quarter hour or so she heard the whoosh of the windmills turning and the voices of people celebrating their arrival to the top. She watched people taking pictures and selfies with the iron sculptures. Some were jubilant and boisterous, others were weeping off to the side. She grew tired of waiting for God to speak again. *Okay, God. I know you're the boss here, but I also don't want to be homeless tonight, so if there's something you need to tell me, can you do it so I can get to an* albergue *before it fills up?* Nothing.

Elizabeth sighed deeply. She took another long pull on her water bottle, looking around, amused to see a food truck nearby. Figuring she might as well take advantage of the opportunity for a snack, she purchased a Snickers bar and walked back to the edge of the activity. She unbuckled her pack, sat down on a patch of grass, and resolved to wait a bit longer. She ate the candy, marveling at how delicious it seemed after the long hike. She breathed deeply, quieting her mind, absorbing all the sights and sounds around her. Out of the peace she felt, she heard, *You carry much anger towards me, Beloved. Will you forgive me?*

Forgive you? But you're God. I don't need to forgive you. You're perfect, right?

Beloved, I'm asking you to trust me. I know what you need. And you need to forgive me. You're angry with me. For your mother's death. For things not working out with Steve. For your distant relationship with your father. For your loneliness. I'll ask again. Will you forgive me?

Elizabeth sat hugging her legs, resting her head on her forearms, weeping at the beauty of a God who would humbly ask her forgiveness. As she wept, she whispered, "I forgive you. Your will be done, Lord. Please." She sat quietly, allowing herself to absorb and enjoy God's healing presence.

The voice came again. *Now, will you forgive yourself? Will you tear down this wall of unforgiveness that hardens your heart, and receive my grace and forgiveness?*

The tears began again, and Elizabeth rocked back and forth as regrets flooded her.

Let me have them, Beloved.

Her head still bowed toward her chest, Elizabeth moaned and spoke aloud the regrets she carried in her heart. "I wasn't there when my mom died, God. Oh God, how could I have been so blind and selfish? How could I have left her? You told me to stay, and I didn't. Mom even tried to tell me she was dying and I wouldn't listen. I was so foolish."

I forgive you. Let me have that. You are beautiful. Your mother is with me, and she is safe. You will see her again. Let me carry that burden.

Elizabeth sighed as though a huge weight had been lifted from her shoulders. She had no idea she'd been carrying that for so many years. She sat awhile longer, listening for more, and reluctant to leave this sacred place of healing, but knowing she needed to make *Puente La Reina* before it got too late. A new peace came over her, and she wiped her face with her bandana. She turned her face to the sky. "Thank you, God. Thank you that you came to give me life and wholeness. Thank you for not giving up on me."

I have good and beautiful plans for you, my child. Plans to prosper you and not to harm you. Plans to give you hope and a future. Get up and walk.

Elizabeth rose to her feet, grabbed her poles, and started walking down the hill. A line from a favorite old song came to her, and she sang out loud, oblivious to the other people nearby, "Prone to wander, Lord I feel it, prone to leave the God I love--Here's my heart Lord, take and seal it, seal it for your courts above." She felt laughter bubbling up inside her as she stepped carefully on the steep downhill path, feeling lighter and more joyful than she could remember feeling in years.

After a few kilometers, her knee seemed to be swelling again, and the pain was increasing. She decided to stop in *Uterga* for the night rather than hike another 10k to

Puente de la Reina, and welcomed the chance to stop earlier than planned. *I can always take a bus if I have to, even though I think I'd feel like I was cheating if I did that.* Dr. Rodriguez's warnings swam into her mind, and she felt chastened. *I've got to be careful. Besides, now I'll have time to do some work since I wasn't able to get online yesterday.*

Elizabeth found space at a new-looking *albergue* with a smiling grandpa acting as *hospitalero*. He introduced himself as *Jaime* and promised to get her a bag of ice for her knee while she settled in. After showering and taking another round of the prescriptions from Dr. Rodriguez, Elizabeth grabbed her laptop and went to the commons room, where she found a good wifi connection and Jaime handed her a bag of ice and an orange Fanta. She dreaded opening her email, knowing she had trespassed Bruce's admonition that she be available at all times. Elizabeth looked in and dozens of emails began populating her screen. She had nearly fifty emails from Bruce, each with an increasingly more snarky subject line than the last. She clicked on the most recent, titled, "Open if you want to keep your job." She groaned as she read.

Elizabeth,

I don't know where you've been for the past 24 hours. The rest of us have been picking up your slack around here so you can be on vacation, and you can't seem to keep up. Email me immediately so I know you've received this, and going forward, be available per our agreement.

Bruce

Elizabeth hastily typed a reply.

Dear Bruce,

I'm so very sorry. I injured my knee quite severely and had to receive medical treatment. Fortunately it's better today and I was able to continue my hike. I stopped hiking early today and will have plenty of time to work. I'm also available by phone for the next several hours should you need to reach me that way.

Thanks for your understanding,

Elizabeth

She began working, editing documents, responding to clients, emailing other members of the firm. New emails pinged into her inbox almost as quickly as she responded to old ones, including an email from Bruce that read simply,

Elizabeth, don't let this happen again. Bruce

Wow, he didn't even ask about my injury. In fact, he doesn't care about me at all. He only cares about what I can produce. Ugh. Well, even so, he is my boss and I need to respect him, so I need to do what he asks. Elizabeth worked steadily into the deepening dusk, taking breaks to eat dinner, get more ice for her knee, and greeting other incoming *peregrinos* who came and went from the commons room.

It was getting late, almost "quiet hours" for the *albergue*, and Elizabeth longed to go to bed. *After all, I stopped early today, so tomorrow's hike is going to be almost 30k. But I do want to keep my job. I kind of wish I hadn't been so quick to say no to John Cunningham. I wonder what it would be like to work for him? Probably a very different experience than working for Bruce Devon!*

Elizabeth looked at her phone. 9:50 pm. She shut down her computer and walked to her room, each step punctuating the stiffness of her knee. She lay down on her bunk, put her pack beside her and propped the injured leg up as well as she could, swallowed the last dose of meds for the night, plugged her ears against the interruptions of snorers, and was asleep in minutes.

13

TO BURGOS

She groaned, as did several others in the room, as an overeager pilgrim's alarm went off before sunrise the next morning. She squeezed her eyes shut, then opened them and let the room swim slowly into focus.

She tried moving her knee. *Argh, this is stiff! Hopefully it will loosen up as I move some. I hope my knee holds up. God, please help my knee hold up, I have 30k today.* She sat up and reached under the bed for her new brace, threaded her leg into it, fastened it, and stood up.

Despite the shorter distance yesterday, the steep grades had aggravated her injury. A sharp pain made her wince as she took a few cautious steps. *I have to do this. There's no way I'm going to make it to Santiago in time if I don't do 30 kilometers today.* After a quick coffee and roll with her leg propped beside the table, she stood up grimacing from pain. She limped to the front door and walked outside. Buffeted by a strong wind, she squared her shoulders and set out. She had to tighten the chinstrap on her hat and pay more attention than usual to planting her steps firmly so as not to blown off balance by the wind. Her knee loosened slightly as she walked, and she was able to walk almost normally after a kilometer. Elizabeth's hair whipped into her face, and she tightened her ponytail, her eyes watering from dust particles in the wind.

Despite the weather, several pilgrims passed her in the first few kilometers of her hike, their greetings of *Buen Camino*!! muffled by the wind. *I must be going pretty slowly with all these people passing me. I need to pick up the pace if I'm going to make it to* Estella *today.* She leaned heavily on her walking poles as she went.

She was startled by a tap on her shoulder. A small man carrying a homemade sack on one shoulder walked beside her. He looked to be about 65 years of age, and his tanned face creased into deep lines and a crooked smile as he looked at her. "No English," he apologized. He pointed to her pack, and gestured for Elizabeth to take it off. She slung it carefully from her shoulders, confused. He positioned his own small knapsack to his chest and put Elizabeth's load on his back, adjusting straps and buckles to fit. "Okay?" he said with a smile as he patted Elizabeth's shoulder.

Overwhelmed by the gesture, she hugged him, and said, "Thank you."

He patted her shoulder again and started walking, letting Elizabeth set the pace. Her knee felt immediate relief with the weight gone. Even though the man was several inches shorter than Elizabeth, he appeared to have no problem carrying the two packs, and hummed happily as he walked. After a couple of minutes she tapped him on the shoulder, pointed at herself, "I'm Elizabeth."

"EE-Leez-a-bet," he repeated, smiling at her and nodding enthusiastically.

"Juan," he said, patting his chest, changing his humming to whistling. Elizabeth whistled with him, and he nodded approval and chuckled.

After a few more kilometers, they stopped to sit on a fallen log, eat a snack and have some water. Juan inhaled deeply as he surveyed the countryside, moved by the surrounding beauty. The expression on his face reminded her of a charcoal drawing that her mother had of Jesus laughing. Pure, childlike joy and trust. *This is how I want to be, Jesus. I want to be like Juan, delighting in my surroundings and caring for people along the way.*

After another few minutes, Juan stood up. Elizabeth reached to take her pack, but he shook his head, pointed to her knee, smiled, and shouldered both packs again. Humbled by his kindness, Elizabeth examined her own heart. *I would never have thought to do something like this for someone, especially someone I can't even speak with. Juan has a deeper level of understanding, of knowing, and somehow I know I can trust him. How many times have I passed people that needed help because I was in too much of a hurry? How many times have I missed opportunities to be kind with a word of encouragement and a smile?*

You are a new creation now, Beloved. Learn from me. I've sent my servant Juan for today to teach you. Elizabeth grinned, and Juan gave her an understanding look.

Though they passed the rest of the way to *Puente la Reina* without talking, they hummed, whistled, laughed, and called out *Buen Camino!* to fellow pilgrims, and a few fell into step beside them, gesturing and chattering in various languages. As the group walked into *Puente la Reina*, Juan stopped in front of an *albergue*.

"Oh, no. I can't stop here," Elizabeth said shaking her head. *"Estella,"* she said, pointing down the path and moving to take her pack.

Juan shook his head confidently and said "No," walked into the *albergue*, and motioned for Elizabeth to follow.

She looked around desperately for someone to help translate, her sense of peace evaporating, and asked the man at the desk, "Do you speak English?" He nodded, and she said, "Can you ask this man to give me my pack? Tell him I need to go to *Estella* today so I can keep my schedule."

The receptionist and Juan spoke Spanish back and forth, and the man turned to Elizabeth. He closed his eyes for a moment, afraid to deliver Juan's message. "Juan wishes for you to stay here tonight. He says God sent him to help you, and if you continue hiking you will severely injure your body. He asks you to please reconsider your plans and join him on a bus in the morning to *Estella*."

Elizabeth looked at little Juan, who stood looking at her with fatherly concern. She put her hands on her hips and looked back at him, frustrated. Even though her knee was screaming, she was determined to stick to her schedule.

"Please tell him I am so grateful for his help and kindness, but I must get to *Estella* tonight. I would like my pack back now, please." The man repeated her request to Juan, who unbuckled the pack and handed it to Elizabeth.

"*Adiós*, EE-Leez-a-bet." He gave her a hug, hung his head, and walked up the stairs, casting one last glance over his shoulder. Elizabeth was grateful to him and meant no disrespect, but walked back out the front door. When she shouldered her pack, pain knifed through her knee, but she resolved to keep walking to *Estella*. She managed just 5km, before she had to stop for a rest in *Cirauqui*, a small medieval village.

A little deli across the square was the only thing in the village that looked open. She looked at her watch. *2 pm. Everyone is taking a siesta.* She hobbled towards the deli. She looked at the offerings in the cold case, and pointed to a sandwich with hardboiled eggs, roasted peppers and some lettuce. She took a Coke Lite from the drink cooler, paid, and asked to use the *servicio.* Sometimes bathrooms were not as appealing as just going along the trail, but she appreciated the privacy of indoor plumbing, especially when trying to manage a leg brace.

Elizabeth took her lunch across the square and sat on the steps of the Church of St. Andrew, where she could elevate her leg on a step above the one on which she sat. She examined her sandwich, removed the wilted lettuce, and threw it away with her trash. She let the cold soda can minister to her knee, as she wolfed down half her sandwich. *Something tastes off here,* she thought as she swallowed. She took a big gulp of soda. *I need to eat to keep going,* she thought, and took another bite, followed by more Coke.

I can't believe I didn't listen to Juan. What was I thinking? God, you clearly sent him to help me, and I rejected your help. I'm so sorry. I totally blew it. As Elizabeth felt more and more guilt, she looked down at her knee that had ballooned to twice its normal size. She finished what she wanted of her sandwich, tears pooling in her eyes, then rolling down her face. *It's over. I should just go home. I can't believe I thought I could do this.*

She sniffed loudly, blew her nose, and put her lunch trash in the bag from the store. She loosened the brace on her knee, re-positioned it, and put most of her weight on her good leg to stand up. As she turned to look for a trash can, a man walked up to her and said, "Elizabeth?"

She looked at him wondering how he knew her name, but could not place meeting him previously. He wore hiking clothes and carried several grocery bags of old clothing. A medium sized black dog sat obediently next to him, gazing up at him with brown eyes. The man nodded and motioned with his hand, and the dog walked over to Elizabeth and began licking her knee. The warm tickle of its tongue brought a fresh torrent of tears and caused her to sit down and hug the dog, but the man seemed neither embarrassed nor hurried. When Elizabeth could speak, she looked up and asked, "How did you know my name? And what is yours?"

"I'm Father Bill, but you can call me Bill," he answered with an accent she recognized as Irish. "God told me come help you, and I read your name there," he chuckled, pointing to the luggage tag on her backpack. Would you please come with me?"

"I-I can't walk," said Elizabeth.

"Not a problem. Paddy will stay with you while I pull the truck around. Paddy, stay." The dog made no movement to follow the man, and Elizabeth wondered again at the strange journey she seemed to be on. She stroked Paddy's head and waited.

Moments later, a small blue truck rattled into the square and pulled up just in front of Elizabeth. Fr. Bill hopped out, opened the passenger door, and helped Elizabeth in. Paddy took his place next to her and laid his silky head in her lap. He put her pack in the back with the bags of clothing, and got behind the wheel. He put the truck in gear, rumbled out of town, and merged onto the highway. Elizabeth glanced at his profile. His bright blue eyes and freckles gave him a boyish look, but his graying hair and whiskers suggested he was in his forties. Fr. Bill hummed and sang to himself, "Be thou my vision, O Lord of my heart, Naught be all else to me, save that Thou art..."

"So, Father Bill..."

"Bill," he interrupted with a smile.

"Bill, can you take me to *Estella*?"

"Nay, I'm supposed to take you to Burgos."

"Burgos!" she exclaimed. "Can you just drop me off in *Estella*? I'd like to start from there tomorrow."

"Elizabeth." Father Bill looked over at her and his eyes bored into hers before focusing again on the highway. "I understand from Holy Spirit that I am to take you to Burgos. Can you trust me?" She stared at the road. "Have there been any recent situations in which someone tried to help and you refused?"

How does he know about Juan? God, did you tell him that, too? I don't want everyone knowing my dirty laundry!

Trust me, Beloved. Let yourself be known.

She squirmed a bit, but agreed, "Okay, Burgos it is." She changed the subject. "So, Father Bill. I mean, Bill. I think I need to tell you something. I'm not Catholic."

Bill laughed, "Not to worry, Elizabeth. Father God is pleased to call you His child, and I am called to give help to all who will receive it. Besides, I already told you, he directed me to walk around to the front steps of the church instead of going to directly to my truck in the back."

"I haven't met many priests like you. Okay, I haven't met ANY priests like you. How is it that an Irishman is a priest in Spain? And where's your priest collar? And how did you get Paddy?"

"Whoa, there. Okay, let me try to answer those questions. I can only remember so much at a time. I'll start with my story. I'm originally from Cork, Ireland. Youngest of seven children, I was a wild child. I spent my teens more drunk than sober, dropped out of university and spiraled deeper into drugs, alcohol, and darkness. One night I passed out cold on a park bench in a small village, and the local priest found me. I woke up in a soft bed with a wicked hangover, so stoned I could hardly move. That priest sat by me for hours without saying anything." Bill's voice wavered and he cleared his throat to keep the story going. "He just sat there for hours, praying, providing for my needs, and being present. After a few days of rest and recovery, I was back out on the streets looking for drugs again.

"But God had begun His work in me, loving me through that little old priest. I started going to Mass, slipping in the back door a few minutes late, leaving early. I didn't want anyone to notice me, see. I was so ashamed; I didn't want to be truly known. So I'd sit back there, smelling like piss and covered in grime, and every time Father Paddy brought out the host, something deep inside me would break, and I would weep. I wanted it so badly, but I didn't know it. You know what I mean?" Elizabeth nodded.

"Anyway," Fr. Bill continued, "one Sunday morning I walked into early Mass and hunched over in the back pew. As Father Paddy processed the cross up the center aisle toward the front, I found myself following behind. It wasn't an altar call or anything, just the regular processional up the center aisle. And there I went, a tramp and outcast, following behind. I couldn't have stopped myself even if I'd wanted to. But I didn't want to. I stayed prostrate before the altar throughout that entire mass. After Mass, I followed the cross back out, and every person at that service introduced themselves, welcomed me, hugged me, despite my filthy appearance.

"Father Paddy took me back into the church and heard my confession, and I told Jesus I wanted to make a new start. Then came the hard work of getting sober. It took me a year, with some relapses, to completely give up drugs and alcohol. Just when I thought I had it, I'd fall off the wagon again. But Father Paddy never gave up on me. He embodied Jesus' grace to me." Bill abruptly stopped talking, and Elizabeth saw him brush away a tear. "Father Paddy died of cancer a few years ago. I still miss him every day." He ruffled the fur on Paddy's head.

"Father Paddy loved dogs and always had one at mass with him. He would be thrilled to know I named my own dog after him. This little four-footed Paddy found me a few years ago. A little skinny, abandoned puppy. He never leaves my side." Bill chuckled and paused for a few moments.

"I think your other question was how I'm here in Spain. After a few years of being sober, I went to seminary to become a priest. I took holy orders, and was commissioned as a missionary priest. I'm on loan from my local diocese in Cork as a missionary to the *peregrinos*. We've noticed that a lot of folks besides Irishmen come to walk the Camino but don't really have a purpose or an answer for why they're doing it. They are more open to hearing about God here for some reason than they are in back home. I've been here ten years, and I hope that in a small way I've been able to show people what they're truly thirsty for, why they are walking.

"So I cover a pretty large area, rotating through a dozen small towns along the Camino, offering prayer for pilgrims, celebrating mass, helping provide for pilgrims' needs, both physical and spiritual. Normally I ride a scooter from place to place, kind of like an updated version of the circuit rider preachers from a century ago in the American old west, but today I have my friend Matteo's truck because I had to pick you up and transport these clothes from St. Andrew's."

Elizabeth looked out the window, still slightly unnerved that Bill seemed to be receiving such clear directives about her. "So, what about you? What made you decide to do this trip?"

144

Elizabeth began telling her story, feeling encouraged by Bill's interest and kindness. He asked lots of questions when she stopped for breath, and she was struck anew by God's goodness and care for her as she remembered the many ways, both big and small, that He had provided since she began this journey.

When she told the part of Saadya, Bill chuckled. "Oh yes, Saadya shows up from time to time when the need is great. Olive skinned, muscular young bloke?"

"Yes!" Elizabeth said excitedly. "How did you know?" "

"Well, I've met him a few times myself, and I've spoken with others who have had interactions with him. There's much more going on that we don't see, but the more we pray to see the world through the eyes of the Spirit, the more He peels back the layers of prejudice and preconceived notions. St. Paul said, 'now we see through a glass darkly, but soon we will see face to face.' He said, 'we only know partially, but someday we will know fully, even as we are fully known.' I love that promise. One of the things I pray every day is that God would give me His heart for the world and people around me. Since I started praying that prayer, things that I used to consider supernatural are actually becoming natural."

"You mean like angels and demons?" Elizabeth said, somewhat skeptically.

"Oh yeah, for sure," said Father Bill. "This life is a battle. Jesus' birth was an invasion into enemy territory. Satan had this world pretty well in his grasp, but God's people were waiting for their savior, during all those years of darkness. And then Jesus showed up in the most unexpected, humble way possible. A handyman from Nazareth and a bunch of fisherman turned this world on its head. And now we get to be part of Jesus' redemptive work in this world. We get to join him, but we still have to fight hard. His Spirit in us does the work. We just have to stay close to Him and let Him shepherd us."

Elizabeth shook her head. She'd never heard someone talk about the spiritual realm this way, and although she was slightly taken aback, she felt an excitement rising inside her as Bill talked. She continued to stroke Paddy's silky head as they came to the outskirts of Burgos, and sat silently, letting what Bill had told her sink in. They joined the traffic entering the city, and Bill pulled up in front of a plain looking building hidden in the shadow of the great cathedral. "I have to deliver these clothes to the sisters that work here. They'll distribute them to the refugee population in Burgos. Bill jogged around to the back of the truck, grabbed the bags, and disappeared into the building. When he came out, he was accompanied by a small woman in an ankle length habit and hiking sandals. As she drew nearer to the truck, Elizabeth let out a cry of recognition.

"Clare!"

The little woman's face lit up with a wide smile. "Elizabeth! I knew I would see you again. I told Father Bill about you after we met in St. Jean, and we've been expecting you!" Clare trotted over, clambered up on the running board, and gave Elizabeth a gentle hug so as not to disturb her knee. Paddy perked up and nosed Clare's hand, and she tugged his ears and ruffled his fur, murmuring a few words in Italian.

"Clare, I didn't know you were a nun! I didn't realize nuns and priests...well, I guess I've never thought of nuns and priests as hikers," she said lamely. Bill and Clare both laughed heartily, and Elizabeth joined in, though she felt slightly foolish for her ignorance.

"Bill and I sometimes joke that we exist to change people's minds about what nuns and priests look like and do. We both spend a large part of our time helping *peregrinos*, and one of the ways we do that is to hike portions of the Camino regularly throughout the year. In the 20 years I've lived in Burgos, I've hiked all of the *Camino Francés* three times, but have lost count of the many other sections I've hiked. How are you?" Clare glanced down at Elizabeth's knee and gasped. "Oh no, you must rest your knee for a few days! You must be in so much pain. I can recommend a very good *albergue* on the outskirts of the city. Bill will drive you back and get you settled, and I will check on you in the morning. Now I have to go help the other sisters with our clothing distribution, but I will see you very soon." Clare patted Elizabeth's cheek, ruffled Paddy's fur again, and jumped down off the truck. She and Bill exchanged a few sentences in Spanish, and Bill climbed back in the truck. Elizabeth's snapped her mouth shut, realizing it had been hanging open since she saw Clare.

Bill laughed at her expression. "Ah, Elizabeth, God has certainly got your number. I love the way He's working in your story." He wheeled the truck around, drove a few blocks to the *albergue*, carried her pack in, then came back to help her. He was carrying a pair of crutches.

"The *hospitalero*, José Maria, keeps these for folk like you. You are welcome to use them for a few days." He propped them against the hood of the truck, then reached up to

147

help Elizabeth down, keeping her steady while he handed her the crutches.

A tall, gangly man with a wide smile and hair pulled back in a ponytail greeted them as they walked in. "Elizabeth, this is *José Maria*. He's going to take care of you. He was able to move a cot to the supply closet on the ground floor so you don't have to walk up the stairs. There is a bathroom with a shower on this level as well. The rest of the pilgrims are at dinner now, so you're welcome to join them. I'll be back to check on you in a couple days."

"Thank you, Bill. I'll never forget you. Thank you for bringing me here and taking care of me." Bending down awkwardly, Elizabeth hugged Paddy around the neck and kissed his silky head. "Thanks for helping me feel better, Paddy." Paddy licked her hand and nudged her leg with his damp nose.

"*Adiós,* José Maria!" Bill waved as he left, and the *hospitalero* smiled at Elizabeth and motioned for her to follow him down the hall. She hobbled after him on her crutches thankful she didn't have to put weight on her injured leg. He opened a door at the end of the hallway and indicated the bathroom, then opened another door and flicked a light on. Elizabeth was touched to see how clean and orderly her small room was. José Maria had set up a little table with towel, washcloth, water, and a small vase of flowers. He pointed to where Bill had propped her pack up in the corner, and then led her back down the hallway to the common room where 15 other pilgrims had begun a meal.

Elizabeth was surprised she didn't feel hungry since all she'd had for lunch was the egg sandwich, but she decided to try eating a little. Her stomach rumbled uncomfortably after a few sips of wine and bites of pasta, so she set her fork down and listened to her fellow pilgrims as they bantered about everything from politics to hiking gear. With a start, Elizabeth remembered she needed to check in with Bruce, so she said good night and bumped back down the hallway to her room.

For the next two hours, she responded to Bruce's queries about various minutiae. It wasn't the first time she had wondered why he needed her to take care of so many unimportant things while she was on vacation. She sighed as she closed her laptop, and realized she needed to ice her knee and take some meds before bed. She found José Maria watering flowers outside, and he happily gave her ice and extra pillows to prop up her leg. After the ice therapy, Elizabeth wrapped her knee securely in the compression bandage, reached over from her bed with the crutch, and flicked off the light switch.

As she waited for sleep to come, Elizabeth thought through the strange events of the day, especially her conversation with Bill about the unseen world around them. *Lord, Let me see people and the world around me the way you do. Thank you for bringing me to Burgos, for Father Bill, and for letting me see Clare again. Please heal my knee so I can continue my walk soon. Thank you for loving me and taking care of me.* She continued praying as she dropped off to sleep, thinking of her father, Ellen, Holly, and others back home.

Elizabeth woke with a queasy stomach the following morning, but was pleasantly surprised to find that her injured knee seemed to be almost normal size. She tested her weight on it and was amazed to find it barely hurt.

It will help to rest it another day. Stay here, Beloved.

I'm already so far behind, though. It would be great if I could just hike a little bit today, maybe even loosen it up. She walked across the hallway, brushed her teeth and washed her face, then walked down to the common room. It was strangely quiet. She was the only person there. *I must have slept really late since there were no windows in my room.*

She heard whistling and found José Maria in the kitchen washing dishes. He beamed at her, motioned for her to sit, and brought her hot coffee and a warm piece of toast. She still had no appetite, but she nibbled the toast and sipped some coffee so as not to hurt his feelings. He sat with her and asked her about her life back in DC, her job, her home. He apologized for his simple English, but explained he appreciated being able to improve by having the conversation with her. His interest and kindness warmed her, and he offered her several English language books from his library since she "needed to rest her knee."

"Actually, my knee is feeling so much better today. I think I'm going to try to walk a bit farther to loosen it up. I love staying here, but I'm already far behind schedule."

"Father Bill wants you to stay here," he said with a concerned look. "And it would be best for you to wait more days until your knee is completely better."

Elizabeth laughed it off, "José Maria, surely I can make it to Rabe! It's only 10 kilometers once I get to Burgos again."

José Maria pursed his lips and stayed silent. "Elizabeth, it is your choice. I cannot force you. But it would be wise for you to stay another day or so. And also my English to be better more and more, yes?" He raised his eyebrows and chuckled.

"Thanks, but I'm going to go. I can't thank you enough for your hospitality!" The *hospitalero* walked her back down to her room, helped her put on her pack, and walked her out the front door, pointing to direct her back to the street that linked to the Camino de Santiago.

"*Buen Camino!*" he said with a smile, and she waved and turned. After a few blocks of walking, she saw a yellow arrow pointing the way. Breathing deeply, she smiled and got her stride. The sky was beautiful, the temperature was mild, and Elizabeth felt immeasurably blessed to be hiking pain free.

As she approached Burgos, her stomach began to churn and cramp slightly. *That's strange. I've barely eaten anything since yesterday. Maybe it's just the coffee.* Looking around for someplace that would have a bathroom, she spotted a little café, ducked in, bought some water, and used the *servicio. Ugh, I thought I would feel better after a bathroom stop. Oh well, this is a short hike today.* The towers of the Cathedral peeked above the trees. It was beautiful. She followed a yellow arrow out of the *albergue's* neighborhood, keeping her eyes fixed on the Cathedral. A wave of nausea swept over her, and she doubled over with cramping.

She sat down on a stone wall, took a sip of water, and hoped it would pass soon. Instead, it got worse. As she stood up to resume walking, she was unable to keep herself from vomiting beside the wall. Thoroughly disgusted, she wiped herself off, swished her mouth out, and tried to keep going. A few motorists drove by, and she turned

151

away, embarrassed. She walked another 100 meters and threw up again, her stomach cramping painfully. Just up the road, she saw a small park, and stepped up her pace to get there, hoping there would be a quiet spot to lie down while she thought about what to do next. She had her cell phone. She could call 112, the Spanish emergency number if she really got desperate, but she wasn't that bad yet. She threw up once more on the way into the garden, and was glad to find it deserted when she entered. She made her way over to the bubbling drinking fountain in the center, knelt down beside it, and splashed cool water on her face. Her stomach cramped again, and she felt an uncontrollable explosion of diarrhea coming. She looked frantically around her, rushed behind a tree in the corner of the garden, and did her best to keep her pants clean, but wasn't totally successful. *Oh, I am so sick! This is so gross.* She fumbled with her pack of tissues, and cleaned herself up as well as she could. Humiliated by her soiled pants, but so weak and doubled over from the cramping she could barely stand, she uttered two words, "Jesus, help," then laid down beside her pack at the fountain near the garden entrance, and cried quietly.

14

INSTRUMENT OF PEACE

Andrés awakened to the rooster's crow in the courtyard, stretched his arms over head and swung his legs out of bed. 5 am. He fell back against the pillows for a moment, wishing he could have one day to sleep in during the summer, but looking forward to serving pilgrims too.

I have a special assignment for you today, my beloved son.

Andrés was used to hearing from God this way, so he waited for more.

I need you to be my hands and feet. Be ready and trust me.

With a sense of anticipation, Andrés dressed and walked to the main building, started the coffee, and began slicing bread for the *peregrinos'* breakfast. He loaded clean oranges into the hopper at the top of the *Zumo* machine, and then got an assortment of cheeses out of the refrigerator. As he sipped his mug of coffee and listened to the *Zumo* squeezing orange juice into a pitcher, he prayed a favorite prayer, penned a thousand years before by St. Francis of Assisi:

> *Lord, make me an instrument of your peace,*
> *Where there is hatred, let me sow love;*
> *Where there is injury, pardon;*
> *Where there is doubt, faith;*
> *Where there is despair, hope;*
> *Where there is darkness, light;*
> *Where there is sadness, joy;*
> *O Divine Master, grant that I may not so much seek to be consoled as to console;*
> *To be understood as to understand;*
> *To be loved as to love.*

He put cheese slices and bread on platters and carried them to a sideboard just as his father came in whistling, followed closely by Rex. *"Buenos días, Papá!"* shouted Andrés cheerily.

"Buenos, Andrés!" replied Matteo as he gave him a big hug.

Andrés put Rex's food in a dish and called him to the corner of the room. The big German shepherd bounded over quickly and sat at attention, waiting for the okay to eat. "Okay, Rex!" The shepherd stood and wagged his way to his food, licking Andrés' hand in appreciation before wolfing it down.

"Papá, café?"

"Yes, please," said Matteo as he sipped from the mug Andrés handed him. "I didn't hear anything from anyone through the night, did you? Thanks for taking the morning duties for me."

"I didn't hear anything from any of our guests, but I did hear from God this morning that He has something for me to do for Him today," he shared smiling.

"That's all you know so far, yes?"

"So far that's it. I will know more when it's time."

Rex finished eating, walked over to Andrés and leaned against his legs where he stood at the worktable. He laughed at the affection. "Are you ready to greet everyone?" said Andrés scratching the dog's ears, and leaning over to receive a wet nose bump on his cheek in return. "Okay, Rex. Go sit and wait."

The shepherd went over to the foot of the stairs and sat at attention as the first two pilgrims walked down, puffy-eyed and stiff. Each one smiled and gave Rex a pat as he nudged their hands with his nose, and Andrés smiled at Rex's ability to soften hearts.

Andrés poured two mugs of coffee and handed them to the German couple with a smile, then directed them toward the food. They loaded their plates with artisan cheese and Miriam's jam, remarking over how delicious and fresh everything was.

"Papá," said Andrés motioning his father to the serving area to speak privately. "I need to go to Burgos to get the truck from Bill. After I clean up from breakfast, I'll cycle over. Do you need me to pick anything up while I'm there?" His father made a list of a few items as Andrés continued to pour coffee, load the toaster, and chat with guests. Each year, the number of pilgrims seemed to increase, and Andrés was thankful his university teaching schedule still allowed him to come back to Spain each summer and work with his father. He loved hearing pilgrims' stories, and was always struck by how open people are to the Spirit on the Camino. He considered it a privilege to tell others about Jesus and help them see He was the answer to their questions.

After breakfast, Andrés cleared the plates, started the dishwasher, and put the leftover food in the refrigerator. *Go quickly,* a voice inside urged him. Rex followed him outside where his father was hanging bed sheets to dry, and Andrés wheeled his bike out of the shed, fastening on his helmet and buckling on his backpack.

Rex wagged his tail in joyful anticipation, and Andrés said, "Papá, Rex and I are leaving! We'll be back soon!" Andrés hopped onto his bike and took off, Rex charging along beside him. As Andrés drew closer to Burgos, he prayed. *Lord, help me see what you see. Keep my heart open to the work you have for me to do.* On a whim, he decided to visit a favorite little park on the outskirts of the city center. His mother had brought him here when he was a boy, and he had enjoyed splashing in the fountain and reading books in the peaceful spot as a welcome break during their walks to and from Burgos.

Stop here, my son. Stop here and pray.

Andrés dismounted and walked in with his bike, unfastening his helmet. With an urgent whine, Rex, ran ahead. "What's wrong, boy?" said Andrés, and then he saw her. Next to the fountain was a woman, beside her a pool of vomit, her clothes soiled with diarrhea. The stench was strong, and Andrés tied his bandana around his nose to keep himself from being sick. Rex nosed the woman's hand, and she stirred slightly, moaning, eyelids fluttering.

Is she drunk? Oh Jesus, what happened? Andrés knelt down next to her, brushed the hair back from her face, and her eyes opened.

"Help me, Jesus," she murmured, then closed her eyes again and moaned.

Quickly, Andrés heard the insistent whisper again.

He pulled a second bandana from his pack, dipped it in the fountain, and wiped the woman's face. She was burning with fever. He spotted her water bottle on the ground beside her, and tried to rouse her so he could give her a drink. As he attempted to lift her to a seated position, she vomited again, splattering the pavement and her pack. Because she was unresponsive, Andrés knew she had reached a severe level of dehydration, and Bill's place was just a half-mile away. He dialed his friend, "Bill, I need your help. just found a young woman in the park who is very sick. I need to get her to a doctor. Can you come right away in the truck and take us to the clinic?"

The priest sighed into the phone. "Is she about thirty, slender, attractive, light brown hair, blue backpack?"

"Yes. You know her?"

"I think our new sister Elizabeth did not heed wise counsel," said Bill resolutely. "I'll be there in ten minutes." Andrés

157

continued to bathe Elizabeth's face, and helped to turn her face sideways as she vomited, and lost control of her bowels yet again. A moment later Bill pulled into the park, screeching to a halt beside Andrés and Elizabeth. The two men wrapped her in a sheet and lifted her into the truck while the dogs supervised, placed Elizabeth's pack and Andrés' bike in the back, and then everyone jumped in as they sped off towards Burgos with the windows down.

"It's 11:00. I know the doctor at the closest clinic. She treats lots of pilgrims. When did you find her?"

Andrés shared the story with Bill, and Bill told Andrés what he knew about Elizabeth. "God is working in her, Andrés, but she's used to doing things her way."

"Aren't we all, Father Bill?" said Andrés, smiling as he looked at Elizabeth and held her head against his shoulder to keep her from falling forward into the dashboard. They parked on the street in front of a small clinic and carried Elizabeth in. The nurse at the front desk glanced up as they entered and immediately took them to the back and put them in their own room. She asked the men to wait outside while she changed Elizabeth's clothes and cleaned her up, then invited them back in to wait for the doctor.

"Bill," said the doctor as she came in, "it's so good to see you, though I'm sorry for the circumstances." Bill rose and gave the doctor a hug, then introduced Andrés.

"Dr. Flavia, this is my friend Andrés Garcia. He and his father, Matteo, own a farm and *albergue* a few kilometers outside Burgos." Dr. Flavia looked down at Elizabeth's prostrate form, now clad in a hospital gown, lying on the bed.

"And who is this?" The men explained what they knew about Elizabeth while the doctor took her vital signs. "She has a very high fever, and she is very dehydrated. All of her symptoms point to salmonella food poisoning. She must have eaten something in the past 36 hours and contracted it. I'll need to give her some fluid to get her back on her feet."

"Doctor, she also has a knee injury. Perhaps you could examine that as well."

"First the fluid," said Dr. Flavia as the nurse started a bag of fluids dripping into Elizabeth's arm. Dr. Flavia probed Elizabeth's knee and bent it gently. "Could be a torn meniscus needing surgery," said Dr. Flavia. "I wonder how long she's been walking on it like this. She must be pretty determined."

"Some might say, 'stubborn'," declared Bill.

"Well, you would know," teased Dr. Flavia. "I'd like her to stay here overnight for observation," she said. "She's very dehydrated."

Take her to Miriam, heard Andrés. Andrés met Bill's eyes and the priest nodded in agreement with the unspoken idea.

"Dr. Flavia, we would like to take her with us to convalesce."

"I do not think that wise, Bill. I am giving her something for the nausea and diarrhea, but she is too ill to care for herself right now. It will be another couple of messy days, and she will need round the clock care from someone to help her in the bathroom and administer medicine."

159

"Dr. Flavia, we will take her to Miriam."

The doctor was silent for a moment, and then said. "She needs to stay here for another two hours, to finish this bag of fluids and perhaps another. Then, I will ONLY release her if you take her straight to Miriam so she can care for her."

"Agreed! I'll stay here so she will see a familiar face when she wakes up, and Andrés will call Miriam to fill her in about her incoming *peregrina*."

15

HEALER

Miriam picked as many peaches as she could carry in her small bucket. She held them up to her face and breathed in the delicious perfume. "Tiggy, these are going to make some *peregrinos* happy tonight! Peach cobbler for dessert!" The little collie responded to her excitement with wags of her tail. Miriam walked over to the clothesline and checked the progress of the freshly washed bed sheets and other laundry items. *Almost dry. I'll wash this fruit and then bring everything inside.*

She looked up at the curtains flapping out of the windows she had opened upstairs to air the rooms used by last night's guests, and noticed the treetops swaying in a breeze coming from the other side of the house. *There could be rain later, I think. Better keep an eye out to the north.*

As she eased the peaches into the sink and turned on the water, she heard, *She's coming today, Beloved.*

Yes, Father, fit me for your plans for Lisbet. Give me your love and grace for her.

Her cell phone rang, and Andrés told her about God's directions for him earlier that morning, and about finding Elizabeth, her condition, and the doctor's agreement to let her come to Miriam for care. "Your reputation as a wise healer has spread, Miriam. What do you say about receiving Elizabeth?"

"You must have taken her to Dr. Flavia. She's a knowledgeable doctor, and has great compassion. We have worked together before. And yes, Father has been whispering to me about Elizabeth for a while now. I am expecting her," affirmed Miriam. "When are you bringing her? Will your father be able to spare you to help me out over here for a couple of days?"

"The doctor says we can pick her up in a couple of hours. Bill is with her, since he met her yesterday in Cirauqui, and I have some shopping to do, so how does 15:00 sound?"

"If you could step in for me with my *peregrinos* between 16:00 and 20:00? That way you can help them with dinner and the evening routine, and I can be with Elizabeth. She will probably need the most help this afternoon and through the first night."

"I already talked to Papá. I'll bring Elizabeth to you then take him the shopping, and bike over to spend the night at your place. He will have Felipe come over to help while I am gone. Do you need for me to pick up anything in town for you?"

"Thank you, Andrés. Just bring Elizabeth and her things,

plus the medicine and instructions from Dr. Flavia. I have everything else. I am glad Father has given us an assignment to work on together. It is a joy to have your help. *Hasta luego*!"

As Miriam began praying for everything Father whispered about the situation, she set about doing all the practical tasks that came to mind. She quickened her prep of the peaches, and a batter, and slid a pan of her grandmother's tasty fruit cobbler into the oven. The big pot of tomato meat sauce simmered on the stove, and she had enough rolls left from the night before. She washed the lettuce, carrots, tomatoes and cucumbers for the salad. Andrés could get help from *peregrinos* to prepare the pasta for the sauce and assemble the salad when it was closer to dinnertime.

Next she set up a cot in her own bedroom so she could give Elizabeth her bed and stay close to her throughout the night. She made up the bed for Elizabeth with a waterproof mattress protector and fresh sheets, and stacked some fresh sheet sets nearby in case there were accidents. She put her tray of cleaning supplies and a stack of old towels in the room, and went out to her kitchen garden to pick several bouquets of rosemary, lavender, and peppermint to put on the table near Elizabeth's bed and throughout the small room. She had one enameled metal bowl on the bedside table for Elizabeth to use in case the nausea medicine failed, and another was for Miriam to make cool, wet compresses infused with some peppermint and lavender oil she would use to bathe Elizabeth's head and neck. She walked from vase to vase of herbs, crushing the leaves gently between her fingers to release their healing fragrances in the room. She got her box of herbal oils down from the shelf where she kept first aid and other things she used with the sick or injured.

Everything that had come to mind was done. Judging from the scrumptious aroma wafting through the house on the breeze, it was time to get that cobbler out of the oven.

16

TO MIRIAM

Bill sat next to Elizabeth's bed and prayed. *Father, forgive her for her foolhardiness. Thank you for your patience with us as you teach us by your love to trust you.* He looked at Elizabeth as he prayed silently. The nurse had washed her hair as best as she could and a damp braid curved around her neck onto her chest. As she lay there, breathing softly and fluttering her eyelids from time to time, Bill could not help but think that she looked like a child. Her color, however, made her look almost corpselike. The priest laid his hand on her forehead and prayed with more fervor.

Two nurses came in and asked Bill to leave so they could take Elizabeth to the bathroom. They could not release her until she proved she could accomplish this with help. Andrés walked into the waiting area and Bill updated him. "I phoned Miriam, and she already knew Elizabeth was coming" said Andrés with a smile. "She's waiting."

"Of course she is," smiled Bill. "So it is with those who live in the Spirit." One of the nurses came to say they could come back in and talk to the doctor.

The nurse handed Dr. Flavia two pill bottles. "These are to help with the vomiting and diarrhea," she said, "and here is some Tylenol to bring her fever down." She handed the three bottles to Fr. Bill, and then said, "You might think I'm being too tough with my warnings, but this young woman was in danger of going into shock when you brought her in. She has accepted all the fluid we gave her, and has demonstrated the ability to empty her bladder with help getting to the bathroom, but her body is still expelling all the toxins in her digestive tract and she's very weak."

Elizabeth was vaguely aware of lying in a bed with a woman in a white coat talking to Bill and a young man she didn't know, but she drifted in and out of sleep, not able or caring to speak. "Do *not* stop anywhere on the way," continued the doctor. "Take her straight to Miriam. I'll be back in thirty minutes to check on her one last time."

The men pulled up chairs and sat down, one on each side of the bed, and Bill took a small vial from his pocket. He let a few drops fall onto his thumb, and then made the sign of the cross on Elizabeth's forehead. Andrés laid his hand on Elizabeth's shoulder while Bill prayed, "Through this holy anointing may the Lord in his love and mercy help you with the grace of the Holy Spirit. May the Lord who frees you from sin save you and raise you up." Fr. Bill put his hands on the top of Elizabeth's head and continued, "Elizabeth, I lay my hands on you in the Name of the Father, and of the Son, and of the Holy Spirit, beseeching our Lord Jesus Christ to sustain you with His presence, to drive away all sickness of body and spirit, and to give you that victory of life and peace which will enable you to serve Him both now and evermore. Amen."

Elizabeth's eyelids fluttered and she moaned, stirring slightly. She coughed, and Andrés grabbed a metal pan just in time to catch another bout of vomiting. He found a tissue, wiped off her face, and took a piece of ice from a cup the nurse had brought. He traced the ice around her fever-cracked lips to moisten her mouth. The men continued to pray silently until Dr. Flavia came back into the room.

"Are you sure you want to take her with you?" she said with a raised eyebrow, glancing at the pan of vomit.

"Yes, we will take her," said Andrés decisively. The men left the room as the nurses helped Elizabeth get dressed and use the bathroom. They helped a half-conscious Elizabeth into a wheelchair and steered her carefully outside where the two dogs were waiting, then lifted her into the truck, and left Burgos. Twenty minutes later they were at Miriam's. She was waiting outside for them, Tiggy by her side.

"Take her to my room," said Miriam. "Everything is prepared." The men carried Elizabeth in and laid her gently in bed and Miriam felt her forehead. Bill and Andrés each laid one hand on Miriam and one on Elizabeth, and Bill prayed, "Holy Father, equip your servant Miriam to care for this, your lamb. Strengthen her and give her stamina. Keep her in your peace. May your healing power flow through Miriam's hands. In Jesus' name, Amen."

"Amen," murmured Miriam and Andrés. Miriam glanced

at Andrés and wrinkled her nose at his vomit stained clothes. "Dear, you need to go home and change. You have done well."

"Thank you, Miriam," said Andrés. "I'll be back as soon as I change, and I'll bring you some produce from our garden when I come."

"Bill," said Miriam. "Thank you for bringing her here. Thank you for not giving up on her."

"Our Lord never gives up on anyone, Miriam. He never gave up on me. Far be it from me to give up on Elizabeth." Miriam patted Bill's shoulder.

"I'm going to stay at Matteo's tonight and he will give me a lift back to town tomorrow. You stay here and we will see ourselves out."

17

LISBET

Elizabeth came back to consciousness to the sound of someone humming. She tried to open her eyes, but her eyelids would not cooperate. She lay still, her entire body aching. The scent of lavender and mint were in the air. *Where am I?* She tried to remember. A park, a fountain, getting sick all over herself, but that was all. She saw flashes of a truck, Spanish voices, nurses and needle pricks, but were those dreams or reality?

She tried to lift her hand, and a musical voice said, "Rest, Lisbet. You are safe here with me at my *albergue*. Father Bill and Andrés brought you." The humming continued, and a hand stroked her hair. Elizabeth felt an overwhelming sense of nausea and fought unsuccessfully to keep it down, vomiting into a pan the woman with the pretty voice held out. She sipped water, eyes still closed, completely embarrassed. The woman continued to stroke her hair, and whispered, "Lisbet, you are so loved. So beautiful and so loved."

Elizabeth began to weep with humiliation. *Lord, help me. I am so weak, so sick.* She felt something warm lying next to her, then a warm tongue on her cheek, and she opened her eyes. A fuzzy sheepdog lay next to her on the bed, licking her face as she cried. Completely disarmed by the dog's sweetness, she put her arms around its neck and buried her face in its fur so she didn't have to meet the woman's eyes.

"Good girl, Tiggy. You are such a little healer. Lisbet, this is Tiggy. I hope you don't mind dogs. This little one is especially gifted at comforting sick people." Elizabeth stared at the sweet face of the dog, petting her head. "One winter I had pneumonia and she never left my bedside." The woman chuckled at the sweet memory.

Tiggy laid her chin down on Elizabeth's chest and sighed. "No, I don't mind at all," croaked Elizabeth through her tears. "I love dogs. I've always wanted one, but I've never been able to have one. She's lovely." Elizabeth looked up at Miriam and was surprised by the depth of love and mercy in the stranger's eyes—today a stormy grey. Elizabeth immediately sensed an inner strength, a knowing, in this woman. Her soft grey hair was pulled back in a simple braid, and she wore a denim skirt and flowered blouse. "I am Miriam," she said. Elizabeth moved to introduce herself. Miriam laid her hand on Elizabeth's head and said, "and you are Lisbet. I've been expecting you."

"My grandmother called me Lisbet." Elizabeth squeezed her eyes shut at the strong emotion she felt, but more tears escaped.

Miriam resumed her soft singing, and Elizabeth's body relaxed. "Just rest, Lisbet. You are God's precious lamb, and He sent you to me to receive His healing." Elizabeth rested her hand on Tiggy and drifted to sleep, comforted by the deep peace in the room.

Miriam looked down at Elizabeth sleeping, continued to bathe her forehead with cool compresses, and felt her cheek. *Fever is down, color is better, and her body more peaceful. Lord, cleanse and heal your dear Lisbet.* She stood up and walked around to the vases of herbs crushing more leaves, and the room freshened. As she moved toward the door Tiggy's ears perked up, but Miriam motioned for her to stay with Elizabeth.

Miriam went down stairs and began slicing vegetables for the evening meal. She had six pilgrims staying with her tonight: two Dutchmen and four Canadians. The Canadians were outside in the cool courtyard with their feet up and smiled welcomingly at Miriam as she joined them outside. "We tossed some laundry in the washing machine like you said we could, Miriam," said Brett, a young man in his twenties with a dark beard and long hair. "Things were starting to get pretty ripe. It's so nice to really be able to wash and dry them."

"Yeah, Miriam, you saved us. If Brett hadn't washed his clothes today, we probably would have left him here with you."

Miriam laughed and said, "Well, I'm glad I could be of service. I'm not sure I could have handled Brett being left here!" She patted Brett on the shoulder and moved around the other side of the table. "Anyone want to help me feed the chickens?" she called over her shoulder.

"I do!"

"So do I!" Brett and the other man in the group, Michael, hopped up and ran up beside Miriam.

Miriam laughed at their enthusiasm. "Okay, boys. Thank you so much!"

As she looked at Brett, she heard, *This one has lost has mother. You have an opportunity to mother him while he is here.* She handed Brett a bucket of chicken feed and Michael a watering can. "Tell me about your families, guys. Where are you from in Canada?"

Michael immediately started talking about his parents and four siblings near Winnipeg, but Brett was silent. As Michael left to fill the watering can, Miriam laid a hand on Brett's forearm. "Are you alright?" she asked, her eyes locking onto his. She was not surprised when his eyes filled with tears. He quickly looked down.

"My family...well, it's just my dad and me. My mom died in car accident a few months ago. We're still dealing with it. I had the opportunity to come with some friends from university on the Camino, and I thought, 'Why not?' So here I am. I still feel guilty leaving Dad back home, but he insisted that I come. I guess I'm here looking for answers." The tears spilled over as he said this, and Miriam sat him down on a bench beside the chicken coop, patiently waiting on him to speak again. Michael came back with water for the chickens, but when he saw what was happening, he set down the water and went back to the courtyard with the rest of the group to give Miriam time with Brett. "I haven't really dealt with this. I haven't even cried yet. Everything was just so sudden, so unbelievable to me. I hugged my mom goodbye after the Easter holidays, thinking I would see her in just a few weeks, and next thing I know, she's gone."

"Oh, Brett. My precious child," Miriam said as she caught Brett's wandering gaze with her own and stroked his back. "I am so very sorry. I can't imagine the pain you and your father have gone through." He laid his head on her shoulder, comforted by Miriam's care. "Would you like me to pray for you?" said Miriam.

"Yes, I think so. I've never really thought much about God. I mean, I guess there is a God somewhere, but it doesn't seem like he or she or it gives a sh** about us. I mean, look at the world we live in. It's a mess. But yeah, it can't hurt for you to pray for me."

Miriam kept her hand on Brett's back, waiting for the Spirit to give her the right words. "Lord Jesus, I know you weep with Brett and his dad. I pray your mercy on these two dear ones. I pray that you would strengthen them and help them in this time of grief and sorrow. Please shepherd and guide them through this dark valley of death and brokenness. Give them a strong sense of your love and presence with them. Surround them with your people to love them and walk with them through this. We pray this in the name of Jesus, who wept with his friends and who does not stand far off, but is near to us. Amen." Brett inhaled deeply, snorted, and wiped his nose on his sleeve.

"Can I tell you something, Brett?" Brett nodded, unable to speak. "When I was a young woman, I left the Netherlands to go to an American university. I met my husband there. We got married, and I moved with him to Washington, D.C., where he had a job as a scientist working for the National Oceanic and Atmospheric Association. We had two children, a boy and a girl.

"There was a lot about the United States that confused me. Why was everything so loud? Why was everyone so friendly? Why were the cars so big, and why were there so few bicycles?" Brett and Miriam both chuckled. "But I loved my family, and I knew that wherever they were was home. One night, my husband was working late. I put the children to bed and kept one eye on the weather, hoping the forecast of an ice storm would hold off until he was home. As the evening wore on and he had not come home, I grew very worried, wondering where he was. At midnight there was a knock on the door. Two police officers stood there. A driver too drunk to be on the roads had lost control of his car in the sleeting conditions and jumped the median. My husband's car was crushed on the driver's side and he died instantly. Our son, who was thirteen at the time, was awakened by the doorbell, and heard every word of the officer's report.

"I was completely stunned. For several months, I couldn't even believe what had happened. I still reached for my husband in the night, still thought he would call to ask me a question about the children's schedules, or whether he could pick something up at the grocery store. It was like a phantom pain, when someone loses a limb. Even though it's gone, they still feel it there."

Tears were pouring down Brett's face again as he stared forward with unfocused eyes, but Miriam continued. "I thought maybe if I went back to Holland, I would be able to heal, so I took my children and moved back to be close to my family in Delft, but still I felt adrift. I grew bitter. Life was so unfair. Why did this happen to me? How could it have happened? Who was this drunk driver, and

174

why did he walk away without a scratch on him, when my husband, the love of my life, was killed? As the years went by, my heart grew harder and darker towards those around me, towards God. My children were afraid of my anger, and I had few friends, because I pushed away those closest to me. One day I woke up and realized I had no purpose in life. My children were at university and didn't need me anymore. I had no husband. I was walking to the market, a shell of a woman, when I saw a poster on a bulletin board at the community center with a beautiful landscape of mountains and vineyards.

"It was my introduction to the Camino de Santiago. Without hope for my life and feeling there was nothing to lose, I researched the Camino, and though I didn't believe in God, I thought it sounded like a good trip to find answers. So off I went. The first day, I thought I was going to die hiking over the Pyrenees, my feet were covered with blisters." Brett laughed with a grimace. "But I got into a rhythm of walking. I met other pilgrims who had also experienced loss. And one day, I came to a small, medieval church. The doors were open, so I walked in. A young boy was singing in a high pure voice, and it was like a phoenix song that went straight to my heart. I sat and listened to that little boy sing while I wept, and something in me grew warm. Then I watched the priest celebrate the mass. In that moment, I knew, as surely as I know you're sitting next to me now, that God was real. After the service, the priest walked over to me and asked if I'd like to talk. He was a funny priest. An Irishman who celebrated the mass in hiking clothes. We talked for several hours, and I realized two things: that God is real, and that He loves me more than I could even imagine. I still didn't understand all of the "why's" and "how's," but somehow I realized that God was the answer to all my questions, and I set out to follow him."

She let a bit of silence grow, and then looked back at Brett. "I was a bitter, sad woman, Brett. I can tell you, before that trip, I never would have thought I'd be running an *albergue* a couple of years later, or having a conversation like this with you. But I'm so grateful that I am. I still wish my husband hadn't been killed by a drunk driver. I miss him so much. In the same way, you will always miss your mom. But I can tell you that as God has walked me through my grief, my heart for people has grown larger. As I've let Jesus come in to heal those broken places, as I've let God show me his understanding of life and death He has increased my capacity to feel more love, and it allows me to understand the pain and needs of others in a new way. I appreciate beauty and sadness, joy and sorrow, darkness and light in ways I never have before. So I'm grateful that in this broken world, we have a Savior who feels our pain and sits with us in it. May I sing a song for you?" Brett nodded, unable to speak.

Miriam began to sing in her resonant alto, and Brett closed his eyes and leaned his head back against the wall of the chicken coop, tears flowing down his cheeks.

> *My Shepherd will supply my need,*
> *Jehovah is His Name;*
> *In pastures fresh He makes me feed,*
> *Beside the living stream.*
> *He brings my wandering spirit back*
> *When I forsake His ways,*
> *And leads me, for His mercy's sake,*
> *In paths of truth and grace.*
> —
> *When I walk through the shades of death*

Thy presence is my stay;
One word of Thy supporting breath
Drives all my fears away.
Thy hand, in sight of all my foes,
Doth still my table spread;
My cup with blessings overflows,
Thine oil anoints my head.

—

The sure provisions of my God
Attend me all my days;
O may Thy house be my abode,
And all my work be praise.
There would I find a settled rest,
While others go and come;
No more a stranger, nor a guest,
But like a child at home.

"You are his precious child, Brett. It's okay if you don't understand, or if you're angry, or scared. Bring those things to Him, and he will give you what you need." Brett looked back at her, his eyes drier but red-rimmed.

"Thank you, Miriam."

"You're welcome. He is always ready to hear you. He loves you." Miriam stopped there, sensing the young man needed time to process their conversation. She stood up and squeezed his shoulder, then said, "I'll be available to talk more if you want. Take as much time as you need, though there are less smelly places to sit than by the chicken coop!" Brett laughed again and squeezed her hand.

"Thanks again, Miriam. We'll talk later." Miriam glanced at her watch and walked back inside to check on Elizabeth and begin supper preparations. Miriam walked back into her bedroom, cracked open her door, and saw that Elizabeth was still sleeping. She laid her hand gently on the younger woman's forehead. She still felt hot, and her skin was clammy. Miriam prayed softly, "Heavenly Father, please work in Lisbet's heart even as she sleeps. May this sleep be restorative and healing, and may I be your hands and feet to her." She backed quietly out of the room as Tiggy laid her chin back down on Elizabeth's chest, looking up at Miriam with soulful eyes from under her bushy, sheepdog eyebrows. "Good girl," Miriam whispered to Tiggy in Dutch as she closed the door behind her.

18

COMMUNITY OF CARE

ndrés and Bill drove back to the Garcia farm, talking quietly. The priest would stay for a night in their *albergue*, then Matteo would drive him back to Burgos in the morning to meet with his bishop. "Bill, do you think you can help my dad with dinner and taking care of the pilgrims tonight? That way I can bike back to Miriam's to help."

"Of course, Andrés. Miriam will need an extra pair of hands. I think she has six staying with her tonight."

"Bill, I don't know what to say about today. I just know God is doing a work, and I'm thankful to be a part of it. And I'll be glad to take a shower and put on some clean clothes," Andrés added with a chuckle.

Bill laughed too, "Yes, Elizabeth is deeply wounded. I know she opened her life to Jesus in Pamplona, but that was just the beginning. Now God is going to start cleaning house and seeing how much space she will let Him move in. That can be a painful process. Elizabeth is going to need people around to help her process and care for her so she doesn't give up. I sense that God in his mercy is bringing her to the end of herself by allowing these injuries and this illness as consequences for a pace and solitary life that are not His best for her."

"Yes, from what you've told me Elizabeth isn't used to receiving help from anyone. That a long time ago, she decided she was going to be strong and not crack, and that underneath the surface, there's a girl who feels it is all up to her."

They pulled into Andrés and Matteo's property, and Rex and Paddy jumped out and started romping, eager to burn off energy from being cooped up all day. Andrés headed straight for the shower while Bill went to find Matteo and fill him in on the details of what had happened that day. As Andrés let the warm water flow over his head, he whispered, "Jesus, show me what my place is here. I feel drawn to Elizabeth, but I don't know if that's from you or if it's something else. Please give me your wisdom."

Andrés' prayers were interrupted by thoughts of Ada. He scrubbed his head with shampoo trying to wash away the hurt. "Help me let her go, Lord," Andrés prayed as he always did when Ada entered his mind. He allowed the painful memories to surface for a moment, hoping that God would have some new, healing insight. He had been surprised to meet another Spaniard when he began graduate studies in economics at Georgetown and was grateful for Ada's friendship, especially in the moments when he felt most homesick.

Ada was from Pamplona, but because Andrés had been a few years ahead of her at the University there, their paths hadn't crossed in Spain. They used to joke that they had to cross the ocean to meet, though they'd been in each other's backyards for years before that. She'd been working on a Ph.D. in art history and Andrés loved talking with her about painting and sculpture, especially in her field of expertise, 16th century Florentine art. It was so different from his field of study. They met regularly to study and talk at coffee shops throughout DC, and as Andrés got to know her better, he found himself caring for Ada more and more deeply. Andrés also admired Ada's beautiful, childlike trust in God, and as the months went by, had a growing clarity that God had led them together. One night, Andrés shared his feelings with Ada. "I'm so grateful for our friendship, Ada, but I sense God has something more for us."

He was shocked when she withdrew and said, "Oh no, Andrés, I'm so sorry. I've never felt anything but friendship for you. I care for you so deeply as a brother and a friend, and I love exchanging ideas with you, but I don't have romantic feelings for you. I'd like to still be friends, though." Andrés was crushed and confused by their opposite feelings about the relationship. He blamed himself for a long time. "I should have been clearer from the beginning," but then gradually came to realize he had done nothing wrong by caring for Ada. Even now, he still cared for her, hence his prayer of letting go. As he prayed, he felt a new sense of peace and closure about his friendship with Ada.

Let me take your hurt and loss, son. All those who sow weeping will go out with songs of joy.

Andrés hummed as he finished his shower, and dressed, packed things for his overnight in his backpack, and found Matteo and Bill at a table downstairs having an afternoon coffee. He poured himself a mug of coffee, and pulled the bowl of almonds over and grabbed a handful. "Papá, I'm going to take some lettuce and potatoes to Miriam if that's okay. The slugs have gotten the best of her greens again."

"Of course, let me put a few things together for you to take." Matteo went to the pantry and the refrigerator and came back to the table with a sack full of freshly washed lettuce and another with potatoes. "I put in a couple of carrots and tomatoes, too. Felipe got a bit carried away harvesting today." The men chuckled at the enthusiasm of the boy who was so eager to please him. "Tell Miriam we will pray for her and Elizabeth in our service here tonight."

Andrés finished his coffee in a gulp and washed his mug in the kitchen. "I'd better go so I can get supper ready while she takes care of Elizabeth." He hugged his Papá, clapped Bill on the shoulder and went out into the yard. *Peregrinos* wandered here and there around the garden in the shade, or soaked their feet in the small pool Matteo had made. *Looks like a pretty full house tonight. I hope they will be okay without me here.* He placed the bags of vegetables into the panniers on his bicycle. Rex trotted over from the garden and sat at attention. Andrés patted him on the head and smiled at the shepherd's eagerness to follow. "Stay, Rex. They need your help here tonight." Rex circled the garden once and lay down in the shade of a hydrangea covered with huge blue flower clusters. *What a good shepherd he is,* smiled Andrés as he coasted out onto the road.

19

CLEANSING

Andrés arrived at Miriam's as she was coming into the courtyard, and she greeted him with a happy wave. "How is she?" he asked as he hopped off his bike and started unpacking the vegetables.

"She's okay. Tiggy is with her. She'll let me know if Elizabeth needs anything."

Andrés laughed, "That dog is filled with the Holy Spirit, Miriam!"

"Well, I've always thought God gives special gifts of discernment to some animals. Tiggy definitely knows who needs the most help and provides a lot of comfort!"

They walked into the kitchen and Miriam stirred the tomato meat sauce on the stove. "Tonight we are serving pasta with meat sauce, a fresh vegetable salad, and peach cobbler. I was hoping you could cook the pasta, assemble the salad, and make some dressing. You know your way around my kitchen so I'll rely on you to take charge. Let me get some help for you."

She went out into the courtyard and rang a little bell, saying, "Time to cook dinner, everyone!" The six pilgrims got to their feet somewhat stiffly and followed Miriam into the kitchen. After introductions, she handed Michael a knife to cut the cucumbers, the two girls took turns whisking the cream for the cobbler, and Brett volunteered to dice tomatoes. Miriam patted his arm as she handed him three tomatoes. "These aren't the prettiest tomatoes you've ever seen, but they are delicious. Just cut out the bad spots, and we will enjoy the rest." He nodded, looked cheerfully into her eyes, and started chopping at lightening speed. The Dutch couple tore lettuce into a big bowl and set the tables while Andrés took the big pot from the shelf and heated water for the pasta. Miriam left Andrés in charge and went to check on Elizabeth.

Tiggy raised her head when Miriam entered. She motioned to the little shepherdess to go out. "You need a break, Tiggs. Go outside for a while. I'll stay with her." The collie trotted to the door, turned to look at Elizabeth and went out. Miriam walked to the bedside. *Father, what does she need?* Elizabeth's eyes were closed and her breathing calm. She had thrown off all her covers, and her clothes and the sheets were soaking wet. *Thank you, Father, for breaking her fever.*

"Lisbet," said Miriam. She repeated her name and stroked her hair until Elizabeth woke up. "Hello, dear girl. Time to get up for a bath, fresh clothes, and water. Your fever is gone, but you must keep drinking water as your body continues to cleanse itself from what made you sick. Let me help you to the bathroom, and when you are ready, I will come back in and help you into the tub for a nice soak. While you are in the tub, I'll put fresh sheets on the bed and set your dirty clothes to wash. First have a good drink of this peppermint tea with your meds. It's not hot, drink it up. The peppermint will help with your nausea, too." Elizabeth obeyed without question, stood up, and leaning heavily on Miriam took slow baby steps toward the bathroom. "Come on, that's right, take your time, I've got you."

Elizabeth was weak, but with Miriam's help she was able to get to the toilet. Miriam gathered the sweat-soaked sheets, wiped down the plastic mattress protector with a disinfectant she had concocted from her herb garden, and opened the windows as wide as possible to air out the room. *Lord, as you blow away all the sickness from the air, blow through Elizabeth's mind and heart. Cleanse her memories and thoughts.* The fresh sheets smelled of the lavender rinse Miriam used on her linens. The fragrance was pleasant, but it also served to deter bedbugs, which are feared by even the hardiest pilgrims. Once the bed was ready again, she walked around the room crushing more of the herbs in their vases, and then tapped on the bathroom door. "Elizabeth, are you ready for your bath?"

"I guess so," answered a faint voice. Miriam came in, plugged the drain, tied a bag of herbs under the faucet, and turned on the water. As the tub filled Miriam helped Elizabeth stand and peel off her sweaty clothes. "I'm so sorry you have to see all of this, Miriam, and smell all of this. I am so disgusting! But I can barely stand up on my own, so thank you, thank you."

Miriam steadied her while she got into the tub. "You

185

are weak, but you are not disgusting. It is a privilege to serve a sister in need. Messes are part of life, but you are improving. A few more days and the illness will be out of your body." Elizabeth leaned against the curve of the tub. "Get ready to be rinsed off." Miriam pointed the hand shower into the tub and turned the lever to divert the faucet water to the shower head. Elizabeth closed her eyes and tilted her head back as Miriam shampooed her hair. "There!" said Miriam, turning off the tap. "I will leave you to soak and rest for 10 minutes. Here is a bar of soap." She gathered the dirty clothes and cracked the door open as she left the bathroom. With the dirty clothes and sheets, Miriam closed her bedroom door behind her and came out into the hallway that led from her private quarters to the kitchen and dining room. She went straight to the laundry room, loaded the washer and then returned to find fresh clothes for Elizabeth.

20

RESCUER

It feels so good to get clean. Elizabeth sighed and relaxed into the water. *Lord, wash away all this gross sickness. I want to be clean inside and out.* She lathered and washed, relishing the beautiful scents of the soap and water. *No spa in the world could offer anything to beat this! Thank you, Lord. Thank you for these people who are taking care of me. I'm sorry I didn't stay in the* albergue *Bill arranged. I have caused trouble for these people who have helped.*

I love you, dear child. I weave all things together into a beautiful tapestry for those I call into a story. Just rest.

Miriam appeared just as she had promised to help Elizabeth stand up, towel off, and help her put on a cotton nightgown. "I think you will be more comfortable in this nightie. It might be a little big on you, but it is very soft and nice, yes?" The gown was old fashioned, but covered her well and was indeed very comfortable. Miriam helped her back to bed, and insisted she drink a glass of water

187

before she lie down. She sipped the cool water while Miriam towel dried her hair, combed out the tangles, and made a loose braid fastened with an elastic. She covered the pillow with a dry towel, and helped Elizabeth lie back. "I'll leave this little bell with you in case you need to get my attention before Tiggy comes back."

"How can you manage helping me when you have pilgrims here? Don't you have lots to be doing?"

"It is true there is much to do as a *hospitalera*, but I have friends to help. Andrés has come to step in for me tonight, and the *peregrinos* here today are a helpful group."

"Who is Andrés?"

"He is the one who found you unconscious. He and Bill took you to the clinic, and then brought you here. He is one God knows will do what He asks."

Elizabeth experienced something pleasant when Miriam said this. As hard as she tried, she could not conjure an image of Andrés, and yet she sensed something going on in her heart. What was it? Appreciation and gratitude toward her rescuer, or something else? She was too weak and tired to think much about it now. "Thank him for me, Miriam, will you?"

"Rest now, dear Lisbet. We will check on you soon."

21

NOT WITHOUT HELP

Miriam walked into the kitchen to find that Andrés had things well in hand. She invited everyone to gather around the table, where she showed them her prayer basket. "Please take a prayer out of the basket and leave one as well. We will also have a time to pray for each other at the evening meal if you'd like. We will serve dinner in about an hour thanks to Andrés and all of your hard work. Please feel free to rest until then."

Miriam asked Andrés to join her in the garden, noticing lots of weeds needing to be pulled. "Ugh! How is it that even though we've had such a drought, the weeds are flourishing? We'd better water everything since we haven't had rain for several days." She looked up as footsteps rustled in the grass, and smiled as Brett approached. "Brett, this is Andrés." Andrés shook the young man's hand warmly, clapping him on the back. "Andrés and his father own an *albergue* a few kilometers down the road, and he's here helping me this evening. We're just doing a bit of gardening. Would you like to help us?"

Brett nodded, and as he knelt down beside Miriam to pull weeds, he said, "I've been thinking a lot about what you said earlier, Miriam…that God will give me everything I need. I don't understand it in my head, but somehow I get it. I understand it in my heart. That probably doesn't even make sense!" Brett laughed as he threw another weed on the compost pile. "I guess I just need some help with the next step. I've been talking with God this afternoon, and I sense His presence. I see Him in you and in Andrés, even though we just met. I want to be like that. I don't want to be bitter and hard. But I don't think I can do it."

Andrés laid his hand on the Brett's shoulder. "Trust me, no one can do anything without God's help. Have you ever heard the story of Lazarus from the Bible?" Brett shook his head no. "Well, Jesus was very good friends with a family who lived not far from his hometown in a little place called Bethany. There were two sisters and a brother in the family, and the sisters sent a message to Jesus saying their brother was ill. Jesus responded in a curious way for a good friend. Instead of going immediately to Lazarus' side and healing him, Jesus stayed where he was. He told his disciples, 'This is for the glory of God, and for your sake I am glad I was not there, so that you may believe.' By the time he got to Bethany, Lazarus was dead. Imagine the feelings of the sisters when they saw Jesus walking toward their house. Sadness, confusion, anger, no doubt. They both said to Jesus, 'Lord, if you had been here, our brother would not have died.' In other words, 'Jesus, WHERE HAVE YOU BEEN?' For a woman back then, the death of a brother, husband, or father was devastating. Lazarus would have been the provider for the family, so Martha and Mary were facing poverty and possibly death themselves. Jesus knew all these things. When he saw his friends weeping, Jesus was deeply moved and wept with the mourners.

"When Jesus got to his friend's tomb, he commanded the stone to be rolled away, and shouted, 'Lazarus, come out!' Lazarus came out, alive and well. The thing is, Jesus knew the whole time he was going to raise Lazarus from the dead. But even so, he wept. He wept at the deep injustice of death, at the sorrow and brokenness of his beloved friends and other people. I'm always struck by how deeply Jesus feels our pain with us. But even though he feels every hurt, all our pain, he is not diminished or weakened by it. He's still God. That's why Jesus says, 'I am the resurrection and the life. He who believes in me, though he die, yet shall he live, and whoever believes in me shall never die.'

"Lazarus still got old and died a second time. But Jesus was showing with this miracle that he is Lord over death. Not only physical death but also the death of souls. Not long after he did this miracle, Jesus himself was crucified. And he went to his death on the cross willingly, so that we could have immortal life with him in his resurrection. Just like you, Brett, I struggled with bitterness after my mother's death. Everything in my soul screamed against the injustice and pain. But I know our true home is with Jesus in heaven. And even though we're separated by death for awhile from those who love Jesus, someday we will see them again because of His goodness to us."

As Andrés finished talking, Brett was staring thoughtfully at the ground. Miriam stayed silent, eyes closed, praying. Andrés leaned closer to him and asked, "Would you like to receive Jesus into your life, Brett?" Brett nodded and bowed his head, and Andrés began praying, "Jesus, thank you that you stand with us, that you know us completely and understand our joys and sorrows. Would you care for my brother Brett here? Help him know the words to say, and show him what he needs to release to you."

Andrés touched his shoulder, and Brett slowly began to pray, "Jesus. God. I'm not sure how to pray. It feels kind of weird. I guess it'll get easier." He laughed, his voice growing stronger. "God, I still don't understand why my mom died. But I want the life and peace you want to give me. I don't want to hold onto this anger any more. I don't want to live my life full of darkness and cynicism. It's not what my mom would have wanted, and I know it's not what you want. I pray that you would teach me how to follow you. And show me how to grieve my mom's death well. Thank you for loving me, Lord. I love you too."

Dinner that evening was a joyful affair. Even though the Canadian group was the age to be at university, they talked and traded jokes easily with the older Dutch couple, who were obviously enjoying themselves. The *peregrinos* appreciated the delicious food, and after gobbling down the whole pan of peach cobbler, everyone sat around the table, contented. When there was a lull in the conversation, Miriam asked if anyone wanted to ask for prayer. "If you prefer not to share it in the group, I'll remind you to write it on a slip of paper and put it in the basket, and I and others will pray for you."

Brett cleared his throat to speak, when the Dutch woman, Annamaria, spoke up. "My husband Adriaan and I have three children about the same age as you four," she said, looking at the Canadians. We came to Spain hoping we'd find some answers about why our relationships with them have become distant. Talking with you tonight has given us hope that we will be able to restore our relationship. Perhaps Adriaan and I have been too hard on them. Thank you for welcoming us and helping us see that. Can you pray for our children, and for us? That whatever the wall is between us will come down, and that we can be close again? Thank you so much." She glanced over at Adriaan, who squeezed her hand and kissed her on the cheek.

Then Brett looked around at everyone at the table and spoke. "I just want to say thank you to my old friends and my new ones. Thank you, Michael," he said, raising his glass to his friend, "for not letting me rest until I agreed to come on this walk with you. Thanks to the rest of you for letting me be angry, for letting me be quiet, for listening to me, and sharing your stories. And thanks to you, Miriam, and you, Andrés, for introducing me to Jesus, and helping me see that God isn't who I thought he was at all. Please pray that I'll be able to share this with my dad when I get back home, and that God will continue to give us peace and comfort as we're missing my mom so much." His voice broke on the last words, and Andrés placed his hand on Brett's shoulder.

"Anyone else?" said Miriam.

Andrés spoke up. "You haven't met her because she's too sick and weak to get out of bed, but there's a woman staying here named Elizabeth who is recovering from salmonella food poisoning, and also has a bad knee injury. She's had a pretty hard time, so I'd like to pray for her." The others nodded their assent, and Miriam said, "Let's pray. Feel free to pray in your own language if you're more comfortable with that." They spent the next 10 minutes or so praying, and as they finished, Miriam passed out slips of paper with the Lord's Prayer and doxology written on them. They prayed and sang favorite songs together, then cleared the table, washed the dishes.

The *peregrinos* filed upstairs to rest. Andrés hugged Miriam and said, "You go check on Elizabeth, and turn in. I'll sleep on the sofa and take the breakfast shift for you. It's always a gift to be here with you, Miriam. I love you."

"I love you too, Andrés. I'll see you in the morning," she said, patting his cheek. "Thank you for your help. Elizabeth asked me to tell you that, too." They grinned at one another, and Miriam closed her hall door behind her.

22

CEASE STRIVING, KNOW ME

E lizabeth was resting peacefully when Miriam entered the bedroom and turned on the tiny nightlight in the bathroom. Her patient's legs moved back and forth, and she was breathing hard. Miriam got ready for bed, and then prepared to wake Elizabeth for the bathroom, more medicine, and more water.

In her dream Elizabeth was running, running as fast as she could. Bruce jeered at her, saying, "Do you want to keep your job?" Then his face changed into that of her father, who said, "Stay strong for us Elizabeth. Be our happy girl." Darkness closed in behind Elizabeth as she ran, but she saw a pinprick of light far ahead. She ran faster and faster, her chest bursting, but suddenly the light was extinguished, and Elizabeth shouted, "No!" She woke up shouting, covered in sweat, and desperate for the bathroom.

She was shaking and clammy, and searched wildly around

her to get her bearings. Tiggy sat up at attention, looked at Elizabeth, and jumped off the bed, running to the bathroom door and barking. In a moment, Miriam was at her bedside helping her to stand. "Miriam, I have to go! Quick, quick!" But she didn't quite make it. Completely humiliated, Elizabeth started weeping again when she realized the mess she'd made for this kind woman to clean up. "I'm so sorry, Miriam. I had a nightmare, and woke up, but..."

"Lisbet, don't worry. Everything can be put right. Besides, if you keep crying, you're just going to get more dehydrated, and we can't have that!" Miriam said with a smile. She handed Elizabeth a towel to clean her legs, then used her cleaning supplies to clean up the floor. "Go ahead and get rid of what you can, and I'll come back in a minute to help rinse you off and get you into a clean nightie."

Elizabeth could not remember ever being this miserable or sick. She relieved herself and called for some help. Miriam helped her undress and turned the tap on, then supported her while she rinsed Elizabeth off with the handheld shower. Elizabeth's legs trembled, and Miriam helped her sit down quickly, not wanting her to collapse. She plugged the drain and turned off the shower to fill the tub.

"Lisbet, I'm going to get you some water and your pills. I'll be right back."

Tiggy lay down next to the tub watchfully, sitting up when Miriam returned with a glass of water and two pills. Elizabeth swallowed the pills, and then leaned her head back against the tub. "Miriam, I'm so sorry about all of this. It's so disgusting. I'm so embarrassed."

"Lisbet, if you say you're sorry one more time, then Tiggy and I will pour cold water on your head!" Miriam said with a smile. "Are you alright here for a bit? I am going to find you another nightgown."

"Thanks, Miriam. I'm sorry I keep apologizing..." Her voice trailed off as Miriam playfully pantomimed dumping a glass of water on Elizabeth's head. "Okay, you win," she surrendered, and forced a smile. Miriam left the room and Elizabeth put her hand on Tiggy's head. "Thank you, for staying with me little friend." Tiggy looked at her lovingly with her soulful brown eyes and thumped the tip of her fluffy tail on the tile floor. "I always wanted a dog," Elizabeth told Tiggy, "but my dad would never let me have one. He said they were too much work. But when I see a sweet one like you, I think any work is worth it, right?" Tiggy continued to thump her tail in response to Elizabeth's voice, then stood up and licked her hand. "Maybe when I get back to DC I'll figure out a way to get a dog, although I'm not sure how Willoughby would feel about that. Or Bruce. BRUCE!" *Oh no, it's been almost two days since I last logged into email. Oh no, oh no oh no--that must have been why I had that dream!*

Elizabeth stood up quickly, then sat down immediately when the room started to spin. Hearing the splash of the water, Miriam came quickly back in. "Lisbet, are you okay? What do you need?"

"Miriam, I have to check my email. My boss told me if I weren't available every day, I'd lose my job. He's going to kill me. He's already threatened to fire me once since I've been gone."

"Okay, Liebchen, slowly, slowly. You are still very weak. Let me help you get dried off and dressed, and then I'll get your computer for you."

Elizabeth got back in bed, and Miriam brought her pack to the bed. She helped her prop up and pulled the laptop from its sleeve, plugging it in next to the bed as Elizabeth turned it on. "Miriam, would you stay here? I'm not sure I want to do this alone."

"Of course. I'm happy to sit with you." She sat down in a chair beside the bed, folded her hands, and fixed her eyes on Elizabeth's face as she logged into her email. Elizabeth inhaled loudly at the 87 new emails, then opened one from Bruce sent an hour ago.

Elizabeth,

As of this morning, you are no longer employed at this law firm. I was very clear about my expectations while you were out of town, and you have disrespected them multiple times. With your priorities out of order, you are no longer welcome at this firm. I will have Donna clean out your desk and send your things by courier to the address you give to her.

Bruce

Elizabeth went pale as she read, "Oh no! I was afraid this would happen! I have to call Bruce! Can you hand me my phone, Miriam?" Miriam handed Elizabeth the phone, and she dialed the firm's number.

Donna answered on the first ring. "Devon, Rice, and Cohen, can you hold please?"

"Yes," she sighed.

After a few minutes, Donna came back on the line. "How may I help you?"

"Donna, it's Elizabeth! I have to talk to Bruce. It's urgent!"

"Elizabeth, so good to hear your voice! I'm sorry, but Bruce isn't in the office right now; he's in court. Are you okay? Can I take a message for you, or would you like to email him?"

"Would you tell him I called, and tell him I'd like a chance to talk with him. I'll send him an email as well."

"Elizabeth, are you okay? You sound really anxious."

"No, I'm not okay. Will you pray for me, Donna? There's a lot going on and I need help."

"Of course, sweetie. Hang in there, and I'll talk to you soon. Send me an email if there are details you want me to know."

They exchanged goodbyes and Elizabeth hung up and looked at Miriam ruefully. "Miriam, what am I going to do if I lose my job? I've poured everything into this job since I graduated from law school. I can't get fired!"

"Lisbet, take a deep breath. Calm yourself. Everything shall be well. Let's write Bruce an email." With Miriam's encouragement, Elizabeth composed a response.

Dear Bruce,

I'm so sorry I've been out of touch and mean no disrespect. I fell ill yesterday morning and have been unable to check email until just now. I called the office, but Donna said you were in court. I would like to explain what happened, and apologize again for being out of touch.

Thank you for understanding,
Elizabeth

Elizabeth read the email aloud to Miriam and, when Miriam nodded her approval, pushed send.

"I am wide awake now. I could tackle some of these other emails while I wait to hear back from Bruce," said Elizabeth.

"I'll take Tiggy out one last time, let her have some water, and be right back."

Elizabeth clicked through her emails, answered all of Bruce's, then moved on. She smiled as she opened one from Holly that contained a selfie of Holly and Willoughby holding a sign that said, "We miss you, Elizabeth!" Elizabeth tapped out a reply.

Holly,

Thank you so much for sending this. Please tell Willoughby I miss him too (and you, of course). I'm currently sick in bed with salmonella food poisoning, and I just heard from my boss that I've been fired! I don't know if you're the praying type, but if you are, please pray that he'll rescind this once I have a chance to talk with him. I never thought I was the praying type until this trip, but that has changed. So much to share, but I better rest now. Give Willoughby a tummy rub for me!

Love,
Elizabeth

Next, Elizabeth opened an email from Ellen, and her panic swelled as she read it.

Dear Elizabeth,

I was so sorry to hear about Bruce's decision to fire you. He announced it at this morning's staff meeting. Please let me know if there's anything I can do to help, or if you'd like to talk.

Yours,
Ellen

Elizabeth shut her laptop as another wave of nausea came, but she managed to hold things down. She reached for the metal bowl and held it in her lap just in case. She closed her eyes and leaned back on her pillows. *I must be getting a little better. What am I going to do about my job? I really hope Bruce calls soon. I hate waiting like this. God, please. Please change Bruce's heart. Please don't let me lose my job.*

I give you my Peace, child. Cease striving. I am God. Know me. Focus your heart and mind on me. I will keep you in perfect peace. Trust me, Beloved.

23

FEELING STRONGER

Elizabeth woke with the morning sun streaming through the curtains, making lacy shadows on the bed coverlet. Tiggy gently crept up next to her face to give her snuffly kisses. She giggled as the collie's fuzzy beard tickled her cheek and chin. She sat up and was thankful her nausea seemed to be gone, though she still felt weak. Tiggy went to the door and barked to call Miriam.

Suddenly Elizabeth thought about her job, and lifted her laptop from the bedside table. She was puzzled to see no emails from Bruce when she logged in. She checked her phone and didn't see a missed call. *This is really strange. Bruce is almost always available by email. I wonder if mine didn't go through.* She looked around the room, noticing some of the details for the first time. Beautiful vases of violets. A picture of a family, Miriam looking to be about Elizabeth's age, a tall man beside her and two elementary school-aged children.

Miriam came in and smiled, bending down to kiss Elizabeth's cheek. "How are you feeling today, Lisbet?"

"Better. Still weak, but not nauseous. Pretty anxious about my job. I didn't hear back from my boss."

"Well, it's 8:00 in the morning here, which means it's 2:00 in DC, so maybe he'll get back to you later today. Try not to worry, Liebchen." She helped her to the bathroom, then waited outside the door while Elizabeth washed her face, brushed her teeth, and used the toilet.

She opened the door, "Miriam, do you think I could try eating something?"

"Yes, I can fix toast and some peppermint tea. How does that sound? All the *peregrinos* have left, so things are quiet for the next several hours. Would you like to try eating at the table, or shall I bring it to you here? "

"I think I'd like to try sitting up and eating if that's okay. Can you wait for me in case I need help getting dressed?" she asked, marveling at how comfortable she was with Miriam in such a short time. *And most of that time I was either passed out or being sick. I guess now that Miriam has seen me at my worst; I don't have anything to hide from her.* She pulled on a fresh pair of hiking pants, long sleeved shirt, and flip-flops.

Miriam combed her hair and braided it as before, then helped her down the hall. Tiggy came bounding back in through the outside door and followed them as they made their slow progress to the common room.

Miriam seated Elizabeth at the table and walked into the kitchen, where someone was whistling and washing dishes. *That's odd. I thought Miriam and I were the only ones here right now.* "Besides you, of course, Tiggy," she said, patting Tiggy where she was resting at Elizabeth's feet after her morning romp. Elizabeth glanced around the plain, but pretty, room. Rough-hewn beams held up the ceiling, and decoration was sparse, but Miriam had placed vases of flowers throughout the room, giving it homey, cheerful look. Beside the door was a small wooden sign with carved words reading, "Come to me, all you who are weary and heavy laden, and I will give you rest. For my yoke is easy, and my burden is light." –Jesus of Nazareth. Elizabeth heard Miriam and a man speaking Spanish softly, then she reappeared holding a plate of toast, glass of water, and a cup of mint tea. She sat down across from Elizabeth and sipped her coffee. "Miriam, who's here?" Elizabeth asked as she nibbled at the toast.

"That's Andrés. He knows you're not feeling well and doesn't want to overwhelm you, but if you'd like to meet him, he can come sit with us when he finishes up the dishes."

Elizabeth paused. Uncertainty washed over her. *He has already seen me...and probably covered in vomit and worse! Oh no! What did I say or do when I was out of it?*

"Um sure, that's fine, no problem," she agreed. Her stomach cramped as she chewed, so she gave up on the toast and sipped some tea and water, willing the toast to stay down.

"So, Liebchen. Tell me about your job. It's very important to you, yes?"

"Yes, I've given my life to that job. I started there right after

I finished at Harvard Law." (Elizabeth waited for Miriam to look impressed, but kept talking when her expression remained unchanged) "My boss is pretty tough, but if I can stay there long enough to make partner, then I'm hoping to open my own firm and work with victims of domestic violence. I ended up coming on the Camino when my doctor ordered me to take a rest."

The corner of Miriam's mouth twitched and she said, "So here you are...resting. It seems even if you don't take it easy, God will be sure that you do."

"Yes, apparently," said Elizabeth without humor. "I'm hoping that I'll be able to continue hiking after I rest up for another day or so. I've already had to change my plans so many times." Miriam raised an eyebrow but said nothing.

Just then, Andrés walked in from the kitchen, drying his hands on a towel, and wearing a cheerful smile. "Buenos Días, Elizabeth! It's so good to see you up!" She looked up at Andrés and her cheeks flamed. Though she had been unconscious while in the park and at the clinic, she recognized his voice and the shame washed over her all over again. She looked down at her plate and said, "Hello." Then she said, "Miriam, I think I need to go lie down again. Can you help me?"

Andrés took in her body language and said, "I think I'll just go out to the garden and start the watering. We're praying you continue to rest well, Elizabeth."

Elizabeth leaned her head on Miriam's shoulder as they walked back to her room. As she sat down on the bed, she said, "Oh, Miriam, I'm so embarrassed. I thought I would never see the men who helped me again. It was bad enough that you had to see me so sick, but having two men see me covered in diarrhea and vomit is more than I can bear right now."

"Elizabeth, God is giving you an opportunity to see what true love and servanthood look like. Andrés is one of the most gentle, compassionate men I know. He would think no less of you for what happened, and neither would Father Bill. This was completely out of your control."

"I know," said Elizabeth as she sank back against her pillow. "That's what makes it so scary. Loss of control." Miriam drew up a chair and sat down beside the bed, taking Elizabeth's hand in both of her own.

"Since the beginning of time, human beings have been trying to take control of their lives out of God's hands. Look at Adam and Eve in the garden. God was so clear in what he told them, and they chose to go their own way. And ever since, even though we continue to pay the consequences, we've followed their example. We choose what seems easy in the moment, or do what we want, rather than listening to God's best for us. If we could see what God sees, or if we even had an inkling of how much He loves us, I expect we'd make different choices. Yet we can't and we choose not to trust him. Is it not better to relinquish control to the One who can see all things?"

Elizabeth gave Tiggy a reflective pat. "Yes. I think so. I guess. Oh, I don't know. I think I need to sleep."

"Of course you do, Liebchen. Here, take your medicine with this water," Elizabeth obeyed. "When you wake up, Tiggy will come find me and we can talk some more. These are hard things."

"Maybe I'll hear something from Bruce later. Maybe sleep will give me a break from worrying about it." Miriam kissed her on the forehead and stroked her cheek. "Rest well, Lisbet." Tiggy snuggled up next to her and she fell asleep quickly.

24

HARD ON OURSELVES

When Miriam walked back into the common room, Andrés was waiting for her, chin in his hands, coffee growing cold beside him. "Well, that didn't go very well, did it? She's too embarrassed to even be in my presence."

Miriam patted his hand. "Andrés, all will be well. She's very ill and exhausted. She has lost her job. And more than that, I sense she has been deeply wounded by men in her past."

"I think so too, Miriam. And the more I pray and talk to God about her, the more drawn I am to her. But since she doesn't want to be in the same room with me right now, I think the best thing I can do is pray for patience."

"It probably wouldn't hurt any of us to pray for patience."

"If you think you can manage now, I should probably

get back to my dad's place and see whether he needs me to help turn the rooms over for this afternoon's pilgrims since he had to drive Bill back to Burgos after breakfast. I'll come back this afternoon after I make sure he's set for tonight. I know Felipe probably helped him some, but you can't always count on a ten year old boy, no matter how well intentioned they are!"

"Thank you, Andrés. God's peace to you."

"And to you, Miriam. Call if you need help sooner." Andrés hopped back on his bicycle and pedaled the few kilometers back to his father's farm. It was a beautiful morning, unseasonably cool, and Andrés was glad for the quiet to reflect on the past 24 hours. He always loved his times with Miriam. In many ways, she was like a mother to him, even though he had only known her since he'd graduated from university. In truth, Miriam was a mother to all she met. Her sacrificial and loving nature put many at ease, but Andrés had seen plenty of pilgrims uncomfortable in her presence. *Then again, Jesus made many people very uncomfortable. And Miriam truly is the hands and feet of Jesus to everyone in her path.* Andrés' thoughts turned to prayers for strength and grace for Miriam, his father, and himself. As he pulled into the driveway on his bicycle, Felipe, was just leaving, Rex at his heels.

"Hello, Felipe!" Andrés called cheerily as the boy walked out of the house. Felipe smiled broadly.

"Andrés! How is you?" he tried in English.

"Almost, Felipe! How *are* you?"

"How are you, Andrés?"

210

"Very well, thank you. And you? How is your family?"

"Mi Mamá, mi Papá, and my..." he paused for a moment, "...seester! are doing very well. Bueno." Andrés smiled and clapped the boy on the back. "And I help Mr. Matteo with everything. Not much left to do."

"Thank you, Felipe. We both appreciate your help. Even though you are young, you're strong and a good worker! Have a nice day!"

"I will, Andrés. I wish you have a good day too!" Felipe trotted off happily, and Andrés smiled after him. He found his Papá out in the garden, humming to himself. "How are things over at Miriam's?" his father asked as he straightened up.

"Things are good. A young man named Brett prayed to receive Jesus last night. Miriam and I both had the opportunity to speak with him. He has good friends traveling with him, and seems excited about sharing the changes with his dad when he gets back to Canada. He recently lost his mother."

"Then you were well-equipped to care for him, Andrés," said Matteo. "You know what it is to be without a mother." Both men were quiet as they thought of Maria. Even though she'd refused more than occasional contact with them since moving to León, her death three years ago had been devastating to both of them. Despite her failings as a wife and mother, both Andrés and Matteo had loved her deeply and hoped for the relationship to be healed. The men hugged one another briefly, then Andrés said, "I met Felipe as I was coming in. He said there wasn't much left to do to prepare for the day's guests. His English is getting better!"

"He's a very intelligent child. Such a quick learner, and so helpful. He's also good company for me when you are away."

"I know, Papá. I miss you. I wish I could be here all the time."

"Oh, son, I didn't mean it like that! Of course I love being with you, but there is not work enough for you here year round. Besides, your work as an economist is very important to Spain and all of Europe. I do look forward to summers though!" said Matteo with a smile. He ruffled his son's hair the way he had when Andrés was a boy, and Andrés smiled back at him.

"So what else do we need to do today? Would you like for me to check the new guests in while you have a siesta?"

"Yes!   Thank you!" His father continued hoeing and Andrés walked back into the house to be sure everything was ready. The large kitchen was spotless; the common room was set and ready for the evening meal. He walked upstairs to the pilgrims' room and saw that the sheets had already been changed, pillows placed on the head of each bed, and blankets folded and stacked next to the door. The bathrooms were clean and in order, toilet paper stocked, fresh paper towels out, and soap dispensers full. Felipe was right. He was doing a great job!

Andrés glanced at his watch. Since it was only 10:00 in the morning, he should have time to catch up on email and do a little writing. He was currently writing a book describing a way out of the recession in Spain and hoped to have the final draft finished by Christmas. Although his initial interest in economics had been precipitated by his desire to improve working conditions for the younger generation in Spain, he found the study of economics fascinating and was thankful to have a job at Georgetown that allowed him to write, do research, and teach. After he'd been writing for an hour, Andrés looked up as a group of 4 pilgrims came in. As Andrés greeted them and stamped their *credenciales*, he learned they were a family from the United States who had been traveling for a month.

The father, Jonathan, looked especially weary, and Andrés learned that he had been struggling with digestive illness. Andrés offered to make him tea with medicinal herbs in the garden, and the man gratefully accepted. "For now, let me show you to the dormitory so you can find your beds and put your packs down. I'll get you tubs to soak your feet and show you the showers."

The mother, who introduced herself as Maggie, said, "Thank you so much for your hospitality, Mr…?"

"Andrés. Just Andrés. I'm happy you're here and glad to help in any way I can. Please be at ease and don't hesitate to ask if you need anything or have any questions." As he led them across the garden to the converted barn, he talked with them about their home in Seattle, their reasons for being on pilgrimage and the highlights of their trip so far. As the family dropped their packs beside the bunk beds, Andrés filled four basins with cold water and drops of Miriam's peppermint oil, and directed his guests to chairs, inviting them to dip their feet in the refreshing soak. He noticed the two teenagers had several bad blisters on their feet and promised to return to give them something for relief.

Andrés promised to be back in a few minutes, went back to the house, and found three women from France waiting to check in. They looked to be in their fifties, and Andrés conversed easily with them in their native language. They were secondary school teachers and had decided to hike the Camino to celebrate their 50th birthdays. One of them laughed and said, "Yes, nothing like blisters and sore legs to celebrate a birthday," but Andrés could tell by their peaceful expressions that they were grateful for this experience.

Over the next two hours, Andrés checked in 10 more pilgrims. *Three more, and we will have reached our capacity for the day. I'll either have to bring our extra cots out into the hallway or send any latecomers on to Miriam. It's always difficult when people have to walk farther, especially when they're so exhausted.* By 15:00, they had a full dormitory of twenty pilgrims, and Andrés called Miriam to see what her count was. He was thankful to find she still had a few spots available in case others showed up, although most pilgrims usually reached their destination by early afternoon. Matteo went upstairs to get a much needed siesta, and Andrés busied himself with making herb poultices for blisters, offering prayer for healing the pilgrims' feet as he applied them, then made Jonathan the promised medicinal tea for digestive health.

Andrés always loved listening to the multilingual pilgrim chatter when they had a full house, and today was no exception. Although English is generally considered the common language of the Camino, today's guests conversed in French, English, Spanish, Czech, and Portuguese. Andrés moved easily among them, conversing fluently in every pilgrim's native language except Czech. "I confess I never have been able to master even a few words in your language, Milos," Andrés said ruefully and handed the old Czech a towel as he lifted his feet out of the basin.

Milos chuckled, his blue eyes twinkling above his red wind-burned cheeks. "Even Czech people struggle to speak our language, my friend," he said laughing. "That's why we all learn English as quickly as possible!"

"English isn't easy either," said Andrés, and several pilgrims rolled their eyes and nodded in agreement. As Andrés finished treating the last of the pilgrim's blisters, Matteo came outside to welcome everyone. He asked if anyone wanted to tour the garden and meet the animals, and the Frenchwomen and Czech men enthusiastically stood up, asking if they could help with anything. Matteo led them across the property to the fenced vegetable garden and animal paddocks, while the rest of the pilgrims continued to take turns with the showers and washing machine.

The American teenagers, Will and Betsy, decided to tag along with Andrés to see if they could help him with dinner preparations. Andrés learned they were sixteen years old, twins, and their parents were both professors at the University of Washington. Their good manners and obvious friendship with one another spoke volumes about the kind of upbringing and values their parents had instilled in them, and Andrés found himself wishing, not for the first time, that he had grown up with a sibling or two. He silently thanked God for the men in a weekly Bible study gathering back in DC; some of them had become like brothers to him.

While Will washed vegetables and Betsy made dessert they both practiced their Spanish with Andrés, who appreciated their desire to learn and their humility as he corrected their mistakes. He laughed as they asked him to translate words such as "vampire," "nerd," "pterodactyl," and "space alien" into Spanish.

"Yeah, our tutor in Seattle doesn't seem to know those words. Then again, she's not actually Spanish. She just went to school over here, but we think people should know this stuff, right?"

"Yes, of course!" Andrés said as he assumed his most serious professor stance and taught them several Spanish jokes and Spanish pick up lines. ("Not that you have *any reason* to know these," he told them sternly, followed by a mischievous smile.) "So you don't have Spanish classes at your high school in Seattle?" he asked. "Is that why you have to hire a tutor?"

"No, it's not that. We're homeschooled," said Betsy. "So for things like Spanish, art, and music, Mom and Dad let us take private lessons or bring someone in to teach us. I mean, Mom's great with Math since she's a math professor ("Sometimes a little too great," interjected Will as Betsy laughed and nodded in agreement), and Dad does a nice job working through our history with us, but it's good they outsource some of the other stuff, especially since Dad is tone deaf. I can only imagine what it would be like if he tried to teach us piano and violin."

"Painful," said Will. Andrés was impressed again by their fondness for their parents and attitude of thankfulness he sensed in them as they talked about their education.

"How did you end up doing school at home?" asked Andrés.

216

Will said, "Well, we were in a great private school for a few years, but because Mom and Dad are both professors and have some flexibility in their schedules, they decided to give homeschooling a go when we were in third grade. They both took sabbaticals that year, and homeschooling gave us an opportunity to do a lot of traveling. After that year, we were hooked and couldn't imagine having to go back to the constraints of a traditional school schedule. It's pretty neat when Mom has a conference in Finland and we go with her and study reindeer, permafrost, and polar bears, or when we go with Dad to England for his British history conferences. I mean, it's way more fun than reading about it in a book."

"So how did you all end up on the Camino?" asked Andrés.

Will jumped in again: "Mom and Dad got serious about their faith in God when they were graduate students. There was a program the local church was doing encouraging young adults to come, hang out with their priest at a pub, and ask him questions about God or anything. Mom and Dad met at one of those groups, and a short time later they both met Jesus. Two years later, they were married, and then we came along a few years after that. Our priest, Father Daniel, did the Camino last year, and raved about it, so my parents decided it would be great to go on a pilgrimage. Plus, Bets and I are going into our senior year, and we have a lot to sort out about our futures. This trip has been a good chance to do it. We walk as a family some, but also spend time alone. It's been great to get away from all the usual distractions and listen for God's whispers."

As Andrés continued the easy conversation with the twins, his father came in with the three Frenchwomen and the Czech men, who were eager to help with the main meal.

Andrés took his father aside and said, "Papá, I'd like to go back to help Miriam once we have things in hand here. Is that okay with you?"

"Of course. Take Rex so he can have a romp with Tiggy. He's been a bit downcast since I took Bill and Paddy back to Burgos this morning."

As Andrés whistled for Rex, and walked outside, a young man limped into the yard and asked in broken English whether they had any room.

"Our bunks are full, but I can set up a cot for you on our porch, or you may come with me to my friend's *albergue* and stay there. It would mean walking another 5 kilometers, though," said Andrés.

"I think I stay here tonight on cot," said the man, and Andrés switched to speaking Italian when he recognized the man's accent.

"Of course! I will sign you in and show you everything! I'm Andrés," he said, extending his hand.

"I am Carlo," said his guest, and as Andrés walked across the yard to show him the dormitory bathrooms and laundry, he noticed blood soaking through the heel of his sock. *This guy has got a serious blister. No wonder he didn't want to go on to Miriam's.*

He told Matteo there was another pilgrim for dinner, and set up a cot in the shade of the porch. Carlo sat down on it with a big sigh, closing his eyes and leaning his head against the wall. Andrés asked if he could have a look at the blister. Carlo removed his boot and gasped in pain.

Andrés immediately saw why. A quarter-sized blood blister, badly infected, covered much of the back of Carlo's heel, and Andrés wrinkled his brow in concern. He went inside and mixed a tepid foot soak with Epsom salts in an enamel bowl, grabbed some liquid antiseptic soap and returned to the porch. He instructed Carlo to soak his foot in the solution for a few minutes, then went back in to the first aid cupboard and found iodine, alcohol, antibacterial ointment, and sterile bandages. Andrés let the foot soak for about fifteen minutes, then put on sterile gloves and washed Carlo's foot carefully with the antiseptic soap. Andrés had seen many such injuries, and was concerned the man may need to stop for medical treatment in Burgos if the infection worsened.

"Carlo, it would be best if you stayed here for a couple of days. I know this is probably an interruption to your plans, but this is a serious infection," said Andrés as he cleaned and bandaged the wound.

"I've been foolish to continue walking without any kind of treatment," said Carlo. "I'm a medical student at the University of Bologna; I should know better."

"We all make unwise choices sometimes, Carlo. Try not to be too hard on yourself," said Andrés as he finished securing the bandage. "May I pray for you?"

"Yes, please. Thank you for helping me," he said as Andrés laid his hands on the young man's shoulders and prayed quietly in Italian. Carlo watched him closely with a smile on his face, and when he finished his prayer said, "Andrés, I have long thought there is much more to the science of medicine than meets the eye. I, too, long to pray for my patients, but I've been strictly forbidden to do so by my professors. Thank you for showing me a way to do it discreetly."

"I'll bring you some food and drink. Stay here and rest." Andrés brought almonds, cheese, water, and tea to Carlo's bedside, and said, "I am going to help my friend Miriam now, but will be back later tonight." Then he signaled Rex and left.

25

GOD'S MERCY, NOT FAILURE

Elizabeth woke after an afternoon nap feeling much better than she had earlier that morning. *Of course, it's not going to help if I have to face Andrés again. That was so embarrassing. It's crazy to have all these people I don't even know seeing me in such a state. I feel like a child. Ugh! I wonder if Bruce has emailed me.*

Trust me, Beloved Daughter. I love you. I care for you. I have numbered the very hairs of your head, I know when you sit up and when you lie down. Before a word is on your tongue, I know it completely. I am the same God yesterday, today, and forever. Let my people Miriam, Andrés, Bill, and Matteo love and care for you.

Elizabeth sat up and swung her legs over the side of the bed and paused, momentarily dizzy. *Okay, God. I'm trying. I'm really trying.*

Cease striving and know that I'm God. Just rest in me. That's all I'm asking. Let yourself be loved and known.

Elizabeth took a deep breath and stood up, holding onto the bed as the room spun momentarily. Tiggy sprang off the bed and stood beside her, looking up and slowly wagging her tail as Elizabeth limped slowly to her pack and extracted her laptop. As she got back into bed and turned it on, Tiggy got up beside her and pushed her head under Elizabeth's hand.

I've got to convince Bruce not to fire me. It'll be fine.

Elizabeth clicked on her email and was dismayed when it didn't open. She pulled the wireless hotspot out of her USB port and saw that some of the metal connectors were bent.

Oh no, what am I going to do? I have to check my email so I can talk with Bruce. I guess I'll try calling him.

She picked her phone up off the nightstand and rang the office, hoping Donna would be able to put her through to Bruce.

"Donna!" Elizabeth shouted when Donna answered the phone.

"Elizabeth, are you alright, dear? What's the matter?"

"I'm sorry, Donna," Elizabeth chuckled. "I probably just about blew out your eardrum. Were you able to give my message to Bruce yesterday?"

"Yes, sweetie, I gave it to him," said Donna, her voice soft.

"Well, he hasn't called me back, and I'm really concerned. I got an email from Ellen saying he had announced my firing at the staff meeting, and it's all a huge misunderstanding. I've been really sick, so I wasn't able to check in with the office the way he wanted me to. I feel terrible about the way everything has happened. This was completely out of my control. I'm sure if I just explain things to him he'll reconsider and understand."

"Elizabeth. Bruce asked me to clean out your desk and send everything to your home address yesterday. I asked him if I could wait until today, but he wanted it done immediately because he was hoping to hire a replacement as soon as possible. I'm so sorry, Elizabeth. I'm afraid there's nothing you, Ellen, or I can do to change his mind."

Elizabeth held the phone silently, letting Donna's words sink in. "Donna, I have to talk to him. I have to make him see…"

"Honey, I know you want to talk to him. I also want you to know that ever since you left, I've been praying for you, and I think it's time for me to share some things with you that God has shown me. Would that be okay?"

Elizabeth nodded numbly, then realized that Donna couldn't see her, and croaked out, "Yes."

"For the past several months, even before you fainted in the office, you've been on my heart and mind. Sometimes God gives me a picture of specific things to pray for, other times I just know I'm to pray for someone but don't have a reason why. With you, I've had a picture of you running, but not just for exercise. You were running *from* something. And as the days went by and I continued to pray, you grew more and more exhausted. You were stumbling, your face covered with dust. And ever since then, I've had the sense that God has something else for you. I don't think you're supposed to keep working for Bruce. I think God wants to give you something better. Even though this firing hurts, it might be God's way of trying to lead you somewhere else."

John Cunningham, her father's former associate, flashed through her mind, but Elizabeth quickly redirected her thoughts. "I can't give up this easily, Donna. Maybe God wants me to stay here and He's just teaching me to persevere! I really need to talk with Bruce. Can you please tell him I'm trying to get hold of him? My email isn't working right now, but I'll try to check in again by phone when I get a chance. I'll try him on his cell too." There was a moment of silence. Donna seemed to be waiting for her to say something. "Donna. Thank you for praying for me. I just have to see this through. Do you understand?"

"Of course I understand. I also know that sometimes the more stubborn we are, the harder we have to fall for God to get our attention. I've been especially concerned about you the past few days. I had a picture in my mind of you lying unconscious in a garden. I've been praying that God would give you rest, wherever you are and whomever you're with."

Elizabeth was stunned that Donna knew about the garden. How was that possible? "I am resting, Donna. I'm sitting in a comfortable bed with a fuzzy sheepdog next to me. I've been taken in by a wonderful woman named Miriam, and she and her dog, Tiggy, have been nursing me. That garden you saw? A man found me there. I had almost gone into shock." Elizabeth proceeded to fill Donna in on the events of the past 48 hours, still feeling embarrassed despite Miriam's admonitions to the contrary.

"Well, I think you need to keep resting Elizabeth. This isn't urgent. This conversation with Bruce can wait."

"You say that, Donna, but you don't know Bruce the way I do. I mean, look, he's already tried to find my replacement, and you and I both know that jobs are in short supply and law school graduates are abundant, especially in the DC area. Bruce has his pick of qualified people to take my place, I'm sure. I really need to talk to him. Will you please tell him I called, and that I'll also try him on his cell?"

"I will, Elizabeth. But please do remember—sometimes what seems like a failure is a mercy. I will continue to pray for you."

"Thank you, Donna. I appreciate it. Really."

Elizabeth hung up the phone, exhausted again. Her thoughts continued to race as she leaned back on her pillow again. *I better go ahead and call Bruce while I'm awake and have the strength.* Tiggy whined slightly and pushed her nose under Elizabeth's hand, then rested her chin on Elizabeth's stomach. "Okay, Tiggy, wish me luck. Here goes." She took a deep breath and dialed Bruce's number.

26

"FURTHER UP, AND FURTHER IN"

Andrés jumped onto his bike, Rex by his side, and pedaled as fast as he could down the dusty road to Miriam's, passing a group of late-hiking *peregrinos*. He called to them in English, asking them if they had accommodations for the night. "We're walking to Burgos," called a tall woman in the front of the group. "We hope to get 50k in today!" she shouted proudly. Andrés shook his head in disbelief but called out, "Okay, Buen Camino!" as he pedaled past them, a cloud of dust in his wake. *I'm always amazed at the people who seem to see the Camino as a challenge to be conquered. Seems like a missed opportunity to slow down and learn to trust.*

As Andrés pulled up to Miriam's, he waved at the group of pilgrims hanging their clothes to dry on the line out front. One of the older women shrank back as Rex bounded in beside Andrés, and Andrés placed his hand on Rex's head, signaling him to settle down so as not to frighten her. He smiled gently and motioned her over, and she petted Rex gently, becoming more enthusiastic as Rex gave her hand a gentle lick and thumped his tail. "Where is Miriam?" he asked the assembled group, and another woman shrugged, saying, "We haven't seen her in a few hours. She showed us how to start dinner and asked that we make ourselves at home," said an older man with a German accent.

Nodding his thanks, Andrés and Rex walked down the hallway to Miriam's bedroom, assuming she was with Elizabeth. He tiptoed softly to the door, not wanting to disturb Elizabeth from sleep. As he approached, he heard muffled weeping, and Miriam's soft voice speaking Dutch. Andrés listened for a moment, leaning his head against the door jamb with his eyes shut, praying for comfort and peace. Rex snuffled at the crack of the door, looking for his friend Tiggy. A few seconds later, the door cracked open, and Miriam squeezed out, her face lined with fatigue. Andrés opened his arms, and she walked into them, leaning her head on his shoulder for a minute as he patted her back. They walked down the hallway towards the kitchen arm-in-arm, and Miriam whispered, "Andrés, she is still so willful. I find myself getting very frustrated with her, because to me it's so obvious what she needs." Miriam put her face in her hands for a moment, inhaled deeply, and looked up at Andrés through eyes swimming with tears. "But weren't we all like Elizabeth? I certainly was. I know I really have no right to be frustrated with her."

Andrés prayed as a few tears slipped down Miriam's cheeks, then said, "Miriam, why don't you go for a walk? I can handle things here with the pilgrims. You need rest, and time to pray on your own. Here, take Rex with you— he'll be glad for the exercise." Miriam squeezed Andrés' hand gratefully, and she and Rex slipped out the front door. Andrés continued down the hallway to the kitchen where some of the pilgrims were already chopping vegetables for the evening meal. He introduced himself, lifted an apron from the hook on the wall, and washed his hands to help with preparations. He pulled two large casserole dishes from the shelves next to the oven and set about making the evening's dessert, a plum cobbler. The elderly lady next to him introduced herself as Hélène, and started chatting with him in French about her grandchildren back in Dijon. Even though she must be in her seventies, she had started out from her hometown, and had been walking for three months.

"This is my sixth time walking the Camino. I have walked every decade since my 20s. I am now 75. This will be my final time walking, and I decided to walk all the way from Dijon this time. Usually I start in St. Jean de Pied de Port."

She grew quiet, and Andrés asked, "Why is this your last time walking? Surely you'll come back when you're 85!" he teased with a half smile as he glanced down at her.

"No," she said quietly. "I will not be on this earth when I am 85. Three years ago I was treated for cancer, and the doctor told me I probably had five more years. I knew God wanted me to make this pilgrimage one more time, and I decided to come now before I get too weak. I wanted to remain with my family, but they knew how much this pilgrimage has meant to me. So they have taken turns walking different portions of the route with me to spend time with me in this way. My son and daughter-in-law arrive in Burgos tomorrow and will take a bus here to meet me and walk the rest of the way to Santiago. Yesterday two of my grandchildren flew home from Burgos after two weeks of walking. Starting out from Dijon, my two daughters walked to St. Jean with me. So you see, Andrés, I am so very rich. Rich in God's provision of a beautiful family. Soon I will be home with Him, and I look forward to that day. But I have to confess, I have loved this world. I have loved the song of birds, the vibrancy of poppies, the beauty of the mountains. I feel as though I am journeying into the unknown. But He has given me peace on this pilgrimage. He is with me, and He will be with me as I come Home."

Andrés had stopped preparing the dessert and was leaning against the counter, unable to look away from Hélène's heavily lined face and bright blue eyes. After some moments, he was able to speak past the lump in his throat. "You have amazing faith, Hélène," he quietly, taking her hand. Then, after a pause, he asked, "Have you ever heard of the Chronicles of Narnia by the English author C.S. Lewis?"

"Yes, of course!" Hélène said excitedly. I read them to my children and grandchildren, in the French translations of course."

"I'm thinking of a part at the end of *The Last Battle…*" Andrés closed his eyes and began translating the beloved words into French as best as he could. "'It was the Unicorn who summed up what everyone was feeling. He stamped his right fore-hoof on the ground and neighed, and then cried: 'I have come home at last! This is my real country! I belong here. This is the land I have been looking for all my life, though I never knew it till now. The reason why we loved the old Narnia is that it sometimes looked a little like this.'" Andrés opened his eyes again to see tears in the eyes of the beautiful woman before him. "The reason you have loved all that is beautiful and good about this world is that it's simply a foreshadowing of the real world." He continued with another Lewis quote: " 'The new Narnia was a deeper country: every rock and flower and blade of grass looked as if it meant more.' Hélène," he continued, "all shall be well. You are brave. You have lived well. And you will continue to live well with Jesus, in His country."

"Yes," said Hélène thoughtfully. "I feel sad for those I'm leaving behind. Even though I rejoice that I'm going home, I grieve the separation from my dear family. But I know in the light of eternity, the separation is only a moment. As Jesus said to his followers in the gospel of St. Jean, 'After a little while the world will behold Me no more; but you will behold Me; because I live, you shall live also. In that day you shall know that I am in My Father, and you in Me, and I in you.'"

"Thank you for sharing your story with me, Hélène," said Andrés, resuming his work on the cobbler. "Will your family be meeting you here tomorrow morning, or somewhere else? If they're coming here, can I meet them and pray with all of you?"

"They'll be coming here," Hélène nodded. "Yes, let's plan to breakfast together, shall we?"

"I would be honored," Andrés replied. They realized they were humming the same song so began singing the words, Andrés in English, Hélène in French, "In mansions of glory and endless delight, I'll ever adore Thee in heaven so bright. I'll sing with the glittering crown on my brow. If ever I loved Thee, my Jesus 'tis now." Andrés slid the cobbler into the oven, hung his apron back on the hook, hugged Hélène, and went back outside to check on the pilgrims who were hanging their clothes to dry on the line.

As he rounded the corner, he bumped into Elizabeth and Tiggy, saying, "Ah, *perdón!*" as he did so. Elizabeth went red in the face and attempted to limp past him, but he steadied her by the shoulders. "Elizabeth, are you alright? I'm sorry; I was on my way outside. Can I get you something?"

Elizabeth mumbled something about needing Miriam, not meeting Andrés' eyes. "Miriam went for a walk, but I can help you with anything you need." She finally looked up at him through bloodshot, puffy eyes.

"I guess I just wanted to talk. It looks like I really did lose my job. My boss finally took my call," she said bleakly. "I don't know what to do. I've given everything to this job since I graduated from law school. And now I have nothing."

Andrés let her lean on his arm and helped her into the common room, seated her on a bench, and handed her a handkerchief. She wiped her cheeks and blew her nose while he filled a glass of water in the kitchen. He set it before her with a piece of fruit and a roll, hoping she'd be able to eat.

Her cheeks were hollow, skin pallid, hair dull and lifeless. Worse than her physical appearance was the dead look in her eyes, the look of hopelessness. Andrés laid his hand on her shoulder and prayed silently. When he opened his eyes, she was looking at him, holding her roll and chewing slowly.

"I'm sorry about your job. It sounds like you're a valuable

employee. It probably feels unfair, doesn't it? I can imagine how difficult this is, since this has been such a big part of your life for so long. It will take time to grieve and process. You do not need to feel ashamed of your feelings. Don't be afraid to be honest."

Elizabeth put her roll down and gulped a few sips of water. "I feel like I haven't been myself for months now. Since the spring, really. I don't know who I am anymore. The old me would never have even taken a trip like this, but here I am. And everything about this trip has gone wrong. Nothing has happened the way I planned it." *Everything has gone wrong, Beloved?* "Okay, maybe not *everything* has gone wrong. I have encountered God in powerful ways here. But this is all so confusing. I see now that God is real, but I'm not sure I like Him. To be honest, He scares me."

"Me too," he said, smiling at her, but Elizabeth didn't smile back.

"I'm serious. Who is He? I mean, look at me. I'm a wreck. I have no job. I can barely walk I'm so weak from this illness. Oh wait, I forgot," she said sarcastically. "I could already barely walk because of my knee injury, which will probably need surgery when I get back to the United States. So I'll be going back to no job and six weeks of lying on my couch rehabbing a bum knee by myself. I say by myself because I have almost no friends, which is what happens when you work 80-hour weeks year in and year out. I just want to say to God, 'Okay, I finally gave in to you. I let you in, and now you've let this happen to me? What is going on here?'" She exhaled in frustration.

Andrés laid his hand on hers and said, "Have you said that to God?"

"No, of course not! How would that sound to the God of the Universe? I mean, He's God, and I'm just some… some…pipsqueak!" Elizabeth did laugh this time, and Andrés joined her, silently thanking God for the release of tension laughter provided.

"Yes, this is true. We are…what did you call it… pipsqueaks?" Elizabeth laughed at his Spanish accent as he tried to pronounce the word. "But the thing is, we have an audience with God. Because of Jesus, He is our Father. We don't have to be afraid of telling Him exactly what we think. He knows anyway, but when we tell Him, it clears the bitterness away and gives Him space to work. And the thing is, even though we know we're pipsqueaks, we still question God in our hearts. We might as well be honest with Him." As he spoke, Elizabeth sensed she had experienced something like this at *Alto de Perdón*.

"I just can't imagine he'd want to hear all that. My father never listened, why would God?" Elizabeth couldn't keep her voice from trembling as she asked the question. She thought of all the times her father had brushed her off and how painful it had been.

Andrés, sensing the pain in her silence, stayed quiet for a few moments, then said gently, "Elizabeth, God isn't like your father. He's always available, always willing, and always loving. I'm sorry for the hurt your father has caused you."

Elizabeth looked away again, both frustrated and encouraged by this man who seemed to know what she was thinking before she even voiced it. Miriam was the same way. It was scary, being vulnerable. *But isn't it better to be known, Child? What do you have to lose? Are you REALLY happy with your life the way it is now?"* "Okay, okay. Things obviously aren't working for me the way I have been doing life so far, huh?" Elizabeth picked her roll back up and sighed deeply.

Sensing she needed some space from such a difficult topic, Andrés said, "So, where do you live?"

"I live in Washington, D.C. Although now I'm not sure. I guess I need to apply for jobs wherever I can."

"You're from Washington! I teach at Georgetown University!"

"You're kidding! That's so funny," Elizabeth said, brightening. "Nice to run into you in Spain! What's your connection here?"

Andrés told her the short version of his story about ending up in Washington, answering Elizabeth's periodic questions. They were enjoying discovering they shared favorite places and favorite restaurants, living in the same city. She was intrigued by the way Andrés saw God's hand in everything, putting His life in the context of a larger story. *Okay, God. Maybe all isn't lost. Maybe something bigger is going on here.* "Well, it's comforting to think maybe I'll have a friend other than my cat-sitter when I get back to DC," said Elizabeth, giving a small smile.

Miriam walked into the room quietly and smiled when she saw Andrés and Elizabeth chatting. She walked over to Elizabeth and laid her hand on the younger woman's cheek. "Lisbet, it is good to see you smiling."

Elizabeth covered Miriam's hand with her own.

"Miriam," she said, meeting the older woman's kind grey eyes. "Thank you so much for everything you've done and are doing for me. I'm thankful to be here."

"We are so very glad to have you, *Liebchen*. Would you like to go to the garden and sit for awhile? I brought a small journal in case you'd like to write some of your thoughts or prayers. That is always a helpful thing for me."

Elizabeth accepted the journal and pen Miriam offered her, and Andrés helped her stand up. "Let me walk you out, Elizabeth." Tiggy and Rex followed, snuffling at their heels. Elizabeth laughed and said, "These dogs are too much! Do you have a dog in DC?"

"Unfortunately, no. Rex stays with my father at our farm a few kilometers down the road. I grew up with German Shepherds around me all my life, so it's very difficult not having one to keep me company back in DC, but I'm not at my apartment enough to give one the attention he needs. Whenever I go for a run, I always stop and ask people if I can pet their dogs. They probably think I'm crazy, chasing them down the way I do."

"So you're a runner? Me too! Well, I used to be. Not sure what to think now that my knee is a wreck," she said sadly.

"You're dealing with a lot of unknowns right now," Andrés observed. "That's a hard place to be. I'll pray for you." He seated her on a stone bench in the garden, stumbling as Rex and Tiggy pelted into him, in the midst of a joyful romp. They both laughed as they watched the two dogs chasing each other through the fields.

"There's something so uplifting about being around

pure, unadulterated joy, isn't there?" Elizabeth said as she watched them wistfully. "I suppose we could learn something from that."

Andrés nodded his assent, and then said, "Okay, I'll leave you here by yourself. Just send Tiggy or Rex if you need anything."

"Andrés. Thank you. For everything you've done for me. For," she paused, suddenly shy, "For rescuing me."

"I'm glad I could be of help." He walked away whistling happily, and Elizabeth closed her eyes, listening to the bees humming around her, feeling the warmth of the sun and the soft breeze on her face.

27

TAPESTRY

Elizabeth sat quietly with her eyes closed, waiting for God to speak to her. Something tickled her injured knee, and she opened her eyes and saw Tiggy licking it vigorously. "Thanks so much for helping, Tiggy, but that's too ticklish! I'm trying to pray here! Leave it!" she commanded halfheartedly, having no idea how to get Tiggy under control. Surprisingly, Tiggy backed off and laid down at her feet, thumping her tail as Rex collapsed beside her, tongue lolling, resting his chin on Tiggy's back. Elizabeth scratched his ears and he leaned into her hand, then moved his chin to her foot and fell asleep, snoring. She laughed out loud at the two dogs sprawled at her feet. *Okay, focus, Elizabeth. You're trying to pray here. Stop letting the dogs distract you!*

Haltingly, she started whispering out loud. "God. Jesus. I'm so frustrated. What is the deal, here? First I don't get promoted. Then I pass out, end up in Spain, hurt my knee, and pass out again." Elizabeth realized she was now almost shouting, but didn't care. "What the hell, God? I poured my life into that job. I was prepared to go back and serve you at work, to do everything for you instead of myself. Instead, Bruce completely shut me out. How could you let that happen? And now I look at my life, and I feel hopeless. I have no job, no friends, no prospects. I don't even know how I'm going to pay my mortgage if I can't work. And frankly, once Bruce Devon fires someone, they get blacklisted, so I'll have to leave town. Even though I don't have a lot of friends in DC, it's still my home, and I want to stay there. Everything else has been pulled out from under me; please don't make me go somewhere else too."

Elizabeth stopped for a moment, breathing hard. "Where would I even go? The last thing I want to do is go back to Atlanta. My dad could care less if I move home since we never even talk anyway, and all the people I grew up with are married with families or have moved away. I don't fit anywhere. And this is your fault, God. What kind of God are you? What kind of God takes everything from someone when they decide to follow Him?"

The kind of God who sacrifices His own Son so you can have life, and have it to the full.

An image of a painting flashed in her mind. She had seen it in the National Gallery on her visit to London years before, and it was by a Dutch painter whose name she couldn't remember. It depicted Jesus being questioned by a man in a turban--the high priest, she remembered--their faces illuminated by a single candle. The expression on Jesus' face of resignation, love, and sadness cut her to the heart. She remembered sitting in front of that painting for an hour as people milled around her, hardly aware of their presence. Now, the image came back to her as she prayed. She sat quietly, focusing on the memory of Christ's face in that painting. Then another image came to mind, another painting she knew well. *The Return of the Prodigal Son* by Rembrandt. She had studied that image in depth while taking an art history elective as an undergraduate, and had been impressed by Rembrandt's mastery of light and shadow. What came back to her now, though was not the prodigal son in the foreground of the painting, but a shadowy figure, almost blending into the background. *The elder brother. He never actually entered into your joy, did he, God?*

She got up, wanting to check her memory of the story. Pain shot through her knee, and Tiggy ran into the house, barking. Andrés came jogging out, dish towel in hand, Miriam's flowery apron covering his torso. Nice apron," Elizabeth chuckled.

"Thank you, it is my favorite," Andrés said with mock politeness, laughing and giving her a curtsy. "Why are you standing up? Can I get you something?"

"I wonder if there's an English Bible anywhere around here? I wanted to check my memory on something."

"Yes, I'm sure there is. I'll be right back. Sit down!" he ordered her in a tone of mock frustration. Tiggy and Rex resumed their romp, having been refreshed by their short nap. A few moments later, Andrés returned holding a tray with a small black book, a glass of water, a banana, and a cup of Miriam's specially blended herbal tea. He had even taken the time to put a small vase of flowers on the tray. Andrés ordered a sharp command in Spanish, and the dogs ran farther out into the field to resume their play. "These dogs are well behaved most of the time, but sometimes they're slightly out of control. Okay, here is your Bible. Please eat this banana right now. I'm not leaving until you do," he said, crossing his arms over his chest.

"Okay, okay, I'm eating! Thanks. "Hey, do you know where the story of the prodigal son is?"

"Ah, yes, in the book of Luke, maybe chapter 15, but there is a concordance in the back of that Bible. An index of terms," he clarified at her questioning look. "You can look up the word 'lost' to check my memory."

"Okay, thanks. And thanks for the flowers," she said as she glanced around at the abundance of flowers surrounding her in the garden.

"Oh," said Andrés, following her gaze. "I guess you didn't need these. Okay, then. I'll go back inside." He seemed suddenly shy, reached to retrieve the vase, but Elizabeth blocked his reach.

"Thanks, Andrés. They are beautiful," she smiled. Andrés grinned, turned, and walked toward the house. Elizabeth watched him go and smiled to herself, then flipped the Bible open to the table of contents, found the book of Luke, and began to read chapter 15. "Now the tax collectors and sinners were all drawing near to hear him," began verse one. *Sheesh, harsh, Luke. Call everyone sinners. Seems judgmental. No wonder people don't like Christians.* She read on to verse 11: "And he said, 'There was a man who had two sons. And the younger of them said to his father, "Father, give me the share of property that is coming to me." And he divided his property between them.'"

Here Elizabeth noticed a footnote, and read the following: "In the ancient near east, for a son to ask for an early inheritance was a travesty. It was the equivalent of saying to the Father, "Father, I wish you were dead. I'm taking my inheritance, leaving, and never coming back." *Speaking of harsh. Wow.* She read on: "Not many days later, the younger son gathered all he had and took a journey into a far country, and there he squandered his property in reckless living. And when he had spent everything, a severe famine arose in that country, and he began to be in need. So he went and hired himself out to one of the citizens of that country, who sent him into his fields to feed pigs. And he was longing to be fed with the pods that the pigs ate, and no one gave him anything. But when he came to himself, he said, 'How many of my father's hired servants have more than enough bread, but I perish here with hunger! I will arise and go to my father, and I will say to him, "Father, I have sinned against heaven and before you. I am no longer worthy to be called your son. Treat me as one of your hired servants." And he arose and came to his father. But while he was still a long way off, his father saw him and felt compassion, and ran and embraced him and kissed him." Elizabeth continued reading, heart pounding, not aware of the tears running, unchecked, down her cheeks. "And the son said to him, 'Father, I have sinned against heaven and before you. I am no longer worthy to be called your son.' But the father said to his servants, 'Bring quickly the best robe, and put it on him, and put a ring on his hand, and shoes on his feet. And bring the fattened calf and kill it, and let us eat and celebrate. For this my son was dead, and is alive again; he was lost and is found.' And they began to celebrate." *This is not the picture I've had of God. When I've thought about him at all, I've pictured him as stern, unloving, and waiting for me to mess up; hating gay people, abortion, and every other religion.*

Out loud, she prayed, "God, I'm like that son. I want to do things my own way. I realize now that's not who you are at all. I'm sorry, God. Please forgive me. All this time, you've just been waiting for me to come home." As she finished saying this, her tears turned to full sobs, but even as she prayed, she felt a weight lift from her shoulders. She breathed deeply, in and out, her heartbeat slowing, the breeze wafting strands of hair around her face.

This is how I rejoice over you, my beloved Daughter. I want to give you the kingdom.

She continued reading, *Now his older son was in the field, and as he came and drew near to the house, he heard music and dancing. And he called one of the servants and asked what these things meant. And he said to him, "Your brother has come, and your father has killed the fattened calf, because he has received him back safe and sound." But he was angry and refused to go in. His father came out and entreated him, but he answered his father, "Look, these many years I have served you, and I never disobeyed your command, yet you never gave me a young goat, that I might celebrate with my friends. But when this son of yours came, who has devoured your property with prostitutes, you killed the fattened calf for him!" And he said to him, "Son, you are always with me, and all that is mine is yours. It was fitting to celebrate and be glad, for this your brother was dead, and is alive; he was lost, and is found."* Elizabeth's heart turned to ice. *You never asked me,* she heard. She took a long sip of water, picked up the journal Miriam had given her and copied the whole of Luke 15 into it. *But now you can ask. Ask me for what you want. Tell me what you need. I love you, and I long to bless you.*

Okay, thanks God. But if I ask and I don't get what I'm asking for, what does that mean? I don't know how to comprehend that. I know you're not some wish-fulfilling genie, and I also know you can see more than I can. But how am I supposed to know what to do when you take away everything I'm hoping for? She paused and thought about an image Miriam had shared with her after her crushing phone call with Bruce. "Liebchen," Miriam had said, as she stroked Elizabeth's hair back and wiped her tears. "Jesus is weaving a beautiful story. A tapestry. And He knows exactly what the design will be, and what needs to happen. Sometimes we see glimpses of it, and sometimes He tells us parts of the design ahead of time. He knows what parts He needs us to play. And when all is dark around us and we can't see, we can cling to the reality that this tapestry will be beautiful."

Elizabeth's cheeks grew warm as she thought about the immaturity of her sharp retort to Miriam, "You don't know about the story God's weaving in my life. How can this possibly be His plan? How dare you speak for Him?" Elizabeth felt a deep pang of remorse at the memory of the pain flickering across Miriam's kind, beautiful face.

"Okay, I will leave you to have some time to think, Elizabeth." It was the first time Miriam had called her by her given name, and that, more than anything, had deflated her.

I have to apologize to Miriam. She's kindness itself. If it weren't for her, I wouldn't even be having this conversation with you. She gave me clothes, her own room, her dog, everything I could have possibly needed, and more. I want to enter into your joy, Father. I don't want to be like the older brother, just trying to earn your love, and standing in the shadows. Teach me what it means to depend on you. A bell rang close to the house, and Elizabeth glanced at her watch. *6:30. It must be time for the evening meal.* Her stomach rumbled. *Wow, I actually feel hungry. I wonder if there's enough for me. I guess I'll leave this tray here for now.* She got to her feet again, feeling refreshed, and limped towards the house.

28

PERDÓN

"Lisbet, why didn't you send Tiggy?" cried Miriam in alarm. "You don't need to be walking in here without support!" Miriam looked down at Elizabeth's knee, face etched with concern, as Elizabeth hobbled into the dining room. Even though she wanted to talk to Miriam privately and ask her forgiveness, Elizabeth saw how busy she was with final dinner preparations, and simply asked, "Miriam, is there enough food for me to join the group for dinner tonight?"

Miriam dropped the pile of napkins she was carrying and rushed over to Elizabeth, kissed her on the cheek, and seated her at the end of the long table. "We'd love to have you, Liebchen. How wonderful! You be careful of that stomach, though! No third helpings until you have had time to get used to solid food again!" she said, shaking her finger and winking at Elizabeth. Elizabeth's eyes filled with tears of gratitude, and she sat down, tasting the sweetness of humility and repentance.

A small, elderly woman sat down next to her, her leathery face creased in a smile, her eyes twinkling. She held Elizabeth's hand for a moment, squeezed it, and then let go to make the sign of the cross over her own chest. Chairs scraped as the other pilgrims laid their dishes on the table and sat down. Elizabeth's mouth watered as the sights and smells of the meal filled her senses. The table groaned as dishes of roast chicken, potatoes, vegetables, lentil stew, fresh baked bread, and pitchers of wine and water crowded it. Miriam and Andrés sat down last, Andrés still wearing his pink, flowery apron. His cheeks reddened slightly above his dark beard as he met her eyes and smiled. She grinned at him from across the table as Miriam clapped to get everyone's attention.

"I'd like to teach you all a simple song for our blessing tonight. Some of you may already know it. I will teach it in English, but if you know it in your native language, please sing in any way you feel comfortable." She closed her eyes and sang the first line, "Our Father, who art in heaven," then beckoned to the guests to repeat the line back to her. Elizabeth closed her eyes and smiled as she listened to the several different languages around her, all beautiful. They sang the rest of the Lord's Prayer, then a chorus of "Amens" filled the room, and glasses clinked as Miriam raised hers and said, "To the King!" Elizabeth raised her glass with the other pilgrims, put it down, and received the bowl of potatoes from the man on her left. She dished herself a small portion, and passed the bowl to the woman on her right, smiling.

"I don't think I know your name," she said as she held out her hand.

"Hélène," the woman said with another bright smile. "I

248

speak no English."

The young man on Elizabeth's left said in heavily accented English, "That's okay, Hélène. I can translate if there's something you would like to talk about. I'm Luc," he added to Elizabeth. Hélène's face brightened after he repeated himself in French, and the three new friends began an animated discussion with Luc as translator.

As they talked, shards of ice seemed to melt from Elizabeth's heart. *So this is what it's like to have friends, to be part of a family. All this time I've thought I didn't need this, but I was wrong. Thank you for showing me this, God.* Throughout the meal, Elizabeth marveled at the delicious food and made a mental note not to keep eating peanut butter out of jars and soup out of cans when she returned home. As the bowls and dishes were wiped clean by the voracious pilgrims, several people sitting around the table started looking drowsy.

"Not yet, my friends," said Miriam playfully as she nudged the older man next to her who had been nodding off. "Please clear your plates but keep your spoons. We have dessert coming!" The pilgrims all got up to help bus the table, but Luc said, first in French, then in English. "Stay seated, ladies. I'll take care of your dishes." Elizabeth smiled her thanks and Hélène patted his hand as he got up. As he walked into the kitchen holding a stack of dishes, Hélène turned to Elizabeth and began to study her face until Elizabeth felt her cheeks grow hot, and looked downward. Hélène finally seemed to come to a conclusion and held out her hand, inviting Elizabeth to join her in prayer. As Hélène prayed in French, Elizabeth was again struck by the paradox of God's kindness juxtaposed with His magnitude. Seeing so many people from different backgrounds, nations, and cultures worshipping him was humbling for Elizabeth.

When Hélène finished praying, she let go of Elizabeth's hand and unwrapped what looked like a bracelet from her tiny wrist. As she held it out to Elizabeth, the younger woman saw that it was a beautiful rosary. She rubbed the polished beads with her thumb, and Luc rejoined them at their end of the table. Hélène said something in rapid French, and Luc looked at her intensely, mouth slightly open. As she continued, he put his face in his hands. Hélène gently grasped one of his hands and nodded in Elizabeth's direction. Luc took a deep breath and said, "This is Hélène's rosary. Her father made it for her mother, who gave it to her. Now she wants you to have it."

Elizabeth continued to rub the plain wooden beads, tears filling her eyes. "Luc, I can't accept this. It is too personal, too precious. Besides, I don't even know how to pray the rosary. Please tell her thank you, a thousand times, but she should give it to someone who will understand it more. Besides, she probably still needs it." Luc relayed this information to Hélène, who raised an eyebrow and put her hand on her hip, an expression needing no translation. She raised her chin and spoke again to Luc, jabbering in rapid French. Luc laughed slightly, but his eyes were moist. Elizabeth looked back and forth between them, wondering what was being said. At last, Hélène stopped and Luc took a deep breath. He seemed to be having trouble speaking and his words were broken with pauses.

"She says it is not a choice for her to give you the rosary. Jesus told her to give it to you. He will show you what to do with it. And," here he paused and swallowed hard, his voice cracking. "She is going to be with Jesus soon, so she won't need this because she will be home." Tears spilled down Elizabeth's cheeks as she raised her eyes from the rosary to Hélène.

"Why?" she whispered, squeezing Hélène's hand, not wanting to let go.

"She has cancer, and it is only a matter of time before it comes back full strength. There is nothing more the doctors can do." Tears were running down Luc's cheeks now, too.

Hélène held both of their hands, eyes bright with tears, but a look of joy on her face. Elizabeth looked again at the rosary, the figure of Jesus on the crucifix rubbed almost completely flat from use.

"Merci," Elizabeth choked out tears pouring down her cheeks. *"Merci beaucoup."*

Hélène stood and drew Elizabeth to her, letting Elizabeth rest her head against her chest. She sat down and started speaking to Luc again, and he said, "She is going to teach us how to pray the rosary while we have our dessert." Miriam came down to the end of the table and hugged Hélène, Luc, and Elizabeth in turn, then said something to Hélène in French. Hélène nodded her assent, and Miriam hurried off. As the cobbler came around, Elizabeth mimicked Hélène as she led them in the praying of the rosary, Luc translating. When they finished, Elizabeth wrapped the rosary around her own wrist, lifted Hélène's tiny, wizened hand and kissed it, then continued to hold it as Miriam stood at the head of the table.

"Now is the time of the night when we take time to pray

for one another. Please write your prayer requests down on a piece of paper, and I will collect them. If you don't want me to read yours out loud, write a star in the upper left hand corner. Please know this time is not mandatory, so if you'd like to go upstairs to your beds, you are welcome to do so. Even if you say goodnight, you may still write a prayer and give it to me."

Andrés passed out slips of paper with pencils, and everyone busied themselves writing. A few pilgrims handed their requests to Miriam and went upstairs, but the rest stayed, so there was a group of six to pray. "I've asked Hélène to lead us this evening." Luc moved to the empty seat next to Hélène, ready to translate the requests into French. They read through them together, Luc whispering in French while the rest of the table sat quietly, heads bowed. When they finished, Hélène stood up, smiled at everyone, and motioned to them to bow their heads and join hands. She prayed in a small but clear voice, and Luc translated into English softly beside her. As Hélène prayed, she lifted her face upwards, her voice increasing in intensity. Miriam began praying in Dutch beside her, and one by one Elizabeth, Andrés, and the other pilgrims joined in until the entire room was filled with multilingual praise. As the prayers continued, Elizabeth slid off her chair onto the ground, stretched out face down before the holy presence of God filling the space. Time seemed suspended as Miriam's rich alto filled the room, singing the doxology. "Praise God from whom all blessings flow; Praise Him all creatures here below. Praise Him above ye heavenly host. Praise Father, Son, and Holy Ghost."

A reverent silence filled the room, and as Elizabeth opened her eyes, she saw every other person in the room lying on the floor in the same position as she. Joyful laughter filled the room as the friends looked around at each other. Andrés was the first to stand, offering his hand to each person in turn to help them up. He came to Elizabeth last, and smiled at her as he pulled her up and helped her back into her chair. "This," he said, still holding her hand. "This is the God we serve, Elizabeth." He squeezed her hand before letting it go, then picked up the empty cobbler pan and headed for the kitchen.

Elizabeth sat still in her chair, reluctant to leave the warmth and security of the dining room, but knew she needed to get plenty of sleep. She caught Miriam's eye as she bustled back into the dining room, having carried the last of the dishes into the kitchen where Andrés was leading the pilgrims in washing up. She smiled as Miriam came over, amazed at how responsive this gentle woman was to anyone in need.

"What can I get you, Lisbet?"

"Nothing, Miriam. Could you sit with me for just a moment?"

"Of course," she said, as she sat on the end of the bench closest to Elizabeth's chair.

"Miriam, I need to ask your forgiveness. I have been prideful, not wanting you to help me, not listening to your words and your advice. You have shown me nothing but kindness, yet I snapped at you earlier when you tried to comfort me about my job. Many people have tried to help me, but I have lashed out at them in my anger. I might never see most of those people again, but I can at least apologize to you. I'm so sorry, Miriam. Will you forgive me?"

Elizabeth met Miriam's eyes, warmed by the tenderness radiating from them. Miriam drew Elizabeth into her arms and stroked her back. "It's very hard to ask for forgiveness, Lisbet. But you do well to ask for it, and to receive it. I forgive you, dear girl. And I love you." Elizabeth rested her head on Miriam's shoulder, wishing she could fall asleep with her head in the older woman's lap, but aware of the many tasks Miriam had to do before she rested for the day.

"Miriam, how much longer are you going to give up your own bed to me? You must be exhausted at the end of every day, and that little cot can't be comfortable. Don't you think you should kick me out?"

"Ah, don't worry Liebchen. Tomorrow night you will sleep in the pilgrims' room, so enjoy your last night in my luxurious bed! Also, tonight I will sleep with pilgrims since you're feeling so much better. That way I will have a regular bed, even if it is a bunk bed," she said with a smirk at Elizabeth. "Even though your knee isn't letting you walk anymore, you are still a pilgrim. A pilgrim is someone who knows that the journey is less about the walk, and more about the inner person. It is about learning to live in community, to live simply, to listen. You are learning to do that, brave girl. I am so proud of you. And I want you to stay here and rest until it's time for you to fly back to the US, okay?" She took Elizabeth's face in her hands and kissed her on the forehead. "Now, let's get you to bed so you can enjoy your own room for one more night, eh?" The two women laughed as they walked down the hallway together.

"Miriam! Elizabeth!" They turned at the sound of Andrés' call as he ran up behind them, panting, still wearing the flowered apron.

"Are you okay, Andrés? What's wrong?" said Miriam.

"Oh!" he said, seemingly surprised at the question. "I'm fine." He looked from Miriam to Elizabeth, eyes widening at the slow smile spreading over Miriam's face. "Well. Yes. I, er, I wanted to say goodnight. Sleep well. Okay. Well, goodnight!" He turned and walked quickly back to the kitchen.

Miriam glanced at Elizabeth out of the corner of her eye and saw the younger woman was also smiling at Andrés' awkward behavior. "Well, well," said Miriam. "It was certainly nice of Andrés to be so thoughtful and wish me good night. He's such a kind young man. And it is so interesting that you live in the same city, isn't it?"

"Yes," smiled Elizabeth, avoiding her eyes. "Yes it is."

29

HIS HEART ON HIS SLEEVE

Andrés leaned against the kitchen counter, breathing heavily. He put his hand over his pounding heart and realized he was still wearing the lacy pink apron. *Well, that was embarrassing. Maybe Elizabeth doesn't mind awkward men.* He took a deep breath and finished putting the dishes away. Miriam came into the kitchen, and Andrés couldn't help but laugh at the knowing look on her face. "Okay, Miriam, you win," he said in Spanish. "I'm wearing my heart on my sleeve. I'm hoping if I keep wearing this apron, she won't be able to resist me." They both laughed, and Rex crowed joyfully. "Okay, quiet down, buddy, people are trying to sleep," said Andrés, scratching Rex's ears. "Besides, I've seen you with Tiggy. Speaking of awkward…" Rex leaned his head against Andrés' leg and sighed, rolling onto his back for a tummy rub.

"She is changing, Andrés. God must have used your words this afternoon."

"I told her it was okay to be angry, and that God could handle whatever she needed to tell Him…" he went on to recount the rest of their conversation, and Miriam's eyes slid shut.

"Thank God! And thank you, Andrés, for giving me time to take a walk this afternoon. You were right to insist on that. I get tired when I try to do things in my own strength, and fail so quickly."

"So do I, Miriam. So do I. That's why we need our friends, right? To be mirrors for us and remind us when we need to take a rest. I guess I'd better head home. Thanks for having me this afternoon."

"Thank you for being here, Andrés. Am I right that I'll be seeing a lot of you over the next several days? Don't worry, I have a lot you can "help" me with." Andrés laughed at Miriam's emphasis the word "help" and playfully snapped her with the dishtowel he was holding.

"Yes, you absolutely need my help. And I won't take no for an answer."

"Okay, don't worry, I wasn't planning to tell you no," said Miriam, eyes shining with mirth. "What time should we expect you tomorrow? Perhaps I should go help Matteo with *his* chores?"

"No, I'll help Papá in the morning and come over after I check the pilgrims in and make sure the evening meal prep is going smoothly."

"Okay, rest well." Miriam gave Andrés a warm hug and flipped the light switch to the kitchen. "I think Father Bill is coming by tomorrow, so I'll send him along to help your Papá after he stops here. It will be good for him and Elizabeth to talk."

"Yes, very good. Even though we both know Father Bill will love Elizabeth no matter what, asking for forgiveness and recognizing consequences of her behavior are important parts of her healing. I continue to pray for repentance, not shame."

"As do I, Miriam. Good night. Oh, can you also pray that I act normally?" Andrés said with a grin.

"Of course, Andrés," chuckled Miriam. "Now, go! If you make me laugh any more, I will have the hiccups and won't be able to sleep!" Andrés waved as he and Rex jogged out the door, and Miriam sang to herself as she tidied the common room.

She lifted the bowl containing the prayer requests off the table, sat down in her favorite rocking chair by the fireplace, and lifted them out one by one, praying silently. When she reached Hélène's, she wept silently as she read the woman's firm but lovely cursive:

> *"Lord, thank you that I get to come home soon and see you. Thank you for taking care of me, and letting me come on this last pilgrimage. Please protect my children and grandchildren from despair and bitterness. Help them not be afraid, and be with them as they grieve. Please make our time together before we are separated rich. And, Lord, help me be brave, even if I'm in pain or tired. Help me to trust you."*

"Ah, Lord," Miriam whispered her prayer out loud. "Protect her and surround her. Release Your healing spirit and Your peace into her life and the life of her family. Thank You for using her powerfully while she is here. Thank You for the privilege of knowing her for even a short time, and for all she has taught those of us who knew her here." Miriam sat in silence for a few more moments, and then checked her wristwatch and bolted out of her chair, knowing the morning would come painfully early. She extinguished the lights on her way upstairs, changed into her pajamas and climbed into her bunk at the end of the sleep room, smiling as she fell asleep to the whiffling snores around her.

30

MAKING ALL THINGS NEW

Miriam opened her eyes to dim grey light coming in through the small skylight in the ceiling. She slipped quietly out of bed, wrapped her sweater around her, and padded downstairs to get dressed. As she came out of the bathroom, she met Elizabeth standing fully dressed in the hallway, Tiggy wagging her tail happily beside her.

"Liebchen, what are you doing up so early?"

"Well," Elizabeth said, almost sheepishly. "I got up early to pray and read my, I mean your, Bible, and try praying my new rosary. I'm feeling a lot better. Can I help you prepare the meal this morning?"

Miriam gave her a warm hug and said, "Of course you can! I'll let you chop up the fruit at the dining room table so you can stay seated while you do it. I still think it's probably best if you stay off that knee."

"I'm not going to argue with you this time, Miriam!" Elizabeth said as she limped after Miriam into the dining room.

"Here, sit there and I'll bring you what you need," she said, indicating the same spot at the end of the table where she had sat last night. Elizabeth sat down, and Miriam brought her a mug of steaming tea, and several oranges, bananas, strawberries, a knife, and a large bowl to put the cut fruit in. "How are you this morning, Lisbet?" Elizabeth knew Miriam was asking about her entire being, not just her physical body.

"I'm well. I'm sort of amazed by what happened last night. What *was* that?" she asked, beginning to peel oranges and put sections in the bowl. Miriam chuckled.

"Lisbet, that was the Holy Spirit. That's what happens sometimes when God's followers pray for Him to work and release His Spirit, and then actually step back and let Him do it. It was beautiful, wasn't it?"

"Yes. Normally that kind of the thing would scare me, but that was incredible. I was thankful I got to witness it." She fingered the rosary around her wrist. "Miriam, did you get to talk to Hélène much?"

Miriam, realizing Elizabeth knew about Hélène's illness, walked into the dining room where she could see Elizabeth's face. "Yes, I did."

"Then you know."

"Yes, I know. I know she is going home soon."

Elizabeth looked up, eyes filled with tears. "Miriam, my mom died of cancer when I was sixteen. It's the hardest thing I've ever gone through, watching her suffer like that. I don't want that for Hélène too."

"Liebchen, let me ask you something," said Miriam, laying her hand over Elizabeth's that was holding the knife, stopping her chopping. "Did your mother know Jesus?"

"Yes, and she tried to tell me about Him, but I didn't want to hear it. All I could see was her suffering. I was too selfish to realize how much she wanted to--what was it Hélène said—"go home." I just wanted her to stay with Dad and me. She was everything to me. My dad was not around much. That hasn't changed. So when Mom died, something in me died too. I think if I could label it, I'd say it was my hope. My hope that there was good in the world. That God was good. Yesterday was the first time I realized how wrong I've been. But, still. That precious, beautiful woman, Hélène. It makes me sick to think of beautiful people like her suffering."

"Elizabeth, I want you to listen to me very carefully," said Miriam. "Do you think it's possible that part of why Hélène is beautiful is precisely because of her suffering? That God's presence in her during her illness is a testament to His power and His love for her?" Elizabeth looked down at the table thoughtfully as Miriam reached for the Bible Elizabeth had absentmindedly carried into the dining room with her. She opened it to the end and began reading, "And I heard a loud voice from the throne saying, 'Behold, the dwelling place of God is with man. He will dwell with them, and they will be His people, and God Himself will be with them as their God. He will wipe away every tear from their eyes, and death shall be no more, neither shall there be mourning, nor crying, nor pain anymore. For the former things have passed away.' And he who was seated at the throne said, 'Behold, I am making all things new.'"

Elizabeth shut her eyes as Miriam read, then opened them when she fell silent. "That sounds familiar. I think the priest may have read that at mom's funeral."

"Elizabeth, you are one of God's people now. Your mother was one of God's people. Hélène is one of God's people. Yes, we still deal with death because of the broken world we live in, but it's only temporary. Does that mean we shouldn't grieve the brokenness? Of course not! Jesus himself wept at his friend Lazarus' graveside. But it's not the end of the story." She squeezed Elizabeth's hands and handed her the knife to continue chopping. Elizabeth sniffed loudly, sipped her tea, and started chopping again.

The women worked in companionable silence for several minutes, then Miriam spoke from the kitchen. "Father Bill is coming today." Miriam heard the knife clatter to the floor and a low moan escape from Elizabeth's lips.

Miriam rushed in to check on her, "What's wrong Lisbet?"

"I have so much to apologize to Father Bill for," she said, squeezing her eyes tight, and shaking her head in resignation of her need to ask forgiveness.

"Oh my goodness, child, don't even start," Miriam said sternly. "Are you glad you asked my forgiveness?" Elizabeth nodded meekly. "Has God worked to heal you as you've realized the consequences of your behavior, and have you started on a new path?" Elizabeth nodded again, feeling very much like a little girl. "Well, then. Jesus doesn't wait until his future return to make all things new. He starts the process here and now. And this is one of the ways he's making you new. Don't go to that place of shame and embarrassment. That's not who you are anymore."

Elizabeth held her hands up in mock surrender. "Okay, okay, Miriam.   won't, I promise!" Both women were giggling when Father Bill came in, Paddy at his side.

"And what is so funny, you two?" he said in his cheerful Irish accent, blue eyes twinkling, hands on his hips. "Well, I must say, you're looking and smelling much better than the last time I saw you, Miss Elizabeth!" Bill said, looking at her with twinkling eyes.

Elizabeth laughed as she watched Paddy and Tiggy bound out through the kitchen door together, and Bill waved his hand in their direction, saying, "Ah, let 'em be. Poor Paddy has been mopey since we went back to Burgos and he's been without his friends. Poor old beast. So!" Bill clapped his hands together and rubbed them in anticipation. "I've been up since 4am and I'm ready to help with breakfast. What can I do, Miriam? And do you have any coffee ready?"

"Do you need anymore coffee, Bill?" said Miriam suspiciously. "It seems like you've had quite a few cups already this morning, but I'm happy to get you some."

Bill bounded into the kitchen and boomed, "Don't be silly, Miriam! I'll get it myself!" Elizabeth and Miriam glanced at each other, shaking with silent laughter.

Bill kept up a steady stream of enthusiastic conversation

with both women as he marched from dining room to kitchen, setting out plates, food, and cutlery. As sleepy pilgrims made their way downstairs, Bill greeted them, "Top o' the morning to ya!" and directed them to their breakfasts. Miriam walked around the table, refilling coffee mugs, giving a word of encouragement, checking on injuries and blisters. As the pilgrims finished their breakfasts one by one and shouldered their packs to leave, Bill walked them out to give a blessing, made the sign of the cross over them, and waved his encouragement.

Hélène lingered longer than the others, having arranged ahead of time with Miriam that she would be meeting her son and daughter-in-law later in the day. She gave Elizabeth a warm hug, then walked out into the garden arm-in-arm with Miriam, speaking to her softly in French.

Father Bill sat down next to Elizabeth and said, "So, Elizabeth, what's been happening since I've left you? I'm happy to see you looking so well!" Elizabeth swallowed hard, then met Bill's kind eyes.

"Bill," she began haltingly. "I want to ask your forgiveness. You tried so hard to help me, and I was so stubborn, I didn't listen to your advice, even when it was clear you were right. Thank you so much for bringing me to Miriam's. I don't know what would have happened to me if it weren't for you and Andrés helping me. Will you forgive me?"

Bill took Elizabeth's hands in both of his and squeezed them. "Elizabeth, I forgive you. Thank you for having the courage to apologize. I'm grateful to know you, and it's a privilege to help you and take part in what God is doing. I trust He will keep at it."

266

Elizabeth smiled broadly, and then said, "So I really want to be of help to Miriam. I know I can't walk anymore, and so I was thinking I would try to do whatever work I can for her while I'm here until I have to fly back home. Can you think of some things that would be helpful for her? Of course, I probably need to stay off my knee as much as possible, but surely there are still things I can do to help."

"Well, today Miriam and Andrés' father, Matteo, have to go into town and get supplies, so perhaps you could be here to check in the pilgrims. I'm sure Miriam would be happy to have someone do that while she's gone for a few hours. Also, there are probably things you could do out in the garden that would be helpful and not too taxing on your knee."

"Great, let's get started!"

Bill laughed at her enthusiasm. "Okay, well, let me finish my coffee, there's a good lass." He and Elizabeth continued to chat companionably while they finished their breakfast, then were startled by joyous barking. Bill stood up and looked out the window, smiling. "Ah, I thought I recognized that bark. Looks like Andrés and Rex have arrived. That means I probably need to leave now to check on Matteo."

"That's strange; I thought Andrés wasn't coming until this afternoon. At least, that's what I thought he said last night. Besides, now that I'm up and about, Miriam will be more free for her usual routines." The corner of Bill's mouth twitched, and he glanced down at Elizabeth where she was still sitting, then out the window again.

"Well, I'm sure Andrés has a good reason for being here," he said as he strode out to greet the younger man. Elizabeth watched the two men hug, then smiled as Bill clapped Andrés on the back in a fatherly gesture. It was a new thing for Elizabeth to see friends love each other so freely, and she wondered how she had lived so much of her life without that kind of community and friendship. *God, I have to make time for this when I get home. Where IS home? I hope it's still DC.* She glanced out the window at Andrés again, wondering what he and Bill were talking about in such animated fashion. They walked towards the house, and Elizabeth absent-mindedly combed through her hair with her fingers, and then laughed at herself. *He's seen me looking a lot worse than this. Things can only get better, right?* Andrés walked into the dining room and Bill waved his goodbye.

"I'm going to go check in with Matteo, Elizabeth. It was so good to see you. I'll stop by again tomorrow on my way back to Burgos."

"Bye, Bill! It was great to see you! Thank you so much for everything!" Bill jogged over to Elizabeth, gave her a quick kiss on the forehead, and ran back out, whistling for Paddy.

"Good morning, Elizabeth," said Andrés as he walked into the room and took a seat next to her.

"Hi Andrés! I almost didn't recognize you without the apron," she winked.

"Don't worry, I'm sure I'll put it on again soon enough."

"Did you rest well?" she said, thinking as she looked at

Andrés' shining eyes and pink cheeks that he certainly looked well.

"Yes, yes, thank you for asking. What about you?"

"Well, I woke up pretty early. I was still thinking about last night. I've never experienced anything like that! And then I practiced praying the rosary that Hélène gave me." She unwound the plain rosary from around her wrist and handed it to Andrés, telling him the story from last night as she did so. Andrés grew somber and fingered the beads, closing his eyes for a moment. "Hélène is a beautiful person," he said finally.

"Yes, she is. Like Miriam. Like Father Bill. Like…" Elizabeth's cheeks reddened and she looked away as Andrés glanced quickly up. They both laughed nervously, then Elizabeth changed topic, "So I was talking to Father Bill about things I could do to help around here. I think it's pretty obvious that I'm not supposed to keep walking on this knee, but Miriam invited me to stay here until it's time for me to fly back to DC, so I want to help in any way I can. I'm still on a pilgrimage, but it looks a lot different from what I expected."

"That's okay," said Andrés. "Having grown up around many, many pilgrims, I can tell you the real pilgrimage often starts when the physical one is over. So you're in good company."

"Bill mentioned Miriam has to go into town with your Dad today, so maybe you can show me how to register pilgrims when they arrive, and also what I can do in the garden."

"Sure, I'd be happy to!" said Andrés enthusiastically, standing up so suddenly that he bumped his knee hard on the table and doubled over in pain.

"Andrés! Are you okay?" said Elizabeth, reaching out to him, trying not to laugh at his clumsiness. Andrés winced in pain, but smiled through clenched teeth.

"Well, soon we'll have twin injuries if I keep this up, right?" As Andrés rubbed his sore knee, Miriam and Hélène walked back in from the garden and smiled to see the pair sitting at the table together.

"Andrés, you're early. How nice to see you! I assume Father Bill already left to go help Matteo? Hélène's family will be here soon to meet her, so she's going to pack her things while I work upstairs. Do you need some ice for that knee?"

"No, no, I'm fine," said Andrés with a wave of his hand. "I was going to take Elizabeth out to the garden and show her what needs to be done, then I thought the two of us could check in tonight's pilgrims while you and Papá drive into town."

"Yes, I think it would be *very* good for you and Elizabeth to do all those activities together today." She and Hélène conspicuously exchanged glances and headed for the stairs.

Elizabeth looked over at Andrés and said, "Well, do you think you can walk out to the garden with me, or do we need to get you some crutches?"

"No, I'll try to pay attention to what I'm doing this time.

Let's go while it's still cool outside." He and Elizabeth walked down the hallway, laughing at their matching limps. As Andrés opened the door for Elizabeth and indicated for her to walk ahead of him into the garden, she inhaled the clean, sweet-smelling air and smiled at the hummingbirds flitting busily in and out of the flowers. "Gosh, this is something I miss about DC. Sometimes I go weeks without really getting outside and enjoying nature," she mused. "Although now that I'm unemployed, I guess I might have quite a bit of time to sit outside and ponder life." She laughed ruefully.

"Do you have any leads of where you might apply for something?" said Andrés. "If you'd rather not talk about it, that's okay," he said quickly.

"No, it's fine. I'm feeling much less stressed than I was yesterday, although I'm sure it'll hit me in a new way when I get home and I don't have my normal routine to go back to. I don't know. I'm kind of thinking I'll deal with it in a few weeks. Maybe that's irresponsible; I don't know."

"I don't think so. I think God has given you a unique opportunity to rest here. Besides, there's not much you can do about it until you get back anyway, right?" said Andrés.

A picture of John Cunningham's job offer from a few weeks before rose into Elizabeth's mind. *There's no way that position is still available. Besides, I just don't feel like opening my email right now and pursuing anything. I need to rest. I haven't rested in…well, it's been awhile.* "Yes, exactly. I actually had a random job offer before I left for Spain from a former associate of my father's, John Cunningham." Elizabeth filled Andrés in on the details of the job offer, and he listened with interest.

"What most appeals to you about this job?"

"When I first got the email, I dismissed it because I was still working for Bruce and hoped I would make partner in the next few years. But, honestly, I've always wanted to do this kind of work. There are so many people who need help getting out of domestic violence situations, and because legal representation is so expensive, they're often trapped. This is actually why I went to law school." Elizabeth smacked her forehead with her hand and said, suddenly panicked, "Andrés, what was I thinking? Why in the world didn't I take that job? That was so stupid!"

Andrés chuckled. "It'll be okay, Elizabeth. Let's do our work in the garden, and then if there's time, we can do some emailing."

"Well, my remote internet thing is broken, so I can't do it."

"My Papá and I have wireless internet at our place, so if you'd like, we can try to find a time to go over to our farm. We might have to wait until tomorrow, though, since Papá and Miriam are using our truck to go to the market today."

"I'm sure one more day won't make a difference at this point, since I already said no," said Elizabeth ruefully. "So, tell me about Georgetown. How did you get that job? How did you end up in DC?"

She and Andrés talked easily as they weeded the vegetables, and Elizabeth was impressed with how comfortably he spoke English, with only a slight Spanish accent. When she remarked on this, Andrés said, "My Papá has relatively good English, but he was convinced it was important for me to be even more proficient. As the unemployment has risen for people of our generation here in Spain, I'm very grateful he insisted I take every opportunity to practice, and growing up on the Camino gave me lots of opportunities. My English and university degrees allowed me to get a job in the United States, even though my heart is still here in Spain in many ways. I'm grateful my teaching position still allows me to be here in the summers and write. In many ways, it's the best of both worlds, and I'm very thankful."

Elizabeth continued to ask questions about Andrés' field of study in economics, and enjoyed his obvious passion for the subject. "So you must be really good at languages. How many do you speak?" Elizabeth asked.

"I speak Spanish and English, and also French, Italian, and Portuguese. Except for English, though, the others are so closely related, being Romance languages, that it's fairly easy to pick them up once you know one well."

"Okay, so you *only* speak five languages. Not Mandarin or Japanese? I'm so disappointed, Andrés!" Elizabeth teased.

"Actually, I've been thinking I should learn Korean because there are so many Koreans walking the Camino now, but I haven't found time. Maybe next summer," Andrés said with a chuckle.

"I'm impressed. I used to do okay with French, but it was not my experience that learning French helped me magically learn four other languages like you're talking about. You must be really gifted in that area," said

Elizabeth.

Andrés inclined his head modestly. "It is an area I've always enjoyed studying. I guess my brain just works that way." He stood up and stretched, gingerly massaging his knee. "I'm going to get the sprinkler so we can do some watering. It's been a dry summer, even for this region." He returned with the hose, and he and Elizabeth took turns watering different sections of the garden. Elizabeth was amazed at the variety of plants and herbs Miriam grew. Andrés tuned out to be an encyclopedia of plants, and she enjoyed quizzing him about the different medicinal herbs and their uses. She learned that Miriam grew echinacea, arnica, aloe, chamomile, witch hazel, St. John's Wort, and many more.

"So in addition to being a linguist and an economist, you're also a botanist?" she said, nudging him with her elbow.

"No, but I grew up on a farm," laughed Andrés. "I've actually learned a lot about medicinal herbs and oils from Miriam. We mainly grow fruits and vegetables on our farm, but when Miriam moved here eight years ago, I started learning from her. I witnessed how Miriam made teas for various illnesses and poultices for blisters from the plants in her garden, and thought it was fascinating. She often sells or trades her tea blends for supplies, and has developed quite a reputation for her expertise. She uses the funds she earns to help support her *albergue*."

"Yes, that tea she gave me when I was so sick was so soothing. Something I'm learning from being here is that there's much more to people than meets the eye. All of you have so many layers! Next thing you know, you're

274

going to tell me Father Bill is a concert violinist," said Elizabeth.

"Wait, how did you know?" said Andrés, but Elizabeth knew by his tone that he was joking. "Actually, I HAVE known Bill to get out his violin, but he's more of a fiddler. I wonder if he has it with him or if he left it in Burgos? We should ask him to play for us. It's impossible not to dance when he gets that instrument tuned up!"

Elizabeth shook her head and looked at her knee. "I'm a terrible dancer, Andrés! Besides, my knee is injured, remember?"

"Yes, yes, I remember. We'll see what happens when Bill gets out the fiddle. I don't think you'll be able to sit still!" Andrés turned off the hose, then looked over the garden. "Okay, I think things are under control out here. Shall we go in? I can show you the main desk where you check in pilgrims."

He and Elizabeth walked back into the house, wiping their muddy shoes carefully on the bristly mat in front of the door. When they walked into the dining room, they met Hélène, Miriam, and a middle-aged couple who had to be Hélène's son and daughter-in-law, all chattering in animated French. Enthusiastic introductions were made all around, and Andrés translated the conversation for Elizabeth so she wouldn't feel left out.

"Thanks, my French from college is *way* too rusty for me to follow this!" she said during a pause. Elizabeth detected anxiety in the countenances of Hélène's children, and prayed silently that God would comfort them and put them at ease. Miriam gestured for everyone to sit, and they joined hands to pray. Andrés stopped translating as they prayed, but Elizabeth was happy to bask in the warmth of the Holy Spirit. Elizabeth squeezed the hand of Hélène's son as he started weeping quietly, and Andrés left the room to fetch him a box of tissues. When he returned, everyone in the circle was laughing and weeping simultaneously, and there was a cacophony of nose blowing and more laughter. As the pilgrims shouldered their packs, Miriam, Andrés, and Elizabeth walked them to the end of the driveway, unwilling to part. Elizabeth felt a pang watching the beautiful, brave Frenchwoman walk away. *But I will see you again. In just a little while.* Hélène turned and waved one last time, and Elizabeth waved back, shouting *"Merci,"* and pointing to the rosary. Hélène nodded and laughed, turned her face westward toward Santiago, joined hands with her family, and walked on.

The three friends stood watching them until they moved around a curve out of sight, then realized they were all still crying. "At moments like these, I can't imagine what I would do without Jesus," said Miriam in a choked voice, and Andrés and Elizabeth nodded in agreement. The three turned, linked arms, and walked slowly back into the house.

31

THE PAST IS PAST

Miriam took out the guest ledger and her *albergue*'s rubber stamp, made sure Andrés and Elizabeth were comfortable with the procedure for checking in pilgrims, and went to make a list of provisions she needed from the markets, humming as she left the room. Elizabeth said, "Andrés, don't you need to go back to your place and help since your dad is coming to pick Miriam up to go to Burgos?"

"No, Father Bill has things under control; I'm sure of it." Just then, Matteo drove up in his ancient pick-up truck, honking the horn happily. He jumped out and received Rex and Tiggy's enthusiastic greeting, then came into the house. Elizabeth was immediately struck by Andrés' resemblance to his father. Although Matteo was taller than Andrés, and had green eyes rather than brown, they had the same smile and facial features, and, on a deeper level, the same gentle spirit.

"You must be Elizabeth! You are feeling better?" said Matteo in his heavily accented English. "Andrés and Bill were very worried about you."

"Yes, I feel so much better, thank you for asking And thank you for sparing Andrés to help Miriam. I don't know what we would have done without him."

"Yes, he is a good boy, isn't he?" ruffling Andrés' hair fondly and smiling.

Andrés laughed modestly and said, "Are you and Miriam taking the dogs?"

"I think yes. They always like a ride in the truck, so we should let them come." Miriam came into the kitchen and greeted Matteo warmly, kissing him on the cheek, then turned to Andrés and Elizabeth.

"Now you two stay out of trouble while we're gone. If you have any questions you can call Matteo on his mobile phone. We'll be back in a few hours." They hopped into the truck with dogs and waved as they pulled out of the driveway, a cloud of dust puffing behind them.

"Why do I feel like a teenager again?" said Andrés with a grin, sitting down at the table and resting his chin in his hands. Elizabeth thought of her own teenage years and forced a laugh, wishing she'd been able to worry about dating instead of her mother's cancer. Andrés noticed the shadow pass over her face, and said quickly, "What's wrong? Are you okay?"

"Yes, I'm fine, it's nothing," said Elizabeth sitting up straighter and making her face a mask.

"How about I make us some lunch?" said Andrés, deciding not to probe. "I think there are leftovers from last night, and Miriam usually keeps bread, cheese and fruit depending on what you think your stomach can handle."

"I think I'd be fine with leftovers. Last night's dinner was delicious, and it seemed to agree with me."

"Yes, your color has improved since you've been able to eat again. You're looking very well," said Andrés, poking his head around the kitchen door and making Elizabeth blush.

As Andrés sang to himself and prepared lunch in the kitchen, Elizabeth tried to shake the melancholy that always came when she thought of her teenage years. She closed her eyes and prayed silently. *Lord, please heal me of these memories. I feel like so much was wasted in my past, but I know you don't want me to be ashamed. Please help me see things the your way.*

Andrés walked back out of the kitchen wearing the flowered apron and carrying two plates. Elizabeth smiled, and Andrés said, "I wore it just for you."

"Thanks, it looks great on you," said Elizabeth as she took the plate from him. He smirked at her and removed the apron, then sat and held his hand out.

"Shall we pray?"

She placed her hand in his and said, "Yes, I'd love to."

"Why don't you pray for us?" said Andrés.

Elizabeth, suddenly shy, said, "God…thanks for this food. Thanks that I can *eat* this food. Thank you for Andrés, Miriam, Matteo, and Father Bill. Please protect Hélène and her children as they walk today. Okay, amen." Andrés didn't immediately release her hand when she finished, but looked at her for a few seconds until her cheeks warmed under his perusal and she pulled her hand away to start eating.

"So what did you think? Does that prayer work? I'm not a professional pray-er like you guys!"

Andrés laughed as he cut up his chicken. "God's not rating our prayers on their eloquence, fortunately! I think it's like any other friendship or relationship. You just talk to him about what's on your heart. You ask Him to guide you, to show you what to pray for, agree with Him in the work He's doing, and tell him how you're feeling. It gets easier with practice." He took a big mouthful of chicken and Elizabeth was quiet for a second, then asked the question that had been on her heart since she'd met Andrés.

"Andrés, what happened to your mom?" Andrés took a few seconds to swallow his mouthful and was silent, but he was neither embarrassed nor did he seem uncomfortable with her question. "She left my dad and me when I was a little boy, and moved to León where her family was from. I only saw her occasionally. She said she didn't like farm life, but that didn't change the hurt. Eventually she filed for divorce from my dad, and he signed the papers, but never stopped loving her." He took another bite and chewed it thoughtfully. "She died three years ago. Even though she wasn't the kind of mother I wish I'd had, my dad and I were both deeply affected by her death. I think while she was living I always hoped somehow God would change her heart and she would come back to us. But that didn't happen. And now she's dead," Andrés said, brushing away a few tears, but speaking without bitterness.

Elizabeth sat frozen, her lunch completely forgotten as Andrés spoke. "Andrés, were you ever angry? Angry at your dad? Angry at God?" she whispered.

Andrés nodded. "Yes, I was. I was angry with my dad for being a farmer. For a long time I felt like it was his fault my mom left. It didn't help that when I did see her, she used to make comments that reinforced my anger. But the older I got, and the closer I got to my dad, I saw my mom had made her own choices, and that she was wrong about my Papá. Then, when I asked Jesus into my heart, He helped me see who my parents really were; that they, too, were broken people in need of His grace. That really helped me heal. It didn't take away the abandonment I felt by my mom, but I was able to forgive her, even though she hadn't asked me to. I don't know why our relationship wasn't restored before she died. I wish it had been. God gives us all the ability to make our own choices, though. She chose not to come back to my Papá and me, even though we asked her to many times, and we prayed for it many times. God doesn't force us into anything, though. We have to accept His invitation."

Elizabeth thought for a few more minutes, then, feeling a nudge in her spirit, decided to be honest with Andrés. "My mom died when I was 16, and she was my world. My dad was never home; he worked so much I barely saw him except on the weekends and late at night if I happened to still be awake when he got home. My mom was incredible. She poured so much love, grace, and kindness into me. But even though she modeled Jesus for me on a daily basis, I still hardened myself to Him, especially when she got sick. I couldn't understand how God could let someone so kind and good suffer. It didn't help that my dad kept saying things like, 'Your mom will be fine. We just have to keep living our lives as usual. We need you to keep a stiff upper lip, Elizabeth.' So I never got to talk to anyone about the fear and doubt I had. Then my mom," Elizabeth's voice broke, but she cleared her throat and kept speaking. "She tried to say good bye to me, but I wouldn't let her. I told her she would be fine, and refused to listen to the last thing she wanted to tell me. I'll never know what that was now because of my stubbornness. She died the next morning while I was out of town, and when I got back, I had to hold everything together. We had the funeral that Wednesday, and then it was back to work for my dad and school for me, like nothing had happened. Like my whole world hadn't just been shattered. My dad has never talked about any of this with me. You'd think it hadn't even happened. When I walked up the Hill of Forgiveness last week, God walked with me. He even asked me to forgive Him and let go of my anger at Him over this. I also forgave my dad, and myself. It was powerful. But I still feel sadness about the whole thing."

Elizabeth looked up from where she had been tracing the grain of the wooden table with her index finger and was surprised to see Andrés' eyes filled with tears again. He grasped her hand, quieting her fingers, and said, "I'm so sorry about your mother, Elizabeth. So sorry." Before she could stop herself, Elizabeth reached out and brushed a tear from Andrés' cheek. He held her hand to his cheek for a moment, then released it.

"Something that has been healing for me is to go back through all the difficult memories I have and ask Jesus to show me where He was in the moment of each one. He almost always gives me a picture of himself, sometimes in unexpected ways. I remember the night my mom left. I was only eight. She had called her sister to come pick her up, and I was so excited to see my Tia Josefina. But when she arrived, she didn't even come into the house to say hello. She honked the horn, and my mom ran out with her suitcase. I ran outside to try to say goodbye, but they had already left. My mama didn't even say goodbye to me; she was so eager to leave. I was crushed. And then I went into the house, and my dad was sitting in his favorite chair, weeping, weeping as if someone had died, which, in a way, she had. I had never seen him emotionally upset like that before. I was so scared and confused. When you're a little child, you think your parents are perfect, and that nothing can go wrong with them, you know? So I didn't know what to do with all of this. I remember going back into my bedroom and standing there like I was dreaming.

"Then I heard a scratch at the door. It was our dog, *Esperanza*. We called her Espie for short. She came into my room and nudged my hand with her nose, almost as if to say, 'It's okay to cry. Don't worry.' And right there, I sank down onto the floor next to her and cried for what seemed like hours. She lay down next to me and let me use her as a pillow while I sobbed, licking the tears off my face. From that moment on, she never left my side unless she absolutely had to. She used to walk me to school, sit outside the classroom window and wait, and then walk me home. For a long time after my mother left, I had nightmares, and Espie was always there to comfort and calm me. So later when I was praying for healing, one of the pictures God gave me was of that dog, reminding me of the comfort He provided through her. By the way, the name Esperanza means 'hope.' "

Elizabeth looked into Andrés' eyes through a haze of tears. "Thank you for telling me that, Andrés." She paused for a few moments and wiped her tears away. "I'm excited to pray in this way. And I'm also excited to get a dog when I get back to DC." Andrés laughed, and Elizabeth smiled, "I'm serious! I'm going to start praying that God sends me just the right one. If I haven't learned anything else on this trip, I've learned that dogs are essential! But I've learned lots of other things too, of course," Elizabeth added hastily.

"Oh, he will send you the right animal. God knows we need animals!"

"I'm not sure my cat will agree, but he'll get over it!" said Elizabeth with a smile. She put another forkful of chicken into her mouth, and Andrés did the same.

"This chicken is cold! Allow me, Madame," he said with an exaggerated French accent, donning his apron and taking her plate back to the kitchen to microwave it.

"You're too good to me, sir!" called Elizabeth into the kitchen.

"So, Elizabeth. If you get a dog, can I come visit it when we get back to DC? And..." his voice trailed off for a moment, then strengthened. "I'd really like to visit you too. Would that be okay?"

"I'd like that very much, Andrés." Andrés started humming in the kitchen again, then reappeared with their reheated lunch.

He raised his water glass to her and said, "To DC! And to

the King of Kings!" Elizabeth laughed as she clinked her glass with his.

32

KINGDOM COME

Matteo and Miriam bumped along in the old Citroën towards Burgos, chatting amicably in Spanish. "What do you think of my son and Elizabeth?" he said with a sideways glance towards Miriam.

Miriam chuckled. "Well, I've tried not to make Andrés too self-conscious, but I can't help laughing at him sometimes. He keeps walking into things and blushing. He's still himself, but seems a little bit undone. It's very amusing to watch him."

"Yes, I've been praying for him," said Matteo. "I want him to meet a nice woman and have a family. He will be a wonderful husband and father. That woman he met at Georgetown a few years back broke his heart, and I was afraid he'd never get over her, so I'm thankful to see this side of him again."

"Yes, and I sense Elizabeth, too, has been hurt in this area of her life. This is the kind of thing that makes me so anxious, even though I know if God wants two people together, nothing either one of them does can mess it up. Funny, that out of all the things I could be thinking about, this is the one most on my heart to pray for."

"Let's pray now, Miriam, for I feel the same way." They spent the rest of the trip to Burgos praying for Andrés and Elizabeth, then for the pilgrims God would send their way that evening, those that had departed earlier in the day, and everyone they would interact with in the city. As they approached the city, the tallest spire of the huge cathedral came into view, and Miriam was struck, as always, by its beauty. Matteo navigated the busy streets with ease, and they arrived at the wholesaler promptly. After they bought their paper and dry goods, they went to the farmer's market for a few supplies.

"Something keeps eating my tomatoes," said Miriam ruefully. "So I need to buy some fresh here."

"Oh, you're welcome to some of mine, Miriam. We have more than enough at our place," said Matteo.

"Okay, well only if you take some of my herbal tea digestive as a trade!" she said with an air of mock bossiness.

"Yes, I promise!" said Matteo with a low chuckle.

"Also, Anneke and Anders are coming to visit tomorrow, and I want to get something special for them. Even though I was a strict mama with them when they were growing up, now I like to spoil them as much as possible!"

"Oh, how wonderful, Miriam! How is Anders' job at the University in Delft? Are he and Johanna adjusting to married life? Is Anneke enjoying being a mamá? How old is little Lars now? Will Anneke's husband be able to get away from the hospital to visit?"

Miriam laughed at the barrage of questions. "I'll tell you what, Matteo. How about you join us for lunch tomorrow and you can ask all these questions yourself?"

"Okay, I'll be there! Thank you for the invitation!"

"Now I need to decide what to serve them," said Miriam, tapping her chin with her index finger.

"You can always get *pulpo*, Miriam," said Matteo, laughing and indicating the huge vat of simmering octopus being served fresh to eager shoppers pausing for a quick lunch at the market.

Miriam shook her head and grimaced, "You Spaniards and your pulpo! This Dutchwoman will *never* get used to it! I was thinking more along the lines of a special dessert, but thank you *very* much for your idea, Matteo! Let's see…something chocolate," she said as she and Matteo walked past a pastry case. "Ah, here we are. Much better than pulpo!" She selected a chocolate mousse torte and the smiling woman behind the counter wrapped it and handed it over the case to Miriam. "See, Matteo? Much better than pulpo."

Matteo laughed, and they divided the rest of the list to finish their shopping more quickly. They met back at the entrance to the market with their bulging shopping bags and hurried back to the little truck where the dogs were waiting patiently in the back. They loaded their purchases and jumped in. Matteo popped the clutch and put the truck in gear. He patted the dashboard affectionately and said, "I love my little truck. I can't believe she's lasted for 20 years."

"Yes, she's a classic for sure, and I am very thankful," said Miriam. When they got back to Miriam's house, there were a few pilgrims already resting in the shade of the trees out front, their packs lined up by the front door in the order of their arrival. They waved happily as Miriam unloaded her parcels and Tiggy jumped out of the back. Matteo honked as he backed out of the driveway.

Miriam greeted the pilgrims warmly and headed into the house, knowing the pilgrims would be content to wait until the mid-afternoon check-in time. She walked into the dining room to find Elizabeth and Andrés deep in conversation, their plates still full of food. Neither of them noticed her arrival until Tiggy ran over and gave them both several snuffly kisses.

"Tiggy!" Miriam said in frustration. "I'm so sorry to intrude, children!"

"Miriam, that's okay," said Andrés, jumping up and taking Miriam's bags. "Let me help you!" They both swept into the kitchen past Elizabeth, and Tiggy looked up at Elizabeth sorrowfully, clearly ashamed because of Miriam's sharp correction.

"It's okay, Tiggy. You were just being a dog, weren't you?" Tiggy thumped her tail slightly and leaned her head against Elizabeth's knee with contrition. Elizabeth laughed. She'd never heard Miriam correct Tiggy that way before.

"Tiggy, I think there might be some scheming going on around here. What do you think?" Tiggy thumped her tail harder, then stood and wagged her whole body when Miriam came back into the dining room, anxious to be forgiven. Miriam took Tiggy's head in her hands and murmured in soft Dutch, and Tiggy trotted after her into the garden.

Andrés came back into the dining room from putting away the food, and he and Elizabeth started laughing. "We have so many helpers, don't we Elizabeth? Maybe we should finish our lunch before we have to start checking pilgrims in." Elizabeth laughed, and they quickly ate, then cleared their places. After checking that everything was in order in the kitchen, Andrés went outside to welcome the pilgrims and let them know it was check-in time. Elizabeth sat behind the desk in the front hallway, recorded their information and stamped their *credenciáles*. Andrés led them upstairs, showed them the bathroom, bunkroom, and foot soak station. He quickly placed Elizabeth's pack on the bottom bunk closest to the door, not wanting her to have to climb up top with her bad knee.

Within thirty minutes, all 10 beds had been claimed, and Andrés hung the "completo" sign on the front door of the house, thinking with a pang of how many footsore pilgrims would be forced to journey another five kilometers back to his own farm to find an available bed. Elizabeth hobbled among the pilgrims, introducing herself, asking them if they needed anything, and handing them small packets of Miriam's herbal footbath, to be combined with cool water to soothe their sore feet. Miriam came back from the garden and led three of their guests outside to check their blisters and show them how to soak their feet, then took a group of volunteers into the kitchen for dinner

291

preparations. As Elizabeth walked among the pilgrims, she was grateful to share in the sense of community, and silently thanked God for the way her trip had gone, realizing it was exactly the one she needed. She had heard somewhere that everyone's time on the Camino looks different, and now she saw the truth of the statement. As she looked at the diverse gathering of people before her, she saw a common bond forged in blisters, sore muscles, and the rhythm of day-to-day life on this unique journey. She realized, *I belong here. I am one of them. Even though I didn't understand what it really meant to be a pilgrim while I was actually walking, now, thanks to Miriam, Father Bill, Andrés, and Matteo, I do. And You, God. You led me here. You used even my mistakes for my healing and my good. Help me end this part of my journey well. Bless others through me, Lord.*

She glanced out the window from where she was setting out cutlery, plates, and napkins and saw a woman pushing what appeared to be a heavy-duty child's stroller. Elizabeth knew by the crushed look on the young woman's face that she had just seen the bright orange sign saying they were full for the night. She caught Andrés' eye and they both walked out the front door. The woman had already turned to continue walking down the path, but they could hear her loud sniffling despite the distance. "Wait," said Andrés, jogging over to her. When she turned, Elizabeth realized she had a sleeping child with her in the stroller and her heart went out to the woman, who looked to be in her late twenties.

"Andrés," Elizabeth said quickly. "Please give her my bed. I'll ask Miriam to set up the cot in the hallway downstairs for me. This woman can't possibly walk any further today." She walked as fast as her sore knee would allow to find Miriam and explain the situation, and the *hospitalera*

292

walked with Elizabeth to the driveway.

Andrés was already walking to the front door with the woman and her child, the former looking extremely relieved and thanking Andrés profusely for lifting her pack from her shoulders to carry inside. Miriam took charge of the stroller and let the young woman lift her boy out to toddle to the entrance. Elizabeth was reminded of the young boy on her flight to Paris, Guillaume. Indeed, as the boy looked curiously up at Miriam, who smiled down at him, Elizabeth noticed that he was clutching a tiny car in his free hand. *I think every little boy loves a toy car,* she thought.

A few moments after the three disappeared in the entrance, Elizabeth and Andrés heard delighted laughter from the child, and a welcoming bark from Tiggy, followed by offers of help and encouragement from the older pilgrims who were inside, shifting kitchen duties to lend the young mother a hand. Elizabeth looked over at Andrés, who was staring at her with a soft expression. She smiled and blushed, "It sounds like Tiggy just made a new best friend." The two of them laughed for a moment before another sound, not from the house, met their ears.

Raucous singing and laughter were coming from a group of pilgrims walking up the road. Elizabeth saw three men, each with a woman hanging on his arm. All of them appeared to be nearing intoxication, and sure enough a closer look revealed bottles in the hands of each of the men. Their voices sounded somewhat familiar, and as they came nearer, one of the men was in fact *very* familiar.

Elizabeth had a sinking feeling in her stomach and wished she could disappear, or that Andrés would at least go inside so he wouldn't see her shame, but despite her shock and a sudden wave of nausea coming over her she couldn't help but exclaim in surprise, "MARCO!"

Sure enough, Marco looked away from the woman leaning against him to see who had called to him and after a moment of concentration a look of exaggerated surprise came over his face. For a moment Elizabeth thought she could see a bit of shame as well, but it passed quickly as he released his hold on the woman next to him to raise both hands into the air. "Elisa! Good to see you on your feet again! You are making good time."

He handed the bottle he had been carrying to Nico, who stood several feet away looking sheepish. The three women looked confused, especially the one Marco left to walk toward Elizabeth, arms extended for a hug. Elizabeth backed away several steps and his smile faded. "What, what's wrong, *chica*?" he asked with a false tone of deepest hurt. "It's been a long time since we've seen each other, we *peregrinos* should act like family!"

Hot anger now replaced her surprise, though she still felt nauseated and ashamed. She stared at him in disbelief and at a loss for words. Her mouth hung open for a moment before she could respond in a thick, trembling voice, "How, how can you even *ask* that? You left me all by myself with a hurt knee after you pushed me to my breaking point." She gestured toward her knee brace. Her cheeks were hot and tears began to spill from her eyes. She really wished Andrés would go inside. "You, you, you said you'd stay with me," she stammered.

Marco dropped the hurt look and his face became a mask. He glanced with bloodshot eyes over at Andrés, who had been listening to the conversation in silence, then said with a wicked smile, "Well, it looks like you've found a new man now. That didn't take very long. Maybe he'll be willing to settle for you."

At this point Andrés stepped between them so quickly it seemed as though he had been waiting to spring. "Marco," he said politely, extending his hand, "I help run this *albergue* and it's already full for the night. Elizabeth is our guest and you are making her uncomfortable, so I can't let you in, but if any of your companions need a place to rest we can make room on our porch for a nap." He looked past Marco to the rest of the group. Elizabeth noticed with a surge of anger that two of the women, including the one who had been attached to Marco, had bandages wrapped around their shins or knees and seemed unsteady on their feet even as they stood still.

Marco grimaced and drew up to his full height, a few inches taller and much more muscular than Andrés. "You think we want to stay here in this boring town? We go to Burgos, and we're going to have a good night!" Nico cheered and one of the women giggled, but Pablo and the other two women stayed silent, listening with longing to the voices of resting pilgrims drifting from the garden.

Marco then dropped his sneer and adopted a brotherly, confidential tone, though he spoke loudly enough to ensure Elizabeth heard every word. "Listen, be careful with this one, she may be beautiful but she turns as cold as ice the moment things don't go her way. Who knows how many men she's had and scared away as soon as they stop doing everything she wants? You'd better keep your distance while you can, take it from someone who knows." Here he raised his eyebrows meaningfully and looked for some reaction from Andrés.

295

Andrés turned to look at Elizabeth, who was now shaking with anger at Marco's words, his face determined, but not angry. Elizabeth saw his eyes narrow as he looked back at Marco and said, "Leave. Now. As I said before, I cannot let you in, but even though we are full, your friends are welcome to rest here."

Elizabeth held her breath, waiting for Marco to shout something or throw a punch, but he did neither. Instead, he looked down angrily at Andrés and said something in Spanish that made the rest of his group gasp, and even Andrés' shoulders tensed at the one word Elizabeth could make out clearly-- "*madre*." Pablo grabbed Marco's arm to draw him quickly back to the road, and the group walked away, Marco muttering in Spanish to the others.

It was a few seconds before Elizabeth could breathe again, but she continued to watch Andrés anxiously, fearing to know his feelings about her history with men. After a moment he sighed and turned back to her, his face sad but peaceful. "Let's go inside, Elizabeth."

"Andrés, I'm so, so, sorry," began Elizabeth in a whisper.

"I don't believe what he said about you," said Andrés without letting her finish. He looked at her, his expression hard to read. "I don't know how well he knows you, but I don't believe anything he said. You must understand that."

"I was stupid, Andrés, I was so stupid when I first started walking, but nothing happened," pleaded Elizabeth, tears forming in her eyes again.

Andrés stopped and looked her in the eye. "I believe you.

Really, I do," he said when she looked down and sighed. "I should get this pack inside, but you must know I really do believe you."

As Andrés carried the young mother's pack upstairs, Elizabeth searched for something to do. Finding nothing, she went outside, lost in thought, and sat heavily on a bench on the porch. With a jolt, she realized she was sitting right next to the young woman for whom she had given up her bed. She introduced herself. The woman, whose blister-covered feet were soaking in one of Miriam's tubs, answered in an accent that sounded vaguely like that of a former classmate who had been from Minnesota.

"My name is Marta, and I am from Sweden. This is my little boy, Gren." She indicated the blonde, chubby-cheeked little boy, who looked to be about three. Elizabeth managed a smile and waved, and was answered with a sweet smile, which widened when Tiggy came out from the house carrying one of her toys in her mouth, a stuffed duck. The collie dropped her duck to sniff Elizabeth and lick her knee a couple of times, then sat and looked at Gren expectantly.

"I think she wants to play with you, Gren," said Elizabeth, her smile now genuine. "It's okay," she assured Marta, who seemed a bit nervous at the prospect of her son leaving her side, "Tiggy is the best nanny you could hope for. If she could take care of me, she can take care of anyone!" Elizabeth gestured to her knee, covered by the brace, and laughed. Marta smiled and told Gren to go play. As soon as he leapt down from the bench, Tiggy snatched up her duck and ran out into the yard, followed by a laughing Gren. Soon all the pilgrims in the yard were giggling at the sight of the dog and little boy playing and running in circles.

Marta watched them with a loving smile and then turned to Elizabeth and said, "How did you find a place for us to sleep? I thought you were all full today."

"No need to worry, Marta. We had an extra cot we could set up, so there is an extra bed for you and Gren in the bunkroom now. Are you two traveling alone?"

Marta looked down sadly and nodded. "My brother was with us at the beginning, but I quickly realized we had to separate. He was more interested in meeting girls and partying than he was interested in walking and hearing God speak to him. It was very sad for me, because it wasn't the way I pictured my time on the Camino."

"I'm amazed that you've been able to push this stroller the whole way!" said Elizabeth. "Did you push that thing over the Pyrenees? I had a rough time on my own walk over the Pyrenees and I can hardly imagine how difficult it would have been if I'd been pushing that too!"

Marta nodded. "I've pushed it the whole way from Le Puy. My brother was with us until we got over the Pyrenees, so he helped me the first few days, but then we separated. It's okay, though. Sometimes Gren walks, and we take lots of breaks. Also, there have been a lot of kind *peregrinos* who have walked with us and have given me breaks from pushing. This trip has been healing for me. It's restored my belief that there are still kind, compassionate, and helpful people in the world."

Elizabeth thought ruefully of Marco and his group, but sensed a story behind the woman's words and asked,

"What prompted you to come on the Camino in the first place?"

"Gren's father, my ex-husband, left us about eighteen months ago. For a few months I was just trying to survive as a single mother. I was working full-time trying to pay our bills and find care for Gren. Fortunately, my family lives nearby in Stockholm, and my parents and sister have been very involved in helping. One of my friends from church walked the Camino and suggested it to me. I dismissed it when she first mentioned it, but she had planted a seed. Then I read something about a woman who walked the Camino with her child. I had some leave saved up at work, so I decided to bring Gren, and my brother volunteered to come along since he would be on a break from university. I realize now he didn't really want to help us, he just wanted to have an adventure. It still hurts. But like I said, God has provided people to help us. People like you, here at this *albergue*. My sister will be meeting me in a few days to walk the rest of the way to Santiago with us. She insisted on coming when she heard I was doing this alone. I tried to tell her I wasn't alone, but older sisters can be bossy!" Marta chuckled. "Oh, my feet feel so much better," she sighed as she wiggled her toes in the footbath. "Thank you for listening, Elizabeth."

"Of course, Marta." Elizabeth had a soft nudge in her heart. "Marta, may I pray for you?"

"I'd like that very much."

"Father, thank you for Marta. Thank you for strengthening her so far. We pray for healing for her feet, for her soul, for her heart and mind. Heal her relationship with her brother, too. We pray for Gren, that you would be his

Father and he would know you." Tears began to roll down Marta's cheek, and Elizabeth stroked her back as she continued to pray. "We thank you for this little boy, and we pray that you would continue to bring people into Marta's life to love her and show her compassion. We thank you that she has been able to walk so far, and we pray that you would give her the strength she needs to continue in whatever way you have for her. Thank you that you are powerful and able to do all things, Lord. We love you." As she opened her eyes, Elizabeth saw Miriam looking at her from the doorway, eyes twinkling with love and pride.

The older woman gave her a slight nod and said, "Who wants to help me in the kitchen?" Four of the pilgrims followed her into the house, leaving Marta, Gren, and Elizabeth alone with Tiggy. Gren walked over to his stroller, extracted a dingy-looking stuffed rabbit, and climbed into Marta's lap, where he popped his thumb into his mouth, and sighed contentedly. Marta kissed his forehead and stroked his hair.

"He's just beautiful," she whispered in Marta's ear. "I'm so glad you came today. It's a gift to have you both."

Marta sighed and leaned her head back against the post supporting her back. "Thank you. We're very glad to be here. Thank you for praying."

Andrés walked over and said, "Marta, I've put your things upstairs for you. If I may, I'll leave the stroller in the shed by the garden."

"Yes, of course, thank you very much. Let me get my flip-flops out of my backpack. I'm not putting those boots back on until I have to!" She glanced at her boots, duct tape on the sides. Andrés told her to stay seated and offered to get her flip-flops for her.

Elizabeth felt another nudge in her heart and said, "Andrés, would you bring my pack when you come back down please?"

Andrés seemed to guess what she was planning to do. "Yes, of course. I'll be right back." He returned quickly with Marta's flip-flops and the pack. Elizabeth opened it and took out her hiking boots.

"Marta, these boots are a size 40. Your feet look to be about the same size as mine. I'd like for you to try these and see if they're more comfortable than your old ones. Also, I have some hiking pants I'd like to give you. Your jeans don't look like they'd be very comfortable once they get sweaty or wet. My pants will probably be a bit long, but you can roll them up."

"But what will you do? I can't take your things!"

"I can't walk any farther, my friend. At least not on this trip!" Elizabeth went on to tell the story of her injuries on the Camino, while Andrés rolled a soccer ball back and forth with Gren, playing keep away from Tiggy.

"Oh, Elizabeth, thank you so much! You are so kind to give me these things."

"Well, if for any reason they don't work, you don't have to take them."

"Elizabeth, you've seen my boots. I think water skis would probably be more comfortable at this point!" she said, laughing. "I will gladly accept. Thank you very much!"

"You're a brave lady, Marta," said Elizabeth, giving her a hug. "Shall we go in and see if dinner is ready yet? I'm sure you and Gren are starving!"

"That child eats more than I do," said Marta. "I don't know where he puts it all!" Andrés heaved a giggling Gren onto his shoulders, and Elizabeth helped Marta dry her feet and stand. "We're quite a pair, hobbling in to dinner like this," observed Marta when she noticed Elizabeth's limp.

"We call it the 'pilgrim shuffle,' Marta," called Andrés over his shoulder. "You're not the first, nor are you the last to be hobbling around like this!"

Marta laughed and glanced over at Elizabeth as Gren hugged Andrés' head and patted his cheek with his chubby hand. She grabbed Elizabeth's hand to let Andrés and Gren go into the house ahead of them and whispered, "Elizabeth, this man is lovely. How did you two meet?"

Elizabeth instinctively answered, "Oh, we're not together, I just met him!"

Marta raised an eyebrow and gave her a skeptical look that reminded Elizabeth of Miriam. "Really? Have you noticed the way he looks at you?"

Elizabeth's cheeks reddened, but she nodded. "I don't know, Marta. I have some pretty serious trust issues because of my past relationships. I'm not sure I can handle the thought of starting something with Andrés right now, and he's seen me at my worst. Just today he found out more about my past relationships than I ever thought he, or anyone here, would, so I'm not sure he would even be interested. He's just a good listener."

"Well, just be open to what God might have for you, okay? Promise?" Marta smiled broadly and squeezed Elizabeth's hand.

"Okay, I promise," said Elizabeth. "You're not the first one who's said something about this!"

"Good, maybe if you hear it enough you'll get the message!" Elizabeth laughed and opened the door for Marta as they walked into the house for dinner. Andrés made sure the two women sat together and rested from their injuries while the other, more able-bodied pilgrims brought steaming dishes to the table and seated themselves. Gren attached himself to Andrés and chattered steadily in Swedish from his position on Andrés' lap, letting Andrés cut his meat and help him with his food while Marta and Elizabeth chuckled at the pair of them. Tiggy stationed herself near Andrés' feet to catch any scraps that fell. The little boy ate quickly, then motioned to Andrés that it was time to go play.

Andrés laughed and said to the women, "I have no idea what he's saying to me, but he doesn't seem to mind. As long as he's happy, I'm happy to spend as much time with him as I can. Is that okay, Marta?"

"That would be a relief, Andrés! Believe me, we've had lots and lots of time together over the past several weeks. I don't think it would hurt either of us to have a bit of a break! Thank you!"

By the time they had finished this exchange, Gren and Tiggy had already gone outside, so Andrés called over his shoulder, "Okay, great!" as he ran to catch up. Miriam came and sat down in Andrés' empty seat.

"That man will make a wonderful father someday," she sighed, looking at the window where Andrés was throwing the ball with Gren.

"Okay, okay, okay! Everyone can stop pressuring me about Andrés now!" said Elizabeth, putting her hands up in mock exasperation.

"Marta, was I talking to Elizabeth?" asked Miriam, feigning innocence. "No, I was simply making a statement of fact. It's so very interesting that you seem so sensitive about the topic, though, Elizabeth!" Marta was covering her mouth to hide her giggles, and Elizabeth snorted in frustration.

"He's just a kind man. We're friends." Miriam and Marta exchanged glances, and Miriam rolled her eyes heavenward.

"Okay, that's nice, Elizabeth. We'll just see how it all turns out, won't we?" She patted Elizabeth's hand and went to get dessert while Marta abandoned all pretenses and laughed aloud at Elizabeth's red cheeks. Elizabeth noticed Miriam looking at her closely as she dished out the dessert, as if the older woman detected her true embarrassment behind the joking. Elizabeth met her gaze with a pleading look, and Miriam nodded slightly, as if to say, "We'll talk later."

By the time dessert was over, Andrés and Gren had come

back in. Gren was still on Andrés' lap, but had his grubby bunny in one hand, his head against Andrés' chest, his eyes closing. Andrés kissed his forehead and laid his cheek on the little boy's silky hair, smiling.

"You're wonderful with children, Andrés," said Marta. "Thank you for spending so much time with Gren. His father hasn't seen him for a year and a half, so he is always drawn to kind men like you. I appreciate your patience."

"It's my joy, Marta," said Andrés. "Shall we go upstairs? I can go ahead and put him in your bunk. Looks like he's out. I'll be right back down, Elizabeth," he said as he stood up slowly so as not to disturb the sleeping child in his arms.

"Good night, Elizabeth! I'll see you in the morning. Thank you so much for everything!" said Marta as she followed Andrés upstairs. Elizabeth sighed and then felt more anxiety creep into her chest. She did love spending time with Andrés, but he was so different from the types of men she'd been with in the past. Ordinarily, Elizabeth was attracted to alpha types: confident men, bordering on arrogant, usually with some sort of high powered job like a lawyer, doctor, or investment banker. Tall, extroverted, outdoorsy. Men like Marco. She didn't know what to make of her attraction to Andrés. There was nothing striking about his looks: he was about her height, medium build, thinning hair, beard. But his eyes had a depth of empathy and kindness she'd seen only in her new friends she'd met on the Camino. He certainly didn't lack confidence, but he had a humility she'd never seen before in a man her age. A humility born of suffering, of faith, of trust. And now he had gotten a glimpse of her past. *I'm so afraid to trust him, Lord. If someone as kind as Andrés hurts me or gives up on me, then I'll completely lose faith in men. I just don't know if I can handle having my heart broken again.*

Let me care for you, Beloved Daughter. Let me love you. Keep your heart open. Don't be afraid.

She heard someone walking down the stairs and returned Andrés' smile when he ducked into the room.

"Elizabeth, I was wondering whether you'd spend the day with me at my farm tomorrow? I can come pick you up tomorrow morning after you've had a chance to meet Miriam's children, and then you can see my Papá and our home. Also, you can spend the night in our guest room. Since Miriam's children will be here, she'll be tight on space and will need the room, so would this be okay with you?"

Trust me, Beloved. "Yes," she said, as she forced a smile back at Andrés. "I'd like that very much."

Elizabeth watched him leave, staring at the door after he left. Miriam came back into the common area and sat down next to her at the table. "Liebchen, I'm so proud of you for giving up your bed for Marta. Already you are learning what a blessing it is to follow the prompts of the Holy Spirit and serve others in His name rather than out of obligation or a need to be strong in yourself. You don't seem to think so, though," she added, looking at Elizabeth's downcast expression.

Elizabeth looked into Miriam's eyes and was once again struck by the love and concern that was always present there. Today her eyes were a clear blue. Slowly, she began to tell Miriam what had happened with Marco, both in Pamplona and that afternoon. "Somehow while I've been here I forgot how dirty I am, all the things I've done wrong. I was going to sleep with him, Miriam! And I *have* slept with other men in America. So now whenever Andrés looks at me or whenever people treat us like we're already a couple, it makes me think, 'Why would he ever be interested in someone like me? He deserves so much better!'"

Miriam sighed and looked with pity at Elizabeth. "Lisbet, what you're feeling is a natural response to the things you've done wrong. Fortunately you didn't sleep with this man, but you intended to. And as you said, you have had relations with others. What you're feeling is the remorse that comes with sin." Elizabeth hung her head. Miriam quickly put her hand on Elizabeth's back and said, "But all of that is washed clean now! That's the power of the cross, dear. Jesus died to ransom us from our mistakes. There's no amount of feeling guilty or doing good things that will earn forgiveness for what any of us have done! You're free from the past, Elizabeth. Jesus forgives you. As far as God is concerned, you are as clean and pure as fresh snow."

Elizabeth felt tears running down her cheeks again. "Then why do I still feel so bad?"

"Liebchen, give your feelings of guilt and shame to Jesus. All of them. He will take them off your shoulders. Sometimes there are consequences we face for our sins, even after forgiveness. That is what happened when Marco and his friends came by today. Also, Satan might try to remind us of our mistakes and condemn us for them. It happens to me often enough!" Miriam chuckled, then looked at Elizabeth intently. "The apostle John wrote to the churches under his care, 'If we claim to have no sin, we deceive ourselves and the truth is not in us. If we confess our sins he is faithful and just to forgive our sins and cleanse us from all unrighteousness. Don't ever let anyone convince you that Jesus didn't pay for *every* single one of your sins. Just give them to him, and when you feel guilt, shame, or find yourself up at night reminded of some mistake, pray, 'Jesus already paid for that.'"

Elizabeth could tell from her voice that Miriam was speaking from personal experience. She nodded and said quietly, "Thank you." Miriam hugged her tightly and held her hand. Elizabeth bowed her head and prayed, "God, I don't even know where to start. I'm sorry I looked for a man to sleep with even on the Camino. I'm sorry for ignoring your voice for so much of my life. I'm sorry for blaming you for all the bad things in my life. I'm..." she trailed off, unable to find words as mistake after mistake flashed through her head.

She saw herself leaving her mother's room in a huff to pack for her soccer game. She felt herself ignoring the initial reluctance she had about spending the night with Steve in college. She heard herself time after time ignoring Donna's feelings and sharply demanding documents or coffee. She even remembered shoving Willoughby off her lap in frustration, harder than she'd meant to, when she received a particularly frustrating email from Bruce late one night. *Jesus, I can't carry this anymore. Please take it, take it all and put it on the cross.*

Instantly she felt lightness in her chest, which before had felt cold and constricted. *Beloved, I forgive you, and I take it all. Now you are free, my* love. Her sobs subsided into peaceful breathing, but tears continued running down her cheeks.

"Thank you, Jesus," she said aloud, hardly knowing where the words came from. Miriam repeated her words, kissed her forehead, and went to bed.

33

FAMILY

Even though Elizabeth spent the night on the little cot in the hallway, she woke feeling refreshed and excited to meet Miriam's children and grandchild and spend the day with Andrés. After receiving a big hug from Marta and exulting in how well her hiking boots and pants fit her new friend, Elizabeth watched as Marta and Gren walked slowly back to the trail, turning to wave before they rounded the curve. Around 10:00 in the morning, a car squealed into the driveway, and two adults quickly got out, chattering in Dutch. Tiggy bounded out the front door, barking joyfully, and jumping in circles. Miriam threw the bunches of herbs she was making into poultices down on the table and ran outside behind Tiggy, throwing her arms around her son and daughter, then lifting a small, blonde baby out of his seat in the back. Joyful laughter wafted through the windows as the family basked in their reunion, and Elizabeth felt a pang of sadness. *Nothing like this has ever happened with my family.*

You have a new family now, Beloved. Be at ease.

As if to reinforce the truth of this assurance, Miriam came in with her arms around her son and daughter, saying, "There is someone very special here I'd like for you to meet. She has become my daughter through Jesus." Elizabeth felt warmth spread through her at the love in Miriam's eyes as she looked at her, and rose to meet the family surrounding Miriam. "This is Anneke, my daughter, and her son Lars, who is one." Anneke moved past Elizabeth's outstretched hand and gave her a warm hug, then turned Lars so he could greet her. Miriam's tall son, Anders, hugged Elizabeth too, and both he and his sister immediately began peppering her with questions. Elizabeth enjoyed seeing how like their mother they were. Anneke, Anders, and Lars had all inherited Miriam's changeable blue-grey eyes, and Anneke and Anders were tall like their mother. They enjoyed swapping Camino stories, and Elizabeth learned that both Anneke and Anders had walked the Camino twice.

"When Mama came back from her Camino, she was a changed woman," said Anders. "She's probably told you some of her story, but when she left, we barely had a relationship. When she returned, she sought us out and immediately asked our forgiveness for the toll her bitterness had taken in our lives, and asked if we could try again. At first we didn't trust her…after all, she hurt us deeply by disengaging after our father died and sinking lower and lower into her own resentment and anger. But gradually, we saw that she really was a new person, and wanted to see what it was that had so changed her. Anneke and I decided to do the Camino together. Then two years ago, I did it and met my wife, Joanna, who unfortunately had to stay in Delft to work and couldn't join us today."

"I walked my second Camino after Mama bought this old farmhouse and converted it into an *albergue*. I walked to Santiago from St. Jean, and then came back to help Mama fix up this place. We spent a whole spring getting it ready for the summer rush, and we finished just in time. Now my husband, Wils and I come back with Lars as often as possible. Like Joanna, Wils was so disappointed not to be here this time. Alas, jobs are necessary, are they not? What do you do back in the States, Elizabeth?"

Elizabeth shared that she was currently jobless, but planning to look for things when she returned to the states. "God will lead you to the right thing," said Anneke confidently. Just then, Matteo's little truck pulled into the driveway behind the rental car and there was another exclamation of joy as Matteo, Andrés, and Rex came into the house and saw their dear friends. Lars squealed with delight when the giant Rex licked his face, and Anneke said, "So much for keeping him clean. As Wils always says, 'The dirtier he is, the better his immune system will be.' Wils is a doctor," she explained to Elizabeth. "I'm not sure whether that fact is scientifically proven or whether he's just trying to make me feel like a better mother. Either way, I find it comforting!" she said with a laugh that sounded just like Miriam's. Everyone else joined in the laughter, and Miriam and Matteo went into the kitchen to make tea while everyone else chatted.

After an hour, Andrés said, "Elizabeth and I should probably get back to the farm, Papá. We need to make sure Felipe finished the chores and be there to check the pilgrims in."

"How much longer will you be in Spain, Elizabeth?" asked Anders.

"I'm spending the night at Andrés and Matteo's place tonight, and then tomorrow night I'll bus to Madrid. I fly out on Sunday."

"Okay, then we'll see you before you go, right?"

"Oh yes, definitely," said Elizabeth, her stomach sinking at the thought of how quickly her time in Spain was coming to a close. She pushed the sadness away. *I want to enjoy the rest of my time here as much as possible.* Andrés ran upstairs and got her pack, and the two of them hopped into the truck for the trip back to the farm. Rex and Matteo would walk home after lunch. As they bumped along the road, Andrés said, "What did you think of Miriam's children?"

"They're lovely," said Elizabeth. "It's been good for me to see that it's possible for children to have relationships with their parents…it gives me hope for my dad and me."

"Yes, although it will likely take some time. But your Papá will see the change in you, Elizabeth."

"Do you think so? Oh, I hope that's true!"

"I've seen a change in you, and I've only known you for a short time. You're a different person than the one I met in the garden that day."

"Well I hope so," said Elizabeth, marveling at how little anxiety she felt about what Andrés had witnessed the previous afternoon. He didn't seem to be treating her any differently. "I'm definitely cleaner!"

"Inside and out," said Andrés laughing. As they pulled into the driveway of the farm, Elizabeth was struck by the beauty of the fields surrounding the house, the light on the stone driveway, the sounds of bells and chickens clucking. Andrés parked the truck, jogged around to Elizabeth's door, and helped her down. He shouldered her pack, and then walked her into the house where they met Felipe coming down the stairs with an armful of dirty sheets to take home. Andrés introduced him to Elizabeth, and Felipe was thrilled to try his English with a native speaker. Elizabeth encouraged him warmly, and the boy strutted out the door with the sheets in a hamper, ready to take them to his mother to wash. Andrés gave Elizabeth a tour of the common room, the kitchen, and pointed to the barn turned dormitory. Matteo could accommodate many more pilgrims than Miriam. Everything was simple, but clean and well kept.

"I thought we could have a quick lunch on the patio," said Andrés. "But first let me show you the guest room." They exited the main building and walked across the driveway to the dorm. "Dad and I have our bedrooms on the top floor of the main house, but the guest room is here." They walked past the tractor, up a narrow staircase, and into a long, narrow hallway. Andrés opened the door at the far end, and showed Elizabeth into a small, clean room with a crucifix on the wall, a handmade quilt on the twin bed, and a small desk in the corner. He placed her pack on the bed and said, "Would you like some time to yourself, or would you like to go ahead and have lunch?"

"Let's have lunch," said Elizabeth, eager to spend as much time with Andrés as possible. Andrés directed her to sit on the patio while he prepared a simple salad, and she reveled in the quiet. Rex came and sat nobly beside her, long ears twitching like antennae. In a fenced yard several meters away from the house, goats wearing bells around their necks munched on the sweet grass. Chickens scuffed and scratched in the dirt near the goats, clucking happily. A huge garden with tomatoes, cucumbers, several kinds of squash, herbs, and much more grew farther out from the house, and beyond, fruit trees in neat rows. She turned to hear Andrés whistling happily, bearing a tray out onto the patio with water, wine, cheese, bread, and salad made from the garden. Elizabeth's stomach rumbled, and she realized she hadn't eaten anything since breakfast. Andrés poured their drinks, placed a plate in front of her, and bowed his head. They joined hands as he prayed, and then Elizabeth tucked into her lunch.

"Andrés, this is the best salad I've ever eaten!" she said between mouthfuls. Andrés laughed at her appetite and said, "My Papá has always prided himself on his home grown tomatoes. He's even managed to create his own variety. He won a prize at the market last year for the best tomatoes."

"It's true; there's nothing better than homegrown tomatoes," said Elizabeth. "But these cucumbers, and this bread! And do you make your own cheese?"

"Yes, Felipe milks the goat every morning for our cheese. It is delicious, isn't it?"

Elizabeth realized she'd eaten her entire salad and several pieces of bread spread with goat cheese in less than five minutes. "Oh Andrés. I'm sorry I ate so fast! Where are my manners?"

"It's no problem! I'm so glad you're enjoying the food.

For dessert we'll have some fresh apricots and almonds. For now, though, we've got plenty of produce if you'd like more salad."

"Well, maybe I'll rest a minute and let this settle a bit," she said, smiling. As they ate, Andrés told her about all the crops they grew, the animals, and the process of planting, harvesting, and selling their goods at the market. "As you saw on the sign when we drove in, we have so many tomatoes and cucumbers right now that we sell them by the road and trust people to leave money. Felipe's mother also helps us with canning, so we'll preserve tomatoes and make jams when the fruit comes into season."

"This all seems so peaceful to me, but I'm sure it's a lot of hard work," said Elizabeth.

"It is," agreed Andrés. "Papá and I are so grateful to have neighbors like Miriam and Felipe's family who help us when times are very busy. Farmers learn to depend on one another for their livelihoods, but it's a beautiful way to be in community with others."

"You must really miss it when you're in DC," said Elizabeth.

"Oh, I do, but I'm grateful that my work schedule still allows me to return in the summers. It's a blessing," said Andrés. He glanced at his watch. "I need to make sure everything is in order for our guests today. Why don't you sit for a while and have some time to yourself? I'll join you once I have everyone checked in."

"Thanks Andrés; that would be lovely!" said Elizabeth. He placed the empty plates on the tray and headed back inside. Elizabeth closed her eyes and leaned her head back, Rex's head in her lap. *Lord, thank you for bringing me to this place. The more I experience your love, the more difficult it is for me to feel afraid.* She sat quietly for a while, then heard two words, *John Cunningham.* She sat bolt upright, remembering that Andrés had encouraged her to email him when she could access the wireless at the farm. Elizabeth limped briskly into the main room where Andrés was just finishing stamping the *credenciáles* of a group of pilgrims from Canada. She stood next to the desk waiting while he explained the location of everything to the group, then noticed a small sign that had the wireless network and password information. She caught Andrés' eye and mimed typing on a keyboard, then went to retrieve her computer. She came back to the main room and sat on the stool next to Andrés while she connected to the network. When she pulled up her email, she saw that she had several new messages-one from her father checking in, one from Holly (and Willoughby), one from Ellen, and one from Donna. She tapped out quick replies to each of them, making a mental note to respond in more detail when she had faster wireless at the airport. She took a deep breath and started a new message to John Cunningham:

Dear John,

Hope you are well! I am writing about your kind offer of a job a few weeks ago. I know you were looking to fill the position as soon as possible, but if it is still open, I hope to talk with you further. I've had a lot of time to think about the direction of my career since I've been in Spain, and would consider it an honor to work in a position like this. If it's still a possibility, please let me know what the next steps are. I return from Spain on August 1st and would be available to talk anytime after that.

Thank you again for thinking of me. I look forward to hearing from you soon.

Sincerely,
Elizabeth Wiltshire

She pressed "send," then shut down her laptop and exhaled. Andrés patted her on the back and said, "Good work. Even it doesn't work out, it could lead to something else."

"Yes, you're right. And I've done what I can do, so now I need to let it go. So, can I feed the goats?"

Andrés laughed hard at her abrupt change in subject and then said, "Well, there's not a lot to do for the goats, but if you're nice I'll show you not only how to feed them, but how to milk Sophia tomorrow morning."

"Andrés, you're so good to me," joked Elizabeth.

"I know, I do so many nice things for you," he said as he stood up from his stool and stretched, yawning.

"Do you want to have a nap or something while I check people in?" she asked eagerly. "That would be fun for me, and if you have other things you need to do, I'm happy to cover things here."

"That would be great, if you don't mind. I need to check in with my editor, send some emails, and maybe sleep a bit. I'll be back in time to help with the evening meal preparations."

"I'm happy to help, Andrés. Take your time!" Andrés

waved gratefully and headed upstairs to his room. Elizabeth checked in a steady stream of pilgrims for the next hour, and by 16:00 they had reached full capacity of 20 guests. Andrés still hadn't reappeared, but Elizabeth thought she'd watched enough at Miriam's place to know where to start. Even though Matteo and Andrés hosted twice as many pilgrims as Miriam did, the principles were the same. Elizabeth opened the refrigerator and pulled out a large tray of thin sliced pork, cucumbers, and lettuce. She found several large boxes of elbow noodles in the pantry, and figured they could serve salad and fried pork with noodles for dinner. She had seen several ripe-looking watermelons in the garden next to the patio, and hoped that would be an acceptable dessert. She started two large pots of water boiling on the stove, and started chopping cucumbers while chatting with Gabriella, a young woman from Sicily who was walking the Camino with her boyfriend.

As she and Gabriella talked happily, Matteo walked into the kitchen, smiling, just as Andrés hurried downstairs and into the kitchen. "Look who fell asleep while you did all this work, Elizabeth!" Matteo laughed and put a loving arm around Andrés to make it clear he was teasing his son.

"Matteo, I *told* Andrés to go take a nap and have a little alone time. He's been working so hard recently." She smiled at Andrés' mussed appearance; he looked like he could have used a few more hours of sleep. "See, look, Gabriella and I have everything under control here. Sautéed pork, pasta, salad, and watermelon for dinner. Sound good?"

"Perfect!" exclaimed Matteo. "Andrés and I will just

head into Burgos and have a drink while you take care of everything, Elizabeth!"

"Haha! Andrés has also promised me I could milk Sophia tomorrow morning. So don't do it yourself!" Elizabeth wagged her finger at both the men.

"Oh, don't worry. I would not want you to miss such an opportunity!" said Matteo, laughing. "Andrés and I will go pick the melons, okay?" While Gabriella and Elizabeth finished making the salad, Gabriella's boyfriend and two other men set out plates, utensils, and napkins. A father and his teenaged son set out glasses and pitchers of wine and water. As the pasta boiled, Elizabeth and Gabriella sautéed the pork and Andrés and Matteo sliced the watermelon. Before long the evening meal was prepared, and the pilgrims sat down while Matteo said a blessing in both English and Spanish.

Elizabeth listened contentedly to the happy chatter around her, trying to push back the steadily increasing melancholy that had been coming on since the morning. The thought of leaving Spain and the people who had become such beloved community was almost more than she could bear. *I will be with you, Beloved. You shall go out with joy and be led forth with peace. I will continue the work I have begun in you, and will hold fast to you.* As she sensed these encouraging words deep in her heart, tears welled up in Elizabeth's eyes as she looked around the table at each pilgrim's face, knowing every soul present had a story to tell, knowing God had beautiful purposes for each one. She looked across the table at Andrés and his tender gaze met hers. Instead of looking away as she usually did, she held his gaze until they were interrupted my Matteo booming, "Time for dessert." Andrés smiled and nodded at Elizabeth, and together they showed the pilgrims how to clean up, and then invited everyone out to the patio for watermelon.

The group continued to chat enthusiastically, and Matteo asked if anyone had something to share about how their Camino had been so far, and if there were ways the group could pray for one another. Elizabeth was struck anew by the relational aspect of Andrés', Matteo's, Father Bill's, and Miriam's faith. This was the first time Elizabeth had met people other than her mother whose faith seemed as natural to them as breathing. She breathed a quiet prayer: *Jesus, keep me rooted in you. Keep me from settling for anything less.*

As she finished praying, she opened her eyes and met Matteo's, recognizing a heart nudge to speak. "I just want to thank Matteo and Andrés for helping me see what Jesus' love means for me. They cared for me when I was too sick and injured to do anything, and they have opened their home to me, as they have to all of you. Before I came to Spain, I was carrying a lot of guilt and shame, too heavy to bear. I was working in a job that was, quite literally, killing me, but I cared about that more than anything in my life. I didn't really have any friends because all I did was work. In fact, the only reason I came to Spain was because I thought I would be able to impress people by showing them my *compostela* so they would know that when I take a vacation, I don't just lie around on a beach somewhere!"

Several pilgrims joined Elizabeth as she laughed. "But God had other ideas. I hurt my knee, and then got so sick that I might have died if Andrés hadn't found me. Since that day, I have seen God's goodness and love in people like Matteo and Andrés. I was fired from my job while

I was here in Spain, and I don't know what is going to happen when I go home, but I know God will take care of me, because He has been teaching me that here. So even though my Camino looked a lot different than I expected, it was exactly the right one for me. God knew what I needed. And He knows what each one of you need too. So thank you, Andrés and Matteo," her voice broke slightly, but she continued. "And thanks be to God for the way he uses you to bless so many." Andrés was beaming when Elizabeth finished, and several of the pilgrims hugged her and asked if she could tell them more details of her story. Others told their stories, some prayed, and Elizabeth stayed on the patio talking with Gabriella, her boyfriend Luca, and a few others until Matteo came to shoo them to bed.

"Tomorrow morning will be early, and we all need to get to bed. Especially since you are milking Sophia, Elizabeth!" Matteo stepped toward Elizabeth and said, "I'm so glad you are here, dear girl. Jesus will be the best friend you will ever have. He is interested in every detail of your life. You can count on Him to always be your advocate." He kissed her on the forehead and Elizabeth squeezed his hand, wishing she could put into words how much Matteo's fatherly touch meant to her, how healing it was.

In a louder voice, Matteo confirmed, "Okay, Elizabeth, Sophia and I will wake you in the morning when it's time to do the milking. If the rooster doesn't wake you first, that is!" They all laughed, and Elizabeth walked outside.

Andrés walked her to the peregrino dormitory entrance, gave her a quick hug, and Elizabeth's stomach dropped at his gentle touch. She said goodnight, went into her room, closed the door, and sat heavily on the bed, realizing her heart was pounding. *This is the scariest thing of all, Lord. This thing with Andrés. I still can't tell what he thinks of me.*

Trust me, Beloved.

Okay, God. Well, I don't really have a choice, do I? She turned her light off, rolled over, smiled, and went to sleep.

34

CAMINO GOODBYES

Elizabeth woke with the dawn and heard a rooster crowing outside her window. *Andrés wasn't kidding was he?* She lay in bed, her quilt pulled up to her chin, then heard a soft knock at the door. "Yes?" she asked.

A cheerful voice from the other side of the door teased, "Elizabeth! "What are you doing, Sleepyhead? Sophia is waiting for us!"

"Okay, okay," give me five minutes. I'll be right out, Andrés." She hurriedly dressed, grabbed her toothbrush, hurried through her morning routine, and joined Andrés in the courtyard.

"Good morning!" he offered.

"I see someone has already had his coffee this morning," commented Elizabeth on his cheerful alertness.

Andrés laughed, grabbed a bucket hanging nearby, and sat down next to the little white goat, who looked at Elizabeth quizzically. He led her over to the fence, clamped her head loosely into a collar over a feed trough, and started cleaning her udder and teats. Before long, Andrés had started sending milk hissing into the little bucket.

"Okay, I want to try," said Elizabeth impatiently.

"Okay," said Andrés. He offered her the milking stool and leaned back against the fence. Elizabeth imitated what she thought she had seen him do, but nothing happened. Sophia looked around at her, but kept munching her feed.

"Wait a second! How in the world did you do this? You make it look so easy! Sorry, Sophia, I'm just an amateur!"

Andrés laughed. "Let me show you. You have to squeeze like this. It takes time to get the feel of it. It's a lot harder than it looks." He showed her in slow motion what he was doing, then knelt next to her, then directed Elizabeth to try again. This time, she got a few drops of milk. Andrés switched with her again, demonstrating the motion again, then let Elizabeth have a final try.

This time she was successful, and said, "I did it!" so enthusiastically that Sophia startled and almost kicked over the bucket of milk. "Maybe you should take it from here, Andrés!" said Elizabeth, laughing. "I've probably traumatized this poor little goat enough for one day."

"No problem," he said, sitting down on the stool. He finished the milking, and unharnessed Sophia from the trough. "We'll just take this into the kitchen and refrigerate it until it's time to make the cheese." Elizabeth nodded her assent, and fell silent. *I'm leaving today.*

After several minutes of silence during breakfast preparations, Andrés asked, "Elizabeth, would you allow me to drive you to Madrid?"

"Oh gosh, Andrés, that is very generous! It is a long way."

"It's only two and a half hours, and I'd like to spend more time with you."

Elizabeth's cheeks warmed, and she said, "Well, I don't have my ticket yet, so if you really don't mind, I'd like that very much. Do you think your Papá can spare you?"

"Spare him from what?" asked Matteo as he came whistling into the kitchen.

"I told Elizabeth I could drive her to Madrid like we talked about, Papá."

"Oh, of course, that's no problem. I'd be happy for you to do that." Matteo smiled and started prepping the *Zumo* machine for orange juice while they made the coffee. "After breakfast, why don't you go to Miriam's to say goodbye, and then you can drive to Madrid?"

Elizabeth felt another pang of sadness at the thought of saying goodbye to Miriam, but breathed deeply and said, "Thanks, Matteo. I would love to do that. Thank you so much." They worked quickly preparing the rest of the breakfast, setting out bread, cheese, and melon with the coffee and orange juice.

Groggy peregrinos filed in and out of the common room

enjoying the delicious breakfast as a good start to their day. The more outgoing pilgrims expressed their gratitude for the nice accommodations, food, and hospitality. Some walked out alone and deep in thought, others laughed and chatted their way down the driveway to the Camino.

"This was a hungry group this morning," said Andrés as they loaded the last of the dishes into the dishwasher and he pressed the "start" button.

"I'll go get the rest of my things from the guest room and be back in a minute."

Matteo walked outside with Elizabeth. "Matteo, thank you so much. Not just for treating me so kindly, but also for working so hard while Andrés was helping Miriam take care of me. I know it was difficult for you to be on your own here without him while I was sick, and I truly appreciate the sacrifices you made. I know you prayed for me a lot too. Thank you for letting Andrés drive me to Madrid. I hope I'll see you again, Matteo." She gave Matteo a warm hug, letting tears trickle down her cheeks without wiping them away.

Matteo pulled back, offered her his handkerchief, and said, "Oh, I think I'll see you again, Elizabeth. I do." He patted her back and pulled her ponytail playfully.

Elizabeth fetched her backpack from her room, and Andrés met her at the dormitory door and loaded it into the truck. Matteo stood in the driveway with Rex and waved as she and Andrés pulled onto the road to Miriam's. A couple of minutes later, Andrés pulled into Miriam's driveway. Tiggy came out and gave them an enthusiastic greeting, and they walked into the dining room to receive hugs from Miriam, Anneke, and Anders.

They shared a light lunch together, then Anders and Anneke hugged Elizabeth and Andrés saying discreetly, "We're going to take Lars outside to the garden if you need anything, Mama."

Miriam nodded, and Andrés said, "I'll clear up from lunch, Miriam. Why don't you and Elizabeth take a little walk together?" Elizabeth stood. The moment she had dreaded, saying goodbye to Miriam, had finally arrived. Miriam put her arm around her, and Elizabeth started shaking with sobs.

"It is so hard to leave. I...just...want...to...stay...here... with...you," she sobbed, leaning her head on Miriam's shoulder. Miriam patted her back, whispering silently in a language Elizabeth had never heard before. "Miriam, I don't know what I would have done without you. Even though you did not know me, you took me in. I was so sick, and you took care of me like a mother would. You prayed for me and loved me when I was completely horrible. How can I ever thank you?"

"God knows, Lisbet. He knows. And I know you are thankful. How can I ever express the joy it has been seeing the work He has done and is doing in you? I know He has good work for you to do for his kingdom back in DC, but yes, it is hard for me to say goodbye, too. I have something to give you." She handed Elizabeth a wrapped package. "There are two things in there. Open it when you get to Madrid."

"I love you...*Mama*."

The word slipped out, and Miriam lifted Elizabeth's chin with her forefinger, then took her face tenderly in her hands. "Lisbet, I love you too. I will never stop loving you. And neither will Jesus. No matter what happens. He will hold you tight and not let you go."

Elizabeth felt a wet nose on her hand, and leaned down to hug and kiss Tiggy. "And *you*, little shepherd. I will never forget you, either."

She straightened, and Miriam said, "Liebchen, we will meet again. Do not worry. God holds us in the palm of His hand." Andrés walked back into the room, and joined hands with the women. Miriam prayed, "Lord, as your daughter Lisbet returns home, we pray that You would become her true home. Make Your presence with her clear on every path she takes, in every building she enters, and in every aspect of her life. By the power of Your Holy Spirit, we ask you to heal her relationship with her father, with her friends, and heal her physical body, especially her knee. We entrust her future to you, knowing that you delight to give good gifts to your children, because you are a good, loving Father. We pray these things in Jesus' name. Amen."

Elizabeth continued to cry silently, and Miriam gave her one last, long, hug. She and Tiggy walked over to the truck to stay their last goodbyes, and as they drove away, Elizabeth looked at Miriam and waved until she couldn't see her anymore. The first half of the drive passed in silence and Andrés seemed to be content to let Elizabeth speak when she was ready.

As they neared Madrid, Elizabeth said, "Andrés, thank you so much for your kindness. Thanks for rescuing me in the garden that day, and taking me to Miriam's. Thank you for listening to Jesus and being so gentle and compassionate towards me. And thank you for driving me to Madrid!"

Andrés seemed to be weighing his words carefully before he spoke. "Elizabeth, I've been thinking a lot about you. About us. And I wanted to ask if you would let me take you to dinner when I get back to DC in a few weeks? My semester starts at the end of August."

This was the moment Elizabeth had most feared. She felt anxiety creeping into her chest again. She searched for words, and finally said, "Andrés, I don't know what you must think of me after meeting Marco the other day. Nothing ever happened with him, but I do have a past. I've been hurt by others, but I've also hurt a lot of people. I just don't want you thinking I had some innocent life apart from being addicted to work." She stopped, afraid to say more.

Andrés glanced over at her. "Elizabeth, I saw you as physically dirty as anyone could be, and God made it clear that He was at work in you. I see Him continuing that work in the way you've helped at Miriam's and my Papá's, in the way you blessed and prayed for Marta and Gren and the others who stayed with us. You have a difficult past, I can only imagine, but Jesus Christ has made you new. Who am I to worry about things you did before I ever even met you? With Jesus, they are forgiven, just as my mistakes are."

Elizabeth breathed a huge sigh of relief. "Thank you, Andrés. You have no idea how much that means to me."

There was a pause, and finally Andrés spoke again. "So... can I take you to dinner?" he asked, chuckling nervously after the last word.

Elizabeth laughed as well, answering, "Andrés, thank you for asking. I...I don't know what to say. I definitely want to see you more. I love spending time with you. But I have to be honest: I don't know if I'll even *be* in DC in a few weeks if I get a job somewhere else. I don't think I could handle starting something if I have to move. Can I think about it and...pray about it, and let you know?"

Andrés looked at her and nodded. "I understand, Elizabeth. I do. I will send you an email when I return to DC with an idea of where to meet, and if you feel ready, we can see each other. Is that okay?"

Elizabeth breathed another sigh of relief. "Yes, that would be perfect. I'm sorry Andrés. I don't want to hurt you, and there's so much uncertainty in my life right now."

"Elizabeth, if God wants us to be in a relationship, He will guide us. It's hard to wait sometimes, but He will care for us in the waiting. I believe that."

"Yes, thank you, Andrés." They were nearing the airport hotel where Elizabeth would stay the night before her early morning flight home. They drove under the portico, and Andrés pressed a business card into her hand.

"This has my contact information on it, as well as my email address. Will you please send me a quick email when you are home safely so I know, and then I will have a way to contact you in a few weeks?"

"Yes, I will. Thank you again for everything, Andrés." Tears threatened to spill over again, so she gave his hand a quick squeeze, grabbed her pack, and shut the door, waving as she walked into the hotel. *Okay, God, it really is just you and me now.*

She checked into her room, then went downstairs to the cafeteria where she forced down a wilted salad and ham for dinner. *I'm going to be spoiled forever after all the great food I had at Miriam's and Matteo's.* She went back to her room and tried to watch a little TV but gave up when she couldn't find an English station. She opened her laptop and checked email, but John Cunningham hadn't written her back, so she responded to all her earlier emails with detailed descriptions of her adventures, the people she had met, and what God had done in her life. She found that writing the story of her trip strengthened her and made her feel less bereft. With a start, she remembered the package from Miriam. *Well, I'm practically at the airport, so I'm going to open it now!*

She tore off the plain brown wrapping paper, and there was the welcome greeting that had been hanging in the dining room, "Come to me, all who are weary and heavy laden…" She held it tenderly and traced the carved letters with her fingers, wiping her tears off the sign as they fell. The second item was the English Bible Miriam had let her borrow. She opened it and saw an inscription in the front:

Dearest Lisbet,

You are the daughter of my heart. Stay rooted in Jesus with His Word. He loves you so much, and so do I.

Love, Miriam

Elizabeth opened the Bible to the book of Psalms, noticing several underlined verses and notes in both Dutch and English. This was Miriam's own Bible. Elizabeth's heart overflowed with thankfulness yet again, and she was able to sleep peacefully that night, feeling hopeful for the first time about returning home.

When Elizabeth woke the next morning to catch her flight, it was still dark outside. The sun was just peeking over the horizon as she boarded the large aircraft and situated her bag in the overhead bin. Elizabeth allowed the pink clouds below to plane to distract her from the tasteless in-flight breakfast and bitter coffee. After the trays were cleared she noticed a wireless icon next to the cabin light above her. *I'm so used to not having internet that I don't even notice when it's available anymore. I guess it wouldn't hurt to start looking for jobs, right God?* She turned on her laptop and waited as it booted up, figuring she'd check email first as a matter of habit. Her heart leapt to her throat when she saw John Cunningham's name in her inbox. She clicked on the email from him.

Dear Elizabeth,

I'm glad you are able to reconsider taking this position. I knew it was supposed to be you. I can't explain that, other than to say I think God is doing something here, and I'm glad we both get to be involved. I'm looking forward to talking with you more. Can we talk at 3:00 on Monday afternoon? My phone number is below. Looking forward to it.

John

Elizabeth leaned her head back, trembling. *I have a job. I have a job! And it's what I've always wanted to do. And I didn't even have to try. God, you just handed this to me. Thank you. Thank you.*

I have work for you to do, Beloved, freeing people from situations of darkness and oppression. I will go before, behind, and beside you.

After Elizabeth had managed to catch her breath, she tapped out a reply:

> *Dear John,*
>
> *I can't begin to tell you how excited and thankful I am for this opportunity. I will call you at 3:00 Monday. Please let me know if there are specific questions you need answered so I can prepare. I look forward to our talk and the work we'll be doing together.*
>
> *Elizabeth*

Too excited to sit still, Elizabeth decided to go ahead and email Andrés.

> *Dear Andrés,*
>
> *I am still somewhere over the Atlantic, but wanted to let you know that I have an email from John Cunningham offering me the job. I'll be staying in DC! So, yes, I'd very much like to see you when you get back. I look forward to it! Thank you for talking through this process with me, and for praying for me about this. Say 'hi' to your dad, and give Rex an ear scratch from me. Please also give Sophia a pat; I'm sure she misses me!*
>
> *Thankful,*
> *Elizabeth*

Despite the distraction of several in-flight movies and

lunch, the rest of the flight seemed to take forever. By the time they landed, Elizabeth was practically bouncing with nervous energy. Fortunately, the line to get through customs wasn't nearly as bad as it could've been, and just as she walked outside, Holly pulled her little red Volkswagen up to the curb. She jumped out and gave Elizabeth an enthusiastic hug, chattering excitedly. "Oh, Elizabeth, you just look beautiful! Willoughby is going to be so happy to see you. He's been sort of happy with me, but I know he misses you. I loved your emails. I'm sure you're tired, but I want to hear everything."

"That's okay, Holly. I'm so glad to see you!" The two friends chatted happily on the drive home, and Elizabeth caught Holly up on everything that had happened. "And I have a new job, Holly. It's unbelievable! I'll find out more on Monday, but God is so good!"

"You keep saying that, Elizabeth, but your trip totally fell apart. Your knee got injured. You got sick. You lost your job."

"Yes, but because of those things I got to know Jesus. I had to learn to let people help me. I learned how much pride I had. I learned how much I'd been trying to do things my own way."

"Well, you seem different, I'll give you that. But I don't know, I think I'd be pissed if it had been me laid up at an albergue for most of the trip." As they pulled up to their building, Elizabeth felt a deep settledness. *I'm home. And I get to stay here. Thank you, God!* Holly opened her apartment door, and Willoughby came running into the room, rubbing against Elizabeth's legs. She scooped him up and laid her head against his soft cheek, listening to his contented purr. "I made a pasta salad for us, Elizabeth. I thought you might be hungry. But if you'd prefer to go straight home, I understand."

"Not at all, I'd love to eat with you. I don't know how great my company will be after traveling, but I'm definitely hungry."

"I think you're probably better company than Willoughby. No offense, buddy," Holly added, watching Willoughby curl up in Elizabeth's lap.

After dinner, Elizabeth unzipped her pack and reached inside for something she had bought at the Barajas airport for Holly. "Here is a bar of Spanish Valor chocolate we can share for dessert!"

Elizabeth caught up on Holly's news from the previous month while they savored the dark chocolate bar. Then Holly helped Elizabeth up to her place, and indicated the stack of mail she'd left on the table. "Nothing looks urgent, so you can probably wait until morning to tackle that."

"Thanks, Holly," said Elizabeth, giving her friend a warm hug. "I can't thank you enough for taking such good care of Willoughby, and for keeping an eye on my place. I'm looking forward to taking you out for a swanky night on the town for a thank you!"

Holly waved goodnight and closed the door behind her, and Elizabeth ran her hand over the kitchen counter, the coffeepot, the stove. It felt odd being back in her own place, almost as if it was someone else's life. She saw the boxes filled with her personal belongings from her office, recalling that Donna had brought them over per Bruce's directive. She peered down at the first box at the nameplate, framed diplomas, and items from her desk, and felt that life had been a lifetime ago.

She opened her pack and took out the little sign Miriam had given her, propping it against the coffeepot where she would see it first thing in the morning. *Things are different now, God. Help me focus on you and this new path.* She got out her oldest, most comfortable pair of pajama pants and a t-shirt dating back to her college days, brushed her teeth, and climbed into bed. Willoughby curled up next to her cheek, still purring. *Thank you, Lord. Thank you for bringing me home safely.*

35

HOME

The next day passed quickly as Elizabeth opened her mail, went to the grocery store, and did laundry. She had three wedding invitations in the mail pile. *Gosh, what's the deal with all these weddings?* Andrés' face swam into her mind, and she blushed at the direction her thoughts were taking. *Hey, maybe he emailed me back. Okay, I need to calm down and not get my hopes up.* She kept up the internal dialogue as she turned on her computer, but her heart started pounding as soon as she opened her email and saw a reply from Andrés.

Dear Elizabeth,

I'm very happy to hear about your job. This is wonderful news! I was able to share with Papá, Miriam, and they are very happy too. We are praising and thanking God for His provision. I also am very much looking forward to seeing you when I return to DC. I fly back on the 28ᵗʰ, and hope to see you as soon as I get back.

With the love of Christ,
Andrés

Elizabeth sat stunned for several seconds, too excited to speak or move. "Willoughby!" she shouted, and Willoughby ran under the table, scared by the volume of her enthusiasm. "Andrés wants to see me. Andrés WANTS TO SEE ME! How am I ever going to wait four weeks? Okay, hopefully John will put me to work right away. That reminds me, I also need to get my knee looked at." While she had her computer on, she made an appointment for Tuesday morning with her doctor. She groaned, thinking about the long road ahead of tests, surgery, and physical therapy. *But if it hadn't been for my knee, I would never have met Manuela. And I wouldn't have met Father Bill. It's weird, though, my knee hasn't been hurting even though I've had to do lots of stairs on the trip home. Well, I should go get it checked out.*

Okay, what am I going to do for the rest of the day? I guess I can update my resume and send all that information to John ahead of our talk tomorrow.

She spent the rest of the evening preparing her CV for John, and catching up on email. She glanced at the clock, saw that it was 9:00 pm, and congratulated herself on being able to stay awake so long. "Okay, Willoughby, we did it! We made it to nine. Let's go to bed now!" They snuggled up together under the downy comforter and Elizabeth sighed. "I missed you, buddy," she said as Willoughby purred into her ear and she drifted off to sleep.

At 3:00 sharp the next day, she called John Cunningham.

They had a good time catching up on the years that had passed since they'd last seen each other, and Elizabeth was thankful he was so easy to talk to.

"Elizabeth, here's what I'm thinking. As I said in my earlier email, we already have a branch of New Hope Law operating in Atlanta, and it has been very successful. We've received the funding we need, but we're still looking for office space in DC, so for the time being, we'd suggest that you work from home. Do you have the capability to do that?"

"Yes, and I would love that," said Elizabeth.

"In the initial stages, as with any start-up, you would wear most of the hats: meeting and representing clients, but also helping us make connections with other firms doing this type of work, whether pro bono or traditional for-profit law firms. We've already identified several contacts, so the best place to start would be for you to call and set up meetings with these folks, explain what we do, and ask them to give us referrals. Some of them might actually become part of our base support. Then, as we build our client base, we can look for additional lawyers to work for us on a full or part time basis. You'd check in with me daily at the beginning, but that will taper off as things get rolling, though I'll always be available if you need me. Since you can practice in Maryland, DC, and Virginia that gives us a lot more options in terms of client base. I will send you the digital files for all of our literature, so you can you can leave it with the different firms with whom we hope to partner. I also had the thought that we could reach out to some women's shelters and offer our services, so I've got those names for you as well.

"So first you'll be doing a lot of legwork until people know about us. Eventually, we hope to have an office, hire you an administrative assistant, and add more lawyers into the mix. You will be directing everything, so the board and I will be open to your feedback. What's working, what's not working, what we need to tweak. How does that sound to you? Oh, and I almost forgot-I didn't mention salary! I know you were probably making a pretty penny working for Bruce Devon." He named a figure that was only $3000 less per annum than her old salary. She hadn't expected nearly so much working for a non-profit. "Hello, Elizabeth, are you still there?" John's voice helped unhinge her tongue.

"John, I can't tell you how wonderful this is. This is exactly why I went to law school. It's such a blessing!" They continued to talk through details, and then Elizabeth said, "One other thing on my to-do list is that I might have to have knee surgery, so this whole working from home thing will be great. Not sure what to do about living in a third floor apartment, but I'll figure it out."

"Let me know how it goes. We'll go at your pace for this, so if you end up being laid up for a bit, we'll work with your schedule. We're happy and proud to have you on our team, Elizabeth. The board will be very pleased when I give them the news. I'll have Sherry, my assistant, send you the employment agreements, insurance info, and all of that. As soon as you get it back to us we can get your salary started. This is going to be huge, Elizabeth. I am excited to set this in motion to start helping women with these needs."

"I am too, John. Thank you again. Also..." she paused, not sure how or whether to ask the question on her mind.

She plunged ahead. "Do you follow Jesus?"

"Yes, I do, Elizabeth. And I assume from your question that you're also a believer. I didn't know, but I'm thankful to hear it. This firm is not specifically Christian, and serves any woman whose needs qualify her as a potential client, but a number of the board members and employees are believers. I think it will be positive for our decision-making for us to be on the same page in that way. Elizabeth, this is great news!"

Tears ran down Elizabeth's face, but she managed to control her voice, "Thank you, John. I'll let you know what the doctor says tomorrow about my knee, so you have the specifics."

"I'll be praying for you and hoping for good news."

"Yes, me too. Take care, John!"

Elizabeth hung up feeling encouraged and hopeful, wanting to celebrate something. She called Holly and asked if she wanted to do the swanky dinner that evening. "I know it's short notice, but we probably won't have too much trouble getting in somewhere since it's a Monday night. There's a place down near Foggy Bottom I was thinking of taking you called the Indigo Duck Tavern. It's a favorite of mine."

"Sounds great, Elizabeth! I'd love to go! We can also say goodbye to my summer vacation from school. I have to start teacher planning days in two weeks. Somehow I'll survive, but this dinner may be my last hurrah for awhile!"

"I'll come down at 7 and we can taxi over."

When they got to the restaurant, Elizabeth told Holly all about her new job, and Holly said, "This calls for champagne with dessert!"

"You're speaking my language, Holly!" she said. The two friends toasted to Elizabeth's new job, to the end of Holly's summer, and to new beginnings. After they both took sips from their glasses, Elizabeth suddenly thought to ask about Holly's fiancé, and if she had news. "So, what have you heard from Jake?" she asked.

Holly's expression darkened, and she said, "One little measly postcard from Morocco. Of course he has posted tons of pictures on his Instagram and Facebook pages. That's pretty much how I know what he's doing. I've sent him a bunch of emails, but he hasn't responded. He didn't even call me on my birthday. But he said when he got back he'd look forward to seeing me, so that's something, isn't it?" she finished hopefully.

A stab of pity went through Elizabeth's heart. "I don't know, Holly. How long have you guys been together again?"

"It'll be three years in September. I wonder if he'll remember our anniversary? We got engaged last Christmas, and were supposed to get married this summer, but then when we started getting serious about the planning, he disengaged. don't know what to think. He keeps telling me he loves me, but he needs more time." Elizabeth squeezed Holly's shoulder, thinking, *Andrés would never do something like that to a woman.*

Aloud she said, "Holly, I'm so sorry. This must be incredibly painful. I'll pray for you, okay?"

"What good does that do?" posed Holly bitterly. "But I guess it can't hurt. It's not like I can stop you." Holly paused realizing she might have offended Elizabeth. "I'm sorry, I don't want to ruin our nice dinner with this. Let's talk about something else that's not so depressing!"

"Well…I'm thinking about getting a dog. I need to see what the doctor says about my knee tomorrow, but now that I know I'll be working from home a lot, I could take care of one." She went on to tell Holly about Tiggy, Rex, and Paddy. "I don't know if I can survive without a dog after being with those three so much in the past month."

"What will Willoughby do?" said Holly, chuckling.

"That's the million dollar question," said Elizabeth. "He may be spending lots of time at your place!"

"Well, you know I love him, so anytime is fine. Hey, let me know what the doctor says tomorrow."

"I will."

"And please know if you end up needing help during the surgery, or need to stay with me afterwards since I'm on the bottom floor, I'd be happy to have you or do anything I can to help."

"Thanks, Holly," said Elizabeth. "You have no idea how grateful I am to have you as a friend."

"Ditto, Lady!" said Holly as they exited the restaurant.

Elizabeth could feel fatigue coming on like a freight train. The taxi dropped them at their building, both of them thankful for the ride and curb service after such a big dinner. They said their goodnights at Holly's front door, and Elizabeth climbed the stairs, thankful that her knee remained pain free, and fell asleep as soon as she got in bed.

36

HEALING

The next morning, Elizabeth arrived at the doctor's office to have her knee assessed for the injuries she incurred in Spain. The nurse took her vitals, and Elizabeth was not surprised to see she'd lost several pounds. *Salmonella food poisoning. A sure fire weight loss plan,* she thought ruefully. Dr. McMillan came into the exam room and greeted her cheerfully. Elizabeth reviewed the symptoms for him, and described the fall she'd had and the miles she'd walked, and about getting the knee brace and help from Dr. Rodriguez in Pamplona.

"It sounds like a torn meniscus," he said, "but there could be some smaller ligaments torn as well. I don't think it's your ACL, although there could be a partial tear there. We'll have to get you an MRI to really see what is going on inside, but I can do a few simple tests now to get a sense of what we're dealing with before I order anything more extensive."

He directed Elizabeth to take off her knee brace and sit on the table, then looked at both her knees. "No swelling. That's surprising, given the amount of trauma your knee received." Elizabeth pulled out her phone and showed the doctor a picture of her ballooned knee when she'd been seen by the doctor in Pamplona. "Yes, from the swelling in that picture and the pain you were having at the time, we're dealing with some sort of soft tissue trauma."

He gently moved the injured knee around. "Pain here?" Elizabeth shook her head no. "What about here?" Again, Elizabeth shook her head no. "That's surprising. Usually with a tear you'd have a lot of pain in those positions." He asked her to stand on one leg. "Any pain when you put all your weight on that leg?"

"No," said Elizabeth, beginning to feel giddy. "I've been wearing my brace for a couple of weeks, but I'm not having any pain walking up and down my stairs, and my limp is gone. Come to think of it, I haven't had any pain since Friday, when my friend Miriam prayed for me."

"Do you have problems with your knee giving out on you, having to walk with a straight leg, anything like that?"

"Well, I did until Friday. But I don't anymore. So…what's going on?"

The doctor removed his reading glasses and looked at her. "Well, I don't pretend to know what's going on. They don't teach us this kind of thing in medical school. I've seen this happen from time to time in my years of practicing. Healing happens in an unexplained way. I used to figure the patient just didn't know what they were talking about, or had been misdiagnosed. Then I realized I was the one who didn't understand. I think you've been healed, Ms. Wiltshire. I don't see any evidence of the injury and trauma you experienced. Of course if you experience any more pain, please don't hesitate to let me know, and I'll order the tests."

Elizabeth sat down on the examining table, mouth hanging open. "Wait…I don't have to have surgery? Are you sure?"

"I'm sure," said the doctor. "Any knee that needed surgery would have displayed symptoms when I did what I was doing just now. You should be fine. I suggest that you be careful for a while and build up your strength slowly. Start with some short walks without the brace to test it out, and then increase the distance. If everything is feeling fine, then you can try running again."

"Thank you, Dr. McMillan! Thank you so much!"

"Thank you, Ms. Wiltshire. It's fun to see things like this from time to time. Helps break me out of my cynicism." Impulsively, Elizabeth threw her arms around the doctor and hugged him, then jumped up and down. The doctor laughed, "Remember to take it easy and slow to test it."

She called Holly on her way home and told her the good news, and then said, "Hey, do you want to come to the animal shelter with me this afternoon? I'm going to look at dogs. Now that I know I can walk one, I want to get one."

"Twist my arm, Elizabeth. I'll go look at puppies with you *if I have to*," Holly joked.

A little while later, they walked into the Animal Rescue League's main building and asked to see dogs ready for adoption.

The woman behind the counter handed Elizabeth forms to fill out, and then explained the adoption process to her. "It might not take as long for you, though, because so many people are taking vacations, fewer people want to get a new dog in the summer."

"Gosh, I hope so. I'm ready!" said Elizabeth enthusiastically.

"We have to do a home visit first, and we'll need to assess what type of dog is right for you."

"Okay, well could I just see them?"

"Sure, especially since no one is here right now." The woman unlocked the door and led them back to the kennels. "If you see one you're interested in, we can let him out to play, and you can get a sense of how he interacts with you."

As they walked down the hallway, the dogs all welcomed them with a chorus of barks and howls. Elizabeth was drawn to the kennel at the end of the row. *This one*, Elizabeth heard, as she read the profile sheet on the gate.

Maggie
German shepherd/lab mix
12 weeks old
Crate trained
Abandoned by family

The puppy was lying in the corner, face turned towards the wall. Even from a distance, Elizabeth could see that her ears and paws were too big for her body. *She's going to be a big girl if she grows into those.* Elizabeth said, "Holly, come here. I think this is the one." At the sound of Elizabeth's voice, Maggie turned her head. When she saw Elizabeth standing at the door, she trotted over to the gate, wagging hopefully. "Can we play with Maggie, please?" Elizabeth asked the volunteer.

"Oh, she's a sweetheart. Such a sad story too. She and her siblings were found in an old barn. All of her siblings have been adopted, but she's still here. I can't figure out why no one's gotten her yet. If I didn't already have three dogs, I'd have taken her home with me the day she got here. You won't find one sweeter."

As she unlocked the door, Maggie loped out to greet Elizabeth. The volunteer looped a leash around Maggie's neck, and Elizabeth took her to the play area. She and Holly sat down on the floor, waiting for Maggie to run around and play with the squeaky toys. Instead, she climbed into Elizabeth's lap, looked into her eyes, and put a paw on her shoulder. Elizabeth's eyes filled with tears. "How soon can I adopt this dog?"

The volunteer laughed. "All of us will be so happy when Maggie gets adopted. But we have to do a home visit. Can you do it today?"

"Yes!" said Elizabeth.

"Then we process your paperwork, and you come pick her up…tomorrow?"

"*Yes!*" said Elizabeth, unaware that she had started bouncing on the balls of her feet.

"Okay, so we should be able to send someone over in about an hour. Does that work?"

"Yes!" said Elizabeth. "Definitely! See you soon!"

Holly and Elizabeth hurried out to the parking lot and jumped in the car. While Elizabeth waited for the home visit volunteer, she returned emails, cleaned her house, and consoled Willoughby, who seemed confounded by the scent of puppy on Elizabeth. "Don't worry, Willoughby, she's sweet. You'll love her."

The volunteer came, pronounced everything in order, and told Elizabeth she'd be getting a call soon. Elizabeth waited anxiously for the phone to ring. She had just eaten dinner, when her phone rang, "You've been approved! Congratulations! What time tomorrow would you like to pick up Maggie?"

"How about around 12:00? That way I can get her some supplies." Elizabeth spent the next morning buying puppy food, collar, leash, bowls, a bed, a crate, and some toys. At noon she walked into Animal Rescue with Maggie's new pink leash and collar. The volunteer led Maggie out, and she wagged her tail joyously. As Elizabeth put her collar and leash on, she snuffled and licked her enthusiastically. She took her for a quick walk, then put her in the car.

"We're going home, Mags," said Elizabeth. "You and me. For good." Elizabeth leaned over and Maggie licked her ear, and lay down on the front seat with her head in Elizabeth's lap. *Every good and perfect gift is from above, from my good Father,* she thought gratefully. She stroked Maggie's silky little head gently. *Thank you Lord. For bringing Maggie and me together. And for bringing us home.*

EPILOGUE

August 28

Elizabeth was thankful for her new work with John Cunningham for many reasons. Helping women trapped in marriages and relationships with abusive partners resonated with her as her true life calling. Though she never wanted to go back to the life she lived working for Devon, Wilson & Moore, she had come to a place of gratitude for all she had learned working for Bruce Devon, and for the network of contacts in legal circles she approached to inform them of the services her organization could offer women in need. Already her caseload was maxed out for the next few weeks, and she was talking with John and their Board about seeking grants to enable them to hire some more staff for the DC branch. Elizabeth was putting feelers out among friends and supportive private sector lawyers to find office space near the Court House.

John was a calm, wise mentor who taught her how to manage client needs in a healthy way, keep sane work hours for herself, and build in margins for recreation, exercise, and friendships. She was learning new work habits from him, which allowed her to grow and find a healthy balance in her life. She still made the most of every minute she blocked out for work hours, but made sure she scheduled time with friends, long walks and short runs with Maggie, who was bigger every day, and time for worship and study groups at the church she had been attending since she had been home. Her friend Ellen had suggested they meet there the first Sunday she was back, and Elizabeth was growing to love the teaching and worship times. The congregation was full of people from diverse cultures, and with many interests, and she was making friends with some people in a house group that met in her neighborhood.

What she was experiencing in the relationships and worship at this church reminded her of the same essence she had known among the dear people in Spain God had used to care for and love her back to health. As Andrés had told her in an email when she described her church experience, "Elizabeth, God's people all share the same Spirit. God puts His Spirit in us when we follow Jesus, and while cultures and individual talents make us different in some ways, we have that in common."

She and Miriam had corresponded once since Elizabeth left for home, but August is the busiest time of the year on the Camino Francés, and Elizabeth knew how difficult it was for Miriam to find internet and send email. More often Andrés relayed messages back and forth when he wrote or talked with Elizabeth. Miriam was busy, as usual in the summer, but was enjoying a season of predictable rhythms at her albergue, which was a respite for Miriam after the time-intensive care Elizabeth needed during her convalescence. Her free time each day was now given to canning the fruit and vegetables from her garden, and gathering herbs for teas and infusions to sell or use throughout the year.

Elizabeth was thankful for God's wake up call, and embraced her new work with energy and passion, but had learned the need to take care of herself. In that spirit, Maggie did her part to keep Elizabeth living in the present, as she needed regular attention throughout the day for walks and play, and she was learning her manners well.

"Andrés is going to get such a kick out of you, Mags!"
You remind me a lot of Rex, but the tips of your ears flop
down," Elizabeth stroked Maggie's velvet ears, and was
rewarded with a little lick of affection. An older and wiser
Willoughby meowed for attention from the windowsill
where he ruled the apartment most days since the arrival
of this very playful puppy. "Yes, he will love you, too,
Willoughby!"

She was more and more grateful for her friendship
with Andrés, which had grown through regular email
correspondence and an occasional Skype call. She was
trying not to look too far ahead for what their relationship
might become, rather stay in the present moment and
enjoy what they had now. She was coming to know more
about Andrés' professional life in DC, as he detailed more
about his faculty position and the Spanish government's
support and expectations of him. The economy of
Spain was suffering greatly in world markets, and the
unemployment rate had continued to rise. Andrés had a
unique opportunity to speak into this desperate time in his
country's history because of his knowledge of economic
systems and his desire to find solutions. She discovered
he was the keynote speaker at many economic summits
throughout Spain, and the manuscript he was editing had
already been purchased by a top publishing house.

"I'm glad to have met him in Spain on his summer break.
I don't know if our friendship would have gotten off the
ground if we had met in a professional way as a professor/
author and lawyer."

Four weeks had flown by as far as work went, but went at

a snail's pace missing him. She re-read the text that had arrived that night:

Dear Elizabeth,

I just got back into DC. Are you still free for dinner tomorrow? I thought we could meet on top of the Kennedy Center at 7:00 pm, then go for tapas at a place I know nearby. I'm looking forward to seeing you!

I am going to sleep early tonight and check in at my office tomorrow morning, and then take a siesta after lunch so I don't fall asleep at dinner. See you at 7.

In Christ,
Andrés

Elizabeth replied,

Hi, Andrés,

Glad you're back! Can't wait to see you!

In Him,
Elizabeth

She woke the next morning thankful for a full day of phone calls and correspondence to fill the time. She and Maggie went for a short run in her neighborhood before it got too hot. She showered, and then plunged into her to-do list.

On every break from her desk, she changed her mind about what to wear. *Let's face it, anything I put on will be an improvement over my Camino clothes! He has never seen me in anything else. I shouldn't be so worried!* At 6pm she made her final decision: a navy blue dress with fitted bodice and pleated skirt, and her favorite orange paisley ballet flats. She kept her makeup minimal, added a squirt of perfume, and looked in the mirror.

"What do you think, guys?" she asked Willoughby and Maggie, who were curled up asleep together on Maggie's bed. Maggie rolled over onto her back and sneezed. "I'll take that as your approval, Mags!" She launched into an inner pep talk, trying to manage her excitement. *Okay. This is Andrés. He is really great, but really easy to be with, and has seen me at my absolute worst on every level. There's nothing to be nervous about.* She took a deep breath, patted Maggie and Willoughby goodbye, walked downstairs, and flagged a taxi to take her to the Kennedy Center.

The sun was easing downward toward the horizon, its golden light shining on the Potomac, and the oppressive heat from earlier in the day softened with an evening breeze. As Elizabeth took the elevator to the roof, her heart pounded with excitement. The doors opened, and she exited the elevator, looking left then right. *Hmmm. Don't see him. I wonder if he is around the corner,* she thought, and took a few steps to the right. A moment later she heard a voice behind her call, "Elizabeth!"

She turned and saw Andrés walking toward her wearing a tan summer suit with light blue tie. His arms were open, and he smiled one of his broad smiles, eyes shining.

"Andrés!" she smiled back at him and walked into his waiting hug.

TRANSLATION HELPS

Spanish & French

St. Jean Pied-de-Port: Traditional starting point in France for pilgrims walking the Camino Francés route

Santiago de Compostela: Pilgrim destination city in the northwest of Spain; site of the great Cathedral of Santiago

Camino Francés: Also known as the *Route Napoléon,* the most popular of many Camino routes; begins in *St. Jean Pied-de-Port, France,* and ends in *Santiago de Compostela, Spain;* a distance of 800k (500 miles)

albergue: The most colorful accommodations on the Camino range from huge dormitory style buildings with rows and rows of bunk beds, to smaller family run albergues offering private rooms.

casa rural: Spanish country home often used by a family in the spring and summer as a second home to escape the heat of the city and grow much of their food; some *casas rurales* along the Camino routes have been converted to albergues during the busy pilgrim seasons.

café con leche: strong coffee with hot milk, the most popular Spanish coffee drink

Buen Camino!: Spanish salutation to pilgrims used when parting company on the Camino as you walk; it is a wish or prayer for the person you salute to have a good pilgrimage

Regardez! Regardez les hommes et les camions: French, Look! Look at the men and trucks!

petite choses: French, little things

Je m'appelle Elizabeth. Et toi?: French, My name is Elizabeth, And yours?

Bon matin! Vous êtes prêt à joue?: French, Good morning! Are you ready to play?

Oui! Je vous aime: French, Yes! I love you!

pèlerin, -e: French, pilgrim

D'accord, allons-y: French, Okay, Let's go!

à bientôt!: French, See you soon!

chica: Spanish, girl

servicio: Spanish, public toilet

Zumo: Spanish, juice

ABOUT THE AUTHOR

Hilary Van Wagenen

Hilary is an adventurer who enjoys reading stories with interesting characters, and has now turned her hand to writing them. She loves playing and listening to many styles of music, hanging out with friends and family cooking and eating delicious food, and tromping through the woods on muddy trails. Hilary resides in Silver Spring, MD with her husband Tom, son Peter, and two dogs, Hamish and Rosie.

ACKNOWLEDGEMENTS

This Is My Father's World, hymn by Maltbie Davenport Babcock and Franklin L. Sheppard

My Shepherd Will Supply My Need, hymn by Isaac Watts and William B. Bradbury

Cover Design: Steve Mast, Photo: Helen Van Wagenen

Photo of the author: Nicole Schmitz, Charlotte, NC

Interior design and layout: Katie McCrillis

Proofreading and story consultation: Hunter, Haley, Wick, and Helen Van Wagenen

Made in the USA
Middletown, DE
06 August 2017